William Maginn, R. W Montagu

Miscellanies - Prose and Verse

Vol. I

William Maginn, R. W Montagu

Miscellanies - Prose and Verse
Vol. I

ISBN/EAN: 9783337078805

Printed in Europe, USA, Canada, Australia, Japan

Cover: Foto ©Andreas Hilbeck / pixelio.de

More available books at **www.hansebooks.com**

MISCELLANIES.

Prose and Verse.

———

VOLUME I.

𝔅𝔞𝔩𝔩𝔞𝔫𝔱𝔶𝔫𝔢 𝔓𝔯𝔢𝔰𝔰

BALLANTYNE, HANSON AND CO.
EDINBURGH AND LONDON

MISCELLANIES:

Prose and Verse.

BY

WILLIAM MAGINN.

EDITED BY

R. W. MONTAGU.

TWO VOLUMES.

VOL. I.

LONDON:
SAMPSON LOW, MARSTON, SEARLE, & RIVINGTON.
CROWN BUILDINGS, 188 FLEET STREET, E.C.
1885

CONTENTS OF VOL. I.

VOL. I.   b

MEMOIR.

WILLIAM MAGINN, the subject of the present memoir, was born in Marlborough Street, in the city of Cork, on the 10th of July 1793. His father, who for many years conducted the most respectable academy in the city, gave him the benefit of careful training; and so rapid was the boy's progress in study that he was sufficiently advanced in learning at the singularly early age of ten years to enter Trinity College, Dublin, where he fortunately came under the personal care of the Right Rev. Dr. Kyle, who, not slow to recognise premonitions of genius, soon conceived a warm regard for his young pupil. Maginn secured the enviable position of favourite of the class; and it is gratifying to record that the relations of esteem thus established were not dissolved by time; Doctor Kyle, who was subsequently raised to the See of Cork, continuing to be to his old pupil "a wise, firm, and judicious friend."

Upon completing his College course Maginn returned to Cork, and assumed the post of classical teacher in the paternal school, which he conducted himself after his father's death in 1813. This assumption of scholastic responsibility was regarded by his associates as radically inconsistent with his rollicking and wit-squandering character. The future had evidently been adumbrated in youth. However, the course of events was even; and in 1816, when he was only twenty three years old, he took the degree of LL.D. The repute of his scholarship had spread far and wide, and pupils were attracted to him thereby, in spite of the absence of what one of his generous biographers periphrastically refers to as " those qualities which are usually supposed to be the distinguishing attributes of a schoolmaster."   It is only too evident that the claims of pedagogy did not consist well with the temperament of one like Maginn ; and although, his assumption of the ferule was attended by success, it is not surprising to learn that he looked around him for more congenial employment.   Yet to his credit be it recorded that he stuck to the school for ten years, the responsibility of maintaining the family circle having devolved upon him since the death of his father.

His pen, it may well be assumed, was not without employment on local topics so provoking to the satiric mind ; but the *Literary Gazette* was the first periodical out of Ireland to which Maginn contributed.   A few of these early efforts are included in this collection.   *Blackwood's Magazine*, however, provided him with the medium exactly suited for the display of the various powers of "The Doctor" in (as Lockhart noted) essay, disquisition, review, romance, ballad, squib, pasquinade, and epigram ; in Greek, Hebrew, Latin, Irish, Italian, English, and Slang.

The story of his connection with *Maga* is strongly marked with the impress of his peculiar mind, always and everywhere resolved to war with the conventional.   This was the way in which Maginn first introduced himself personally to William Blackwood in May 1820 :

" I called at the shop in Princes Street, and just as I was going in, I recollected that poor Dowden and Jennings, and one or two more in whose names I had written squibs for the magazine, were after writing very wicked notes to Blackwood demanding the author's address ; so I had a clear stage for some sport.   I asked if Mr. Blackwood could be seen, and was introduced to his private office.   I made a rather formal bow, and, giving him a touch of the Cork brogue, said, ' Ye'r Misther Blackwood, I presume, sir?' ' Yes, sir,' was the answer, ' at your service.' ' Be Gor, sir,' said I, ' if you were only at my service a week ago, you'd have saved me a journey; but, be my conscience, as I'm here I'm very glad entirely that you *are* at my service at last.' ' Pray, sir, may I ask,' he said, ' what I can do to oblige you, or how have I displeased you? Our establishment is very punctual in replying to all letters.' ' Sir, sir, listen to me now,' I said; ' there's some rascal in Cork— you know Cork, don't you?—Well, there's some blackguard there after making use of my name in your old thrump of a magazine; and I must know who he is.' ' Oh, sir!' said Blackwood, ' I deny your right to ask any such questions, and those requests cannot be granted without delay and consideration.' ' Consideration indeed!' I cried. ' Aren't you after writen to one Scott there!' ' I really cannot answer you, sir.' ' May be it's going to deny what you wrote you are. May be you'll deny this, and this, and this,' said I, throwing a bundle of his letters on the table before him. ' May be you'll say they're not to the man that writes for you; and may be you'll say that I'm not the man himself.'"

This interview, though conducted by Maginn on the basis of what he called fair quizzification, was not distasteful to the sagacious Blackwood, whose guest he became for six weeks, during which he luxuriated in the society of Wilson, Lockhart, Gillies, Hamilton, and others of literary note in Edinburgh. Indeed, it is recorded that the publisher was " delighted with his wild Irish assistant; " or, as another hand figuratively deposes, they were at once " up to the elbows in friendship." Maginn's social qualities—his constitutional gaiety, his convivial pleasantry, and the ceaseless flow of his conversation, at once learned, witty, and wise— were such as could not fail to render him a favourite in circles of culture. Let us look at the picture drawn of him about this period:

"All were standing, all were listening to some one who sat in the middle of a group. A low-seated man, short in stature,

was uttering pleasantries and scattering witticisms about him
with the careless glee of his country. His articulation was
impeded by a stutter, yet the sentences he stammered forth
were brilliant repartees uttered without sharpness, and edged
rather with humour than with satire. His countenance was
rather agreeable than striking ; its expression sweet rather than
bright. The grey hair, coming straight over his forehead, gave
a singular appearance to a face still bearing the attributes of
youth. He was thirty or thereabouts ; but his thoughtful brow,
his hair, and the paleness of his complexion gave him many of
the attributes of age. His conversation was careless and off-
hand, and, but for the impediment of speech, would have had
the charm of a rich comedy. His choice of words was such as
I have rarely met with in any of my contemporaries."

In 1823 he married a lady of the name of Cullen ; and
soon after, whether because the revenue derived from the
school was not adequate for the support of a wife and a
prospective family, or whether his appetite for social life on
a somewhat wider scale than that provided by his native
city had been inflamed by his recent visit to Edinburgh, he
resolved to give up the school and to devote himself to
literature, and solicited the favour of his friends both in
Edinburgh and in London to procure for him some per-
manent employment. *John Bull* had been started at
the close of 1820. As this was only a weekly (Saturday)
paper, Theodore Hook, proficient in the arts of political
warfare, was anxious to have a journal published on
Wednesday, for the due reinforcement of the arguments of
Saturday. Accordingly some half-dozen newspapers then
in the market were purchased for the sum of three hundred
guineas, and upon their ruins was erected the new property,
which was intrusted to the direction of Maginn. To *John
Bull* it has been positively asserted that Maginn contributed only one article, in spite of the current tradition that
he was Hook's vigorous coadjutor. Anyhow, the new venture was abandoned after a few months at a heavy loss.
Such also was the fate of the *London Literary Journal*, a

review upon the plan of Jerdan's *Literary Gazette*, set up also at the instigation of Hook, with which Maginn was associated. The highest tribute to his powers, however, was the fact that, immediately upon receipt of intelligence of the noble poet's death, John Murray selected Maginn for the task of bringing out the memoirs, journals, and letters of Lord Byron. Here was an enterprise worthy of Maginn ; all the materials were put into his hands ; but the destruction of the autobiography occasioned such a gap that it was not then deemed advisable to proceed with the work ; and, as we know, it was finally intrusted to Moore. About this time Maginn's pen found exercise in the pages of the *Quarterly Review*.

The establishment of the *Representative*, that effort in the shape of a daily newspaper which involved the spirited magnate of Albemarle Street in the loss of twenty thousand pounds in the short space of six months, enlisted Maginn as Paris correspondent ; and in this connection it may be noted that his failings had evidently begun to manifest themselves ; for in a letter of Lockhart's addressed to Wilson on 23d December 1825 occurs this ominous passage : " Maginn is off for Paris, where I hope he will behave himself. He has an opportunity of retrieving much if he will use it." That with his facility of composition he availed himself of the columns of the *Age* and of the *True Sun*, by way of eking out his income, is only too probable. His pen could, if only he would apply himself, produce excellent work off-hand. The letterpress to the " Gallery of Illustrious Characters," with which was connected the pictorial skill of his fellow-townsman, Daniel Maclise, was hit off, we know, at a moment's notice, and in the course of a few minutes. But steady devotion to business evidently was not to be expected of Maginn. The square peg cannot be adjusted to the round hole, lament the matter as we may.

Ultra-Tory as he was, upon the foundation in 1828 of

the *Standard* newspaper, under the able editorship of Dr. Stanley Lees Giffard, father of Lord Chancellor Halsbury of our own day, Maginn obtained the post of junior editor. "Whitehall, or the Days of George IV.," was the title of a novel published by him anonymously about this time, in which all the leading personages of the period, ranging from the King down to Jack Ketch, were sketched with an unrestrained freedom of wit and humour; its special purpose being the satire of Horace Smith and his novel of "Brambletye House." The annuals of those days were costly publications, enriched with beautiful steel plates, to which men of the first literary eminence were in the habit of contributing. As representative of Maginn's style in this sphere, in which he had to accommodate himself to delicacy of taste, we give "A Vision of Purgatory" from "The Literary Souvenir." This, we may add, was designed as a specimen of "Tales of the Talmud," which, though repeatedly announced as nearly ready, never emerged from the realm of projects into the light of day.

Hitherto Maginn had not faltered in his allegiance to *Blackwood*. The "Noctes," we may remark in passing, were his suggestion; and his contributions thereto, including the famous Greek motto with its intensely free translation, were numerous. Several of the brightest of the songs embedded in the rich prose were his; and it has been recorded on weighty authority that the whole of No. 4 of the series, in which Byron and Odoherty at Pisa are the only speakers, was written by Maginn.

A difference seems to have arisen about this time between Blackwood and the Doctor; and this estrangement, synchronising with the introduction of the latter to the familiar friendship of Hugh Fraser,* a typical Bohemian of the

* An incident at the funeral of his friend (in 1841) is recorded as an instance of exception to Maginn's generally unromantic character. The obsequies took place at Bunhill Fields, and at the conclusion of the

period, led to the founding of *Fraser's Magazine.* The preliminary steps were characteristic of the two associates. Having looked up their papers, and put some of them into their pockets, they strolled through Regent Street in search of a publisher. Arriving at number 215, Maginn exclaimed: "Here's a namesake of yours, Fraser ; let's try him." They entered the shop and submitted the proposal, which was at once adopted : and in February 1830, in pursuance of the agreement thus made, appeared the first number of *Fraser's Magazine for Town and Country :* the title "Fraser" being derived, not from the publisher, but from the projector ; the former of whom, by way of resenting this baptismal distinction, would allow no one in his employment to refer to it otherwise than as "The Town and Country," under which appellation he further took care that it should be referred to in all his business communications and books. Maclise's cartoon of the Fraserians is a pictorial record of the proud position soon attained by "Regina ;" and the early volumes attest the inexhaustible variety of its literary excellence ; not the least attractive feature being the "Gallery of Illustrious Literary Characters," pages of spicy text from the ever-ready pen of Maginn, illuminated by admirable portraits from the cunning hand of Maclise. As exemplifying the range and the depth of the learning which his native vigour of mind never suffered to become oppressive to its owner, the articles upon Farmer's essay " On the

ceremony the Doctor bade the gravedigger show him the tomb of Bunyan. The gravedigger led the way, and was followed by Maginn, who appeared particularly thoughtful. As they approached the spot, he turned to the person who accompanied him, and, tapping him on the shoulder, said "Tread lightly." Bending over the grave for some time in melancholy mood, while the bright sunshine poured around him, he seemed unconscious of any one's presence. At length he recovered from the fit of pensive absorption, and, turning away from the scene, exclaimed in deep and solemn tones: "Sleep on, thou Prince of Dreamers."

Learning of Shakespeare," together with the study of Lady Macbeth, are included in this collection. They show what he might easily have achieved in the shape of serious work, could he only have schooled himself to the requisite application. But sustained effort was against the grain. Only by fits and starts it was that he could work, the ardour of composition under difficulties having an irresistible fascination for his radically discursive intellect.

No better illustration could be given of this defect or peculiarity than that supplied by the review of " Berkeley Castle." It happened that the book was sent in towards the end of the month; matter was wanted to fill up some pages of the next number of the magazine; the author, if not a Radical, certainly was a Whig. What an auspicious conjunction of circumstances! Maginn was in his element. He set to work at once, under the inspiration of adverse surroundings, with the double purpose of vexing the publisher and of smashing the author of the novel; the result being the famous review which brought down upon the luckless Fraser the terrible ire of Grantley Berkeley. Proceeding to Fraser's shop in Regent Street in the company of his brother, whom he left to guard the door by way of providing against interruption, Grantley Berkeley belaboured the publisher most unmercifully about the head and neck with a heavy riding-whip, while Craven Berkeley urged him on to prolongation of the murderous assault with encouraging cries of "Give it him, Grantley; give it him well." The details of this outrage, perpetrated by a powerful man upon one who, besides being physically inferior to his assailant, was at the time in a delicate condition of health, are shocking to read; yet the action brought in the Court of Exchequer to recover damages resulted in the award of only one hundred pounds, the jury being apparently influenced by the very remarkable defence set up by Mr. Thesiger (afterwards Lord Chelmsford) " that his client could not be called upon to measure the quantity and quality of the blows he gave."

Maginn's part in the matter has now to be narrated. Upon hearing of the assault on his publisher, he lost no time in avowing the authorship of the offensive review, and in intimating, in accordance with the usage of the period, that his friend Mr. Hugh Fraser was prepared to receive a message. A hostile meeting was arranged ; the combatants met in a field in the Barnet Road ; and three shots were exchanged, at the last fire Maginn's bullet grazing the collar of his adversary's coat, and the bullet of the latter striking the ground beside Maginn's boot. Upon this third ineffectual exchange of shots, the account runs, the seconds interfered, and the parties, bowing to each other, left the ground without explanation.

With the reputation thus earned, it is not surprising to find that all the slashing papers in *Fraser* were attributed to him. In the number for April 1837 appeared a severe criticism upon a drama entitled " The Student of Padua," which provoked in the columns of the *Metropolitan Conservative Journal* the grossest abuse of Maginn, who, besides being branded as a coward (which he assuredly had proved himself not to be), was denounced as "a slanderer, a backbiter, and a dastardly calumniator by profession." Maginn, however, was not the author of the critique ; and an action for libel against the printer of the journal (in which Sergeant Talfourd was for the plaintiff, and Mr. Thesiger—who was gracious enough to admit that, however degraded a man might be, he had a right to seek compensation for any libel upon him—for the defendant) secured damages to the extent of one hundred and fifty pounds with costs. The *Examiner's* brief report of the case exhausts comment in the heading " Pot *v*. Kettle."

Of the " Homeric Ballads," in which the solidity of Maginn's scholarship (especially in the notes) is to be found

in close union with the vigorous vivacity of his common
sense, the late Professor Conington observed that the author
"may be esteemed the first who consciously realised to
himself the truth that Greek ballads can be really represented in English only by a similar measure. This is his
great praise, and will continue after the success of his execution shall have been ratified by other workmen in the same
field."   Mr. Gladstone bears testimony to "their admirably
turned Homeric tone;" and that most exacting of critics,
Mr. Matthew Arnold, is pleased to speak of them as "genuine
poems in their own way." A complete version of the "Iliad"
and the "Odyssey" was said to have been contemplated.
Indeed, he has himself recorded that he had made considerable progress with such a translation; but, as usual,
we learn no more about it. The man who seldom wrote
except in company and generally in the midst of tumult,
who in the middle of a sentence would relieve the strain of
thought by throwing himself back in his chair and telling a
humorous story, and who then would suddenly break off
in his talk and resume his pen, could not possibly con-
centrate his powers for the production of steadily continuous
work.

As might have been anticipated, Maginn's intemperate
habits had by this time dissolved several literary engagements; and his life may be said to have been weighed
down with grief and care, no small portion of it, in fact, being
passed either in imprisonment for debt, or in concealment
in obscure retreats from the sheriff's officer. Captain
Shandon in "Pendennis" is a memorable sketch of the
Doctor; and let us not omit to record the fact that
Thackeray, with characteristic generosity, came to the relief
of the distressed scholar. "He lent," says James Hannay,
"or in plainer English gave, five hundred pounds to poor
old Maginn when he was beaten in the battle of life, and,
like other beaten soldiers, made a prisoner in the Fleet."

Of the systematic imprudence which had served, in conjunction with his devotion to the bottle, to conduct him to
so pitiable an end, we have a singular illustration in the following anecdote. A friend at his table was complimenting him
on the fine flavour of the wine, and begged to be informed of
the merchant's name. "Oh, I get it from a house close by,
just as I happen to want it," replied the host; "the London
Tavern." "Indeed!" exclaimed the other; "a capital
cellar unquestionably. But have you not to pay rather
an extravagant price for it?" "I don't know—I don't
know," returned the Doctor. "I believe they put down
something in a book." Beyond that little affair of book-
keeping Maginn's interest in his connection with the London
Tavern did not extend. His witty sallies, too, it must be
remembered, could not fail to alienate the regard of powerful
patrons. His humiliation of Croker is an intensely neat
example of the way in which he could, when so minded,
abate and dissolve pomposity. At a dinner-party graced
by the presence of a great Tory lord, the conversation
turned on the proper mode of calling a peer, whether he
should take his title from a castle or locality, or whether he
should be created by his family name. Opinions differed,
and Croker with habitual assurance propounded his view.
"For my part," he said, "Lyneham is the place where the
Crokers were first settled; and, if I am made a peer, I
shall have myself gazetted, not as Lord Croker but as Lord
Lyneham." No sooner had Croker delivered himself of
this oracular statement than up jumped Maginn in ecstasy
roaring out, "Stop — stop — stop, Mr. Croker!" The
company, hitherto observant of the stiffest propriety, were
amazed at the outbreak; nor was their astonishment
lessened when Maginn, fixing his eyes on his host, exclaimed: "Don't do that—don't do that, Mr. Croker;
for you'd then have to be re-gazetted as Lord *Penny-a-
line-'em!*"

Broken in health and saddened in spirit, Maginn, after recovering his liberty through the medium of the Insolvent Court, retired in 1842 to Walton-on-Thames, where he expired of consumption, in the arms of his attached friend Edward Vaughan Kenealy, on 21st August. It was a lamentable close of his career in the forty-ninth year of his age. As the fearless and persistent champion of Toryism for a quarter of a century, he had reckoned upon reward when his party came into power. A minor diplomatic post at Vienna was talked of being assigned to him. But what his party did not do for him was done with all delicacy and promptitude by the man whose pro-Catholic policy of 1829 Maginn, animated by the strong feelings of an Irish Orangeman, had denounced with unsparing severity, and whose personal motives he had assailed, as Lockhart notes, "with unwearied pertinacity, especially in rhymes only less galling than the fiercest of Swift's." Sir Robert Peel was his benefactor. When, a few years before Maginn's death, a private subscription was set on foot for his relief, Sir Robert, casually hearing of it, sent £100 as a contribution to the fund, with a stipulation for secrecy; and again, on learning of the deathbed wants of the wild son of genius, the noble-hearted statesman forwarded a similar amount.

This memoir may fitly close with the epitaph, full at once of pathos and of wit, written by Lockhart:

> "Here, early to bed, lies kind William Maginn,
> Who with genius, wit, learning, life's trophies to win,
> Had neither great lord, nor rich cit of his kin,
> Nor discretion to set himself up as to tin :
> So, his portion soon spent, like the poor heir of Lynn,
> He turn'd author while yet was no beard on his chin ;
> And whoever was out, or whoever was in,
> For your Tories his fine Irish brains he would spin,
> Who received prose and rhyme with a promising grin—
> 'Go ahead, you queer fish, and more power to your fin !'
> But to save from starvation stirr'd never a pin.
> Light for long was his heart, though his breeches were thin,

> Else his acting for certain was equal to Quin :
> But at last he was beat, and sought help from the bin
> (All the same to the Doctor, from claret to gin),
> Which led swiftly to gaol, with consumption therein ;
> It was much, when the bones rattled loose in his skin,
> He got leave to die here, out of Babylon's din.
> Barring drink and the girls, I ne'er heard of a sin :
> Many worse, better few, than bright, broken Maginn."

No stone, it may be finally added, marks the place of his repose in the churchyard of Walton-on-Thames. Let this collection of his writings, exhibiting every variety of literary excellence, serve to perpetuate his memory.

MISCELLANIES.

SOME ACCOUNT OF THE LIFE AND WRITINGS OF ENSIGN AND ADJUTANT ODOHERTY

(LATE OF THE 99TH REGIMENT).

I.

IF there is something painful to the feelings in the awful ceremonial of consigning a deceased friend to the grave, there is something equally consolatory to our affection in perpetuating the remembrance of his talents and virtues, and gathering for his grave a garland which shall long flourish green among the children of men. This may indeed be termed the last and highest proof of our regard, and it is this task which I am now about to discharge (I fear too inadequately) to my deceased friend, Ensign and Adjutant Odoherty, late of the 99th or King's Own Tipperary regiment. In offering to the public some account of the life and writings of this gentleman, I have pleasure in believing that I am not intruding on their notice a person utterly unknown to them. His poems, which have appeared in various periodical publications, have excited a very large portion of the public curiosity and admiration; and, when transplanted into the different volumes of the Annual Anthology, they have shone with undiminished lustre amid the blaze of the great poetical luminaries by which they were surrounded. Never was there a man more imbued with the very soul and spirit of poetry than Ensign and Adjutant Odoherty. Cut off in the bloom of his years, ere the fair and lovely blossoms of his youth had time to ripen into the golden fruit by which the autumn of his days would have been beautified and adorned, he has deprived the literature of his country of one of its brightest ornaments, and left us to lament that youth, virtue, and talents should afford no protection from the cruel hand of Death.

Before proceeding to the biographical account of this extraordinary person, which it is my intention to give, I think it proper previously to state the very singular manner in which our friendship had its commencement. One evening, in the month of October 1812, I had the misfortune, from some circumstances here unnecessary to mention, to be conveyed for a night's lodging to the watch-house in Dublin. I had there the good fortune to meet Mr. Odoherty, who was likewise a prisoner. He was seated on a wooden-stool, before a table garnished with a great number of empty pots of porter.* He had a tobacco-pipe in his mouth, and was talking with great gallantry to two young ladies of a very interesting appearance, who had been brought there under similar circumstances to himself. There was a touching melancholy in the expression of his countenance, and a melting softness in his voice, which interested me extremely in his favour. With all that urbanity of manner by which he was distinguished, he asked me "to take a sneaker of his swipes." I accepted the invitation, and thus commenced a friendship which ended only with his life, and the fond remembrance of which shall cease only with mine.

Morgan Odoherty was born in the county of Kilkenny, in the year 1789. His father acted for many years as a drover to the Right Honourable Lord Ventry, at that period an eminent grazier; and, on that gentleman's being raised to the peerage, he succeeded to a very considerable portion of his business. He had certainly many opportunities of

---

. * We beg leave to hint to our Irish correspondent that, if the *pots* were empty, they could scarcely be termed *pots of porter*.

amassing wealth; but the truth is, he only provided *meat* for others, with the view of getting *drink* for himself. By his wife he had acquired a small property in the county of Carlow, which it was his intention to have kept as a provision for his family. His business, however, gradually decreased, and on the last settlement of his accounts, when he came to liquidate the claims of his creditors on his estate, he found, to his astonishment, that he had long since *liquidated* his own. The discovery was fatal. The loss of his credit with the world he might have survived, but the loss of his credit with the *whisky merchant* drove him to despair. He died in the year 1798; a melancholy monument of an ill-spent life.

Of his mother Mr. Odoherty was ever in the habit of talking with gratitude and respect, and the manner in which she discharged the duties of her situation to himself and his three sisters, I have every reason to believe, was highly ex-emplary. And with the exception of the circumstance of a posthumous child making its appearance about fourteen months after the death of her husband, there occurred nothing which could raise a doubt of her being the most virtuous of her sex. Being endowed with a considerable taste for letters, Mrs. Odoherty determined that her son should receive a *liberal* education, and accordingly sent him to a charity school in the neighbourhood. At this school I have reason to believe he remained about four years, when, by the interest of his uncle, Mr. Dennis Odoherty, butler to the Right Honourable Lord Muskerry, he was received into his lordship's family as an under-domestic. In this noble family Ensign and Adjutant Odoherty soon became a universal favourite. The sweetness of his temper, the grace and vigour of his form, which certainly belonged more to the class of Hercules than the Apollo, rendered him the object of the fervent admiration of the whole female part of the family. Nor did he long remain in a menial situation. By the intercession of Lady Muskerry, he was appointed under-steward on the estate, and on his lordship's being appointed

colonel of the Limerick Militia in 1808, his first care was
to bestow a pair of colours on Mr. Odoherty. Never surely
did a gift bestow more honour on the giver, and Lord
Muskerry had the satisfaction of raising, to his proper
station in society, a youth whose talents were destined to
do honour not only to the Limerick Militia, but to his country
and the world. In this situation, it is scarcely necessary to
state, he was the very life and soul of society wherever he
was quartered. Not a tea-party could be formed, not an
excursion could be planned in the neighbourhood, without
Mr. Odoherty's being included in it. In short, he was like
the *verb* in a sentence, quite impossible to be wanted. I
have been informed by several officers of the regiment that
he was the greatest promoter of conviviality at the mess.
His wine, to use their own expression, was never lost on
him, and, towards the conclusion of the third bottle, he
was always excessively amusing. When quartered with his
regiment at Ballinasloe, in the year 1809, he became smitten
with the charms of a young lady of that city, who, from
what I have heard of her person and temper, was all

" That youthful poets fancy when they love."

Her father was a man of considerable wealth, and what is
called middle-man or agent to several of the noblemen and
gentlemen of the country. Her name was Miss Augusta
M'Craw, and her family were believed to be descended from
the M'Craws of Inverness-shire, a house which yields to
none in the pride of its descent, or the purity of its blood.
Mr. M'Craw, indeed, used to dwell, with great complacency,
on the exploits of an ancestor of the family, Sir John M'Craw,
who flourished in the reign of James III., who not only
defeated a Sir James M'Gregor in a pitched battle, but
actually kicked him round the lists, to the great amusement
of the king and all his court. In this exercise, however,
there is a tradition of his having dislocated his great toe,
which ended in a whitlow, of which he died about three
years afterwards, leaving his fate as a lesson to his successors,

of the consequences attending such unknightly behaviour. To this lady, as I already mentioned, Mr. Odoherty formed a most devoted attachment, and he accordingly made her an offer of his heart and hand. The young lady returned his attachment with sincerity, but her father and mother were most unaccountably averse to the connection. On stating to them the affection he entertained for their daughter, and soliciting their consent to its legal consummation, he was treated with the utmost indignity, and desired to quit the house immediately. On his remonstrating against this improper treatment, the brother of the lady attempted to pull him by the nose, and Mr. Odoherty retreated with the very proper resolution of demanding the satisfaction of a gentleman. He accordingly sent him a message the next day, and a meeting was the consequence. On this occasion Ensign Odoherty behaved with all the coolness of the most experienced veteran. They fired nine shots each without effect; but, in the tenth round, Mr. Odoherty received a wound in the cheek, which carried off three of his jaw teeth, and entirely demolished one of his whiskers. On receiving the wound, he raised his hand to his face, and exclaimed, with the greatest coolness, "A douce in the chops, by God!" By this wound he was unfortunately ever afterwards much disfigured, and was afflicted with a stiffness in the neck, from which he never recovered. Miss Augusta M'Craw was married, a short time afterwards, to a lieutenant of artillery, and Mr. Odoherty very feelingly expressed his regret and sorrow on the occasion, by two odes on the inconstancy of women, which appeared in the Irish newspapers, and were afterwards recorded in the *Lady's Magazine* for October 1811.

Let it not be supposed, however, that, in the progress of the events which I have been relating, his poetical talents had remained dormant. Although we do not find, in his pieces of this period, the same lofty degree of excellence which was afterwards so prominent in his more mature productions, yet they are all imbued with very considerable spirit and imagination. They had hitherto been generally rather of a light and amatory nature ; but of his talents for satire I believe the following epigram, on a certain amorous dowager, will afford not an unfavourable specimen :—

> If a lover, sweet creature, should foolishly seek
>   On thy face for the bloom of the rose,
> Oh tell him, although it has died on thy cheek,
>   He will find it at least on thy *nose*.
>
> Sweet emblem of virtue ! rely upon this,
>   Should thy bosom be wantonly prest,
> That if the rude ravisher gets but a kiss,
>   He'll be ready to *fancy the rest !*

I also find, among his papers, an unfinished Tragedy, which, I conjecture, must have been composed about this time. It is entitled " Euphemia," and, in my opinion, displays an uncommon degree of genius. I shall only extract part of one scene, which strikes me as being executed in the most masterly manner. The Princess Euphemia is represented as passing a sleepless night, in consequence of the imprisonment of her lover Don Carlos. Towards morning, she breaks out into the following impassioned reflections :—

> *Euphemia.* Oh, 'tis a weary night ! Alas, will sleep
> Ne'er darken my poor day-lights ! I have watched
> The stars all rise and disappear again ;
> Capricorn, Orion, Venus, and the Bear :
> I saw them each and all. And they are gone,
> Yet not a wink for me. The blessed Moon
> Has journeyed through the sky : I saw her rise
> Above the distant hills, and gloriously
> Decline beneath the waters. My poor head aches
> Beyond endurance. I'll call on Beatrice,
> And bid her bring me the all-potent draught
> Left by Fernando the apothecary,
> At his last visit. Beatrice ! She sleeps
> As sound as a top. What, ho, Beatrice !
> Thou art indeed the laziest waiting maid
> That ever cursed a princess. Beatrice !
>   *Beatrice.* Coming, your highness. Give me time to throw
> My night-gown o'er my shoulders, and to put
> My flannel dicky on ; 'tis mighty cold
> At these hours of the morning.
>   *Euphem.* Beatrice !
>   *Beat.* I'm groping for my slippers ; would you have me

Walk barefoot o'er the floors?   Lord, I should catch
My death of cold.
   Euphem. And must thy mistress, then, I say, must she
Endure the tortures of the damned, whilst thou
Art groping for thy slippers?   Selfish wretch !
Learn, thou shalt come stark-naked at my bidding,
Or else pack up thy duds, and hop the twig.
   Beat. Oh, my lady, forgive me that I was so slow
In yielding due obedience.   Pray, believe me,
It ne'er shall happen again.   Oh, it would break
My very heart to leave so beautiful
And kind a mistress.   Oh, forgive me !   (*weeps.*)
   Euphem. Well, well ; I fear I was too hasty :
But want of sleep, and the fever of my blood,
Have soured my natural temper.   Bring me the phial
Of physic left by that skilful leech Fernando,
With Laudanum on the label.   It stands
Upon the dressing-table, close by the rouge
And the Olympian dew.   No words.   Evaporate.
   Beat. I fly !   [*Exit.*
   Euphem. (*sola.*) Alas, Don Carlos, mine own
Dear wedded husband ! wedded ! yes ; wedded
In th' eye of Heaven, though not in that of man,
Which sees the forms of things, but least knows
That which is in the heart.   Oh, can it be
That some dull words, muttered by a parson
In a long drawling tone, can make a wife,
And not the——

Enter BEATRICE.

   Beat. Laudanum on the label ; right :
Here, my lady, is the physic you require.
   Euphem. Then pour me out one hundred drops and fifty,
With water in the glass, that I may quaff
Oblivion to my misery.
   Beat. 'Tis done.
   Euphem. (*drinks.*) My head turns round ; it mounts into my
I feel as if in paradise !   My senses mock me :   [brain.
Methinks I rest within thine arms, Don Carlos ;
Can it be real?   Pray, repeat that kiss !
I am thine own Euphemia.   This is bliss
Too great for utterance.   Oh, ye gods
Of Hellespont and Greece !   Alas ! I faint.   [*faints.*

The heart of Mr. Odoherty was of the tenderest and most
inflammable description, and he now formed an attachment
to a Lady Gilhooly, the rich widow of Sir Thomas Gilhooly,
knight, who, on account of some private services to the state,

was knighted during the lieutenancy of Lord Hardwicke. His love to this lady was of the most modest and retiring nature, and he never ventured to make a personal declaration of his passion.   He has commemorated it, however, in the following beautiful and pathetic stanzas :—

> Oh, lady, in the laughing hours,
>   When time and joy go hand in hand ;
> When pleasure strews thy path with flowers,
>   And but to wish is to command ;
> When thousands swear that to thy lips
>   A more than angel's voice is given,
> And that thy jetty eyes eclipse
>   The bright, the blessed stars of heaven ;
> Might it not cast a trembling shade
>   Across the light of mirth and song,
> To think that there is one, sweet *maid*,
>   That loved thee hopelessly and long ;
> That loved, yet never told his flame,
>   Although it burned his soul to madness ;
> That lov'd, yet never breathed thy name,
>   Even in his fondest dreams of gladness.
> Though red my coat, yet pale my face,
>   Alas ! 'tis love that made it so,
> Thou only canst restore its grace,
>   And bid its wonted blush to glow.
> Restore its blush ! oh, I am wrong,
>   For here thine art were all in vain ;
> My face has ceased to blush so long,
>   I fear it ne'er can blush again !

This moving expression of passion appears to have produced no effect on the obdurate fair one, who was then fifty-four years of age, with nine children, and a large jointure, which would certainly have made a very convenient addition to the income of Mr. Odoherty.   He now resolved on volunteering into the Line.   He was unwilling that his services should be confined to the comparatively inactive and inglorious duties of a militia officer, and he therefore determined to wield his sword, or, as he technically called it, his *spit*, wherever the cause of his country should demand it.   He was soon after appointed to an ensigncy in the 44th regiment, then in the West Indies ; and, on the 14th of

August 1814, he embarked at Dover in the schooner *John Dory*, Captain Godolphin, for Jamaica. He experienced a tedious passage, and they were unfortunate enough to fall in with an American privateer, from which, however, after a smart action, they had the good luck to escape. The following *jeu d'esprit* gives so favourable a specimen of his talent for humour that I cannot refuse the reader the pleasure of submitting it to his perusal :—

Captain Godolphin was a very odd and stingy man,
Who skipper was, as I'm assured, of a schooner-rigged West Indiaman ;
The wind was fair, he went on board, and when he sailed from Dover,
Says he, " This trip is but a joke, for now I'm half-seas over ! "

The captain's wife, she sailed with him, this circumstance I heard of her,
Her brimstone breath, 'twas almost death to come within a yard of her ;
With fiery nose, as red as rose, to tell no lies I'll stoop,
She looked just like an admiral with a lantern at his poop.

Her spirits sunk from eating junk, and, as she was an epicure,
She swore a dish of dolphin fish would of her make a happy cure.
The captain's line, so strong and fine, had hooked a fish one day,
When his anxious wife *Godolphin* cried, and the dolphin swam away.

The wind was foul, the weather hot, between the tropics long she stewed,
The latitude was 5 or 6, 'bout 50 was the longitude,
When *Jack* the cook once spoilt the *sauce*, she thought it mighty odd,
But her husband bawl'd on deck, " Why, here's the *Saucy Jack*,* by God."

The captain sought his charming wife, and whispered to her private ear,
" My love, this night we'll have to fight a thumping Yankee privateer."
On this he took a glass of rum, by which he showed his sense ;
Resolved that he would make at least a *spirited* defence.

The captain of the *Saucy Jack*, he was a dark and dingy man ;
Says he, " My ship must take this trip, this schooner-rigged West India-
    man.
Each at his gun, we'll show them fun, the decks are all in order ;
But mind that every *lodger* here must likewise be a *boarder*."

No, never was there warmer work, at least I rather think not,
With cannon, cutlass, grappling-iron, blunderbuss, and stink-pot.
The Yankee captain, boarding her, cried, " Either strike or drown ; "
Godolphin answered, " Then I strike," and quickly knocked him down.

The remaining thirty verses of this poem, giving an account of the action and the subsequent voyage to Jamaica,

* A celebrated American privateer.

of how Mrs. Godolphin was killed by a cannon-ball lodging in her stomach, and how Captain Godolphin afterwards died of the yellow fever, I do not think it necessary to insert. It is sufficient to say, they are fully equal to the preceding, and are distinguished by the same quaintness of imagination and power of ludicrous expression.

On his arrival at Jamaica, he found it the rendezvous of the force destined for the attack of New Orleans, under the command of the brave though unfortunate Sir Edward Packenham. Of this force the 44th regiment formed a part, and the heart of Mr. Odoherty throbbed with delightful anticipation of the high destiny to which he felt himself called. A circumstance now occurred, however, which bid fair to cloud his prospects for ever. On the evening before the sailing of the armament for its destination, Mr. Odoherty had gone on shore. He there chanced to meet with an old schoolfellow, who filled the situation of slave-driver or whipper-in to a neighbouring plantation. This gentleman invited him to his house, and they spent the night in pouring forth the most liberal libations of new rum, which they drank fresh from the boilers. The consequence was that next morning, on the sailing of the fleet, Mr. Odoherty was absent. His friend the whipper-in, however, who was less drunk than his guest, had the good sense to foresee the consequences of his being left behind on so pressing an occasion. He hired a couple of negroes to row after the fleet, had Ensign Odoherty carried insensible to the boat, and he was conveyed to his ship, as he himself humorously termed it, "as drunk as David's sow." The commanding officer immediately placed him under an arrest, and it was only on his expressing the most sincere contrition for his folly, joined with many promises of amendment, that he was again allowed to perform the duties of his situation. After this, few of the officers of the regiment thought proper to associate with him; and with the exception of some, who had formerly been his companions in the militia, he was placed in Coventry by the whole corps.

II.

It is not my intention, in this paper, to recapitulate the various calamities of the siege of New Orleans. That the armament was utterly inadequate to accomplish the object of the expedition, is now generally admitted. Fitted out for the express purpose of *besieging* one of the strongest and most formidable fortresses of America, it was not only unprovided with a battering-train, but without a single piece of heavy ordnance to assist in its reduction. Sir Edward Packenham, therefore, on his arrival at Jamaica found himself under the necessity of awaiting the tedious arrival of reinforcements from England, or of undertaking the expedition with the very inadequate means at his disposal. Listening rather to the suggestions of his gallantry than his prudence, he decided on the latter. If he erred in undertaking the expedition, it must be owned that he displayed the most consummate skill in the conduct of it. On his arrival at New Orleans, he established himself immediately on the peninsula guarded by the fortress, and so vigorously did he push his operations that on the third night he determined on giving the assault. The honour of heading the storming party was allotted to the 44th regiment, then under the command of the Honourable Lieutenant Colonel Mullins, son to Lord Ventry, patron to our hero's father, and who did not at all congratulate himself, however, on his good fortune. The 44th regiment were driven back at the commencement of the attack ; and, on Sir Edward Packenham's inquiring for the commanding officer, it was discovered that both he and Ensign Odoherty had remained in the rear. On search being made for them, Colonel Mullins was discovered under an ammunition waggon, and Ensign Odoherty was found in his tent, apparently very busy searching for his snuff-box, the loss of which, he solemnly declared, was the sole reason of his absence. In consequence of these circumstances, Colonel Mullins was brought to a court-martial, and dismissed the service; and such, most probably, would likewise have been the fate of Ensign Odoherty, had he not, by the most humble intercessions, prevailed on the officers of the regiment to suppress their charges, on condition that he rid them of his presence by an immediate exchange into another regiment. I am far from wishing to justify the line of conduct adopted in this instance by Mr. Odoherty, in yielding to the prejudices against his character which the officers of the regiment appear so gratuitously to have entertained. Knowing him as I do, to have been as brave a man as ever pushed a bayonet to the throat of an enemy, I cannot but sincerely regret that any change of circumstances should have occurred to give a different complexion to his character in the opinion of the world. But such regrets are useless. Who, when gazing on the brightness of the sun, can suppose his effulgence to be diminished because, when viewed through a telescope, a few trifling spots are discernible on his disk?

Having entered into this arrangement, in order to effect his exchange Mr. Odoherty took advantage of the sailing of the first ship to return to England, and accordingly embarked in the *Beelzebub* transport for that purpose. On their voyage home they encountered a severe storm when off the river Chesapeake, which broke the bobstay of the *Beelzebub*, and did considerable injury to her mainmast. To crown the misfortune of this unlucky voyage, they were captured by the American frigate *President*, in lat. 35^c 40' long. 27° 14', and carried into Boston as prisoners of war. Mr. Odoherty bore his misfortunes with the greatest philosophy and calmness; and, as a proof of the happy equanimity of his temper, I give the following extract from an extempore address to a whale, seen off Long Island on the 14th June 1814:—

> Great king of the ocean, transcendent and grand
> Dost thou rest 'mid the waters so blue ;
> So vast is thy form, I am sure, on dry land,
> It would cover an acre or two.

> Thou watery Colossus, how lovely the sight
>   When thou sailest majestic and slow,
> And the sky and the ocean together unite
>   Their splendour around thee to throw.
>
> Or near to the pole, 'mid the elements' strife,
>   Where the tempest the seaman appals,
> Unmoved, like a continent pregnant with life,
>   Or rather a living St Paul's.
>
> Thee soon as the Greenlander fisherman sees,
>   He plans thy destruction, odd rot him !
> And often, before thou hast time to cry Pease,
>   He has whipped his harpoon in thy bottom.

Here unfortunately a hiatus occurs, which, I am sure, will be regretted by every lover of what is sublime in conception, grand in description, and beautiful in imagination. Odoherty is not the only author of high genius whose vivacity exceeded his perseverance. We may say of him what Voltaire said of Lord Bacon, "*Ce grand homme a commencè beaucoup de choses que personne ne peut jamais achever.*"

On his arrival at Boston, he received orders to proceed to Philadelphia, the station allotted for his residence by the American Government. In this great city the manly graces of his person, and the seductive elegance of his manners, gained him the notice and attention of all ranks. But, notwithstanding the kindness and hospitality which he experienced from his American friends, his pecuniary circumstances were by no means in the most flourishing condition. He found, to his astonishment, that American merchants, however kind and liberal in other respects, had a strange prejudice against discounting Irish bills, nor could any offers, however liberal, of an extraordinary percentage reconcile their minds to the imaginary risk of the transaction. Under these circumstances, Mr. Odoherty was obliged to confine his expenses to his pay, a small part of which was advanced to him, with much liberality, by the British agent for prisoners of war in that city, to whose kindness he was, on several occasions, much indebted. It was in Philadelphia that

Ensign Odoherty had the misfortune to form a connection with a lady of the name of M'Whirter, who kept a well-known tavern and smoking-shop. Her husband had taken an active part in the rebellion of 1798 in Ireland, of which country he was a native, and had found it prudent to escape the consequences of his conduct by a flight to America. He accordingly repaired to Philadelphia, where he opened the "Goat in Armour" tavern and hotel, and soon after married a female emigrée from the Emerald Isle; an act which, I believe, he had only once occasion to repent. He died in a few years, and the "Goat in Armour" lost none of its reputation under the management of his widow. In this house did Mr. Odoherty take up his residence on his arrival at Philadelphia; and, it is almost needless to add, he soon made a complete conquest of the too susceptible heart of Mrs. M'Whirter. In the present difficulty of his pecuniary affairs, this circumstance afforded him too many advantages to be neglected or overlooked. Disgusting as she was in her person, vulgar in her manners, weak in her understanding, and unsuitable in years, he determined on espousing her. He accordingly made his proposals in form, and Mrs. M'Whirter was too much flattered with the idea of becoming an ensign's lady, not to swallow the bait with avidity. They were privately married, and continued to live together with tolerable harmony, until the peace of 1815 restored Mr. Odoherty once more to liberty. He was now heartily sick of the faded charms and uncultivated rudeness of his new wife, and accordingly determined once more to pursue the current of his fortune in another hemisphere. He accordingly possessed himself of as much ready money as he could conveniently lay his hands upon, and secretly embarked on board a ship then on the point of sailing for England. The astonishment, rage, and grief of his wife, at the discovery of his flight, may be more easily conceived than described. She has indeed embodied them all with the greatest fidelity in an address to her husband, which, I have reason to believe, she composed immediately after his elopement. I shall only

give the first verse, which possesses certainly much energy
if not elegance :—

"Confusion seize your lowsy soul, ye nasty dirty varment !
  Ye goes your ways, and leaves me here without the least preferment ;
  When you've drunk my gin, and robbed my till, and stolen all my pelf, ye
  Sail away, and think no more on your wife at Philadelphy."

I shall certainly not presume to offer the delicate and
refined reader any further specimen of this coarse and vulgar,
but surely pathetic and feeling, poem. Gray's "Bard" has
been often and justly admired for the beautiful and unexpected abruptness of the opening stanza, the sudden
vehemence of passion in which strange curses are imprecated
on the head of the devoted monarch. It begins with the
beautiful line

"Ruin seize thee, ruthless king ;"

but how inferior is this to the commencement of Mrs.
Odoherty's poem, which I have just extracted ! How
emphatically it addresses itself to our feelings ! How
dreadful the curse which it invokes !

"Confusion seize your lowsy soul !"

The blood runs cold at the monstrous imprecation,—
we feel an involuntary shuddering, such as comes on us
when poring over the infernal caldron of Macbeth, and
listening to unearthly and hellish conjurations. Such are
the proudest triumphs of the poet !

Mr. Odoherty arrived in England after a short and prosperous passage. The following piece was composed on
sailing past Cape Trafalgar in the night. I mistake if it
does not exhibit the strongest traces of powerful and wild
imagination, and only leaves room to regret that, like most
of his poetical effusions, it is unfinished. It reminds us of
some of the best parts of John Wilson's "Isle of Palms :"—

Have you sailed on the breast of the deep,
When the winds had all silenced their breath,
And the waters were hushed in as holy a sleep,
And as calm, as the slumber of death;

When the yellow moon, beaming on high,
Shone tranquilly bright on the wave,
And careered through the vast and impalpable sky,
Till she found in the ocean a grave,
And, dying away by degrees on the sight,
The waters were clad in the mantle of night?

'Twould impart a delight to thy soul,
As I felt it imparted to mine,
And the draught of affliction that blackened my bowl
Grew bright as the silvery brine.
I carelessly lay on the deck,
And listened in silence to catch
The wonderful stories of battle or wreck
That were told by the men of the watch ;
Sad stories of demons most deadly that be,
And of mermaids that rose from the depths of the sea.

Strange visions my fancy had filled,
I was wet with the dews of the night ;
And I thought that the moon still continued to gild
The wave with a silvery light.
I sunk by degrees into sleep,
I thought of my friends who were far,
When a form seemed to glide o'er the face of the deep,
As bright as the evening star.
Ne'er rose there a spirit more lovely and fair,
Yet I trembled to think that a spirit was there.

Emerald green was her hair,
Braided with gems of the sea ;
Her arm, like a meteor, she waved in the air,
And I knew that she beckoned on me.
She glanced upon me with her eyes ;
How ineffably bright was their blaze !
I shrunk and I trembled with fear and surprise,
Yet still I continued to gaze ;
But enchantingly sweet was the smile of her lip,
And I followed the vision and sprang from the ship.

'Mid the waves of the ocean I fell,
The dolphins were sporting around,
And many a triton was tuning the shell,
And ecstatic and wild was the sound ;
There were thousands of fathoms above,
And thousands of fathoms below ;
And we sunk to the caves where the sea lions rove,
And the topaz and emerald glow,
Where the diamond and sapphire eternally shed
Their lustre around on the bones of the dead.

And well might their lustre be bright,
For they shone on the limbs of the brave,
Of those who had fought in the terrible fight,
And were buried at last in the wave.
In grottoes of coral they slept,
On white beds of pearl around,
And near them for ever the water-snake crept,
And the sea-lion guarded the ground,
While the dirge of the heroes by spirits was rung,
And solemn and wild were the strains that they sung.

Dirge.

Sweet is the slumber the mariners sleep :
Their bones are laid in the caves of the deep,
Far over their heads the tempests sweep,
That ne'er shall wake them more.
They died when raved the bloody fight,
And loud was the cannons' roar ;
Their death was dark, their glory bright,
And they sunk to rise no more,
They sunk to rise no more.
But the loud wind past
When they breathed their last,
And it carried their dying sigh
In a winding-sheet,
With a shot at their feet ;
In coral caves they lie,
In coral caves they lie.
Or where the syren of the rocks
Lovely waves her sea-green locks,
Where the deadly breakers foam
Found they an eternal home !

Horrid and long were the struggles of death,
Black was the night when they yielded their breath :
But not on the ocean, all buoyant and bloated,
The sport of the waters, their white bodies floated.
For they were borne to coral caves,
Distant far beneath the waves ;
And there on beds of pearl they slept,
And far over their heads the tempests swept,
That ne'er shall wake them more,
That ne'er shall wake them more.

On his arrival in England he repaired immediately to
London, and effected an exchange into the 99th or King's
Own Tipperary regiment, and set off immediately to join
the depôt then stationed in the Isle of Wight.   In order to

cover the reason of his leaving his former regiment, and to prevent the true cause of his exchange from becoming publicly known, he addressed the following stanzas to the officers of the 44th regiment, and took care to have them inserted in all the newspapers, with the signature of Morgan Odoherty. They are as follows :—

> Come, push round the bottle ; one glass ere we part
> Must in sadness go round to the friends of my heart,
> With whom many a bright hour of joy has gone by,
> Whom with pleasure I met, whom I leave with a sigh.
>
> Yes, the hours have gone by : like a bright sunny gleam,
> In the dark sky of winter they fled like a dream ;
> Yet, when years shall have cast their dim shadows between,
> I shall fondly remember the days that have been.
>
> Come, push round the bottle ; for ne'er shall the chain
> That has bound us together be broken in twain,
> And I'll drink, wheresoever my lot may be cast,
> To the friends that I love, and the days that are past.

This *ruse de guerre* had the desired effect, for nobody could possibly suspect that the author of this sentimental and very feeling address had just been kicked out of the regiment by these very dear friends whom he thus pathetically lauds. Soon after his arrival at the depôt of the 99th regiment, he was ordered to proceed on the recruiting service to Scotland, and arrived in Edinburgh in the summer of 1815. Here new and unexpected honours awaited him. He had hitherto been a stranger to literary distinctions, and, notwithstanding his writing in the different periodical publications attracted much of the public admiration, he had hitherto remained, in the more extended signification of the word, absolutely unnoticed. This, however, was at length to cease ; and though Mr. Odoherty was by birth an Irishman (to the shame of that country be it spoken), it was Scotland which first learned to appreciate and reward his merit. Soon after his arrival at this metropolis, he was voted a member of the "Select Society." Here he distinguished himself by his eloquence in a very eminent degree ; and as the gentlemen of this Society seemed to pride themselves more on the quantity than the quality of their orations, and seemed to meet with much greater success in the multiplication of their words than in the multiplication of their ideas, to correspond with them, Mr. Odoherty, from his natural volubility, soon succeeded in casting his rivals in the shade. In particular, I am told he made a speech of four hours and a half on the very new and interesting question of whether Brutus was justified in the assassination of Cæsar ; which was carried in the affirmative by a majority of one, and may therefore be considered as being finally settled. He likewise made a long speech on the question of the propriety of early marriages, and clearly established, in a most pathetic and luminous oration, that Queen Elizabeth was by no means justified in the execution of Mary. It was impossible that these elaborate displays of the most extraordinary talent could long remain unnoticed. In consequence of his giving a most clear and scientific description of a Roman frying-pan, found in the middle of a bog in the county of Kilkenny, he was immediately elected a member of the Society of Scottish Antiquaries, and read at their meetings several very interesting papers, which were received by his brother antiquaries with the most grateful attention. He was likewise proposed a member of the Royal Society, and unfortunately black-balled. Candour induces me to state, for the credit of that learned body, that this rejection was not understood to proceed on the personal unfitness of Mr. Odoherty for the proposed honour, but was simply owing to the circumstances of several Irish members who had been recently chosen having bilked the Society of their fees, which made them unwilling to add to their number. To make amends for this disappointment, the same week in which it occurred he was proposed in the Society of Dilletanti, and admitted by acclamation into that enlightened body. The evenings which he spent at their meetings in Young's Tavern, High Street, were often mentioned by him as among the most

radiant oases in the desert of his existence.   He composed
a beautiful ode to the keeper of the tavern where they
assemble, of which we cannot at present quote more than
the three opening stanzas—

> Let Dandies to M'Culloch go,
>   And Ministers to Fortune's hall ;
> For Indians Oman's claret flow,
> In John M'Phail's let lawyers crow,—
> These places seem to me so so :
>   I love Bill Young's above them all.
>
> One only rival, honest Bill,
>   Hast thou in Morgan's whim ;
> I mean Ben Waters, charming Ben,
> Simplest and stupidest of men ;
> I take a tankard now and then,
>   And smoke a pipe with him.
>
> Dear Ben ! dear Bill ! I love you both,
>   Between you oft my fancy wavers ;
> Thou, Bill, excell'st in sheepshead broth ;
> Thy porter-mugs are crowned with froth ;
> At Young's I listen, nothing loth,
>   To my dear Dilletanti shavers.
>   Oh scene of merriment and havers,
>   Of good rum-punch, and puns, and clavers,
>   And warbling sweet Elysian quavers !—
> Who loves not Young's must be a Goth.

III.

THE ode to Messrs. Young and Waters, with part of which
we closed our last notice of Mr Odoherty's life, has a
merit which is far from being common among modern lyrics
—it expresses the habitual feelings of the author.   The
composer of an ode, in these times, is usually obliged to
throw himself out of his own person into that of some
individual placed in a situation more picturesque than has
fallen to his own share ; he is obliged to dismiss all recollection of his own papered parlour and writing-desk, and to
imagine himself, *pro tempore*, a burning Indian, a dying
soldier, or a love-sick young lady, as it may happen.   He

thus loses that intense air of personal emotion, which forms
the principal charm in the stern heroics of Pindar, the elegant
drinking-songs of Horace, the gay *chansons* of Deshoulieres,
and the luxurious erotics of Tom Moore. Odoherty wrote
of Young and Waters in his own person ; the feelings which
he has embodied in verse are the daily, or rather nightly,
visitants of his own bosom. If truth and nature form the
chief excellence of poetry, our hero may take his place among
the most favoured children of the Muse.

Those taverns were, however, far from being the scenes
of mere merriment and punch-drinking. The bowl was
seasoned with the conversation of associates, of whom it is
sufficient to say that they were indeed worthy to sit at the
board with Ensign and Adjutant Odoherty. The writer of
this has no personal knowledge of these distinguished persons ;
but from the letters and poems of the Ensign's, composed
during his stay in Edinburgh, it is evident that those upon
whom he set most value were the following gentlemen :
James Hogg, Esq., the celebrated author of " The Queen's
Wake," " Pilgrims of the Sun," " Mador of the Moor," and
other well-known poems. Of this great man Odoherty
always wrote with rapture. Take the following specimen :—

> While worldly men through stupid years
>   Without emotion jog,
> Devoid of passions, hopes, and fears,
>   As senseless as a log,
> I much prefer my nights to spend,
>   A happy ranting dog,
> And see dull care his front unbend
>   Before the smile of Hogg.
>
> The life of man's a season drear,
>   Immersed in mist and fog,
> Until the star of wit appear,
>   And set its clouds agog.
> For me, I wish no brighter sky
>   Than o'er a jug of grog,
> When fancy kindles in the eye,
>   The good grey eye of Hogg.
>
> When Misery's car is at its speed,
>   The glowing wheels to cog ;

> To make the heart where sorrows bleed
>   Leap lightly like a frog ;
> Gay verdure o'er the crag to shower,
>   And blossoms o'er the bog,
> Wit's potent magic has the power
>   When thou dost wield it, Hogg !

In the escritoir of the Ensign his executors found, among letters from the first literary characters of the day, many excellent ones from Mr Hogg ; and the following beautiful lines formed the postscript to that one in which he returned thanks to our poet for the above tribute to his own kindred genius :—

> O hone, Odoherty !
> I canna weel tell what is wrang ;
> But oh, man, since you gaed frae me,
> The days are unco dull and lang.
> I try the paper and the sclate,
> And pen, and cawk, and killivine ;
> But nothing can I write of late,
> That even Girzzy ca's divine.
>   O hone, Odoherty !
>   O hone, Odoherty !
> Oh weary fa' the fates' decree,
> That garred the Captain part frae me.
>
> O hone, Odoherty !
> Come back, come back to Ettrick lake,
> And ye sall hear, and ye sall see,
> What I'se do for the Captain's sake.
> I'll coff tobacco o' the best,
> And pipes baith lang and short I'se gie ;
> And the toddy-stoup sall ne'er get rest,
> Frae morn till night, 'tween you and me.
>   O hone, Odoherty !
>   O hone, Odoherty !
> O welcome sall the moment be
> That brings the Captain back to me.

Next to the Ettrick Shepherd, the member of the Dilletanti who shared most of Ensign Odoherty's confidence and affection was William Allan, Esq. This gentleman's genius as a painter does not require any notice on the present occasion. He has, we understand, done justice to his own feelings, and to his friend, by introducing a striking likeness of Odoherty's features into one of his principal pieces. Reader, the Cobbler in the Press-gang is Odoherty! To Mr Allan, Odoherty frequently addressed humorous epistles in verse. We prefer, however, to quote the following eulogy, which is written in the Adjutant's best serious manner :—

> When wondering ages shall have rolled away,
> And that be ancient which is new to-day ;
> When Time has pour'd his warm and softening glow
> O'er that pale virgin's * throbbing breast of snow,
> And lent the settled majesty of years
> To those grim Spahis, and those proud viziers ;
> From distant lands the ardent youth shall come
> To gaze with admiration—breathless, dumb,
> To fix his eyes, like orbs of marble *there !*
> And let his soul luxuriate in despair.
> Posterity ! Ah, what's a name to thee?
> What Raphael is, my Allan then shall be.

As the writer of the present notice intends to publish in a separate form the poetical verses of Odoherty, with authentic portraits of his friends, it is not necessary to quote any more of these effusions now. The pleasantry of the Ensign was always harmless, and his very satire was both dart and balsam. He never condescended to personalities, except in one solitary instance, in a song entitled "The Young Man of the West," composed upon Mr James Grahame, the famous anti-Malthusian philosopher. This song he used to sing with great humour, to the tune of " A Cobbler there was," &c.; but though frequently urged to do so, he never would print it ; and on his own manuscript copy there is this note, " Let the Young Man of the West be destroyed ;" an injunction which has since been scrupulously complied with.

During one of those brilliant evenings at the Dilletanti, which, says our bard in a letter to the present writer, "will for ever live in the memory of all who enjoyed them," the conversation ran upon the Italian improvisatori. Odoherty remarked that the power which appeared to many so wonderful was no way uncommon, and offered to recite, or

* Circassian captive.

write down *currente calamo*, a poem upon any given subject. The president proposed "An Elegy, by a Young Lady in a Ball-room disappointed of a Partner," and the Adjutant wrote down the following twenty four-line stanzas in fifty-three minutes nineteen seconds by a stop-watch. Such an achievement throws the Admirable Crichton into the shade :—

ELEGY WRITTEN IN A BALL-ROOM.

The beaux are jogging on the pictured floor,
  The belles responsive trip with lightsome heels ;
While I, deserted, the cold pangs deplore,
  Or breathe the wrath which slighted beauty feels.

When first I entered glad, with glad mamma,
  The girls were ranged and clustered round us then ;
Few beaux were there, those few with scorn I saw,
  Unknowing Dandies that could come at ten.

My buoyant heart beat high with promised pleasure,
  My dancing garland moved with airy grace ;
Quick beat my active toe to Gow's gay measure,
  And undissembled triumph wreathed my face.

Fancy prospective took a proud survey
  Of all the coming glories of the night ;
Even where I stood my legs began to play—
  So racers paw the turf e'er jockeys smite.

And "who shall be my partner first?" I said,
  As my thoughts glided o'er the coming beaux :
"Not Tom, nor Ned, nor Jack." I tossed my head,
  Nice grew my taste, and high my scorn arose.

"If Dicky asks me, I shall spit and sprain ;
  When Sam approaches, headaches I will mention ;
I'll freeze the Colonel's heart with cold disdain :"
  Thus cruelly ran on my glib invention.

While yet my fancy revelled in her dreams,
  The sets are forming, and the fiddles scraping ;
Gow's wakening chord a stirring prelude screams,
  The beaux are quizzing, and the misses gaping.

Beau after beau approaches, bows, and smiles,
  Quick to the dangler's arm springs glad ma'amselle ;
Pair after pair augments the sparkling files,
  And full upon my ear "THE TRIUMPH" swells.

I flirt my fan in time with the mad fiddle,
  My eye pursues the dancers' motions flying ;
Cross hands ! Balancez ! Down and up the middle !
  To join the revel how my heart is dying.

One miss sits down all glowing from the dance,
  Another rises, and another yet ;
Beaux upon belles, and belles on beaux advance,
  The tune unending, ever full the set.

At last a pause there comes.   To Gow's keen hand
  The hurrying lackey hands the enlivening port ;
The misses sip the ices where they stand,
  And gather vigour to renew the sport.

I round the room dispense a wistful glance,
  Wish Ned, or Dick, or Tom would crave the honour ;
I hear Sam whisper to Miss B., "Do dance,"
  And launch a withering scowl of envy on her.

Sir Billy capers up to Lady Di ;
  In vain I cough as gay Sir Billy passes ;
The Major asks my sister ; faint I sigh,
  "Well, after this—the men are grown such asses !"

In vain ! In vain ! Again the dancers mingle,
  With lazy eye I watch the busy scene,
Far on the pillowed sofa sad and single,
  Languid the attitude, but sharp the spleen.

"La ! ma'am, how hot !" "You're quite fatigued, I see ;"
  "What a long dance !" "And so you're come to town !"
Such casual whispers are addressed to me,
  But not one hint to lead the next set down.

The third, the fourth, the fifth, the sixth, are gone,
  And now the seventh, and yet I'm asked not once !
When supper comes must I descend alone ?
  Does Fate deny me my last prayer—a dunce ?

Mamma supports me to the room for munching,
  There turkey's breast she crams, and wing of pullet ;
I slobbering jelly and hard nuts am crunching,
  And pouring tuns of trifle down my gullet.

No beau invites me to a glass of sherry ;
  Above me stops the salver of champagne ;
While all the rest are tossing brimmers merry,
  I with cold water comfort my disdain.

Ye bucks of Edinburgh ! ye tasteless creatures !
  Ye vapid Dandies ! how I scorn you all !

> Green slender slips, with pale cheese-paring features,
>   And awkward, lumb'ring, red-faced boobies tall.
>
> Strange compounds of the beau and the attorney!
>   Raw lairds! and schoolboys for a whisker shaving!
> May injured beauty's glance of fury burn ye!
>   I hate you, clowns and fools! But hah! I'm raving!

We shall now take leave, for the present, of Odoherty and the Dilletanti Society, with an extract from his longest and latest poem, entitled " Young's Night Thoughts" (a humorous allusion to the before-mentioned celebrated tavern). Lively as this strain is, we can scarcely read it without tears ; for it was, we repeat, the very last of his works here below. The following poem, copied by a female hand on hot-pressed gilt paper, is intended to explain the great leading object of the poem :—

> There was a time when every sort of people
>   Created, relished, and commended jokes ;
> But now a joker's stared at, like a steeple,
>   By the majority of Christian folks.
> Dulness has tanned her hide to thickness triple,
>   And Observation sets one in the stocks,
> When you've been known a comic song to sing,
> Write notices, or any harmless thing.
>
> This Edinburgh, Edina, or Dunedin
>   ('Cleped, in the Bailie's lingo, " the Good Town ;"
> But styled " Auld Reekie " by all Celts now treading
>   Her streets, bows, wynds, lanes, crescents, up and down,
> Her labyrinths of stairs and closes threading
>   On other people's business or their own—
> Those bandy, broad-faced, rough-kneed, ragged laddies,
> Those horny-fisted, those gill-swigging caddies)—
>
> This Edinburgh some call Metropolis,
>   And Capital, and Athens of the North—
> I know not what they mean. I'm sure of this,
>   Tho' she abounds in men of sense and worth,
> Her staple and predominant qualities
>   Are ignorance and nonsense, and so forth ;
> I don't like making use of a hard word,
> But 'tis the merest *hum* I ever heard.
>
> There's our Mackenzie : all with veneration
>   See him that Harley felt and Caustic drew ;

'There's Scott, the pride and darling of his nation,
  Poet and cavalier, kind, generous, true ;
There's Jeffrey, who has been the botheration
  Of the whole world with his glib, sharp Review,
And made most young Scots lawyers mad with Whiggery ;
There's Leslie, Stewart, Alison, and Gregory.

But these and some few others being named,
  I don't remember one more great gun in her ;
The remanent population can't be blamed
  Because their chief concern in life's their dinner.
To give examples I should be ashamed,
  And people would cry, "Lord ! that wicked sinner !"
(For all we gentry here are quite egg-shells,
We can't endure jokes that come near "*oorsells.*")

They say that knowledge is diffused and general,
  And taste and understanding are *so* common ;
I'd rather see a sweep-boy suck a penny roll
  Than listen to a criticising woman.
And as for poetry, the time of dinner all,
  Thank God, I then have better things to do, man.
Exceptions 'gainst the fair were coarse and shocking :
I've seen in breeches may a true blue-stocking.

Blue-stocking stands, in my vocabulary,
  For one that always chatters (sex is nothing)
About new books from June to January,
  And with re-echoed carpings moves your loathing.
I like to see young people smart and airy,
  With well-dressed hair and fashionable clothing.
Can't they discourse about ball, rout, or play,
And know reviewing's quite out of their way?

It strikes me as a thing exceeding stupid
  This conversation about books, books, books.
When I was young, and sat 'midst damsels grouped,
  I talked of roses, zephyrs, gurgling brooks,
Venus, the Graces, Dian, Hymen, Cupid,
  Perilous glances, soul-subduing looks,
Slim tapering fingers, glossy clustering curls,
Diamonds and emeralds, cairngorms and pearls.

On Una that made sunshine in the shade,
  And Emily with eye of liquid jet,
And gentle Desdemona, and the maid
  That sleeps within the tomb of Capulet
Hearts love to ponder.   Would it not degrade
  Our notion of a nymph like Juliet,
To be informed that she had just read through
Last number of the *Edinburgh Review?*

> Leave ye to dominies and sticker stibblers,
> And all the sedentary generation,
> The endless chitter-chatter about scribblers,
> And England's melancholy situation.
> Let them be still the customary nibblers
> Of all that rule or edify the nation ;
> Leave off the Corn-bill, and the law of libel,
> And read the Pilgrim's Progress or your Bible.

From the poem itself we quote the following stanzas, without any remarks, convinced that their simple elegance and unaffected grace stand in no need of the critic's recommendation :—

> I rose this morning at half-past nine,
>   At breakfast coffee I consumed *pour quatre*,
> Unnumbered rolls enriched with marmalade fine,
>   And little balls of butter dished in water,
> Three eggs, two platesful of superb cold chine
>   (Much recommended to make thin folks fatter) ;
> And, having thus my ballast stowed on board,
> Roamed forth to kill a day's time like a lord.
>
> How I contrived to pass the whole forenoon,
>   I can't remember though my life were on it ;
> I helped G. T. in jotting of a tune,
>   And hinted rhymes to G——s for a sonnet ;
> Called at the Knox's shop with Miss Balloon,
>   And heard her *ipse dixit* on a bonnet ;
> Then washed my mouth with ices, tarts, and flummeries,
> And ginger-beer and soda, at Montgomery's.
>
> Down Princes Street I once or twice paraded,
>   And gazed upon these same eternal faces ;
> Those beardless beaux and bearded belles, those faded
>   And flashy silks, surtouts, pelisses, laces ;
> Those crowds of clerks, astride on hackneys jaded,
>   Prancing and capering with notarial grace ;
> Dreaming enthusiasts who indulge vain whimsies
> That they might pass in Bond Street or St. James's.
>
> I saw equestrian and pedestrian vanish—
>   One to a herring in his lonely shop,
> And some of kind gregarious, and more clannish,
>   To club at Waters' for a mutton-chop ;
> Myself resolved for once my cares to banish,
>   And give the Cerberus of thought a sop ;
> Got Jack's, and Sam's, and Dick's, and Tom's consent,
> And o'er the Mound to Billy Young's we went.

I am not nice, I care not what I dine on,
　A sheep's head or beef-steak is all I wish.
Old Homer! how he loved the ἐρυθρὸν οἶνον :
　It is the glass that glorifies the dish.
The thing that I have always set my mind on
　(A small foundation laid of fowl, flesh, fish)
Is out of bottle, pitcher, or punch-bowl,
To suck reviving solace to my soul.

Life's a dull, dusty desert, waste and drear,
　With now and then an oasis between,
Where palm-trees rise, and fountains gushing clear
　Burst 'neath the shelter of that leafy screen.
Haste not your parting steps when such appear,
　Repose, ye weary travellers, on the green.
Horace and Milton, Dante, Burns, and Schiller,
Dined at a tavern—when they had "the siller."

And ne'er did poet, epical or tragical,
　At Florence, London, Weimar, Rome, Maybole,
See Time's dark lanthorn glow with hues more magical
　Than I have witnessed in the Coffin-hole.
Praise of antiquity a bam and fudge I call,
　Ne'er past the present let my wishes roll ;
A fig for all comparing, croaking grumblers,
Hear me, dear dimpling Billy, bring the tumblers.

Let blank verse hero, or Spenserian rhymer,
　Treat Donna Musa with chateau-margout,
Chateau-Lafitte, Johannisberg, Hocheimer,
　In tall outlandish glasses green and blue.
Thanks to my stars, myself a doggrel-chimer,
　Have nothing with such costly tastes to do ;
My muse is always kindest when I court her
O'er whisky-punch, gin-twist, strong beer, and porter.

And oh, my pipe, though in these dandy days
　Few love thee, fewer still their love confess,
Ne'er let me blush to celebrate thy praise,
　Divine invention of the age of Bess !
I for a moment interrupt my lays
　The tiny tube with loving lip to press :
I'll then come back with a reviving zest,
　And give thee three more stanzas of my best.

(I smoke.)

Pipe ! whether plain in fashion of Frey-herr,
　Or gaudy glittering in the taste of Boor,
Deep-darkened Meer-schaum or Ecume-de-mer,
　Or snowy clay of Gowda, light and pure.

Let different people different pipes prefer,
   Delft, horn, or catgut ; long, short, older, newer ;
Puff, every brother, as it likes him best :
   De gustibus non disputandum est.

Pipe ! when I stuff into thee my canaster,
   With flower of camomil and leaf of rose,
And the calm rising fume comes fast and faster,
   Curling with balmy circles near my nose,
And all the while my dexter hand is master
   Of the full cup from Meux's vat that flows—
Heavens ! all my brain a soft oblivion wraps
Of wafered letters and of single taps.

I've no objections to a good cigar,
   A true Havannah, smooth, and moist, and brown ;
But then the smoke's too near the eye by far,
   And out of doors 'tis in a twinkling flown ;
And somehow it sets all my teeth ajar,
   When to an inch or so we've smoked him down ;
And, if your leaf have got a straw within it,
You know 'tis like a cinder in a minute.

I have no doubt a long excursive hooker
   Suits well some lordly lounger of Bengal,
Who never writes or looks into a book, or
   Does anything with earnestness at all.
He sits, and his tobacco's in the nook, or,
   Tended by some black heathen in the hall,
Lays up his legs, and thinks he does great things
If once in the half-hour a puff he brings.

I rather follow in my smoking trim
   The example of Scots cottars and their wives,
Who, while the evening air is warm and dim,
   In July sit beside their garden hives ;
And, gazing all the while with wrinkles grim
   To see how the concern of honey thrives,
Empty before they've done a four-ounce bag
Of sailors' twist, or, what's less common—shag.

IV.

THIS winter was indeed a memorable one in the life of
Odoherty. Divided almost in equal proportions between
the Old and the New Town of Edinburgh, the society of
Hogg, Allan, and the Dilettanti on the one hand, and that
of the female and fashionable world on the other, and thus
presenting to the active mind of the Ensign a perpetual

succession or, rather, alternation of the richest viands, it produced the effects which might have been anticipated. and swelled considerably the bulk of two portfolios, respectively set apart for the prose and verse compositions which. at this period of his career, our bard was so rapidly pouring forth to the admiration of his numerous friends and the public.

His morning hours were devoted to attend several courses of lectures in the University ; for Odoherty was never weary of learning, and embraced with ardour every opportunity that was afforded him of increasing the stores of his literary acquisitions and accomplishments. His remarks upon the different lectures which he now attended possess all his characteristic acuteness, and would have done honour to a more practised critic. But these we reserve for the separate publication of his works. To insert any mutilated fragments of them here would be an act of injustice to the illustrious Professors, Brown, Playfair, Leslie, Hope, Ritchie, &c., no less than to their distinguished disciple. Great and illustrious as is the fame of these philosophers, it is possible that the names of some of them may live in distant ages chiefly because of their connection with that of Odoherty. The Ensign may be to them what Xenophon has been to Socrates ; he may be more, for it is possible that none of them may have a Plato.

The gay world of the northern metropolis, which during this remarkable winter was adorned by the graceful and ingenious Ensign, seems, we are constrained to observe, to have found less favour in his eyes than in those of most other visitors with whom we have had an opportunity of conversing. In one of those inimitable letters of his, addressed to the compiler of the present sketch, he comments with some little causticity on the incidents of several balls and routes which he had just attended. "The gaieties of Edinburgh," writes the Ensign, "are a bad and lame caricature of those of London. There is the same squeeze, the same heat, the same buzz; but, alas ! the ease, the elegance, the nonchalance are awanting. In London the different orders of society are so numerous that they keep themselves totally apart from each other; and the highest circles of fashion admit none as denizens except those who possess the hereditary claims of birth and fortune, or (as in my own case) those who are supposed to atone for their deficiencies in these respects by extraordinary genius or merit. Hence there are so few stones of the first or even of the second water that recourse is necessarily had to far inferior gems, not unfrequently even to the transitory mimicries of *paste*. You shall see the lady of an attorney stowing away her bedsteads and basinstands, dismantling all her apartments, and turning her whole family topsy-turvy once in a season, in order that she may have the satisfaction of dispersing two hundred cards, with ' *At home* ' upon them. It is amusing enough to see with what laborious exertion she and her daughters, sensible people that attend to domestic concerns, plainwork, &c., for three parts of the year, become for a few short weeks the awkward inapt copyists of their far less respectable betters. It is distressing to see the faded airs with which these good *bourgeoises* endeavour to conceal their confusion in receiving the curtsy of a lady of quality, who comes to their houses only for the purpose of quizzing them in some corner, with some sarcastic younger brother," &c. The rest of the letter, consisting chiefly of rapturous descriptions of particular young ladies, is omitted from motives of delicacy. Two fair creatures, however, a most exquisite petite blonde, and a superb sultana-like brunette, who seem to have divided for several weeks the possession of the sensitive heart of Odoherty, may receive, upon personal application to the publisher, several sonnets, elegies, &c., which are inscribed with their names in the above-mentioned portfolio of their departed admirer, faint and frail memorials of unripened affections,—memorials over which they may now drop a tear of delightful pensiveness, which they may now press to the virgin bosom without a hope, and therefore, alas! without a blush.

About this period their Imperial Highnesses the Arch-dukes John and Lewis of Austria arrived in the Caledonian metropolis.   Although they received every polite attention from the military, legal, and civic dignitaries of the place, these elevated personages were afflicted, notwithstanding, with considerable symptoms of ennui in the course of the long evening which they spent at M'Culloch's, after returning from the pomps and festivities of the day.   It was then that, their Highnesses expressing some desire to partake of the more unceremonious and week-day society of the Northern Athens, various characters of singing, smoking, and scientific celebrity were introduced to their apartment, through the intervention of a gentleman in their suite.   Among these, it is scarcely necessary to observe, was Odoherty.   The Ensign, with that happy tact which a man of true genius carries into every situation of life, immediately perceived and caught the air, manner, &c., in a word, whatever was best adapted for captivating the archiducal fancy.   His proficiency in the German tongue, the only one which these princes spoke with much fluency, was not indeed great ; but he made amends for this by the truly Germanic ferocity with which he smoked (for the Ensign was one of those who could send the cloud *ad libitum* through the ears and nostrils, as well as the mouth), by the unqualified admiration which he testified for the favourite imperial beverage of Giles' ale ; but, above all, by the style of matchless excellence in which he sung some of his own songs, among which were the following :—

SONG I.

Confusion to routs and at homes,
    To assemblies, and balls, and what not ;
'Tis with pain e'er Odoherty roams
    From the scenes of the pipe and the pot.
Your Dandies may call him a sot,
    They never can call him a spoon ;
And Odoherty cares not a jot,
    For he's sure you won't join in the tune.

    With your pipes and your swipes,
    And your herrings and tripes,
You never can join in the tune.

I'm a swapper, as every one knows,
  In my pumps six feet three inches high ;
'Tis no wonder your minikin beaux
  Have a fancy to fight rather shy
Of a Gulliver chap such as I,
  That could stride over troops of their tribes,
That had never occasion to buy
  Either collars, or calves, or kibes,
    My boot wrenches and pinches,
    Though 'tis wide twenty inches,
And I don't bear my brass at my kibes.

When I see a fantastical hopper,
  A trim little chip of the *ton*,
Not so thick as your Highness' pipe-stopper,
  And scarcely, I take it, so long,
Swaddled prim and precise as a prong,
  With his ribs running all down and up,
Says I, Does the creature belong
  To the race of the ewe or the tup ?
    With their patches and their scratches,
    And their plastered mustaches,
They are more of the ewe than the tup.

SONG II.

That nothing is perfect has frequently been
  By the wisest philosophers stated untruly ;
Which only can prove that they never had seen
  The agreeable Lady Lucretia Gilhooly.
Where's the philosopher would not feel loss of her ?
  Whose bosom these bright sunny eyes would not thaw ?
Although I'm a game one, these little highwaymen
  Have rifled the heart of poor Major M'Craw.

Cook sailed round the world, and Commodore Anson
  The wonders he met with has noted down duly ;
But Cook, nor yet Anson, could e'er light by chance on
  A beauty like Lady Lucretia Gilhooly.
Let astronomer asses still peep through their glasses,
  Then tell all the stars and the planets they saw ;
Damn Georgium Sidus ! we've Venus beside us,
  And that is sufficient for Major M'Craw.

Delighted with this mirthful evening, the illustrious strangers, before breaking up, insisted that Odoherty, the principal source of its hilarity, should accompany them next day to the literary, mercantile, and manufacturing city of Glasgow. Here the Ensign was received in the most distinguished manner, not more on account of the company in which he travelled than of the individual fame which had already found its way before him to the capital of St. Mungo. The party put up at the Buck's Head, to the excellent hostess of which (Mrs. Jardine) the Ensign addressed a pathetic sonnet at parting. At the dinner given by the provost and magistrates, the Ensign attended in full puff, and was placed among the most illustrious guests, at the upper end of the table. He sung, he joked, he spoke ; he was the *sine quâ non* of the meeting. At the collation prepared for the imperial party by the Professors of the University, he made himself equally agreeable ; and indeed, upon both of these occasions, laid the foundations of several valuable friendships, which only terminated with his existence. Among his MSS. we have found a paper which purports to contain the words of a *programma* affixed to the gate of the college on the morning preceding the visit of the Archdukes. We shall not hesitate to transcribe this fragment, although, from our ignorance of the style and ceremonial observed on similar occasions by the Scottish universities, we are not able to vouch for its authenticity. The Ensign kept his papers in much disorder—*seria mixta jocis,* as his Roman favourite expresses it.

Q. F. F. Q. S.

Senatus Academicus Togatis et non Togatis Salutem dat.—Ab altissimo et potentissimo Principe Marchione de Douglas et Clydesdale, certiores facti quod eorum altitudines imperiales Archiduces Joannes et Ludovicus de Austria hodie nos visitatione honorare intendunt, hasce regulas enunciare quomodo omnes se sunt gerere placuit nobis, et quicunque eas non volunt observare severrime puniti erunt postea.

1*mo.* Eorum altitudines imperiales Archiduces Joannes et Ludovicus de Austria capient frigidam collationem in aula priori cum principali et professoribus (cum togis suis) et quibusdam generosis hominibus ex urbe et vicinitate, et signifero Dochertiade et alia sequela eorum circa horam meridianam, impensis Facultatis.

2. Studentes qui barbas habent tondeant et manus et facies lavent sicuti in die dominico.

3. Studentes omnes indusia nitida induant velut cum Dux Montis-Rosarum erat hic.

4. Studentes Theologici nigras braccas et vestes et pallia decentia induant quasi ministri.

5. Omnes studentes in casu sint videri per Archiduces et Marchiones et honorabiles personas qui cum iis sunt; et Hibernici et Montani supra omnia sibi oculum habeant et omnes pectantur.

6. Studentes duas lineas faciant decenter et cum quiete intra aulam priorem et aulam communem cum processio ambulat, et juniores ni rideant cum peregrinos vident.

7. In aula communi Professor . . . (name illegible) qui olim in Gallia fuit Franciscc illis locutus erit nam Professor . . . est mortuus.

8. Deinde aliquis ex Physicis sermonem Anglicam pronunciabit et Principalis Latine precabitur.

9. Sine strepitu dismissi estotis cum omnia facta sunt.

It is to be regretted that several leaves are awanting in the Ensign's diary, which probably contained an account of the rest of the tour which he performed in company with the scions of the house of Hapsburg. Their custom of smoking several pipes every evening after supper took from him, it is not unlikely, the leisure that might have been necessary for composing a full narrative; but, however slight his *precis* might have been, its loss is to be regretted. The sketches of a master are of more value than the most elaborate works of secondary hands; the fragment of an Angelo surpasses the *chef-d'œuvres* of a West. But to return. At Dublin, the festivities with which the arrival of the party was celebrated surpassed in splendour and variety, as might be expected, everything that had been exhibited in the cities of Scotland. After spending several days in a round of gaieties, the Archdukes set sail for Liverpool. Odoherty, from the pressure of his professional engagements, found himself compelled to go no farther in the train of the princely travellers. The parting was one of those scenes which may be more easily imagined than described. Although the Ensign lingered a day or two in the midst of the most brilliant society of Dublin, although he spent his mornings with Phillips, and his evenings with Lady Morgan, his spirits did not soon recover their usual tone and elasticity. The state of gloom in which his mind was thus temporarily involved extended no inconsiderable portion of its influence to his muse. We do not wish to prolong this article beyond the allowable limit; but we must make room for a single specimen of the dark effusions which at this epoch flowed from the gay, the giddy Odoherty.

THE ENGLISH SAILOR AND THE KING OF ACHEN'S DAUGHTER.

A TALE OF TERROR.

Come, listen gentles all,
And ladies unto me,
And you shall be told of a sailor bold
As ever sailed on sea.

'Twas in the month of May,
Sixteen hundred sixty and four,
We sallied out, both fresh and stout,
In the good ship *Swiftsure*.

With wind and weather fair
We sailed from Plymouth Sound;
And the Line we crossed, and the Cape we passed,
Being to China bound.

And we sailed by Sunda Isles,
And Ternate and Tydore,
Till the wind it lagged, and our sails they flagged,
In sight of Achen's shore.

Becalmed, days three times three,
We lay in the burning sun;

Our water we drank, and our meat it stank,
 And our biscuits were well nigh done.

Oh ! then 'twas an awful sight
 Our seamen for to behold,
Who t'other day were so fresh and gay,
 And their hearts as stout as gold.

But now our hands they shook,
 And our cheeks were yellow and lean,
Our faces all long, and our nerves unstrung,
 And loose and squalid our skin.

And we walked up and down the deck
 As long as our legs could bear us ;
And we thirsted all, but no rain would fall,
 And no dews arise to cheer us.

But the red red sun from the sky
 Lent his scorching beams all day,
Till our tongues, through drought, hung out of our mouth,
 And we had no voice to pray.

And the hot hot air from the South
 Did lie on our lungs all night,
As if the grim Devil, with his mouth full of evi
 Had blown on our troubled sprite.

At last, so it happed one night,
 When we all in our hammocks lay,
Bereft of breath, and expecting death
 To come ere break of day,

On a sudden a cooling breeze
 Shook the hammock where I was lain ;
And then, by Heaven's grace, I felt on my face
 A drop of blessed rain.

I opened my half-closed eyes,
 And my mouth I opened it wide ;
And I started with joy from my hammock so high,
 And " A breeze, a breeze ! " I cried.

But no man heard me cry,
 And the breeze again fell down ;
And a clap of thunder, with fear and wonder
 Nigh cast me in a swound.

I dared not look around,
 Till, by degrees grown bolder,
I saw a grim sprite, by the moon's pale light,
 Dim glimmering at my shoulder.

He was drest in a seaman's jacket,
  Wet trousers, and dripping hose,
And an unfelt wind I heard behind,
  That whistled among his clothes.

I looked at him by the light of the stars,
  I looked by the light of the moon ;
And I saw, though his face was covered with scars,
  John Jewkes, my sister's son.

" Alas ! John Jewkes," I cried,
  " Poor boy, what brings thee here ? "
But nothing he said, but hung down his head,
  And made his bare skull appear.

Then I, by my grief grown bold,
  To take his hand endeavoured ;
But his head he turned round, which a gaping wound
  Had nigh from his shoulders severed.

He opened his mouth to speak,
  Like a man with his last breath struggling,
And, before every word, in his throat was heard
  A horrible misguggling.

At last, with a broken groan,
  He gurgled, " Approach not me !
For the fish have my head, and the Indians my blood,
  'Tis only my ghost you see.

" And dost thou not remember
  Three years ago to-day,
How at aunt's we tarried, when sister was married
  To Farmer Robin, pray ?

" Oh ! then we were blythe and jolly,
  But none of us all had seen,
While we sung and we laughed, and the stout ale quaffed,
  That our number was thirteen.

" And none of all the party,
  At the head of the table, saw,
While our cares we drowned, and the flagon went round,
  Old Goody Martha Daw.

" But Martha she was there,
  Though she never spake a word ;
And by her sat her old black cat,
  Though it never cried or purred.

" And she leaned on her oaken crutch,
  And a bundle of sticks she broke,

And her prayers backward muttered, and the Devil's words uttered
  Though she never a word out spoke.

  "'Twas on a Thursday morn,
  That very day was se'nnight,
I ran to sweet Sue, to bid her adieu,
  For I could not stay a minute.

  " Then crying with words so tender,
  She gave me a true lover's locket,
That I still might love her, forgetting her never—
  So I put it in my pocket.

  " And then we kissed and parted,
  And knew not, all the while,
That Martha was nigh on her broomstick so high,
  Looking down with a devilish smile.

  "So I went to sea again,
  With my heart brimfull of Sue ;
Though my mind misgave me, the salt waters would have me,
  And I'd take my last adieu.

  " We made a prosperous voyage
  Till we came to this fatal coast,
When a storm it did rise, in seas and in skies,
  That we gave ourselves up for lost.

  " Our vessel it was stranded
  All on the shoals of Achen ;
And all then did die, save only I,
  And I hardly saved my bacon.

  " It happed that very hour,
  The Black King, walking by,
Did see me sprawling, on my hands and knees crawling,
  And took to his palace hard by.

  " And finding that I was
  A likely lad for to see,
My bones well knit, and my joints well set,
  And not above twenty-three,

  " He made me his gardener boy,
  To sow pease and potatoes,
To water his flowers, when there were no showers,
  And cut his parsley and lettuce.

  "Now it so fell out on a Sunday
  (Which these pagans never keep holy),
I was gathering rue, and thinking on Sue,
  With a heart full of melancholy,

"When the King of Achen's daughter
Did open her casement to see ;
And, as she looked round on the gooseberry ground,
Her eyes they lit upon me ;

" And seeing me tall and slim,
And of shape right personable ;
My skin so white, and so very unlike
The blacks at her father's table,

"She took it into her head
(For so the Devil did move her),
That I, in good sooth, was a comely youth,
And would make a gallant lover.

" So she tripped from her chamber so high,
All in silks and satins clad,
And her gown it rustled, as down she bustled,
With steps like a princess sad.

" Her shoes they were decked with pearls,
And her hair with diamonds glistened,
And her gimcracks and toys, they made such a noise,
My mouth watered the while I listened.

" Then she tempted me with glances,
And with sugared words so tender,
(And though she was black, she was straight in the back,
And young and tall and slender).

" But I my love remembered,
And the locket she did give me,
And resolved to be true to my darling Sue,
As she did ever believe me.

" Whereat the princess waxed
Both furious and angry,
And said, she was sure I had some paramour
In kitchen or in laundry.

" And then, with a devilish grin,
She said, 'Give me your locket '—
But I damned her for a witch, and a conjuring bitch,
And kept it in my pocket.

" Howbeit, both day and night
She did torture and torment,
And said she, ' If you'll yield to me the field,
' I'll give thee thy heart's content.

" ' But give me up the locket,
' And stay three months with me,

' And then, if the will remains with you still,
  'I'll ship you off to sea.'

  "So I thought it the only way
  To behold my lovely Sue ;
And the thoughts of Old England, they made my heart tingle, and
  I gave up the locket so true.

  "Thereon she laughed outright
  With a hellish grin, and I saw
That the princess was gone, and in her room
  There stood old Martha Daw.

  "She was all astride a broomstick,
  And bid me get up behind ;
So my wits being lost, the broomstick I crossed,
  And away we flew, swift as the wind.

  "But my head it soon turned giddy,
  I reeled and lost my balance,
So I tumbled over, like a perjured lover,
  A warning to all gallants.

  "And there where I tumbled down
  The Indians found me lying ;
My head they cut off, and my blood did quaff,
  And set my flesh a-frying.

  "Hence, all ye English gallants
  A warning take by me,
Your true love's locket to keep in your pocket
  Whenever you go to sea.

  "And, O dear uncle Thomas,
  I come to give you warning,
As then 'twas my chance with Davy to dance,
  'Twill be yours to-morrow morning.

  "'Twas three years agone this night,
  Three years gone clear and clean,
Since we sat down at Aunt's at the wedding to dance,
  And our number was thirteen.

  "Now I and sister Nan
  (Two of that fatal party)
Have both gone from Aunt's with Davy to dance,
  Though then we were hale and hearty.

  "And, as we both have died
  (I speak it with grief and sorrow)
At the end of each year, it now is clear
  That you should die to-morrow.

" But if, good uncle Thomas,
   You'll promise, and promise truly,
To plough the main for England again,
   And perform my orders duly,

" Old Davy will allow you
   Another year to live,
To visit your friends, and make up your odd ends,
   And your enemies forgive.

" But, friend, when you reach Old England,
   To Laure'ston town you'll go,
And then to the Mayor, in open fair,
   Impeach old Martha Daw.

" And next you'll see her hanged
   With the halter around her throat ;
And, when void of life, with your clasp-knife
   The string of her apron cut.

" Then, if that you determine
   My last desires to do,
In her left-hand pocket you'll find the locket,
   And carry it to Sue."

The grisly spectre thus
   In mournful accents spoke,
By which time, being morning, he gave me no warning,
   But vanished in sulphur and smoke.

Next day there sprang up a breeze,
   And our ship began to tack,
And for fear of the ghost, we left the coast,
   And sailed for England back.

And I, being come home,
   Did all his words pursue ;
Old Martha likewise was hung at the 'size,
   And I carried the locket to Sue.

And now, being tired of life,
   I make up my mind to die ;
But I thought this story I'd lay before ye,
   For the good of posterity.

Oh never then sit at table
   When the number is thirteen ;
And, lest witches be there, put salt in your beer,
   And scrape your platters clean.

This "Tale of Terror" was composed at the express request of a distinguished female, nearly related (by marriage and genius) to its no less distinguished author. In return this matchless female christened a lovely and promising boy, of whom she was delivered, during the stay of the Ensign, after the name of Odoherty; an appellation the ideas suggested by which will be agreeable, or otherwise, to its bearer, according as he shall, in future years, inherit or not inherit some portion of the genius in whose honour it was originally conferred. Of the various *genethliaca* composed upon the occasion the most admired was the following :—

TO THE CHILD OF CORINNA !

O boy ! may the wit of thy mother awaking
  On thy dewy lip tremble when years have gone by ;
While the fire of Odoherty, fervidly breaking,
  In glances and gleams, may illume thy young eye.

Oh, then such a fulness of power shall be seen
  With the graces so blending, in union endearing,
That angels shall glide o'er the ocean green,
  To catch a bright glimpse of the glory of Erin !

Oh, sure such a vision of beauty and might,
  Commingling, in splendour, by him was exprest,
The old Lydian sculptor, the delicate sprite,
  That in Venus' soft girdle his Hercules drest.

On his return to Edinburgh we find the indefatigable mind of the Ensign earnestly engaged in laying the plan and preparing the materials for a weekly paper, upon the model of the *Tatler*, the *Spectator*, and the *Saleroom*. His views in regard to this publication were never fully realised ; but we have open before us a drawer which contains a vast accumulation of notes and *esquisses* connected with it. We insert a few of the shortest in the meantime, and may perhaps quote a few dozens of them hereafter.

I.

There is nothing in this world more likely to produce a
good understanding in families and neighbourhoods than a
resolution to be immediately entered into by all the several
members of the same, never again, from this time forward,
upon any occasion or pretence whatever, in speech or
writing, to use the monosyllable *I*.   This will no doubt cause
some trouble and inconveniences at first, especially to those
who are not half so intimate with any other pronoun ; but
by the help of a small penalty to be strictly levied upon
every transgression, that will soon be got over, and this most
wicked and pernicious monosyllable effectually banished
from the world.   The Golden Age will then re-descend on
earth, and many other things will happen, of the particulars
of which the curious reader may satisfy himself by referring
to Virgil's Eclogue.   Among the most interesting circumstances of this great revolution (which, however, is not
specified in the place referred to) will be the total abolition
of both metallic and paper currency.   *Money will be no more.*
Those that have will give to those that want ; and the
redundant population will not, on having the matter properly
explained to them, object to removing themselves by some
convenient and gentle method of suicide, rendering war,
famine, pestilence, and misery (so politely called by Mr.
Malthus by the somewhat endearing term, *checks*) utterly
unnecessary.   Who would not wish to accelerate to mankind
the approach of this blessed era?   The simple and sure
means are above stated ; and, if the world does not forthwith
proceed to make itself happy, it can no longer shelter itself
under the pretence of not knowing how to set about it.

II.

Of all the Natural Sciences, that of Scandal has been the
most universally cultivated in every civilised country, and
the most successfully in our own.   Modern scandalographers

have comprised it under two great divisions, open or direct scandal, and implied or indirect scandal.

Instances of the first are now less common in society than formerly. This perhaps arises more from an artificial refinement in our manners than from any real refinement in our minds. There still exist many who would not hesitate, under favourable circumstances, to make use of the direct scandal; and there are many more who would not be ashamed to listen to it. But in all circles, whether public or private, there are, for the most part, three or four men and women, who are as different from the surrounding mass of starched neck-cloths and satin slips "as red wine is from Rhenish." These humane and gentle beings check the growth of direct scandal, which, notwithstanding the fostering care of its vulgar disciples, is generally "no sooner blown than blasted." Being prevented from lifting its malignant head into the liberal air, it strikes downward, and, spreading its obscure ramifications underground, gives rise to the indirect or implied scandal.

This is the more dangerous kind, in as far as it is more difficult to eradicate or guard against it. In polished society, where it most frequently occurs, it has neither a local habitation nor a name. It is "an airy tongue, that syllables men's names," without pronouncing them distinctly; and the labour of the metaphysical chemist has been unequal to the discovery of any sure test for its detection. It is also, on that account, more fondly cherished by the disciples of the science, because the practical gratification arising from it is in consequence so much the greater. Thus a scandalous assertion, if made directly, cannot be frequently repeated, because the mode of its expression admits of little variety; whereas your implied scandal is capable of being varied almost infinitely, and thus affords a pleasant and continued opportunity of showing off to advantage the ingenuity of the malicious man, without vexing the dull ear of the drowsy one. Under the name of personal talk, it may be regarded as constituting the essence of conversation in society at the present period.

III.

There are few subjects on which men differ so much as in regard to blue-stockings. I believe that the majority of literary men look upon them as entirely useless. Yet a little reflection will serve us to show the unphilosophical nature of this opinion. There seems, indeed, to be a system of exclusive appropriation in literature, as well as in law, which cannot be too severely reprobated. A critic of the present day cannot hear a young woman make a harmless observation on poetry or politics without starting; which start, I am inclined to think, proceeds from affectation, considering how often he must have heard the same remark made on former occasions. Ought the female sex to be debarred from speaking nonsense on literary matters any more than the men? I think not. Even supposing that such privilege was not originally conferred by a law of Nature, they have certainly acquired right to it by the long prescription. Besides, if commonplace remarks were not daily and nightly rendered more commonplace by continual repetition, even a man of original mind might run the hazard of occasionally so far forgetting himself and his subject as to record an idea which, upon more mature deliberation, might be found to be no idea at all. This, I contend, is prevented by the judicious interference of the fair sex.

At the same time "a highly polished understanding," in an ugly woman, is a thing rather to be deprecated than otherwise. A pretty girl may say what she chooses, and be "severe in youthful beauty" with impunity, for no one will interrupt her solely to criticise the colour of her stockings; but I think that a plain one should reflect seriously before she "cultivates her mind assiduously."

IV.

One solitary death's head, all of a sudden grinning on us in our own bed-room, would be a much more trying sight than millions of skulls piled up into good large houses of three stories. Architecture of that kind is less impressive than could be imagined. There is a tolerable specimen of it at Mucruss Abbey, Killarney; but the effect is indifferent. Skulls, somehow or other, do not build well. Perhaps they would look better in mortar. As they are arranged at Mucruss Abbey, they look like great clusters of the wax of the humble-bee; and after heavy rain the effect of the water dripping from the jaw-bones and eye-holes is rather ludicrous than pathetic. They are all in the melting mood at one time, and apparently for no sufficient reason; while the extreme uniformity of their expression may, without much impropriety, be said to be quite monotonous. It may be questioned if a stranger, unacquainted with this order of architecture, would, at first sight, perceive the nature of its material. Perhaps he would, for a while, see the likeness of one or two skulls only, and wonder how they got there; till, by degrees, the whole end-wall would laughably break out, as it were, into a prodigious number of vacant faces, and wholly destroy the solemnity of that otherwise impressive religious edifice. Yet it is not to be thought that an Irishman could contemplate such a skullery with unmoved imagination. Where be all their brogue and all their bulls now? A silent gable-end of O'Donohues and Maggilli-cuddies! Walls with long arms—but sans eyes, sans nose, sans ears, sans brains! A mockery of the live population of the county Kerry! A cairn of skulls erected over the dry bones of the buried independence of the south of Ireland! Yes, thanks to the genius of the Lake of Killarney, there is not here the skull of a single absentee.

If the reader has ever been in the kingdom of Dahomey, he will remember the avenue leading up to the king's palace. For nearly a mile it is lined on each side by a wall of skulls twenty feet high; and how nobly one comes at last on the skull palace! Yet the scene cloys on the spectator. One comes at last to be insensible to the likeness between the head on his own shoulders and those that compose the skull-work of the royal residence; and he might forget it entirely, were it not that he occasionally sees a loose skull replaced by a head belonging the night before to one of his friends. It is understood that the present king of Dahomey is about to remove these walls, and distribute the old materials through his kingdom, now greatly in want of inclosures. There is also some talk of taking down the ancestral palace itself, and of building another of fresh skulls. It is calculated that three hundred thousand adult skulls, and three hundred thousand infant ones, will be sufficient for a very handsome palace; and fifty thousand annually have been cheerfully subscribed for six years. It will be finished, most probably, about the same time with the college of Edinburgh; and report speaks highly of the beauty and grandeur of the elevation.

From Mucruss and Dahomey the transition is easy and natural to the catacombs of Paris. They are on a larger scale, and consequently so much the less terrifying. One "skull by itself skull" may be no joking matter; but, after remaining unmolested for a few minutes among some billions of pericraniums, we come to feel a sovereign contempt of the whole defunct world, and would not care a straw though a dozen of them were to jump down and attempt to kick our shins. One takes out a skull, and puts it back again into its place, just as one would a common book from the shelves of a library; and, what is far worse, every skull is *verbatim et literatim* the same empty performance, and, not being bound in Russia leather, worm-eaten through and through. A man in the catacombs may indeed be said to be in a brown study.

A night passed in a vaulted cell, with one or even two skeletons, especially if they were well known to have been able-bodied men when alive, might well occasion a cold sweat, and make the hair to stand on end. There would be something like equal terms there, one quick against two dead; and no man of spirit could refuse the encounter, though the odds were against him, guineas to pounds. A ring would have to be formed, the odd ghost bottle-holder

and umpire.   But in a populous Place of Skulls—a Cranio-
polis like the catacombs, containing so enormous an "in-
habitation" that no regular census has ever been made—any
accidental visitor might contrive, surely, to while away a few
hours without much rational perturbation, and, unless very
much disposed indeed to pick a quarrel, might suffer the
thigh-bones to lie at rest, as pieces of ornamental furniture,
never intended to be wielded as weapons either of offensive
or defensive warfare.

A night passed in a small, black, bleak, musty old church,
not far from the catacombs, would be worse by far than the
catacombs themselves.   One would sit there full of the
abstract image of skulls ; and, beyond all doubt, several skulls
would come trundling in during the course of the night.
Of old, when a hero was dubbed knight, he sat up during
the dark hours in a church, where an occasional ghost or
two might touch him, when gliding by, with its icy fingers.
It would have required but a small share of chivalrous feeling
to have kept watch in an intrenchment of skulls, seemingly
impregnable.   It asks more courage to fight the champion
of an army in single combat than to dash into the lines.

v.

The toils of the day were now near a close, and the
Editor with his Contributors was about to leave the tent
for an evening walk along the Dee and its "bonny banks of
blooming heather," to indulge the most delightful of all
feelings, such namely as arise from the consciousness of
having passed our time in a way not only agreeable to ourselves, but useful to the whole of the widespread family of
man, when John Mackay came bouncing in upon us like a
grasshopper : "Gots my life, here are twa unco landloupers
cumin dirdin down the hill—the tane o' them a heech
knock-kneed stravaiger wi' the breeks on, and the tither,
ane o' the women-folk, as roun's she's lang, in a green

joseph, and a tappen o' feathers on her pow." At the word " women-folk," each contributor

"Sprang upwards like a pyramid of fire ;"

and we had some difficulty in preventing a sally from the tent. "Remember, gentlemen," quoth we, "that you are still under literary law—be seated." We ourselves, as master of the ceremonies, went out, and lo ! we beheld two most extraordinary itinerants.

The gentleman who was dressed in brown-once-black had a sort of medico-theological exterior—which we afterwards found to be representative of the inward man. He was very tall and in-kneed *—indeed, somewhat like Richmond the black about the legs ; the squint of his albino eyes was far from prepossessing ; and stray tufts of his own white hair here and there stole lankly down from beneath the up-curled edge of a brown caxon that crowned the apex of his organisation. He seemed to have lost the roof of his mouth, and, when he said to us, "You see before you Dr. Magnus Oglethorpe, itinerant lecturer on poetry, politics, oratory, and the *belles lettres,*" at each word his tongue came away from the *locum tenens* of his palate with a bang like a piece of wet leather from a stone (called, by our Scottish children, "sookers :" we forget the English name), each syllable indeed, standing quite *per se,* and not without difficulty to be drilled into companies or sentences.

But we are forgetting the lady. She was a short, fat, " dumpy woman "—quite a bundle of a body, as one may say—with smooth red cheeks, and little twinkling roguish eyes ; and, when she returned our greeting, we were sensible of a slight accent of Erin, which, we confess, up in life as we are, falls on the drum of our ear

"That's like a melody sweetly played in tune."

---

* It was upon this gentleman that the celebrated punster of the West made that famous pun, " the Battle of the Pyrenees (the pair o' knees)."

She was, as John Mackay had at some distance discovered, in a green riding-habit, not, perhaps, much the
worse, but certainly much the smoother for wear,—and,
while her neat-turned ankles exhibited a pair of yellow laced
boots which nearly reached the calf of her leg, on her head
waved elegantly a plume of light-blue ostrich feathers. The
colours altogether, both those of nature and of art, were
splendid and harmonious, and the Shepherd, whose honest
face we by chance saw (contrary to orders) peeping through
a little chink of the tent, whispered " Losh a day, gin there
binna the queen o' the fairies ! " We requested the matchless pair to walk in ; but Dr. Magnus, who was rather dusty,
first got John Mackay to switch him, behind and before,
with a bunch of long heather, and we ourselves performed
the same office, with the greatest delicacy, to the lady.

The improvement on both was most striking and instan-
taneous. The Doctor looked quite fresh and ready for a
lecture, while the lady reminded us—so sleek, smooth,
and beautiful did she appear—of a hen after any little
ruffling incident in a barn-yard. We three entered the
tent—" Contributors ! Dr. Magnus Oglethorpe and lady on
a lecturing tour through the Highlands." In a moment
twenty voices entreated the lady to be seated. Dr. Morris
offered her a seat on his bed, which, being folded up, he
now used as a chair or sofa. Wastle bowed to the antique
carved oak arm-chair that had been sent from Mar Lodge
by the Thane. Tickler was lifting up from the ground an
empty hamper to reach it across the table for her accommoda-
t'on. Buller was ready with the top or bottom of the whisky
cask, and we ourselves insisted upon getting the honour of
the fair burden to the Contributor's Box. Seward kept
looking at her through his quizzing-glass. " Deuced fine
wumman, by St. Jericho ! demme if she b'nt a facsimile of
Mary-Ann Clarke, only summat deeper in the fore-end—
one of old Anacreon's βαθυκολ.ποι."

Her curtsy was exceedingly graceful, when all of a
sudden, casting her eyes on the Standard-bearer who,

contrary to his usual amenity towards the sex, stood sour and silent in a corner, she exclaimed, " By the powers, my own swate Morgan Odoherty!" and jumping up upon the table, she nimbly picked her steps among jugs, glasses, and quechs (upsetting alone Kempferhausen's ink-horn over an Ode to the Moon), and in a moment was in the Adjutant's arms. Mrs. M'Whirter, the fair Irish widow whom the Ensign had loved in Philadelphia, stood confessed. There clung she, like a mole, with her little paws to the Standard-bearer's sides, striving in vain to reach those beguiling lips which he kept somewhat haughtily elevated about six feet three inches from the ground, leaving an unscalable height of at least a yard between them and the mouth of the much flustered, deeply injured Mrs. M'Whirter. The widow, whose elegant taste is well known to the readers of " Blackwood," exclaimed, in the words of Betty (so she called him),

> " Ah ! who can tell how hard it is to climb
> The steep where love's proud temple shines afar ? "

" Never mind the money, my dearest Morgan. Och! I have never known such another man as your sweet self since we parted at Philadelphia."

The Adjutant looked as if he had neither lost nor won, still gently but determinedly repelling the advances of the warm-hearted widow, whose face he thus kept, as it were, at arm's length. At last, with a countenance of imperturbable solemnity, worthy of a native of Ireland and a contributor to " Blackwood," he coolly said : " Why, Mr. Editor, the trick is a devilish good one, very well played, and knowingly kept up; but now that you gentlemen have all had your laugh against Odoherty, pray, Mrs. Roundabout Fat-ribs, may I ask when you were last *bateing hemp*, and in what house of correction?" "Och! you vile Sadducee." "I suspect," said Tickler, "that you yourself, my fair Mrs. M'Whirter, were the seducee, and the Ensign the seducer." "Why, look ye," continued Odoherty, "if you are Molly M'Whirter, formerly of Philadelphia, you have the mark of a murphy (*Hibernicè*, potato) on your right side, just below the fifth rib, and of a shamrock or, (as these English gentlemen would call it) a trefoil, between your shoulders behind, about half-way down —— "

Here Mrs. M'Whirter lost all temper, and appealed to Dr. Magnus Oglethorpe, if Odoherty was not casting foul aspersions on her character. The Doctor commenced an oration with that extraordinary sort of utterance already hinted at, which quite upset the Adjutant's gravity; and the lady, now seizing the "tempora mollia fandi," said with a bewitching smile: "Come now, my dearest Morgan, confess, confess!" The Standard-bearer was overcome, and, kissing his old friend's cheek in the most respectful manner, he said: "I presume Mrs. M'Whirter is no more, and that I see before me the lady of Dr. Magnus Oglethorpe, in other words, *Mrs. Dr.* Oglethorpe." "Yes, Morgan, he is indeed my husband; come hither, Magnus, and shake hands with the Adjutant; this is the Mr. Odoherty of whom you have heard me so often spake." Nothing could be more delightful than this reconciliation. We again all took our seats, Dr. Magnus on our own left hand, and Mrs. Dr. Magnus on our right, close to whom sat and smiled, like another Mars, the invincible Standard-bearer.

It was a high gratification to us now to find that Odoherty and Mrs. M'Whirter had never been united in matrimony. It was true that in America they had been tenderly attached to each other, but peculiar circumstances, some of which are alluded to in a memoir of the Adjutant's life elsewhere published, had prevented their union, and soon after his return to Europe the M'Whirter had bestowed her hand on a faithful suitor whom she had formerly rejected, Dr. Magnus Oglethorpe, lecturer on poetry, politics, oratory, &c.; a gentleman famous for removing impediments in the organs of speech, and who, after having instructed in public speaking some of the most distinguished orators in the House of Representatives, United States, had lately come over to Britain to retard, by his precepts and his practice, the decline and fall of eloquence in our island. As we complimented the Doctor on the magnificent object of his pedestrian tour, he volunteered a lecture on the spot, and in an instant, and springing up as nimbly upon the table as Sir Francis Burdett or Mr. John Hobhouse could have done, the American Demosthenes (who seemed still to have pebbles in his mouth, though far inland), thus opened it and spake :—

LECTURE ON WHIGGISM.

Ladies and Gentlemen,—Fear is "Whiggism," hatred is "Whiggism"—contempt, jealousy, remorse, wonder, despair, or madness, are all "Whiggism."

The miser when he hugs his gold, the savage who paints his idol with blood, the slave who worships a tyrant, or the tyrant who fancies himself a god—the vain, the ambitious, the proud, the choleric man, the coward, the beggar, all are "Whigs."

> " The ' Whig,' the lover, and the poet,
> Are of imagination all compact.
> One sees more devils than vast Hell can hold—
> The madman."

"Whiggism" is strictly the language of *imagination ;* and the imagination is that faculty which represents objects, not as they are in themselves, but as they are moulded, by *other* thoughts and feelings, into an infinite variety of shapes and combinations of power. This language is not the less true to nature, because it is false in point of *fact ;* but so much the more true and *natural,* if it conveys the impression which the object under the *influence of passion* makes on the mind. Let an object, for instance, be presented in a state of agitation or fear, and the imagination will distort or magnify the object, and convert it into the likeness of whatever is most proper to encourage the fear.

Tragic "Whiggism," which is the most impassioned species of it, strives to carry on the feeling to the utmost point, by all the force of comparison or contrast—loses the sense of present suffering in the imaginary exaggerations of it, exhausts the terror by an unlimited indulgence of it, *grapples with impossibilities in its desperate impatience of restraint.*

When Lear says of Edgar, nothing but the unkind "ministry" could have brought him to this, what a *bewildered* amazement, what a *wrench* of the imagination, that cannot be brought to conceive of any other cause of misery than that which has bowed it down, and absorbs all other sorrow in its own!   His sorrow, like a flood, supplies the sources of all other sorrow.

In regard to a certain Whig, of the unicorn species, we may say—How his passion lashes itself up, and swells and rages like a tide in its sounding course, when, in answer to the doubts expressed of his returning "temper," he says—

> " Never, *Iago*.   Like to the Pontic Sea,
> Whose icy current and compulsive course
> Ne'er feels retiring ebb, but keeps due on
> To the Propontic and the Hellespont ;
> Even so my 'frantic' thoughts, with violent pace,
> Shall ne'er look back, ne'er ebb to humble 'sense,'
> Till that a capable and wide revenge
> Swallow them up. "

The pleasure, however, derived from tragic "Whiggism," is not anything peculiar to it as Whiggism, as a fictitious and fanciful thing.   It is not an anomaly of the imagination. It has its source and groundwork in the common love of "power" and strong excitement.   As Mr. Burke observes, people flock to "Whig meetings;" but, if there were a public execution in the next street, the "house" would very soon be empty.   It is not the difference between fiction and reality that solves the difficulty.   Children are satisfied with stories of ghosts and witches.   The grave politician drives a thriving trade of abuse and calumnies, poured out against those whom he makes his enemies for no other end than that he may live by them.   The popular preacher makes less frequent mention of Heaven than of Hell. Oaths and nicknames are only a more vulgar sort of " Whiggism."   We are as fond of indulging our violent passions as of reading a description of those of others. We are as prone to make a torment of our fears as to luxuriate in our hopes of "mischief." The love of power is as strong a principle in the mind as the love of pleasure. It is as natural to hate as to love, to despise as to admire, to express our hatred or contempt as our love and admiration.

> " Masterless passion sways us to the mood
> Of what it likes or loathes."

Not that we like what we loathe, but we like to indulge our hatred and scorn of it (viz., Toryism), to dwell upon it, to exasperate our idea of it by every refinement of ingenuity and extravagance of illustration, to make it a bugbear to ourselves, to point it out to others in all the splendour of deformity, to embody it to the senses, to stigmatise it in words, to grapple with it in thought, in action, to sharpen our intellect, to arm our will against it, to know the worst we have to contend with, and to contend with it to the utmost.

Let who will strip nature of the colours and the shapes of "Whiggism," the "Whig" is not bound to do so; the impressions of common sense and strong imagination—that is, of passion and "temperance"—cannot be the same, and they must have a separate language to do justice to either. Objects must strike differently upon the mind, independently of what they are in themselves, so long as we have a different *interest* in them, as we see them in a different point of view, nearer or at a greater distance (morally or physically speaking), from novelty, from old acquaintance, from *our ignorance* of them, from our fear of their consequences,—from contrast, from unexpected likeness; hence nothing but Whiggism *can* be agreeable to nature and truth.

This lecture gave universal satisfaction; but Dr. Magnus is a man of too much genius not to acknowledge unreservedly his obligations to other great men; and, after our plaudits had expired, he informed us that he claimed little other merit than that of having delivered the lecture according to the best rules and principles of oratory, for that the words were by his friend Mr. Hazlitt. " In the original," said he, " Mr. Hazlitt employs the word ' Poetry,' which I have slightly changed into the word ' Whiggism,' and thus an excellent lecture on politics is procured, without the ingenious essayist having been at all aware of the ultimate meaning of his production. As the lecture was but short, will you have another ? " " No, no, enough is as good as a feast," quod Odoherty. " Perhaps, Mr. Editor, if you request it, Mrs. Magnus will have the goodness to make tea." There was not only much true politeness in this suggestion of the Adjutant, but a profound knowledge of the female character ; and, accordingly, the *tea-things* were not long of making their appearance, for in our tent it was just sufficient to hint a wish, and that wish, whatever it might be, that moment was gratified. Mrs. Magnus, we observed, put in upwards of thirty spoonfuls, being at the rate of two and a half for each contributor, and the lymph came out of the large silver tea-pot "a perfect tincture," into his third and last cup of which each contributor emptied a decent glass of whisky ; nor did the Lady of the Tent, any more than the Lady of the Lake, show any symptoms of distaste to the mountain dew. The conversation was indeed divine, and it was wonderful with what ease Mrs. Morgan conducted herself in so difficult a situation. She had a word or a smile for every one, and the Shepherd whispered to Tickler, just loud enough to be heard by those near the Contributor's Box, "sic a nice leddy wad just sute you or me to a hair, Mr. Tickler. Faith, thae blue ostrich plumbs wad astonish Davy Bryden, were he to see them hanging o'er the tea-pat at Eltrive Lake, wi' a swurl."

After an " excellent new " song read by the Bailie, said Mrs. Magnus :—

" My dear Mr. Odoherty (for they treated each other with infinite respect), will you give us something amatory ? " " I gives my vice, too, for something hamatory," pertly enough whiffled Mr. Tims ; when the Standard-bearer, after humming a few notes, and taking the altitude from the pitch-key of Tickler (which he carries about with him as certainly as a parson carries a corkscrew), went off in noble style with the following song, his eyes all the while turned towards Mrs. Magnus Oglethorpe, whose twinklers emanated still but eloquent responses not to be misunderstood :—

INCONSTANCY; A SONG TO MRS. M'WHIRTER.

BY MR. ODOHERTY.

I.

" Ye fleeces of gold amidst crimson enrolled
   That sleep in the calm western sky,
Lovely relics of day float—ah ! float not away !
   Are ye gone ? Then, ye beauties, good-bye ! "
It was thus the fair maid I had loved would have staid
   The last gleamings of passion in me ;
But the orb's fiery glow in the soft wave below
   Had been cooled—and the thing could not be.

2.

While through deserts you rove, if you find a green grove
   Where the dark branches overhead meet,
There repose you a while from the heat and the toil,
   And be thankful the shade is so sweet ;
But if long you remain it is odds but the rain
   Or the wind 'mong the leaves may be stirring :
They will strip the boughs bare—you're a fool to stay there—
   Change the scene without further demurring.

3.

If a rich-laden tree in your wanderings you see
   With the ripe fruit all glowing and swelling,
Take your fill as you pass—if you don't you're an ass,
   But I daresay you don't need my telling.
'Twould be just as great fooling to come back for more pulling :
   When a week or two more shall have gone,
'These firm plums very rapidly, they will taste very vapidly,
   —By good luck we'll have pears coming on !

4.

All around Nature's range is from changes to changes,
   And in change all her charming is centered—
When you step from the stream where you've bathed, 'twere a dream
   To suppose't the same stream that you entered ;

Each clear crystal wave just a passing kiss gave,
    And kept rolling away to the sea,
So the love-stricken slave for a moment may rave,
    But ere long, oh! how distant he'll be!

5.

Why—'tis only in name, you, e'en you, are the same
    With the SHE that inspired my devotion:
Every bit of the lip that I loved so to sip
    Has been changed in the general commotion—
Even these soft gleaming eyes that awaked my young sighs
    Have been altered a thousand times over;
Why? oh why, then complain that so short was your reign?
    Must all Nature go round but your lover?

The tears flowed in torrents from the blue eyes of Mrs.
Magnus, during the whole of this song; and when Mr. Tims,
who was now extremely inebriated (he has since apologised
to us for his behaviour, and assured us that when tipsy on
tea he is always quite beyond himself), vehemently cried,
" Hangcore! hangcore!" the gross impropriety of such un-
feeling conduct was felt by Mr. Seward, who offered, if
agreeable to us, to turn him out of the tent; but Tims
became more reasonable upon this, and asked permission
to go to bed; which being granted, his friend Price assisted
the small cit to *lay* down, and in a few minutes, we think,
unless we were deceived, that we faintly heard something
like his own thin tiny little snore.   Mrs. Magnus soon
recovered her cheerfulness; for being, with all her vivacity,
subject to frequent but short fits of absence, she every now
and then, no doubt without knowing what she was about,
filled up her tea-cup, not from the silver tea-pot, but from a
magisterial-looking bottle of whisky, which then, and indeed
at all times, stood on our table.   She now volunteered a
song of her own composition; and after fingering away in
the most rapid style of manipulation on the edge of the
table, as if upon her own spinnet in Philadelphia, she too
took the key from Tickler's ready instrument, and chanted in
recitativo what follows; an anomalous kind of poetry :—

CHAUNT.—BY MRS. M'WHIRTER.

*Tune—The Powldoodies of Burran.**

1.

I wonder what the mischief was in me when a bit of my music I prof-
    fered ye !
How could any woman sing a good song when she's just parting with
    Morgan Odoherty?
A poor body, I think, would have more occasion for a comfortable quiet can,
To keep up her spirits in taking lave of so nate a young man ;
Besides, as for me, I'm not an orator like Bush, Plunkett, Grattan, or Curran,
So I can only hum a few words to the old chaunt of the Powldoodies of
    Burran.
        Chorus—Oh ! the Powldoodies of Burran,
            The green green Powldoodies of Burran,
            The green Powldoodies, the clean Powldoodies,
            The gaping Powldoodies of Burran !

2.

I remember a saying of my Lord Norbury, that excellent Judge,
Says he, never believe what a man says to ye, Molly, for believe me 'tis all
    fudge ;
He said it sitting on the Bench before the whole Grand Jury of Tipperary.
If I had minded it, I had been the better on't, as sure as my name's Mary ;
I would have paid not the smallest attention, ye good-for-nothing elf ye,
To the fine speeches that took me off my feet in the swate city of Philadelphy.
        Oh ! the Powldoodies of Burran, &c. &c.

3.

By the same rule, says my dear Mr. Bush one night when I was sitting
    beside Mausey,
" Molly, love," says he, " if you go on at this rate, you've no idea what
    bad luck it will cause ye ;
You may go on very merrily for a while, but you'll see what will come on't,
When to answer for all your misdeeds, at the last you are summoned ;
Do you fancy a young woman can proceed in this sad light-headed way,
And not suffer in the long run, tho' manetime she may merrily say,
        Oh ! the Powldoodies of Burran," &c. &c.

4.

But I'm sure there's plenty of other people that's very near as bad's me,
Yes, and I will make bould to affirm it, in the very tiptopsomest degree ;

---

* The POWLDOODIES OF BURRAN are oysters, of which more may be said
hereafter.

Only they're rather more cunning concealing on't, tho' they meet with
    their fops
Every now and then by the mass, about four o'clock in their milliners' shops ;
In our own pretty Dame Street I've seen it—the fine lady comes commonly
    first,
And then comes her beau on pretence of a watch-ribbon, or the like I purtest.
               Oh ! the Powldoodies of Burran, &c. &c.

5.

But as for me, I could not withstand him, 'tis the beautiful dear Ensign I
    mean,
When he came into the *Shining Daisy* * with his milkwhite smallclothes
    so clean,
With his epaulette shining on his shoulder, and his golden gorget at his
    breast,
And his long silken sash so genteelly twisted many times round about his
    neat waist ;
His black gaiters that were so tight, and reached up to a little below his knee,
And showed so well the prettiest calf e'er an Irish lass had the good luck
    to see.
               Oh ! the Powldoodies of Burran, &c. &c.

6.

His eyes were like a flaming coal-fire, all so black and yet so bright,
Or like a star shining clearly in the middle of the dark heaven at night ;
And the white of them was not white, but a charming sort of hue,
Like a morning sky, or skimmed milk, of a delicate sweet blue ;
But when he whispered sweetly, then his eyes were so soft and dim,
That it would have been a heart of brass not to have pity upon him.
               Oh ! the Powldoodies of Burran, &c. &c.

7.

And yet now you see he's left me like a pair of old boots or shoes,
And makes love to all the handsome ladies, for ne'er a one of them can
    refuse ;
Through America and sweet Ireland, and Bath and London City,
For he must always be running after something that's new and pretty,
Playing the devil's own delights in Holland, Spain, Portugal, and France,
And here too in the cold Scotch mountains, where I've met with him by
    very chance.
               Oh ! the Powldoodies of Burran, &c. &c.

8.

When he first ran off and deserted me, I thought my heart was plucked
    away,
Such a tugging in my breast, I did not sleep a wink till peep of day—

---

   * The *Shining Daisy* was the sign of Mrs. M'Whirter's chop-house at
Philadelphia. Sir Daniel Donelly hoisted the same sign over his booth the
other day at Donnybrook Fair.—*Editor.*

May I be a sinner if I ever bowed but for a moment my eye-lid,
Tossing round about from side to side in the middle of my bid.
One minute kicking off all the three blankets, the sheets, and the counter-
pane,
And then stuffing them up over my head like a body beside myself again.

     Oh ! the Powldoodies of Burran, &c. &c.

9.

Says I to myself, I'll repeat over the whole of the Pater Noster, Ave-Maria,
and Creed,
If I don't fall over into a doze e'er I'm done with them 'twill be a very un-
common thing indeed ;
But, would you believe it ? I was quite lively when I came down to the
Amen,
And it was always just as bad tho' I repeated them twenty times over and
over again ;
I also tried counting of a thousand, but still found myself broad awake,
With a cursed pain in the fore part of my head, all for my dear sweet
Ensign Odoherty's sake.

     Oh ! the Powldoodies of Burran, &c. &c.

10.

But, to cut a long story short, I was in a high fever when I woke in the
morning,
Whereby all women in my situation should take profit and warning ;
And Doctor Oglethorpe he was sent for, and he ordered me on no account
to rise,
But to lie still and have the whole of my back covered over with Spanish
flies ;
He also gave me leeches and salts, castor-oil, and the balsam capivi,
Till I was brought down to a mere shadow, and so pale that the sight would
have grieved ye.

     Oh ! the Powldoodies of Burran, &c. &c.

11.

But in the course of a few days more I began to stump a little about,
And by the blessing of air and exercise, I grew every day more and more
stout ;
And in a week or two I recovered my twist, and could play a capital knife
and fork,
Being not in the least particular whether it was beef, veal, lamb, mutton, or
pork ;
But of all the things in the world, for I was always my father's own true
daughter,
I liked best to dine on fried tripes, and wash it down with a little hot brandy
and water.

     Oh ! the Powldoodies of Burran, &c. &c.

12.

If I had the least bit of genius for poems, I could make some very nice songs
On the cruelties of some people's sweethearts, and some people's sufferings
    and wrongs ;
For he was master, I'm sure, of my house, and there was nothing at all at all
In the whole of the *Shining Daisy* for which he could not just ring the bell
    and call ;
We kept always a good larder of pigeon-pies, hung beef, ham, and cowheel,
And we would have got anything to please him that we could either beg, bor-
    row, or steal.

                Oh ! the Powldoodies of Burran, &c. &c·

13.

And at night when we might be taking our noggin in the little back-room,
I thought myself as sure of my charmer as if he had gone to church my bride-
    groom ;
But I need not keep harping on that string and ripping up of the same old
    sore,
He went off in the twinkling of a bed-post, and I never heard tell of him no
    more,
So I married the great Doctor Oglethorpe, who had been my admirer all
    along,
And we had some scolloped Powldoodies for supper ; and every crature
    joined in the old song,

                Oh ! the Powldoodies of Burran, &c. &c.

14.

Some people eat their Powldoodies quite neat just as they came out of the
    sea,
But with a little black pepper and vinegar some other people's stomachs
    better agree ;
Young ladies are very fond of oyster *pates*, and young gentlemen of oyster
    broth,
But I think I know a bit of pasture that is far better than them both :
For whenever we want to be comfortable, says I to the Doctor, My dear man,
Let's have a few scolloped Powldoodies, and a bit of tripe fried in the pan.
        Chorus—Oh ! the Powldoodies of Burran,
             The green green Powldoodies of Burran,
             The green Powldoodies, the clean Powldoodies,
             The gaping Powldoodies of Burran.

After Mrs. Magnus had received those plaudits from the tent due to this exhibition of native genius, the learned Doctor somewhat anxiously asked us what sort of accommodation we had for him and his lady during the night? We told him that the tent slept twenty easily, and that a few more could be stowed away between the interstices. "But give yourself no uneasiness, Dr. Magnus, on that score; we are aware of the awkwardness of a lady passing the night with so many contributors, and of the censoriousness of the world, many people in which seem determined, Doctor, to put an unfavourable construction on everything we do or say. Besides, your excellent lady might find our tent like the Black Bull Inn of Edinburgh as it was twenty years ago, when Dr. Morris first visited it, 'crowded, noisy, shabby, and uncomfortable.' Now the inn at Braemar is a most capital one, where the young ladies of the family will pay every attention to Mrs. Magnus. We have already despatched a special messenger for Dr. Morris' shandrydan, and as it is a fine moonlight night, you can trundle yourselves down to bed in a jiffey." The sound of the shandrydan confirmed our words, and we all attended Mrs. Magnus and her husband to the road, to see them safely mounted. Our readers have all seen Peter's shandrydan, a smart, snug, safe, smooth, roomy, easy-going concern, that carries you over the stones as if you were on turf; and where, may we ask, will you see a more compact nimble little horse than Peter's horse, Scrub, with feet as steady as clock-work, and a mouth that carries his bit with a singular union of force and tenderness? "I fear that I cannot guide this vehicle along Highland roads," said Dr. Magnus; "and I suspect that steed is given to starting, from the manner in which he keeps rearing his head about, and pawing the ground like a mad bull. My dear, it would be flying in the face of Providence to ascend the steps of that shandrydan." While the orator was thus expressing his trepidation, the Standard-Bearer handed Mrs. Magnus forward, who, with her nodding plumes, leapt lightly up beneath the giant strength of his warlike arm, and took her seat with an air of perfect composure and dignity; while Odoherty, adjusting the reins with the skill of a Lade or Buxton, and elevating his dexter hand that held them and the whip in its gnostic grasp, caught hold of the rail of the shandrydan with his left, and flung himself, as it were, to the fair side of her who had once been the mistress of his youthful heart, but for whom he now retained only the most respectful affection. " Mount up behind, Dr. Magnus," cried the Adjutant, somewhat impatiently; "your feet will not be more than six inches from the ground, so that in case of any disaster, you can drop off like a ripe pease-cod; mount, I say, Doctor, mount." The Doctor did so; and the Standard-Bearer giving a blast on Wastle's bugle, and cutting the thin air with his thong several yards beyond Scrub's nose, away went the shandrydan, while the mountains of the Dee echoed again to the rattling of its wheels.

Note from Mr. Odoherty.

My dear Editor,—The report of my death, a report originally created by the malevolence of a fiend, has, I am sorry to observe, gained considerable currency through the inadvertence of you, a friend. Had my body been really consigned to the dust, you should have received intelligence of that event, not from the casual whispers of a stranger, but from the affectionate bequest of a sincere admirer; for, sir, I may as well mention the fact that, by a holograph codicil to my last will and testament, I have constituted you sole tutor and curator of all my MSS.; thus providing, in case of accidents, for these my intellectual offspring the care of a guardian who, I am well aware, would super-intend, with a father's eye, the mode of their introduction into public life.

I flatter myself, however, that you will not hear with indifference of my being still in a condition to fulfil this office in *propriâ personâ*. On some future occasion I shall describe to your readers, in, I hope, no uninteresting strains, the strange vicissitudes of my fate during the last two years: among these not the least amusing will be the narrative of those very peculiar circumstances which have induced me to lie *perdue*, a listener to no less than two succeeding historians of my life, supposed to be terminated, and eulogists of my genius, no less falsely supposed to have been swallowed up in the great vortex of animation. But of all this anon.

I enclose, in the meantime, as the first offerings of my

reacknowledged existence, three several productions of my muse. The first (The Garland) was composed by me a few weeks ago, on the following occasion.

I happened to be in Hawick at the moment when the celebrated giantess, Mrs. Cook, passed through that town on her way from the South. Animated with that rightful spirit of curiosity which has been pronounced to be the mother of all knowledge, I immediately hastened to wait upon her. The vast stature of this remarkable woman, her strength (for with a single squeeze she had well nigh crushed my fingers to dust), the symmetry of her figure, but above all, the soft elegance of her features,—these united attractions were more than sufficient to make a deep impression on the mind of one who has never professed himself to be "a stoic of the woods." After spending a comfortable evening at Mrs. Brown's, I set out for Eltrive, the seat of my friend Mr. Hogg, and in the course of the walk composed the following lines, which I soon afterwards sent to Mrs. Cook. It is proper to mention that the fair daughter of Anak enclosed to me, in return, a ticket of free admission for the season, of which I shall certainly very frequently avail myself after my arrival in Edinburgh.

The other two poems, the Eve of St. Jerry, and the Rime of the Auncient Waggonére, were composed by me many years ago. The reader will at once detect the resemblance which they bear to two well-known and justly celebrated pieces of Scott and Coleridge. This resemblance, in justice to myself, is the fruit of their imitation, not of mine. I remember reciting the Eve of St. Jerry about the year 1795 to Mr. Scott, then a very young man ; but as I have not had the pleasure of seeing Mr. Coleridge, although I have often wished to do so, and hold his genius in the highest estimation, I am more at a loss to account for the accurate idea he seems to have possessed of my production, unless, indeed, I may have casually dropt a copy of the MS. in some bookseller's shop in Bristol, where he may have found it.—Meantime, I remain, dear Editor, your affectionate servant,

MORGAN ODOHERTY.

ELTRIVE LAKE, *Feb.* 29*th*, 1819.

ODOHERTY'S GARLAND.

IN HONOUR OF MRS. COOK, *THE GREAT.*

Let the Emerald Isle make O'Brien her boast,*
  And let Yorkshire be proud of her "strapping young man ;"
But London, gay London, should glory the most,
  She has reared Mrs. Cook, let them match her who can ;
This female Goliah is thicker and higher
  Than Italian Belzoni, or Highlandman Sam.
Yet the terrible creature is pretty in feature,
  And her smile is as soft as a dove or a lamb.
When she opens her eyelids she dazzles you quite
  With the vast flood of splendour that flashes around ;
Old Ajax, ambitious to perish in light,
  In one glance of her glory perdition had found.
Both in verse and in prose, to the bud of a rose
  Sweet lips have been likened by amorous beau ;
But her lips may be said to be like a rose-bed,
  Their fragrance so full is, so broad is their glow,

---

* Charles O'Brien, the person here alluded to, measured exactly eight feet two inches in his pumps. His countenance was comely, and his chest well formed, but, like the " Mulier Formosa" of Horace's Satire, or (what may be considered as a more appropriate illustration) like the idol of the Philistines, he was very awkwardly shaped in the lower extremities. He made a practice of selling successively to many gentlemen of the medical profession, the reversion of his enormous carcase. It is said that one of these bargains—viz. that contracted between him and the celebrated Liston of Edinburgh—was reduced to a strictly legal shape. It is well known that, according to the forms of Scots law, nothing but movables can be conveyed by *testament;* every other species of property requires to be transferred by a deed *inter vivos.* The acute northern anatomist, doubting whether any court of law would have been inclined to class O'Brien's body among *movables*, insisted that the giant should vest the *fee* of the said body in him (the surgeon), saving and retaining to himself (the giant) a right of usufruct or liferent. We have not heard by what *symbol* the doctor completed his infeftment. [The skeleton of O'Brien, the Irish giant, is preserved in the Museum of Trinity College, Dublin.]

The similitudes used in king Solomon's book,
  In laudation of some little Jewess of old,
If we only suppose them devised for the Cook,
  Would appear the reverse of improper or bold.
There is many a tree that is shorter than she,
  In particular that on which Johnston was swung ;
Had the rope been about her huge arm, there's no doubt
  That the friend of the *Scotsman* at once had been hung.

The cedars that grew upon Lebanon hill,
  And the towers of Damascus might well be applied,
With imperfect ideas the fancy to fill,
  Of the monstrous perfections of Cook's pretty bride.
Oh ! if one of the name be immortal in fame,
  Because round the wide globe he adventured to roam,
Mr. Cook, I don't see why yourself should not be
  As illustrious as he without stirring from home !
QUOTH ODOHERTY.

THE EVE OF ST. JERRY.

[The reader will learn with astonishment that I composed the two following ballads in the fourteenth year of my age, *i.e.* A.D. 1780. I doubt
if either Milton or Pope rivalled this precocity of genius.—M. O.]

Dick Gossip the barber arose with the cock,
  And pulled his breeches on ;
Down the staircase of wood, as fast as he could,
  The valiant shaver ran.

He went not to the country forth
  To shave or frizzle hair ;
Nor to join in the battle to be fought
  At Canterbury fair.

Yet his hat was fiercely cocked, and his razors in his pocket,
  And his torturing irons he bore ;
A staff of crab-tree in his hand had he,
  Full five feet long and more.

The barber returned in three days' space,
  And blistered were his feet ;
And sad and peevish were his looks,
  As he turned the corner street.

He came not from where Canterbury
  Ran ankle-deep in blood ;
Where butcher Jem, and his comrades grim,
  The shaving tribe withstood.

Yet were his eyes bruised black and blue ;
   His cravat twisted and tore ;
His razors were with gore imbued—
   But it was not professional gore.*

He halted at the painted pole,
   Full loudly did he rap,
And whistled on his shaving boy,
   Whose name was Johnny Strap.

Come hither, come hither, young tickle-beard,
   And mind that you tell me true,
For these three long days that I've been away,
   What did Mrs. Gossip do?

When the clock struck eight, Mrs. Gossip went straight,
   In spite of the pattering rain,
Without stay or stop to the butcher's shop,
   That lives in Cleaver Lane.

I watched her steps, and secret came
   Where she sat upon a chair :
No person was in the butcher's shop—
   The devil a soul was there.

The second night I spied a light
   As I went up the Strand,
'Twas she who ran, with pattens on,
   And a lanthern in her hand ;

She laid it down upon a bench,
   And shook her wet attire ;
And drew in the elbow-chair, to warm
   Her toes before the fire.

In the twinkling of a walking-stick,†
   A greasy butcher came,
And with a pair of bellows he
   Blew up the dying flame.

And many a word the butcher spoke
   To Mrs. Gossip there ;
But the rain fell fast, and it blew such a blast
   That I could not tell what they were.

---

   * We have no wish to injure the reputation of this gentleman ; but, from the above stanza, it is evident that his hand was liable to tremor, whether from natural nervous debility, or the effect of brandy, we cannot take upon us to determine.—M. OD.

   † From this line it is to be inferred that the oaken saplings of our ancestors rivalled in elasticity the bamboo canes of our modern dandies.—M. OD.

The third night there the sky was fair,
    There neither was wind nor rain ;
And again I watched the secret pair
    At the shop in Cleaver Lane.

And I heard her say, " Dick Gossip's away,
    So we'll be blithe and merry,
And the bolts I'll undo, sweet butcher, to you,
    On the eve of good St. Jerry." *

" I cannot come, I must not come "—
    " For shame, faint-hearted snarler,
Must I then moan, and sit alone,
    In Dicky Gossip's parlor?

" The dog shall not tear you, and Strap † shall not hear you,
    And blankets I'll spread on the stair ;
By the blood-red sherry, and holy St. Jerry,
    I conjure thee, sweet butcher, be there."

" Though the dog should not tear me, and Strap should not hear me,
    And blankets be spread on the stair,
Yet there's Mr. Parrot, who sleeps in the garret,
    To my footsteps he could swear."

" Fear not Mr. Parrot, who sleeps in the garret,
    For to Hampstead the way he has ta'en :
An inquest to hold, as I have been told,
    On the corpse of a butcher that's slain."

He turned him round, and grimly he frowned,
    And he laugh'd right scornfully,
" The inquest that's held, on the man that's been killed,
    May as well be held on me.

" At the lone midnight hour, when hobgoblins have power,
    In thy chamber I'll appear ;
With that he was gone, and your wife left alone,
    And I came running here."

Then changed, I trow, was the barber's brow,
    From the chalk to the beet-root red :
" Now tell me the mien of the butcher thou'st seen,
    By Mambrino I'll smite off his head."

---

* We have in vain scrutinised the kalendar for the name of this saint.—
M. OD.

† After his master's misfortune, this gentleman settled in the North, and
was the great-grandfather of that Strap so honourably noticed by Smollett.

" On the point of his nose, which was like a red rose,
    Was a wart of enormous size ;
And he made a great vaporing with a blue and white apron,
    And red stockings rolled up to his thighs." *

" Thou liest, thou liest, young Johnny Strap,
    It is all a fib you tell,
For the butcher was taken, as dead as bacon,
    From the bottom of Carisbrook well."

" My master, attend, and I'll be your friend,
    I don't value madam a button ;
But I heard Mistress say, Don't leave, I pray,
    Sweet Timothy Slaughter-mutton."

He oped the shop door, the counter he jumped o'er,
    And overturned Strap,
Then bolted up the stair, where he found his lady fair,
    With the kitten on her lap.

" Now hail, now hail, thou lady bright,—
    Now hail, thou barber trim,
What news from Canterbury fight,
    What news from bloody Jem ?" †

" Canterbury is red with gore,
    For many a barber fell ;
And the mayor has charged us for evermore
    To watch the butcher's well."

Mrs. Gossip blushed, and her cheek was flushed,
    But the barber shook his head ;
And having observed that the night was cold,
    He tumbled into bed.

Mrs. Gossip lay and mourned, and Dicky tossed and turned ;
    And he muttered while half asleep,
The stone is large and round, and the halter tight and sound,
    And the well thirty fathoms deep.

The gloomy dome of St. Paul's struck three,
    The morning began to blink,
And Gossip slept, as if his wife
    Had put laudanum in his drink.

---

* This was no doubt a bold and masterly attempt of the butcher to imitate plush breeches.—M. OD.

† It is astonishing that Hume and other historians make no mention of this bloody encounter, which threatened to exterminate the whole shaving generation, or at least scatter them like the twelve tribes of Israel.—M. OD.

Mrs. Gossip drew wide the curtains aside,
　The candle had burned to the socket,
And lo! Timothy stood, all covered with blood,
　With his right hand in his pocket.

" Dear Slaughter-mutton, away," she cried,
　" I pray thee do not stop."
" Mrs. Gossip, I know who sleeps by thy side,
　But he sleeps as sound as a top.

" Near Carisbrook well, I lately fell
　Beneath a barber's knife ;
The coroner's inquest was held on me—
　But it did not restore me to life.*

" By thy husband's hand was I foully slain,
　He threw me into the well,
And my sprite in the shop, in Cleaver Lane,
　For a season is doomed to dwell."

Love mastered fear.　" What brings thee here?"
　The Love-sick matron said ;
" Is thy fair carcase gone to pot?"
　The goblin shook his head.

" I slaughtered sheep, and slaughtered was,
　And for breaking the marriage bands,
My flesh and bones go to David Jones,†
　But let us first shake hands."

He laid his left fist on an oaken chest,
　And, as she cried, " Don't burn us ; "
With the other he grasped her by the nose,
　And scorched her like a furnace.

There is a felon in Newgate jail,
　Who dreads the next assize ;
A woman doth dwell in Bedlam cell,
　With a patch between her eyes.

The woman who dwells in Bedlam cell,
　Whose reason is not worth a button,
Is the wife of a barber in Newgate jail,
　Who slaughtered Slaughter-mutton.

---

* It seems to us an unconscionable expectation of the butcher, that the inquest of the coroner was to restore the " vis vitæ."—M. OD.

† Apparently one of the slang names for the " hangman of creation," omitted by Burns in his address to that celebrated personage.—M. OD.

THE RIME OF THE AUNCIENT WAGGONERE.

IN FOUR PARTS.

Part First.

It is an auncient Waggonere,
    And hee stoppeth one of nine :
" Now wherefore dost thou grip me soe
    With that horny fist of thine?"

" The bridegroom's doors are opened wide,
    And thither I must walke ;
Soe, by your leave, I must be gone,
    I have noe time for talke ! "

Hee holds him with his horny fist—
    " There was a wain," quothe hee—
" Holde offe, thou raggamouffine tykke."
    Eftsoones his fist dropped hee.

Hee satte him down upon a stone,
    With ruefulle looks of feare ;
And thus began this tippyse manne,
    The red-nosed waggonere.

" The waine is fulle, the horses pulle,
    Merrilye did we trotte
Alonge the bridge, alonge the road,
    A jolly crewe, I wotte."
And here the tailore smotte his breaste,
    He smelte the cabbage potte !

" The nighte was darke, like Noe's arke,
    Oure waggone moved alonge ;
The hail poured faste, loude roared the blaste,
    Yet still we moved alonge ;
And sung in chorus, 'Cease, loud Borus,'
    A very charminge songe.

" ' Bravoe, bravissimoe,' I cried,
    The sounde was quite elatinge ;
But, in a trice, upon the ice,
    We hearde the horses skaitinge.

" The ice was here, the ice was there,
    It was a dismale mattere
To see the cargoe, one by one,
    Flounderinge in the wattere !

Marginal glosses:

An auncient waggonere stoppeth ane tailore going to a wedding, whereat he hath been appointed to be best manne, and to take a hand in the casting of the slippere.

The waggonere in mood for chat, and admits of no excuse.

The tailore seized with the ague.

He listeneth like a three years and a half child.

The appetite of the tailore whetted by the smell of cabbage.

The waggenere, in talking anent Boreas, maketh bad orthographye.

Their mirthe interrupted.

And the passengers exercise themselves in the pleasant art of swimminge, as doeth also their prog. to witte, great store of colde roasted beef: item, ane beef-stake pye; item, viii choppines of usquebaugh.

" With rout and roare, we reached the shore,
    And never a soul did sinke;
But in the rivere, gone for evere,
    Swum our meate and drinke.

The waggonere hailethe ane goose, with ane novei salutatione.

" At lengthe we spied a good grey goose,
    Thorough the snow it came;
And with the butte ende of my whippe
    I hailed it in Goddhis name.

" It staggered as it had been drunke,
    So dexterous was it hitte;
Of brokene boughs we made a fire,
    Thomme Loncheone roasted itte."—

The tailore impatient to be gone, but is forcibly persuaded to remain.

" Be done, thou tipsye waggonere,
    To the feaste I must awaye."
The waggonere seized him bye the coatte,
    And forced him there to staye,
Begginge, in gentlemanlie style,
    Butte halfe-ane-hour's delaye.

THE RIME OF THE AUNCIENT WAGGONERE.

Part Second.

The waggonere's bowels yearn towards the sunne.

" The crimson sunne was rising o'ere
    The verge of the horizon;
Upon my worde, as faire a sunne
    As ever I clapped eyes onne.

The passengers throwe the blame of the goose massacre on the innocent waggonere.

" 'Twill bee ane comfortable thinge,"
    The mutinous crewe 'gan crye;
" 'Twill be an comfortable thinge
    Within the jaile to lye;
Ah! execrable wretche," saide they,
    "Thatte caused the goose to die!

The sunne sufferes ane artificial eclipse, and horror follows, the same not being mentioned in the Belfaste Almanacke.

" The day was drawing near ittes close,
    The sunne was well nighe settinge;
When lo! it seemed as iffe his face
    Was veiled with fringe-warke-nettinge.

Various hypotheses on the subject, frome which the passengeres draw wronge conclusions.

" Somme saide itte was ane apple tree,
    Laden with goodlye fruite,
Somme swore itte was ane foreigne birde,
    Some said it was ane brute;
Alas! it was ane bumbailiffe,
    Riding in pursuite!

" A hue and crye sterte uppe behind,
   Whilke smote oure ears like thunder,
Within the waggone there was drede,
   Astonishmente and wonder.

Ane lovelye sound ariseth; ittes effects described.

" One after one, the rascalls rann,
   And from the carre did jump ;
One after one, one after one,
   They felle with heavy thump.

The passengers throw somersets.

" Six miles ane houre theye offe did scoure,
   Like shippes on ane stormye ocean,
Theire garments flappinge in the winde,
   With ane shorte uneasy motion.

" Their bodies with their legs did flye,
   Theye fled withe feare and glyffe ;
Why star'st thoue soe ?—With one goode blow,
   I felled the bumbailiffe ! "

The waggonere complimenteth the bumbailiffe with ane Mendoza.

THE RIME OF THE AUNCIENT WAGGONERE.

Part Third.

" I feare thee, auncient waggonere,
   I feare thy hornye fiste,
For itte is stained with gooses gore,
   And bailiff's blood, I wist.

" I fear to gette ane fisticuffe
   From thy leathern knuckles brown ;
With that the tailore strove to ryse —
   The waggonere thrusts him down.

The tailore meeteth Corporal Feare

" ' Thou craven, if thou mov'st a limye,
   I 'll give thee cause for feare ; '
And thus went on, that tipsye man,
   The red-billed waggoner.

" The bumbailiffe so beautifull !
   Declared itte was no joke,
For, to his knowledge, both his legs
   And fifteen ribbes were broke.

The bailiffe complaineth of considerable derangement of his animal economye.

" The lighte was gone, the nighte came on,
   Ane hundrede lantherns' sheen
Glimmerred upon the kinge's highwaye—
   Ane lovelye sighte, I ween.

Policemen with their lanthernes, pursue the waggonere.

    "' Is it he,' quoth one, 'is this the manne?
      I'll laye the rascalle stiffe;'
   With cruel stroke the beak he broke
      Of the harmless bumbailiffe.

Steppeth 20 feete in imitatione of the Admirable Crichtoun.

   "The threatening of the saucye rogue
      No more I coulde abide.
   Advancing forthe my goode right legge,
      Three paces and a stride,
   I sent my lefte foot dexterously
      Seven inches through his side.

Complaineth of foul play, and falleth down in ane trance.

   "Up came the seconde from the vanne;
      We had scarcely fought a round,
   When some one smote me from behinde,
      And I fell down in a swound:

One acteth the parte of Job's comforteru.

   "And when my head began to clear,
      I heard the yemering crew—
   Quoth one, 'This man hath penance done,
      And penance more shall do.'"

THE RIME OF THE AUNCIENT WAGGONERE.

Part Fourth.

The waggonere maketh ane shrewd observation.

   "O Freedom is a glorious thing!
      And, tailore, by the by,
   I'd rather in a halter swing
      Than in a dungeon lie.

The waggonere tickleth the spleen of the jailer, who daunces ane Fadango.

   "The jailere came to bring me foode,
      Forget it will I never,
   How he turned up the white o' his eye
      When I stuck him in the liver.

Rejoicethe in the fragrance of the aire.

   "His threade of life was snapt: once more
      I reached the open streete;
   The people sung out 'Gardyloo'
      As I ran down the streete.
   Methought the blessed air of heaven
      Never smelte so sweete.

Dreadeth Shoan Dhu, the corporal of the guarde.

   "Once more upon the broad highwaye,
      I walked with feare and drede;
   And every fifteen steppes I tooke
      I turned about my heade, .
   For feare the corporal of the guarde
      Might close behind me trede!

" Behold, upon the western wave
 Setteth the broad bright sunne ;
So I must onward, as I have
 Full fifteen miles to runne.'

" And should the bailiffes hither come
 To aske whilke waye I've gone,
Tell them I took the othere road,
 Said hee, and trotted onne."

The tailore rushed into the roome,
 O'erturning three or foure ;
Fractured his skulle against the walle,
 And worde spake never more ! !

The waggonere taketh leave of the tailore, to whome ane small accidente happeneth. Whereupon followeth the morale very proper to be had in minde by all members of the Dilettanti Society when they come over the bridge at these houres. Wherefore let them take heed and not lay blame where it lyeth nott.

Morale.

Such is the fate of foolish men,
 The danger all may see
Of those who list to waggonere,
 And keepe bad companye.

Christabel.

The Introduction to Part the Third.

LISTEN ! Ye know that I am mad,
   And ye will listen !—wizard dreams
   Were with me—all is true that seems!
From dreams alone can truth be had—
In dreams divinest lore is taught,
For the eye, no more distraught,
Rests most calmly ; and the ear,
   Of sound unconscious, may apply
Its attributes unknown, to hear
   The Music of Philosophy !

Thus am I wisest in my sleep,
For thoughts and things which daylight brings
   Come to the spirit sad and single ;
But verse and prose, and joys and woes,
   Inextricably mingle
When the hushed frame is silent in repose !
Twilight and moonlight, mist and storm,
Black night, and fire-eyed hurricane,
And crested lightning, and the snows
That mock the sunbeams, and the rain
Which bounds on earth with big drops warm,
All are round me while I spell
The legend of sweet Christabel !

CHRISTABEL.—PART THIRD.

Nine moons have waxed, and the tenth in its wane
Sees Christabel struggle in unknown pain !

For many moons was her eye less bright,
For many moons was her vest more tight.
And her cheek was pale, save when, with a start,
The life-blood came from the panting heart
And, fluttering o'er that thin fair face,
Past with a rapid, nameless pace;
And at moments a big tear filled the eye,
And at moments a short and smothered sigh
Swelled her breast with sudden strain,
Breathed half in grief and half in pain,
For hers are pangs on the rack that wind
The outward frame and the inward mind.
And when at night she did visit the oak,
She wore the Baron's scarlet cloak
(That cloak which, happy to hear and to tell,
Was lined with the fur of the leopard well).
And as she wandered down the dell,
None said 'twas the Lady Christabel.
Some thought 'twas a weird and ugsome elf;
Some deemed 'twas the sick old Baron himself,
Who wandered beneath the snowy lift
To count his beads in solemn shrift
(For his shape below was wide to see,
All bloated with the hydropsie).
Oh, had her old father the secret known,
He had stood as stark as the statue of stone
That stands so silent and white and tall
At the upper end of his banquet-hall!

Am I asleep, or am I awake?
In very truth I oft mistake,
As the stories of old come over my brain,
And I build in spirit the mystic strain.
Ah! would to the Virgin that I were asleep!
But I must wake, and I must weep!

Sweet Christabel, it is not well

That a lady, pure as the sunless snow
That lies so oft on the mountain's brow,
That a maiden of sinless chastity
In child-birth pangs should be doomed to die,
Or live with a name of sorrow and shame,
And hear the words of blemish and blame!
For the world that smiles at the guilt of man
Places woman beneath its ban.
Alas! that scandal thus should wreak
Its vengeance on the warm and weak;
That the arrows of the cold and dull
Should wound the heart of the beautiful!

Of the things that be, did we know but half,
Many and many would weep who laugh!
Tears would darken many an eye,
Or that deeper grief (when its orb is dry,
When it cannot dare the eye of day)
O'er the clouded heart would stray
Till it crumbled like desert dust away!
But here we meet with grief and grudge,
And they who cannot know us judge!
Thus souls on whom good angels smile
Are scoffed at in our world of guile.
Let this, Ladie, thy comfort be:
Man knows not us; good angels know
The things that pass in the world below.
And scarce, methinks, it seems unjust
That the world should view thee with mistrust;
For who that saw that child of thine,
Pale Christabel, who could divine
That its sire was the Ladie Geraldine?

But in I rush, with too swift a gale,
Into the ocean of my tale!
Not yet, young Christabel, I ween
Of her babe hath lighter been.

—"'Tis the month of the snow and the blast,
And the days of Christmas mirth are past,
When the oak-roots heaped on the hearth blazed
      bright,
Casting a broad and dusky light
On the shadowy forms of the warriors old,
Who stared from the wall, most grim to behold;
On shields where the spider his tapestry weaves,
On the holly boughs and the ivy leaves,
The few green glories that still remain
To mock the storm and welcome the rain,
Brighter and livelier 'mid tempest and shower,
Like a hero in the battle hour!
Brave emblems o'er the winter hearth,
They cheered our fathers' hours of mirth!

Twelve solar months complete and clear
The magic circle of the year!
Each (the ancient riddle saith)
Children two times thirty hath!
Three times ten are fair and white,
Three times ten are black as Night;
Three times ten hath Hecatè,
Three times ten the God of Day:
Thus spoke the old hierophant
(I saw her big breast, swelling, pant)
What time I dreamed, in ghostly wise,
Of Eleusinian mysteries;
For I am the hierarch
Of the mystical and dark,
And now, if rightly I do spell
Of the Lady Christabel,
She hates the three times ten so white,
And sickens in their searching light;
And woe is hers—alas! alack!
She hates the three times ten so black;

As a mastiff bitch doth bark,
I hear her moaning in the dark !

'Tis the month of January :
Why, lovely maiden, light and airy,
While the moon can scarcely glow
Through the plumes of falling snow,
While the moss upon the bark
Is withered all, and damp and dark,
While cold above the stars in doubt
Look dull, and scarcely will stay out,
While the snow is heavy on beechen bower,
And hides its namesake, the snowdrop flower,
Why walk forth thus mysteriously ?
Dear girl, I ask thee seriously.
Thy cheek is pale, thy locks are wild—
Ah, think how big thou art with child !
Though the baron's red cloak through the land hath no fellow,
Thou shouldst not thus venture without an umbrella !

Dost thou wander to the field of graves
Where the elder its spectral branches waves ;
And will thy hurried footsteps halt
Where thy mother sleeps in the silent vault ?
Where the stranger pauses long to explore
The emblems quaint of heraldic lore,
Where, though the lines are tarnished and dim,
Thy mother's features stare gaunt and grim,
And grinning skull and transverse bone,
And the names of warriors dead and gone,
Mark Sir Leoline's burial-stone :
Thither go not, or I deem almost
That thou wilt frighten thy mother's ghost !
Or wilt thou wend to the huge oak-tree,
And, kneeling down upon thy knee,
Number the beads of my rosary ?

Nine beads of gold and a tenth of pearl,
And a prayer with each, my lovely girl,
Nine and one shalt thou record ;
Nine to the Virgin and one to the Lord !
The pearls are ten times one to behold,
And ten times nine are the beads of gold :
Methinks 'tis hard of the friar to ask
On a night like this so weary a task !

'Tis pleasant, 'tis pleasant, in summer time,
In the green wood to spell the storied rhyme,
When the light winds above 'mong the light leaves are
    singing,
And the song of the birds through your heart is ringing ;
'Tis pleasant, 'tis pleasant when happily humming
To the flowers below the blythe bee is coming !—
When the rivulet, coy and ashamed to be seen,
Is heard where it hides 'mong the grass-blades green,
When the light of the moon and each starry islet
Gives a charm more divine to the long summer twilight,
When the breeze o'er the blossomy hawthorn comescheerful,
'Tis pleasant—with heart, ah ! how happy though fearful—
With heaven-beaming eyes where tears come while smiles
    glisten
To the lover's low vows in the silence to listen !

'Tis pleasant too on a fine spring day
(A month before the month of May)
To pray for a lover that's far away !
But, Christabel, I cannot see
The powerful cause that sways with thee
Thus, with a face all waxen white,
To wander forth on a winter night.

The snow hath ceased, dear lady meek,
But the night is chill and bleak ;

And clouds are passing swift away
Below the moon so old and grey—
The crescent moon, like a bark of pearl,
That lies so calm on the billowy whirl ;
Rapidly, rapidly
With the blast
Clouds of ebony
Wander fast.
And one the maiden hath fixed her eye on
Hath passed o'er the moon and is near the horizon !
Ah, Christabel, I dread it, I dread it,
That the clouds of shame
Will darken and gather
O'er the maiden's name,
Who chances unwedded
To give birth to a child, and knows not its father !

One—two—three—four—five—six—seven—eight—nine—
ten—eleven !—
Tempest or calm, in moonshine or shower,
The castle clock still tolls the hour,
And the cock awakens, and echoes the sound,
And is answered by the owls around ;
And at every measured tone
You may hear the old baron grunt and groan.
'Tis a thing of wonder, of fright, and fear,
The mastiff bitches' moans to hear ;
And the aged cow in her stall that stands,
And is milked each morning by female hands
(That the baron's breakfast of milk and bread
May be brought betimes to the old man's bed,
Who often gives, while he is dressing,
His Christabel a father's blessing)—
That aged cow, as each stroke sounds slow,
Answers it with a plaintive low !
And the baron old, who is ill at rest,
Curses the favourite cat for a pest ;

For let him pray, or let him weep,
She mews through all the hours of sleep,
Till the morning comes with its pleasant beams,
And the cat is at rest, and the baron dreams.
Let it rain however fast,
Rest from rain will come at last,
And the blaze that strongest flashes
Sinks at last, and ends in ashes!
But sorrow from the human heart,
And mists of care—will they depart?
I know not, and I cannot tell,
Saith the Lady Christabel;
But I feel my bosom swell!
In my spirit I behold
A lady—call her firm, not bold—
   Standing lonely by the burn:
Strange feelings through her breast and brain
Shoot with a sense of madness and pain.
   Ah, Christabel, return, return;
Let me not call on thee in vain!
Think, lady dear, if thou art drowned,
That thy body will be found.
What anguish will thy spirit feel
When it must to all reveal
What the spell binds thee to conceal!
How the baron's heart will knock 'gainst his chest
When the stake is driven into thy breast,
When thy body to dust shall be carelessly flung,
And over the dead no dirge be sung,
No friend in mourning vesture dight,
No lykewake sad—no tapered rite!

Return, return, thy home to bless,
   Daughter of good Sir Leoline;
In that chamber a recess,
   Known to no other eye than thine,
   Contains the powerful wild flower wine

That often cheered thy mother's heart;
Lady, lovely as thou art,
Return and, ere thou dost undress
And lie down in thy nakedness,
Repair to thy secret and favourite haunt
And drink the wine as thou art wont,
Hard to uncork and bright to decant!

My merry girl—she drinks—she drinks;
  Faster she drinks and faster;
My brain reels round as I see her whirl:
She hath turned on her heel with a sudden twirl,
  Wine, wine is a cure for every disaster;
For when sorrow wets the eye,
Yet the heart within is dry.
Sweet maid, upon the bed she sinks:
May her dreams be light, and her rest be deep;
Good angels guard her in her sleep!

Billy Routing.

A LYRICAL BALLAD.

FIT subject for heroic story,
  I sing a youth of noble fame;
Town and country, ten miles round,
Awaken at the glowing sound
  Of gallant Billy Routing's name!

Who wanders 'mid the summer landscape,
  To scare the crows, for ever shouting?
Who makes that sweet harmonious noise,
Surpassing far the raven's voice?
  By heavens 'tis he, 'tis Billy Routing!

Billy Routing walketh lamely—
  Lamely, lamely walketh he;
Billy Routing cannot work;
You'd swear his leg is made of cork
  (I never saw him bend his knee).

The doctors say he's paralytic
  Fair certificate he showeth;
Billy limpeth through the town,
Hawking ballads up and down;
  Up and down, where'er he goeth.

Billy Routing hath a staff,
  Measuring inches forty-three:
Its head is smooth; with leathern string
I've seen it from his button swing—
  (Some say it grew upon a tree!!!)

Billy Routing is a sportsman :
  In summer I have seen him trouting.
A poet also is the youth ;
A player too, for I, in truth,
  In country barns have heard him spouting.

Billy hath a goodly great-coat,
  I'll take my oath it once was green,
Though now it shines of many a hue ;
A lovelier coat, I'm certain, you
  On human back have never seen.

Now to my tale :—It chanced that Billy
  Was seven months from his home away ;
And no one of him heard or saw,
Till on the top of blue Skiddaw
  He landed on a summer day.

It chanced on that eventful morning,
  While walking forth upon the plain,
I saw him with my telescope,
I saw him on the mountain top,
  Holding a donkey by the mane !

Oh ! where have you been, Billy Routing ?
  We dreaded much that thou wast lost ;
Long did we drag each pond and river,
Fearing that thou wert gone for ever,
  And stuck handbills on every post.

And hast thou been in Fairyland,
  This many a month, this many a day ?
And hast thou seen the Danish boy ?
The idiot lad, or Betty Foy ?
  Old Goody Blake, or Lucy Gray ?

Or hast thou been in Nor-ro-way,
    Among the mountains gathering leeches?
That is a lovely beast of thine;
I'm sure its skin would make a fine
    Soft easy pair of leathern breeches.

Now Billy, tell me all your tidings,
    Now Billy, haste and tell me true.
What was his answer, can you tell?
With the bold front of Peter Bell,
    He crowed aloud, "Tu-whit, too-whoo!!!"

Note.—Further to illustrate this interesting subject, I have only to observe, that Mr. Routing was a person of an "aspetto nobile;" in his youth he suffered a severe attack of the "eruptio popularis," commonly hight small-pox; which, it must be confessed, had somewhat impaired the "contorno del suo viso." From being so much in the sun, his countenance had acquired a tawny—I had almost said—a נפרית colour. The most objectionable feature of his inward man, was the "auri sacra fames," which sometimes "αγαγε αυτον" to make free with "les oiseaux domestiques" about farm-yards. I remember on speaking to him on this subject, in a friendly manner, he defended himself with this quotation from Plato de Republica, lib. 2. cap. 4. "εαν ἐχωμεν χρημαθ, ἐξομεν φιλους." I have always chimed in with that opinion, that the sayings of great men, however trivial, are worthy of eternal commemoration. *Vide* Boswell's Life of Johnson, Hayley's Cowper, &c.

Rydal Mount.   W. W.

John Gilpin and Mazeppa.

HAD the poem of "John Gilpin" appeared immediately after that of "Mazeppa," we should have believed, in this age of parody, that Cowper wished to have his joke upon Lord Byron. As it is, we cannot help suspecting that his lordship has been aiming a sly hit at the bard of Olney; and though his satire is occasionally rather stiff and formal, it cannot be denied that on the whole the Hetman of the Cossacks is a very amusing double of the train-band captain of the Cockneys.

"John Gilpin" has always appeared to us a very fine chivalrous poem. Unquestionably, the author sometimes indulges in a strain of humour which, to fastidious minds, lessens the sublimity of the principal character and of his destinies; yet we believe that by more philosophical readers this mixture of the ludicrous with the terrible is felt to present a more true and affecting picture of human life.

In childhood and early youth we are, after all, the best judges of representation of human passion. We see objects, incidents and events, as they really are; we estimate their effect on the agents engaged with them free from all bias; and mere words, mere poetry, however much they may delight us, are, during that wise and blessed age, unable to pervert our judgment, or mislead the natural affections of our heart.

Accordingly, "John Gilpin" is that poem which has drawn from youth more tears and smiles than, perhaps, any other in the whole range of English poetry. It is treasured up in every amiable and sensitive heart, and that man is little to be envied whose conjugal affection would not kindle at the inn of Edmonton, or whose filial piety would not grow warmer at the calendrer's house at Ware.

It is not our intention to give an elaborate analysis of "John Gilpin," or a philosophical exposition of the principles on which that great poem is constructed. This would necessarily lead us into a discussion of the principles of all poetry, which we prefer giving some months hence, in a separate treatise. Mr Wordsworth has, to be sure, done this already, in his preface to the "Lyrical Ballads;" but, unless we are greatly mistaken (*ni fallor*), he has not exhausted the subject, and we do not fear that among the numerous quartos yet to be written thereupon, ours can fail of attracting some portion of that public regard which we gratefully acknowledge to have hitherto been so lavishly bestowed on our lucubrations.

It seems to have been Lord Byron's intention to show what John Gilpin's feelings would in all probability have been had he been placed in circumstances different from those in which he found himself on the anniversary of his marriage with Mrs. Gilpin ; and surely the least imaginative reader will be of opinion that the noble lord has attained this difficult object in Mazeppa. After the perusal of the two works, we all feel that if John Gilpin's stars had permitted it, he was just the man to have become the monarch of the Ukraine; and *vice versa*, that Mazeppa, but for the accident of his birth, &c., might have established a highly respectable firm in Cheapside.

Cowper has not given us any account of the ante-nuptial loves of John Gilpin, but introduced him at once to our acquaintance as a married man with a considerable family, and in a thriving trade. Mazeppa, on the other hand, had involved himself, early in life and the poem, in a very improper intrigue. But human nature is the same in all countries ; and no good objection could have been brought against either bard, though John Gilpin had been described as gallanting a citizen's wife on a water-party to Richmond, and Mazeppa comfortably settled with a wife and family in

some mercantile town on the frontiers of Poland.   As Mr.
Wordsworth remarks, "similitude dissimilitude" is one of
the chief sources of the sublime in poetry.

That principle being once admitted, Mazeppa will probably
seem to every one sufficiently like John Gilpin in character
and situation in life.   Let us next look at the two gentlemen
after they are fairly mounted.   There is no occasion to quote
the whole description of John, for it is probably familiar to
our readers.   Suffice it to remind them that

> " John Gilpin, at his horse's side,
>   Fast seized the flowing mane."

And that afterwards,

> "Then over all, that he might be
>   Equipped from top to toe,
>   His long red cloak, well brushed and neat,
>   He manfully did throw."

Lord Byron is more minute in his description ; and from
it we suspect that, on the whole, Mazeppa was better
mounted than John Gilpin.

> " Bring forth the horse—the horse was brought.
>   In truth he was a noble steed,
>   A Tartar of the Ukraine breed."

John Gilpin's horse was, we have reason to know, an Irishman—his friend the calendrer having imported him from
the county of Tipperary.*   On the other hand, though
better mounted, Mazeppa was worse dressed, for he was

> "In nature's nakedness."

This being the case, he was probably in the long run no
better off than John Gilpin, of whom it is written that

> "The snorting beast began to trot,
>   Which galled him in his seat."

Hitherto the similarity between the Hetman and the

---

* He was bred by —— Blennerhasset, Esq.   See *Sporting Magazine* for
that year.

Linen-draper has been sufficiently apparent; but it is much more striking after they have fairly started.

> "So, fair and softly, John he cried,
>   But John he cried in vain;
> That trot became a gallop soon,
>   In spite of curb or rein.
>
> So stooping down, as needs he must
>   Who cannot sit upright,
> He grasped the mane with both his hands,
>   And eke with all his might.
>
> His horse, who never in that sort
>   Had handled been before,
> What thing upon his back had got,
>   Did wonder more and more."

Nothing can be finer and more headlong than this, except what follows :—

> " 'Away, away! my breath had gone,
> I saw not where he hurried on!
> 'Twas scarcely yet the break of day,
> And on he foamed, away, away!'"

In one very remarkable particular, John Gilpin is distinguished from Mazeppa.

> "So stooping down, as needs he must
>   Who cannot sit upright,
> He grasped the mane with both his hands,
>   And eke with all his might."

On the contrary, Mazeppa says:

> "With sudden wrath I wrenched my hand,
>   And snapped the cord, which to the mane
> Had bound my neck in lieu of rein."

It would appear, therefore, that on first starting Mazeppa (it will, no doubt, be said *involuntarily*) had his arms round his horse's neck, but afterwards held them more like a gentleman who had taken lessons in riding, whereas John Gilpin first of all probably attempted to elevate his bridle-hand, but afterwards conceived it more salutary to embrace the neck of his Bucephalus. This, however, is a circum-

stance scarcely worth mentioning. Lord Byron then goes
on to say :

> " Away, away, my steed and I,
> Upon the pinions of the wind !"

And Cowper in like manner writes:

> " Away went Gilpin neck or nought,
> Away went hat and wig."

Which last line does, we confess, convey to our mind a more
lively idea of the rapidity of motion than any single image
in Mazeppa.

It is impossible, however, to admire sufficiently the skill
with which Lord Byron has contrasted the general features
of Mazeppa's ride with those of John Gilpin's. John's steed
gallops along the king's highway, and Mazeppa's through the
desert. Yet, if danger or terror be one source of the sublime,
we humbly hold that there is a sublimity in the situation of
the London cit far beyond that of the Polish gentleman.
For in the first place Mazeppa, being securely bound to his
horse, need entertain no apprehensions of a severe fall,
whereas John's adhesion to his nag seems to the reader
almost in the light of a continued miracle, little accustomed
as he must have been to that sort of exercise. Secondly,
would not any person whatever prefer galloping along turf,
sand, or dust, to a causeway leading from the metropolis of
a great empire? Nothing surprises us so much in the poem
of John Gilpin as that the calendrer's horse does not come
down, which would almost force us to suspect that John was
a better horseman than the world in general gives him credit
for. Indeed, though not much of a metaphysician ourselves,
having read little on that subject, save some of the works of
the celebrated Macvey Napier, Esq., we think that we may
venture to assert that a considerable portion of the delight
with which we peruse (or rather pursue) John Gilpin arises
from our admiration of his skill in horsemanship. This
admiration of the rider is also blended with affection for the
man :

" We love him for the dangers he is passing,
And he loves us because we pity them."

And this leads us, in the third place, to remark that those
dangers are of the most formidable kind. We may safely
assert that before he reached Edmonton, he had brushed by
at least 200 carriages, coming and going, of all sorts, from
the broad-wheeled waggon to the shandrydan. Yet it does
not appear that he drove any of them into pieces, or in any
one instance transfixed his friend's galloway on the pole of
a carriage coming up to town. He seems to us to be a
man under the protection of Providence. And then, what
majestic calmness and composure are his! Why, Mr. Editor,
not two men in eight millions, that is to say, no other man
but John Gilpin, in the whole then population of England,
would have exhibited such heroism. Mazeppa, too, no
doubt had his difficulties to contend with, but they were
not of so formidable a description. His feelings must have
been very uncomfortable as he "neared the wild wood,"
"studded with old sturdy trees," and he probably laid his
account with many a bang on the shins; but Lord Byron
ought not to have told us that the trees "were few and far
between ;" for, in that case, the forest must have been very
pretty riding.

" He rustled through the leaves like wind,
Left shrubs, and trees, and wolves behind."

It would almost seem from these lines as if Mazeppa
were under such alarm as to imagine the shrubs and trees
to be chasing him, as well as the wolves. This is a touch
of poetry beyond anything to be found in John Gilpin.
His dangers were of another sort :

" The dogs did bark, the children screamed,
Up flew the windows all"—

The extreme folly of thus suddenly throwing open their
windows (an ugly trick, by which many an honest man has
come to an untimely end) is almost redeemed by the deep

interest which these worthy but thoughtless people take in
the fortunes of the flying Cockney :

> " And every soul cried out, Well done !
> As loud as he could bawl."

We never read this agonising poem (for the interest is so
intensely kept up as to be indeed agonising) without blessing
ourselves for the fortunate delusion of the various turnpike-
men by which John Gilpin was saved the necessity of taking
many dangerous leaps, one or other of which would in all
human probability have proved fatal.

> " He carries weight—he rides a race ! "

This exclamation, borne before him, and just before him,
on the wings of the wind, gives one a truly awful idea of
velocity, and well might Cowper exclaim :

> " 'Twas wonderful to view,
> How in a trice the turnpikemen
> Their gates wide open threw."

No sooner did the public mind take up the belief " he
rides a race," than by a wonderful process of thought it
discovers the amount of the wager he had laid :

> " 'Tis for a thousand pound "

—an immense sum at that time, when horse-racing had not
nearly reached its meridian splendour, and when only a
very few numbers, if any, of the *Sporting Magazine* had
been published.   In all this Cowper has manifestly the
advantage over Byron.   Compared with the fine passages
now quoted from Gilpin, how tame are the following words
of Mazeppa :—

> " Untired, untamed, and worse than wild,
> All furious as a favoured child
> Balked of its wish, or fiercer still,
> A woman piqued, who has her will."

Here Mazeppa's gallantry altogether forsakes him, nor
can we imagine a more inelegant compliment to the mistress
whom he was then leaving than to compare her, or indeed

any of her sex, to a wild Tartar horse, on whom he was then
tied "in nature's nakedness."

It does not appear that Gilpin lost his senses or his
presence of mind during any portion of the Excursion, a
Poem. Mazeppa, on the other hand, was completely done
up, and absolutely fainted:

> " He who dies
> Can die no more than then I died,
> O'er-tortured by that ghastly ride."

Presence of mind is a quality indispensable in the character
of a true hero. We pity Mazeppa, but we admire Gilpin.

Mazeppa complains frequently of hunger during his ride;
but no such weakness degrades Gilpin, who seems almost
raised above all the ordinary wants of nature:

> " Stop, stop, John Gilpin !—here's the house,
> They all at once did cry—
> The dinner waits, and we are tired ;
> Said Gilpin—So am I !"

Not a single word of regret does he utter for the want of
that dinner which has so long waited for him, but which,
from the impatient appetites of Mrs. Gilpin and the children,
he well knows is then trembling on the brink of destruction.
One solitary exclamation is all that proceeds from his lips
as he hurries by below the balcony:

> " So am I !"

An ordinary writer would have filled his mouth with
many needless words. Lord Byron has evidently very
closely copied this sublime passage in an early part of
Mazeppa's career:

> " Writhing half my form about,
> Howled back my curse ; but 'midst the tread,
> The thunder of my courser's speed,
> Perchance they did not hear nor heed."

It may be questioned, however, if this, fine as it is, does
not want the concise energy of the original.

The dangers which Gilpin and Mazeppa encounter arise not only from land but water. Thus quoth the Pole:

> "Methought the dash of waves was nigh,
> The wild horse swims the wilder stream."

In like manner we are told by Cowper:

> "Thus all through merry Islington
> These gambols he did play,
> Until he came unto the Wash,
> Of Edmonton so gay;
>
> And there he threw the wash about
> On both sides of the way,
> Just like unto a trundling mop,
> Or a wild goose at play."

These images are homely, but they are not, on that account, the less expressive. That of the "trundling mop" simply expresses the appearance of the "wash" thrown off on both sides of the way by the pony *en passant;* that of the wild goose at play makes a direct appeal to the imaginative faculty, and suggests, to our minds at least, a much more poetical feeling of a good galloper than his lordship's images of the crying baby or the scolding mistress. It gives one a momentary flash of the higher and hidden powers of that roadster, and convinces us that his owner would not part with him for a very considerable sum of money. This is one of those sudden and unexpected touches so characteristic of Cowper, and that prove what great things he might have accomplished had he turned his genius more systematically to the cultivation of the higher provinces of poetry.

After swimming the river, Mazeppa's horse is not in the least degree tired, but

> "With glossy skin, and dripping mane,
> And reeling limbs and reeking flank,
> The wild steed's sinewy nerves still strain
> Up the repelling bank."

Here Lord Byron strictly follows the original:

> "But yet his horse was not a whit
> Inclined to tarry there," &c.

And, what is still more strikingly similar, the two horses have
the very same motive for their conduct :

> :" For why? His owner had a house
> Full ten miles off at Ware."

Mazeppa's horse had hitherto been accustomed to lead a
free-and-easy life rather more than ten miles off in the
Ukraine, and thither accordingly he set off at score, making
play all the way, pretty much after the fashion of a steeple-
hunt. It may perhaps be worth while to quote, for a
particular reason, the following verse :

> " So like an arrow swift he flew,
>   Shot by an archer strong;
> So did he fly—which brings me to
>   The middle of my song."

Now it is very remarkable, and we think the coincidence
cannot be accidental, that the corresponding passage in
Mazeppa also occurs just about the middle of the poem ;
which satisfactorily shows that the original structures of the
two great works do in their dimensions exactly coincide.

The termination of Gilpin's excursion, therefore, evidently
suggested that of Mazeppa's. But Byron has contrived to give
quite a new turn to his poem, so that in the final catastrophe
he almost seems to lose sight of the original. At Ware,
Gilpin's horse stands stock-still at the door of his master's
house, which, by the by, proves that he had not that unchancy
trick of bolting into the stable, "*sans ceremonie*," which has
incommoded many a sober-headed gentleman. Mazeppa's
horse, in like manner, falls down the instant he reaches home,
so we observe that the transition from motion to repose is in
both cases equally abrupt. Mazeppa's sufferings are now at
an end, and, being put instantly into a good warm bed, he
soon comes to himself, marries, and in good time becomes
the father of many children, and Hetman of the Cossacks.
Gilpin, on the other hand, has scarcely had leisure to put
on a new hat and wig before off he sets again without ever
drawing his bit ; but it is unnecessary to follow him farther

with any minuteness.   Conclude we cannot without recalling to the memory of our readers one stanza which ever awakens in our minds a profound sense of the depth of Mrs. Gilpin's conjugal affection, and of the illimitable range of the imagination when flying on the wings of terrified love:

> "Now Mrs. Gilpin, when she saw
> Her husband posting down
> Into the country far away,
> She pulled out half-a-crown."

That one line, "into the country far away," gives to us a vaster idea of distance, of time and space, than the whole 1000 lines of Mazeppa.   The reader at once feels how little chance there is of the post-boy overtaking Gilpin, and owns that the worthy man ought to be left entirely to himself and his wild destinies.

We need pursue the parallel no farther.   But we may remark that, though we have now proved John Gilpin to have been the prototype of Mazeppa, yet the noble author has likewise had in his recollection the punishment which used sometimes to be inflicted on criminals in Russia.   They were bound on the back of an elk, and sent into Siberia or elsewhere.   We refer our readers to the *Sporting Magazine*, where they will find a very affecting picture of a gentleman on his elk.   It was always the practice to shave the criminal before he mounted, and, in the picture we speak of, he has a beard of about six inches long, which informs us that he had been on his travels probably several weeks.   *Ut pictura poesis.*

Song,

"THAT I LOVE THEE, CHARMING MAID,"

To its own tune.

THAT I love thee, charming maid, I a thousand times have
    said,
  And a thousand times more I have sworn it;
But 'tis easy to be seen in the coldness of your mien
  That you doubt my affection, or scorn it.
                         Ah me!

Not a single pile of sense is in the whole of these pretences
  For rejecting your lover's petitions;
Had I windows in my bosom, oh! how gladly I'd expose 'em
  To undo your phantastic suspicions.
                         Ah me!

You repeat I've known you long, and you hint I do you
    wrong
  In beginning *so late* to pursue ye;
But 'tis folly to look glum because people did not come
  Up the stairs of your nursery to woo ye.
                         Ah me!

In a grapery one walks without looking at the stalks,
  While the bunches are green that they're bearing;
All the pretty little leaves that are dangling at the eaves
  Scarce attract even a moment of staring.
                         Ah me!

But when time has swell'd the grapes to a richer style of
       shapes,
  And the sun has lent warmth to their blushes,
Then to cheer us and to gladden, to enchant us and to
       madden,
  Is the ripe ruddy glory that rushes.
                               Ah me!

Oh 'tis then that mortals pant, while they gaze on Bacchus'
       plant,
  Oh 'tis then—will my simile serve ye?
Should a damsel fair repine, though neglected like a vine?
  Both ere long shall turn heads topsy-turvy.
                               Ah me!

Ode to Mrs. Flanagan.

BY AN IRISH GENTLEMAN, LATELY DECEASED.

SIR,—A friend of mine died last month in Tralee. *Sit illi terra levis.* He left behind him a large quantity of MSS. His wife, a woman of singular judgment, appointed me to prepare them for the press; and before I finally commit them entire to the public, I think it right to give a specimen of the poetical part. Your Magazine has been pointed out to me as the vehicle. The public in this incredulous age might not wish to purchase a couple of folios without some sample of their contents. I give, therefore, the first that comes to hand.

It happens to be a poem, written about 1817, to a Mrs. Flanagan of Youghall. Various passages in it requiring elucidation, I submitted it to the people who could give me most information on its topics. I have to thank Mr. Roderick Mulshenan, Eugene Falvey, mariner; Lieutenant Duperier, Mr. Leigh Hunt, &c. The last gentleman took a very kind interest in the concern, as will appear by the notes furnished by himself and his friends; and I hereby return him my most grateful thanks. Every gentleman who assisted me in my commentary is duly mentioned, after the laudable custom of those *viri clarissimi*, the Variorum editors.

I shall send you some more of these papers in prose and verse, with a life of the author, at some future opportunity.— I remain, sir, your most obedient and very humble servant,

PHILIP FORAGER.

DRUMANIGILLIBEG, *Feb.* 29, 1820.

P.S.—I understand that it is conceived by some of the critics who have perused this piece that the hint is taken from Horace.   Perhaps so ; I accordingly subjoin the ode. I have some notes and annotations on the Latin text, which I at first intended to send to you, but, on mature reflection, I have transmitted them to Mr. Kidd, who has promised to publish them in his Curæ Posteriores in Horatii Carmina.

HORATII, *Carm. Lib.* iii. *Od.* 7.	MSS. No. I.
Asteriem consolatur de Gygis absentia, et ad fidem hortatur.	*To Mrs. Kitty Flanagan, comforts her on the absence of her husband, Jerry Flanagan, mate of the* Jolly Jupiter, *and drops a hint about a light dragoon.*
QUID fles, Asterie, quem tibi candidi	WHY do cry, my sweet Mrs. Flanagan,
Primo restituent vere Favonii,	When you will soon have your own dear man again,
Thynâ merce beatum,	
Constanti juvenem fide,	Whom the first wind will bring home from the Delaware,
	Brimful of sovereigns, and such other yellow ware ?
Gygen? Ille, Notis actus ad Oricum	He's driven in to some port to the west of us
Post insana Capræ sidera, frigidas	(A thing that might happen, dear, to the best of us),
Noctes, non sine multis	
Insomnis lacrimis, agit.	Where he is sighing, sobbing, and chattering, Night and day long of his own dear Catherine,
Atqui sollicitæ nuncius hospitæ,	Although his landlady, one Mrs. Gallagher,*
Suspirare Chloën, et miseram tuis	Wants him to quit you, the rogue, and to follow her.
Dicens ignibus uri,	
Tentat mille vafer modis.	She tells him the tale of the wife of old Potiphar,†
Ut Prœtum mulier perfida credulum	
Falsis impulerit criminibus, nimis	Relating a fact that will ne'er be forgot of her ;

---

* Mrs. Gallagher (pronounced more Hibernico, Gollagher) keeps the sign of the Cat-and-Bagpipes in Dingle, a woman irreproachable in her conduct, amatory in her disposition, fair in her dealings, and a good hand in *running* spirits.   Touching the colour of her hair, it is red, and she was a widow (at the time of this poem) of her third husband for nearly three months : she has been since married.   Miss Skinandbone, a maiden lady in Dingle, tells me that her treatment of Flanagan was kind, and that he was *no* Joseph— but this may not be authenticated.—P. F.   She appears to be a woman of taste and reading, by having my poem in her house.—LEIGH HUNT.   It was left at her house by a Cockney barber, who was running away from his creditors, and taking ship on board the *Yankiedoodle* in Dingle ; he left it with Mrs G. as pledge for a tumbler of punch.—RODERICK MULSHENAN. Perhaps he found it too *heavy* to carry it any further.—Z.

† This allusion to Scripture I think profane and reprehensible.—LEIGH HUNT.   So do I.—BYRON.   So do I.—WM. HONE.   So do I.—BEDFORD. So do I.—SUSSEX.   So do I.—T. MOORE.   So also many more Whig wits,

Casto Bellerophonti
  Maturare necem, refert.

Narrat penè datum Pelea Tartaro,
Magnessam Hippolyten dum fugit
    abstinens :
  Et peccare docentes
    Fallax historias monet :

Frustra ; nam scopulis surdior Icari
Voces audit, adhuc integer. At, tibi
  Ne vicinus Enipeus
    Plus justo placeat, cave ;
Quamvis non alius flectere equum
    sciens
Æquè conspicitur gramine Martio ;
  Nec quisquam citus æquè
    Tusco denatat alveo.

Primâ nocte domum claude : neque
    in vias
Sub cantu querulæ despice tibiæ :
  Et te sæpè vocanti
    Duram, difficilis mane.

Who, from a feeling malignant and sul-te-ry,
Had Joseph near hanged for eschewing adul-
    tery :
And from this basest, this vilest of women, he
Gets Mr. Hunt's smutty story of Rimini,*
By which, 'tis plain, she hopes to a surety,
Soon to corrupt his natural purity ;
But he resists her arts and her flattery,
Deaf and determined, just as a battery.†
But there's a sergeant, one Patrick Hennessy,‡
Keep away, Kitty, from all such men as he,
Though he's so smart that he's always
    employed as
Rough-rider to the old Marquis of Drogheda's.§
Though there are few so brawny and big, my
    dear,
Or far better at dancing a jig, my dear,
Close down your windows when he comes caper-
    ing,
Shut both your doors and your ears to his
    vapouring,
Mind not the songs or sighs of this Hannibal,
But, looking at him, cross as a cannibal,
Cry, " Come, be off as light as a tailor, man,
I will be true to my own dear sailor-man."

---

men conspicuous for respect for the Scriptures. Nobody understands profaneness better than they.—P. F.

  * The clear shown bay of Dingle rises on my soul with springy freshness from this circumstance. Mrs. Gallagher made the use I intended of my poem. A rational piety and a manly patriotism should prompt a writer to excite those passions which nature has given us, and which tend to increase the population of the country. By smutty is meant that I resemble Rembrandt in being dark, gloomy, and grand ; it is a dear coming-round metaphorical expression, quite feet-on-the-fenderish, and reminds one of a poker in the fire, and a chimney-corner.—LEIGH HUNT.

  † Deaf as a battery is not the proper phrase : it must have been put in *rythmi gratia*. I suggest the following ;—

      " But he's as deaf—as deaf as the postesses
      To the designs and the arts of his hostess's."
                  —JOHN KEATS.

Postesses, in the Cockney tongue, signifies *Posts*.—P. F.

  ‡ There is no such sergeant or rough-rider in the 18th Hussars.—H. DUPERIER, Lieutenant and Adjutant.

  There must then be some mistake in the business, which I cannot account for.—P. F.

  § The most noble Charles, Marquis of Drogheda, K.S.P., is colonel of the 18th Hussars.—H. D., Lieutenant and Adjutant.

Ode to Marshal Grouchy on his Return.

BY AN IRISH GENTLEMAN, LATELY DECEASED.

SIR,—I send another specimen of my deceased friend's poetry, and, *mirabile dictu*, it, as well as the former, bears a similitude to an Ode in Horace. Indeed, I believe he wrote a set of parallel Carmina to the Horatian, and if Archdeacon Wrangham were to see them, I think he would give up for ever the idea of attempting to lay his versions before the public, for which reason I hope he never will see them.

I am working away arranging the papers, and in a month or so they will be prepared finally. Another month will be occupied in writing my friend's life, so that I shall be ready to face the booksellers by next October.

I should say more, but that I am in a hurry, being called away to attend a coroner's inquest over the body of one Timothy Regan *alias* Tighe a Breeshtha, who was killed yesterday, fighting at a fair in a feud, a *bellum intestinum*, between the Shanavests and Caravats. I can only add that I have procured fewer notes for this than for the former Ode. I remain, sir, your humble servant,   PHILIP FORAGER.

DRUMMANIGILLIBEG, *August* 6, 1820.

<table>
<tr><td>HOR. Od. 7, Lib. ii.</td><td>MSS. No. II.</td></tr>
<tr><td>AD POMPEIUM.
*Felicem ex infelici militiâ reditum
gratulatur.*</td><td>*To Marshal —— on his Return;
or, Congratulatory Address by
Mons. ——.*</td></tr>
</table>

I.

O sæpe mecum tempus in ultimum	O WELCOME home, my marshal, my
Deducte, Bruto militiæ duce,	colleague true and good,
Quis te redonavit Quiritem	When under brave Napoleon we
Dis patriis, Italoque cœlo,	dabbled long in blood;

Pompei, meorum prime sodalium?
Cum quo morantem saepè diem mero
  Fregi, coronatus nitentes
    Malobathro Syrio capillos.

Who brought you back to Paris in
  Bourbon's royal days?
Was it Madame Bonaparte's man, our
  own Monsieur De Cazes?*

2.

Tecum Philippos et celerem fugam
Sensi, relictâ non benè parmulâ ;
  Cum fracta virtus, et minaces
    Turpe solum tetigere mento.

With thee I robbed through Prussia,
  through Portugal and Spain ;
With thee I marched to Russia, and
  then—marched back again ;
With thee I faced the red-coats awhile
  at Waterloo ;
And with thee I raised the war-song
  of jolly † *sauve qui peut.*

3.

Sed me per hostes Mercurius celer
Denso paventem sustulit aëre :
  Te rursus in bellum resorbens
    Unda fretis tulit æstuosis.

I took the oaths to Louis, and now,
  with face of brass,
I bawl against the royalists all in the
  Chambre Basse ;
But you, my lad, were exiled ; a
  mighty cruel thing,
For you did nothing surely but fight
  against your king.

4.

Ergo obligatam redde Jovi dapem,
Longâque fessum militiâ latus
  Depone sub lauru meâ, nec
    Parce cadis tibi destinatis.

Then drink a health to the Emperor,
  and curse Sir Hudson Lowe ; ‡
And decorate with stolen plate your
  honest-earned chateau ;
And merrily, my marshal, we shall
  the goblet drain :
'Tis a chalice § that I robbed oneday
  out of a church in Spain.

---

* Hodie Duc de Cazes, olim secretary to Madame Mere, the imperial mother of all the Bonapartes.—P. F.

† Jolly ! Quoi? Jolly ! Ma foi, voila une epithete assez mal appliqué.—MARSHAL GROUCHY.

‡ Sir Hudson Lowe is a very bad man in not letting the Emperor escape.—LAS CASES. He is a man of no soul. The world cannot decide whether Bonaparte or Wellington is the greater general—I am sure the former is, without a second battle of Waterloo; and here we have a simple knight preventing the solution of the question. He is an imbecile. I am sure he never had the taste to read my Amyntas.—LEIGH HUNT.

§ It was an instrument of superstition ; and I, therefore, although a water-drinker, approve of its being turned to any other use, just as I approved of the enlightened revolutionists of France turning the super-

5.

Oblivioso levia Massico
Ciboria exple ; funde capacibus
   Unguenta de conchis. Quis udo
    Deproperare apio coronas

Fill, fill the bumper fairly ; 'tis Cham-
   bertin,* you see,
The Emperor's favourite liquor, and
   chant in pious glee
A song of Monsieur Parny's,† Miladi
   Morgan's bard,
And curse the tasteless Bourbons who
   won't his muse reward.

6.

Curatve myrto? quem Venusarbitrum
Dicet bibendi? Non ego sanius
   Bacchabor Edonis : recepto
    Dulce mihi furere est amico.

Then, with our wigs all perfumed, and
   our beavers cocked so fierce,
We'll throw a main together, or troll
   the amorous verse ;
And I'll get as drunk as Irishmen, as
   Irishmen *morbleu*,
After six - and - thirty tumblers ‡ in
   drinking healths to you.

---

stitious bells of Paris into cannon, although, on principle, a declared enemy
of war.—SIR R. PHILLIPS.

   * Bonaparte was fond of Chambertin.—Teste TOM MOORE. I prefer
whisky.—P. F.

   † A pet poet of Lady Morgan's.—*Vide* her France. I wonder what the
medical Knight, her *caro sposo*, says, when he catches her reading "La
Guerre des Dieux."—P. F.

   ‡ On this I must remark, that six-and-thirty tumblers is rather hard
drinking. My friend, Rice Hussey, swears only to six-and-twenty, though
he owns he has heard he drank two-and-thirty, but could not with propriety
give his oath to it, as he was somewhat disordered by the liquor. There is
not a Frenchman in France would drink it : I will lay any wager on that.
In fact, I back Ireland against the world. A few years ago the Northumberland, a very pretty English militia regiment, commanded by Lord
Loraine, who endeared himself wherever he went in Ireland by his affable
and social manners, arrived in the city of Cork. His lordship gave a dinner
to thirty officers of his regiment, who each drank his bottle. When the bill
was called for, he observed to the waiter with a smile that the English
gentlemen could drink as well as the Irish. "Lord help your head, sir,"
said the waiter, "is that all you know about it? Why, there's five gentlemen next room who have drank one bottle more than the whole of yees, and
don't you hear them bawling like five devils for the other cooper?——coming,
gentlemen!"—P. F. In Horace it is Edoni, not Irishmen ; but that is
quite correct. The Irish are of Scythian descent, so were the Thracians.—
THOS. WOOD, M.D.

Extracts from a Lost (and Found) Memorandum Book.

To Christopher North, *Esq.*

Sir,—While lately travelling through part of England, a thing which is customary with me twice a year for the transaction of business, I happened, in the stage between Bath and ——, to meet with a circumstance which is the occasion of my now addressing you.

As I do not happen to be of the melancholic temperament, and am rather fond than otherwise of society, it is not unusual for me, as I am a bachelor, and have the happiness or misery of travelling alone, when I fall in with a landlord of genteelish manners and good nature, to ask him to a participation of my supper. By good luck it fell out that I here found a man to my mind. After supper was discussed, and our rummers charged for the second time, the spirit of my host began to expand; and, in the midst of his hilarity, he let me in to numerous anecdotes of his own; some of which might have been spared, and many of which were entertaining enough. I shall confine myself to that which is the subject of my present epistle.

About two years ago, a military gentleman, of what rank he could not learn, except that his companions sometimes called him General, took up abode with him for eight days; and lived, during the whole of that time, to use a proverbial expression, "at rack and manger." Every stranger that arrived within that time, at the inn, seemed to be of his acquaintance; or, if they were unknown to him, a friendship was soon begun and cemented; and ere they were a couple of hours together, one could have sworn that they had been

born in the same village, educated at the same school ; or,
to bring forward a still stronger link of association, which
the author of " Rob Roy " has mentioned, " had read from the
same Bible at church." Whoever was with him, whether
the social or the serious, he regularly obliged them to sit
till three in the morning, when he sent them, or, more
properly speaking, led them, to their bed-rooms.

At length, having ordered breakfast one morning, he
disappeared, and the landlord could never afterwards find
one token or trace of him.   He left behind him a green-net
purse (containing more than the amount of his bill), and
the chambermaid drowned in tears.   He was remarkably
tall, of rather a spare habit of body, wore neatly-curled
brown whiskers, a grey surtout, Wellington boots with spurs,
and a South-Sea cap with a gold band.   He had no baggage
with him ; and the only relique of his visit was a little book,
which he had inadvertently left in his bed-room.

I begged a sight of this relique from my host, and was
not a little struck with its contents.   It is a small volume,
in red binding, fastened with tape.   On the back, in gilt
letters, is marked " Memorandum Book."   After looking
over a few pages, I was highly amused with its contents, and
expressed myself so to my host, who obligingly told me it
was of no use to him, and that I was most welcome to it.
Its contents are of a most miscellaneous nature, and written,
in some parts, in a rather illegible hand.   I have made one
of my young men transcribe a piece from it, here and there,
which you will receive along with this, and which you may
make public if you please.   Should I observe this to be the
case, I may transmit you a few further extracts from time to
time.—I remain, yours, &c.,

J—— T——N.

February 10, 1821.

EXTRACTS.

No. I.

STRICTURES ON POLITICAL ECONOMY, WHEREIN A REMEDY
FOR THE POOR LAWS IS DIVULGED.

Insula, sole occidente, viridi, seculis plurimis elapsis, præclarus vir mili-
taris apparebitque florebit. Ille non modo omni sapientiæ re, sed omni
philosophiæ discet et docebit ; poeta etiamque celebris.
—*Frag. MS. Vet. apud Vatican.*

IT is only of late years that political economy has raised
itself to the dignity of a science. Doctrines that men
believed to be as true as Father Paul's history of the Council
of Trent were nevertheless neglected ; and other theories, as
unsubstantial as the morning mist, though known and
acknowledged to be false, substituted in their stead, and
acted on. As Jeffrey said of Wordsworth's "Excursion," "this
would never do." The chaff has been sifted from the wheat
—the truth has been purified from the error—and the facts
that before were scattered, like the twelve tribes of Israel,
over the face of society, have been brought together, and
cemented into a regular and almost complete fabric, under
the auspices of Malthus, Godwin, Weyland, Say, James
Graham, M'Culloch, Jeremy Bentham, and the writer of
the present article.

But what is the rising of the stocks to him who has no
capital ? What is the question about the balance of trade to
him who has no merchandise ? And what is the worth of
our knowing the right principles, if we find it impossible to
act on them ? It is of no use to know the nature of the
disease, if we have not a plaster to apply, or a remedy to
prescribe.

We cannot make as good silks in England as we can get
from India, nor can we afford to sell them as cheap ; we
want *materiel.* But then it would overpower the feelings of
our humanity to ruin the 40,000 families that are employed
in that branch of manufacture. The silk spun in this

country is by no means so good; whether it be the case that the silk-worm does not keep its health in our northern latitudes, or not, I have too little confidence in my own opinion to say: but this I can tell from experience, that we are more apt to be mistaken as to the animal itself, thereby rendering all our labour fruitless and our efforts abortive. The writer of this article bought several papers full of the embryos of the silk-worm, but, after waiting in eager expectation for a twelvemonth, to his utter consternation and astonishment they turned out to be nought else but common maggots.

The poor-rates are a great bore in this country, but it is all owing to the excess of population, and for this I have before suggested a remedy. If the overplus of the population were to be called together, and some able speaker, say one of the advocates of the Scottish bar, selected to address them, and lay down to them in a placid and precise manner the hardships they entail on society, and the impropriety of their ever having been born, unquestionably then the overplus of population, provided they consisted of well-educated, decent, and sensible people, could have no objection either to be transported beyond seas, or despatched in as gentle a manner as could be devised. Until a great national meeting is called for the purpose, we must be content to put up with many evils. Mendicity is not the least of these, and to the public in general we recommend the following plan, which is as yet in private circulation, and does not seem to have reached the ear of the Society for the Suppression of Begging. It originated from the ingenuity of one of that useful class of the community, a French cook; but as he had been for several years domesticated in this country, no other realm can presume to come in for a share of the honour, which is purely national. It is said that M. Say, Benjamin Constant, and Carnot claim it for France; but this is only a report.

The house in which this ingenious French cook served was infested from morning to night, and the court-yard literally swarming with beggars, as "thick as the motes that people the sunbeams." The proprietor was dunned with petitions, and the watch-dog, which was chained at the outer gate, had actually worn down his teeth to the stumps in biting the intruders. No further service could thus be expected from him. Long did the French cook ponder, during his evening reveries over his tumbler by the kitchen fire, what could be done in the present unfortunate dilemma. For a long series of evenings he beat his brains to no purpose ; at length, after a long hour's silence, he one night started up, and almost severed, with his heel, the butler's gouty toe from his body, exclaiming "Eureka! I have found it !"

He set about preparing a most hellish decoction, which he seasoned with cayenne pepper (the Capsicum Annuum of Linnæus), until it was enough, without a metaphor, to set the stomach on fire, and cause an "interna conflagratio."

Next morning he set about putting his project in practice, and the first beggar that approached he beckoned him to come in, shut the kitchen door, and, having filled out a bumper, bade him whip it off, and be gone, lest his master should appear. The mendicant, glad of the treat, turned up his little finger in a twinkling, and retreated as fast as his legs could carry him, but not far ; for his eyes threatened to start from his head, and the saliva ran from the corners of his mouth, after the fashion of a waterspout. Thus was one despatched ; he came no more. Again—again —a hundred times was the project tried, and uniformly with the same success ; till in less than three weeks not one beggar was to be seen in that country side. The French cook is, we understand, at present putting in for a patent, which we have no doubt will be granted.

By this time the public may observe that the way to get quit of beggars is by the immediate use of the hellish decoction, and not by following the vain, void, visionary, childish, and nugatory schemes at present inculcated by the writers on political economy.   M. O.

July 10*th.*—Settled with Bullock and Badcock for the "Poems by a Military Amateur." Balance in my favour of £3, 15s. 11½d. Very bad concern. Cost me three months' severe composition. Cannot fathom what the reading public of this age would swallow: what I write most carelessly they relish best. Hope I shall succeed better with my "Treatise on the Education of Young Ladies."

July 12*th.*—Went to Newmarket. Bet three to one, at starting, on the blue body and buff sleeves; fairly taken in, as he came last; or rather never came in, being distanced. Gulled out of a guinea and half, and got very angry. Run, after the race, a foot match with Lieutenant Finch; shammed lameness at first, and then beat him hollow, running the last fifty yards backwards. Out of pocket by this excursion, 10s. 6d.

13*th.*—Played three hours at billiards with a knowing one, who took me in. Proposed whist, at which I am a dead hand, and fairly came paddy over him. Rose in a passion, and broke off farther connection with me, swearing there was foul play. Gained by my acquaintance with him £2, 10s. 3d. Got drunk.

14*th.*—Headache in the morning. Wrote sonnet to Despondency, ditto to Despair. Got up and shaved, felt better; went out at twelve to a match at cricket, returned successful; a dinner and drink at stake, dressed at five, excellent claret, got drunk. Returned home, and read Rogers' Human Life—did not much like it—too wirewove. Took up Story of Rimini—thought more highly of it—last book admirable.

15*th.*—Dreamt all night of Cockaigne—terrible jargon these fellows speak. Felt squeamish; but after despatching a bottle of soda-water, sate down and composed the following letter and love-song.

LOVE SONG,

By a Junior Member of the Cockney School.

TO THE EDITOR OF LA BELLE ASSEMBLÉE.

(This letter is private, so you must not print it.)

SIR,—As I am not at all pleased with the strain of sentiment and affectation that disfigures and runs through the love poems of Burns and Byron, I have endeavoured to hit on a key somewhat nearer to the well-head of the human heart, and somewhat truer to the feelings of domestic nature, mutual endearment, and connubial felicity.   Descriptions of simple life and rural nature are very well to those who have had an opportunity of seeing them; but to me, and the multitudes like me who live in the great city, it is but just that the writers of the present age should adopt something that would come home to our feelings and businesses. A friend of mine, that came off a far journey last week, very jauntily told me that cabbages grew on fir trees, that cows can eat potatoes, and that they feed sheep on cider in Kent; but I was not such a spoony as to believe him.   If the accompanying poem be adapted to your miscellany, please insert it, and believe me,

Your most obliged Friend,
WM. TIMS GOODENOUGH.

Oh! lovely Polly Savage,
  Oh! charming Polly Savage,
Your eye beats Day and Martin,
  Your check is like red cabbage.

As I was going down the Strand,
  It smote my heart with wonder
To see the lovely damsel,
  A sitting at a vinder.
      Oh! lovely Polly Savage, &c.

Oh! once I loved another girl,
  Her name it was Maria;
But, Polly dear, my love for you
  Is forty-five times higher.
      Oh! lovely Polly Savage, &c.

We'll take a shop in Chicken Lane,
  And I will stand prepared
To sell fat bacon by the pound,
  And butter by the yard.
      Oh! lovely Polly Savage, &c.

And when at five o'clock, my love,
  We sit us down to dine,
How I will toast your darling health,
  In draughts of currant *vine.*
      Oh! lovely Polly Savage, &c.

Oh, then our little son shall be
  As wanton as a spaniel,
Him that we mean to christened be
  Jacques Timothy Nathaniel.
      Oh! lovely Polly Savage, &c.

And if we have a little girl,
  I'm sure you won't be sorry
To hear me call the pretty elf,
  Euphemiar Helen *Laurar.*
      Oh! lovely Polly Savage, &c.

Then fare-thee-well a little space,
  My heart can never falter,
And next time when I see your face,
  'Twill be at Hymen's *haltar.*
      Oh! lovely Polly Savage, &c.

18th. Wet morning; could not venture to stir abroad; just shows us how much men alter. A few years ago, when my country demanded my services, I braved the dangers of every clime, the torrid heats of a Spanish summer, and the damp atmosphere of the United States. Dare say, however, that I could do so again, if occasion required. Took a chair by the fire, and read over again Crabbe's Borough. Think the reverend gentleman shows pluck, but do not remember, in all his pictures of human life, ever observing the portrait of one butcher introduced. Pondered whether I might venture to remedy this defect, and send him my delineation to be hung up in the Gallery of Portraits in the next edition of his admirable work.

Wrote what follows in twenty minutes and copied it verbatim as under:

THE SOMNAMBULATORY BUTCHER.

An Episode.

Reflections—birth—parentage—boyish tricks—education—change of
dress—apprenticeship—bladders and Dr. Lavement—bad habits—ditto
cured by his mother—caution—and moral.

Men's legs, if man may trust in common talk,
Are engines put in motion when men walk ;
But when we cross our knees, and take a chair
Beside the fire, they're not in motion there :
So this we learn by wisdom, art, and skill,
That legs are made to stir, or to sit still.
Yet sometimes I have heard that, when the head
In woollen cap lay snoring on the bed,
The legs, without the sanction of the brain,
Were fond to wander on the midnight plain,
Pursue, mid darkness, tasks of common day,
Yet come, as willed caprice, unharmed away ;
Which to illustrate, let the reader bend
A willing ear, and list his warning friend.

James Neckum Theodore Emmanuel Reid
Was meanly born, and was ignobly bred,
Lived upon pottage, slept within a shed ;
His mother,—but it were in vain to look—
Hers was no marriage by the Session book ;
His mother, fool, had never taken pains
To gird her neck with matrimonial chains,
And he, her leman, seeing what would be,
Turned a blue-necked marine, and crossed the sea ;
So in neglect and wrath the child was born,
While neighbours chuckled with their looks of scorn ;
But fast he throve, and fat he grew, and that
Was felt most keenly by the tortured cat,
Whose ears he pinched, whose tail he drew, until
'Twas forced, when fairly vanquished, to lie still ;
The chickens, too, no sinecure of life
Had with the boy, who pulled their necks in strife,
Till from the sockets started their black eyes,
And died their vanished voice in feeble cries.

At length a cap upon his head was braced,
Shoes shod his feet, and breeches girt his waist ;
Tall as a leek he grew, his hair was long,
And through its folds the wild winds sang a song ;
From mother's clutches oft would he elope,
And little knew his morning face of soap ;

Till, having spent the morn in game and play
With comrades dirty, frolicsome, and gay,
As duly as the village clock struck two,
As duly parted he from ragged crew,
And homewards wended fast, and nothing loth
To dip his whispers in his mother's broth.

The boy grew strong ; the master of the school
Took him in charge, and with a birch did rule ;
Full long and oft he blubbered ; but at length,
Within a week, he learned to letter tenth ;
And ere six moons had waxed and waned and set,
He had reached z, and knew his alphabet.

His education finished, choice he made
Of a most lucrative and wholesome trade ;
The leathern cap was now dismissed ; and red,
Yea fiery, glowed the cowl upon his head ;
And, like a cherry dangling from the crown,
A neat wool tassel in the midst hung down ;
Around his waist, with black tape girded tight,
Was tied a worsted apron, blue and white ;
His Shetland stockings, mocking winter's cold,
Despising garters, up his thighs were rolled,
And, by his side, horn-handled steels, and knives,
Gleamed from his pouch, and thirsted for sheep's lives.
For, dextrous, he could split dead cows in halves,
And, though a calf himself, he slaughtered calves.
But brisker looked the youth, and nothing sadder,
For of each mother's son he got the bladder,
And straight to Galen's-head in joy he bore it,
Where Dr. Lavement gave a penny for it.

But he had failings, as I said before ; ⎫
So, duly as his nose began to snore,   ⎬
His legs ran with his body to the door ; ⎭
And forth he used to roam, with sidelong neck,
To—as the Scots folks term it—lift the sneck.
All in his shirt and woollen cap he strayed,
Silent, though dreaming ; cold, but undismayed.
The moon was shining 'mid the depth of heaven,
And from the chill north fleecy clouds were driven
Athwart its silver aspect, till they grew
Dimmer and dimmer in the distant blue ;
The trees were rustling loud ; nor moon, nor trees,
Nor cloud could on his dreaming frenzy seize,
But, walking with closed eyes across the street,
He lifted handsomely his unshod feet,

Till nought, at length, his wandering ankles propt,
And head and heels into the pond he dropt.

Then rose the loud lament ; the earth and skies
Rung with his shouts and echoed with his cries ;
The neighbours, in their night-caps, thronged around,
Called forth in marching order at the sound ;
They haled young Neckum out, a blanket rolled
Around his limbs with comfortable fold,
Hurried him home, and told him, cursing deep,
" That if again with cries he broke their sleep,
Him they would change into a wandering ghost,
Draw from the pond, but hang him on a post."

Oh ! reader, learn this truth most firm and sure,
That vicious practices are hard to cure ;
That error girds up with a serpent fold,
Hangs on the youth, but clings about the old.—
Night after night, if rainy, cold, or fair,
Forth went our hero, just to take the air ;
Ladies were terrified, and, fainting, cried,
A ghost in white had wandered by their side !
The soldier home his quaking path pursued,
With hair on end, gun cocked, and bayonet screwed,
And frightful children run to bed in fear,
When mothers said the ghost in white was near !

'Twas a hard case, but Theodore's mother quick
Fell on a scheme to cure him of the trick.
Hard by his bed a washing-tub she placed,
So, when he rose, it washed him to the waist ;
And loud he roared while, startled at the sound,
Old women bolted from their beds around—
" Save, save a wandering sinner, or he's drowned ! ! ! "

He rose no more, as I'm informed, in sleep,
But duly felled down cows, and slaughtered sheep,
Took to himself a wife, a pretty wench,
Sold beef by pounds, and cow-heel on a bench ;
In ten years had seven boys and five fair girls,
With cheeks like roses and with teeth like pearls ;
Lay still in bed like any decent man,
Pursued through life a staid and honest plan,
And lived beloved, while honours thickened o'er him,
Justice of Peace and Custos Rotulorum.

So all my readers from this tale may learn
The right way from the wrong way to discern ;
Never by dreams and nonsense to be led,
Walk when they wake, and slumber when in bed !

———Read last night a volume of the Heart of Mid-Lothian. The author's name as well known to me as if he had put it on the title-page. "None but himself can be his parallel." Well may we say, as my friend Ovid said of Telamon Ajax,

"None but himself, himself could overthrow."

This book knits my heart more firmly than ever to the "land of the mountain and the flood." When sitting in my chamber, I am transported there in a twinkling; the scenes rise before me in all their native majesty, the Castle, the High Street, and the Porteous mob. Am most pleased with the scenes at Davie Deans' cottage, Leonard's Hill, and Arthur's Seat. Many a time have I, reclining among the ruins of St. Anthony's Chapel, surveyed, in ecstatic admiration, the magnificent prospect around; the blue and castellated majesty of Dunedin, "throwing its white arms to the sea;" the variegated succession of woodlands, and pasture, and green fields; the broad expanse of the Forth, with its multitude of gliding sails; and, far in the north, the pale green, or the remoter hazy blue, mountains of Fife and Stirling-shire. At my feet, the palace of Holyrood, the habitation of kings, the mansion of the Stuarts, with the Gothic ruins of its chapel, its grey towers, and its desolate garden, spotted with dark green shrubs and melancholy flowers; and, stretching around me in emerald smoothness, the far-extending park, with its well-trodden pathway. Often have I, returning half cut from dining at the mess of my fellow-soldiers at Piershill, felt an inward trepidation in entering that park, and instinctively grasped my sword when I thought on the ghost of Ailie Mushat, who is said yet to

"Visit the glimpses of the moon,
Making night hideous."

N.B.—A good subject for poetry; to remember it the first idle hour.

(After a few pages commemorative of a battle between two of the Fancy, written in the cant style, the review of a corps of sharpshooters, with whose manœuvres the writer finds great fault, and an elaborate criticism on a charity sermon which had been recently preached, we find this promise fulfilled to the letter as follows):—

AILIE MUSHAT'S CAIRN.

A Vision-like remembrance of a Vision.

The night was dark; not a star was viewed
'Mid the dim and cloudy solitude;
I listened to the watchman's cry,
    And to the midnight breeze, that sung
Round the ruins of St. Anthony,
    With dismal and unearthly tongue:
I scarcely felt the path I trode;
    And I durst not linger to look behind,
For I knew that spirits were abroad,
    And heard their shrieks on the passing wind;
When lo! a spectacle of dread and awe
With trembling knees and stiffening hair I saw!

A grave-light spread its flames of blue,
    Its flames of blue and lurid red,
And in the midst a hellish crew
    Were seated round the stony bed
Of one whom murder robbed of life!
I saw the hand that held the knife,
It was her husband's hand, and yet
With the life-gore the blade was wet,
Dripping like a fiery sheath,
On the mossy cairn beneath!
The vision changed; and on the stones,
    With visage savage, fierce, and wild,
Above the grave that held her bones,
    The ghost of Ailie Mushat smiled:
It was a sight of dread and fear—
    A chequered napkin bound her head,
Her throat was cut from ear to ear,
    Her hands and breast were spotted red;
She strove to speak, but from the wound
Her breath came out with a broken sound!

    I started! for she strove to rise,
And pierced me with her bloodshot eyes;
She strove to rise, but fast I drew
    Upon the grass a circle round;

> I said a prayer, and she withdrew
>   Slowly within the stony mound—
> And trembling and alone I stood
> In the depth of the midnight solitude.

Aug. 4.—Am glad to observe from the philosophical journals, the newspapers, and other authentic sources, that several of the barbarous tribes are paying attention to literature and the fine arts. The Japanese poem I have seen pleases me extremely, though the subject can scarcely be said to be well adapted for poetry. My translation is not so bad. M. Titsingh's Latin paraphrase is also very good. The English is literal.

HORÆ SINICÆ. NO. II.

ODE ON THE DEATH OF YAHMAHSSEERO, COUNCILLOR OF STATE.

Japanese.

Kee rah ray tah vah
Bah kah to see yo ree to
Kee koo tah fah yah
Yah mah mo o see ro mo
Sah vah goo sin bahn.

Latin.

Præcidisse
Consiliarium minorem
Nuper audivi,
In montis castello
Turbas excitantem, novum custodem.

English.

I have just learned that one of the new guards has excited a tumult in the castle, by assassinating a councillor in his folly.

Free Translation.

Pray, have you heard the news?
   One of the footguards drew
His cutlass ; in a rage
His anger to assuage,
   A councillor he slew !

II.

Yah mah see ro no
Ser ro no o ko so day
Tshay mee so mee tay
Ah kah do see yo ree to
Fee to vah yoo nahr.

II.

Yahmahsseero
Candidam togam
Cruore tinctam
Rubentemque consiliarium
Omnes viderunt.

The white robe of Yahmahsseero is stained with blood, and all call him the red councillor.

Yahmahsseero's robe
   Is stained with fiery gore,
And each that doth him meet
Calls him upon the street,
   The crimson councillor.

III.

Ah soo mah see no
Sahn no no vah tahree nee
Mee soo mah see tay
Tah no mah mo kee ray tay
O tsoo too yah mah see ro.

The current which, on the eastern road, crosses the village Sahnno, has swelled, and penetrated the dyke round the fen, and the high castle of the mountain has fallen.

IV.

Fah tsee oo yay tay
Oo may gah sah koo rah ta
Sah koo fahn mah vo
Tah ray tah kee tsoo kay tay
Sahn no mee kee ray say tah.

Who has cast into the fire the plum and cherry trees?—valuable trees, which are planted in boxes, for the sake of their agreeable flowers? *Sahnno* has cut them down.

V.

Kee rah ray tah vah
Bah kah do see yo ree to
Yoo oobay kay mee
Sahn no sin sah yay mee moo
Ho ray gah ten mei.

A councillor in his madness hath been overthrown ; if ever such an event was heard of, it may be said to be a judgment from heaven.

III.

In via orientali
Per vicum *Sahnno* irruentes,
Aquæ profluentes,
Terram lacunæ perfosserunt
Ruitque *montis* castellum.

The current to the east
  By Sahnno, little town,
Hath overflown, and burst the dyke
With fury, and the castle, like
  A fool, hath fallen down.

IV.

Pretiosas in vasis arbores,
Prunos et cerasos
Floribus amœnas
Quis in ignem projecit?
Sahnno quidem eas præcidit.

Who has felled the cherry trees?
  And who has felled the plum?
Trees planted in neat boxes,
And anything but hoaxes
  For odoriferous gum.

V.

Præcidit (consiliarium)
Vesanus consiliarius.
Dicere possumus,
Si prius talia unquam audiverimus,
Hoc fuisse *Cæli Mandatum*.

A councillor hath been knocked
  From off his legs,—most true ;
If ever such a thing was heard,
It may most safely be averred
  That it hath been—adieu !

Aug. 8.—Blue-stockings are not to my taste, unless their attention be only paid to polite literature—the play that is just to come out, or the last new poem.

Last night's party, however, the most agreeable of the kind that I have met, if the young lady with the blue eyes could have been contented with only smiling and showing us her fine teeth, and not disturbed herself about the alteration in the criminal laws, and the effects which the Corn Bill might have had. Rather too theatrical in the other young lady, Miss ——, to recite Coleridge's Ode to the Departing Year with such emphatic pith and such vehemence of gesticulation. The MS. poems handed round insufferably bad. Elegies in the measure of "Oh, Miss Bailey, unfortunate Miss Bailey," and odes in which sound gave sense no opportunity of coming forward in self-defence. Must learn the particulars of that sweet, modest, and melancholy young creature who sate on the end of the sofa nearest the door. Am certain that I caught her sighing several times. Must be at the bottom, having been teazing myself whether the unfortunate passion, the theme of the stanzas which she handed about as her picnic share of the literary banquet, can be only an effusion of sentiment, or whether they have originated in dread reality. At all events, she may wait long enough till her verses come round to her again, as, in the heat of conversation, I stowed them along with my snuff-box into my waistcoat-pocket. They are not amiss.

STANZAS.

Oh mine be the shade, &c.

Oh mine be the shade where no eye may discover
    Where in silence and sorrow alone I may dwell;
Give scorn to the maid who is false to her lover;
    A tear unto her who has loved but too well!
Alas for the heart, when affection forsaking
    The vows it hath pledged and has cherished through years;
For no refuge remains to that lone heart but breaking,
    The silence of grief, and the solace of tears!

Farewell the bright prospects that once could allure me
    To think this poor earth was a promise of Heaven;
Since he, who once doated, no more can endure me,
    Too much with the darkness of fate I have striven;
The flowers with their odours, the birds with their singing,
    The beauties of earth, and the glories of sky,
Dear, sad recollections are constantly bringing,
    And all that remains upon earth is—to die!

To die—or to be married. It is a lottery indeed; but still

"I have stout notions on the marrying score," to use the words of an eminent poet. Truly I am not a little taken with this sweet young creature ; and perhaps, after all, this

> " Was *not* taught her by the dove,
> To die, and know no second love."

If I thought so, I do not know but that I might make proposals ; if she has any rhino, so much the better ; let her put it in her pocket, and it will prevent the wind from blowing her away. But the deuce is, I am afraid of that evil genius of mine, Mrs. M'Whirter. What misery a rash step entails upon us ! I wish a hurricano would blow her and the lecturer to the river of the Amazons for ever and a day.

*   *   *   *   *   *

Familiar Letter from the Adjutant,

CONTAINING PROJECTS, PROMISES, AND IMITATIONS.

DEAR KIT,—I write this in the earnest hope of its finding you less molested by your inveterate enemy in the great toe, and brimful of the delight which your modesty and diffidence cannot prevent you feeling, in hearing it acknowledged from all quarters that yours is the most excellent work of its kind which has appeared in any country since the invention of printing. Do let me know what the *Edinburgh Review* people are saying about it, or if they are at last fairly beat to a standstill, and seriously thinking of giving up the concern. I heard, indeed, that a meeting of their contributors has been lately convened, either for that purpose, or perhaps for petitioning you to make your journal a general receptacle for speculations of all kinds; and that thus such of them as were capable might be transferred to the legion of *Blackwood*, and not utterly cast destitute. But this is a matter, friend North, on which I would advise you to proceed with cautious circumspection—it might prove like marriage—alas! the day—a step not easy to be remedied. Many of your supporters would find a delicacy in making common cause with the generality of these folks, as they have uttered such a quantity of unsound and unsatisfactory stuff in every branch and department of human knowledge, and ridiculed everything worthy of respect and veneration. *Exempli gratia*, but that's a trifle, there is your humble servant, who could not, with any degree of honour, act in concert with men who depreciated the late glorious war, and every battle in it, mid whose bloodshed and under whose " sulphrous canopy " he plucked a leaf of laurel for his brow. But we shall drop the subject as not worth speaking about, conscious that where the glory of his country and the reputation of his work are concerned, no man will direct the helm with a more intrepid spirit, or maul the invaders with a more unerring hand, than yourself, the redoubted Christopher North, Esquire.

You asked me in your last, if I ever now-a-days read any; and, if so, what books occupy my attention and time? A question with a vengeance. Do you think that my knowledge comes to me by intuition? After having written above half a hundred articles to you, in every department of human knowledge, you ask me if ever I read any. That reminds me of the tower of Babel—you might as well ask it if it reared itself. But, in writing so, I doubt not you have only made a *lapsus linguæ*, or at any rate a joke on my multitudinous researches. All kinds of books come welcome enough to me. I have a capacity of digestion rather ostrich-like, and capable of managing a great farrago, and assimilating the same into solid nourishment. I like the drama very much; and Alexander Macpherson, being now in the middle of the fifth act, will soon show whether or not the genius of the drama loves me. Novels are " an appetite and a feeling " which I cannot resist. Political economy I like better than I do some of its professors. Metaphysics are excellent food for me, and over a ten-hours' mathematical proposition I am as cool as a cucumber; but *entre nous*, theological controversy is my favourite study, but don't mention this, as the Roman Catholic clergy like nothing better than to have a bull-baiting with me; and in spite of all my asseverations and protestations to the contrary, they will insist that I am a little loose both in my moral and religious principles, but I am thoroughly convinced that they are wrong.

When you see Wastle, tell him I have found it quite out of my power to be over, according to promise, at the walking of the Commissioner; but hope yet to have that honour al ong with him. At all events, I am determined to be over at the Edinburgh races, as I have got possession of as fine a bit of horse-flesh as ever put hoof to turf; and I would like to know what success Salamanca would have in taking a few rounds for the Hunter's Plate. If he be successful, it will be a good speculation; if not, I will sell him the next day at Wordsworth's out of pure vexation, although I had him as a present from a military friend of mine, who rode him at the battle of Waterloo. He has not yet lost tooth-mark, and gallops like a fury. The best of it is, that the longer he runs he continues to improve; and, if there be above three four-mile heats, I never saw the horse, mare, or gelding that I would not back him against at considerable odds. He is a little stiff for the first mile or so after starting; but, when he begins to warm, you never beheld a finer personification of the fine idea which Lord Byron has applied to denote the beauty and swiftness of Mazeppa's charger,

> " Who looked as though the speed of thought
> Were in his limbs."

I have him in training already, and hope to show him off in style to you in July. If I was not so lengthened in the nether extremities, I would not care much to jockey him myself; but that, to be sure, is an after consideration.

Do give us a paper from your editorial pen on the Pope and Bowles controversy. I cannot fathom what Campbell and Byron would be at. Lord Byron compares the poetry of Pope to a Grecian temple, and the poetry written by Campbell, Scott, Wastle, Southey, Wordsworth, Hogg, Coleridge, himself, myself, &c., to the tower of Babel. A pretty comparison of a surety; but it is all in my eye, Betty Martin, that men like Campbell and Byron should imagine that the essence of poetry consisted in the manners and morals of society; in drawing pictures of merchants with spectacles, and goose quills stuck behind their ears, pondering over their ledgers; of awfully ancient spinsters, leering from behind their fans, and looking unutterable things; of grocers' apprentices sanding the sugar, watering the tobacco, and then walking aloft to prayers; of the lackadaisical exclamations of boarding-school misses, and the pettifogging dandyism of lawyers' clerks; and yet, that these poets, in hostility to their own doctrines, should write of such natural personages as a Corsair with "one virtue, and a thousand crimes;" of a Lord Lara, who, seeing a ghost, broke out into a perspiration, and then spoke Gaelic or some other outlandish tongue; of Count Manfred, alias Dr. Faustus, jun., who

> "Saw more devils than vast hell can hold,
> The madman;"

of the Giaour, who turned an infidel monk because he ran away with another man's wife, who was sewed up in a sack and thrown into the sea; or of such a true and natural person as Andes, "Giant of the western star," sitting with his cheek reclined on his dexter hand, and a flambeau in his left fist, looking over in the dark from America to Europe; or of a gentleman of the second sight, begging his master not to go to battle, as he had a presentiment that he would be much safer at home; and a thousand other things, well enough adapted to poetry, in my humble opinion, but having as slight an application to the practice of life as can well be imagined. Sir Walter Scott must immediately send Lord Cranstoun's goblin page an errand to the Red Sea, and let him be for ever "lost! lost! lost!" And as for his redoubted namesake, Michael, the flag-stone must be no more lifted from his grave; Coleridge must tie the Auncient Marinere to a stake, and have a shot at *him* with the cross-bow, as he so treated the "harmless Albatross;" and as for the Lady Christabel, he must, without delay, scribble four dozen of letters, inviting his friends to her funeral—let him employ a patent coffin, as she is rather a restless and unruly subject. Wordsworth must despatch the Danish Boy to the land of shadow; and Hogg should purchase a pennyworth of saddle-tacks, and with a trusty hammer nail the ears of the Gude Grey Catte to his stable-door to frighten away the rats, as she will no longer be able to act as governess to the seven daughters of the laird of Blair. As for Miss Kilmeny, when she comes back at the end of the next seven years, let him give her a furlough, specifying perpetual leave of absence. Dr. Southey ought to send a specimen of a petrified Glendoveer to the College Museum, ere the species becomes utterly extinct, that future antiquaries may not be completely puzzled if their bones be found, like those of the mammoth, in a fossil state; and he ought to give the witch Maimuna in Thalaba, that was perpetually singing, a half-crown's worth of the most choice ballads, to set her up in a decent line of trade, and have done with her. Thomas Moore's Veiled Prophet, without the nose, should get a proper certificate, and be sent to the Chelsea Hospital; and, on proper representation being made, the Peri, who had neither house nor hold, may be received into the Charity-Workhouse. Do, North, convince both Mr. Campbell and his lordship that the world is tolerably well contented with the poetry they have foolishly thought proper to give it; that though Mr. Campbell's criticism is sometimes a little vapid, yet that his verses are generally excellent; and that, if Lord Byron's system of moral and ethical poetry be after his old way, that is, if Beppo and Don Juan, like the brick of the pedant in Hierocles, are specimens of the materials of which it is to be composed, we should think that the world will be contented with the specimens it has already enjoyed. Enough is as good as a feast; "where ignorance is bliss, 'tis folly to be wise;" and, as I am tired of it, I will drop the subject.

Friend North, I have a crow to pluck with you. You are as strange a fellow as ever fell within the circle of my acquaintance, always excepting Mrs. M'Whirter, for she beats cockfighting. You will pretend, now, that you did not know to whom the memorandum-book belonged out of which you treated your readers, or rather the world, for all the world are your readers, a month or two ago. Really this is provoking, and I do not take it altogether well at your hands.

Would it not have been more creditable to you, instead of creating a few smiles at my expense, to have written to the wandering sinner of a bagman into whose hands my book fell, that you knew the proprietor; and that you would thank him to transmit it to you, that you might transmit it to the proper owner? It would not surprise me much, though you were yet to write me a letter professing your entire ignorance of the whole transaction; and that you are free to give your oath that you had not so much as the smallest suspicion that the memorandum-book could possibly belong to me. Do you think me innocent enough to believe any stuff of this sort? Though I am not a Highlander, I have enough of the second sight to see clearly through trifles of this kind. But I will waste no more words on the subject; and, though we are hundreds of miles apart, our hearts are always together. I can take a joke, and can give one; so we will shake hands and forget the whole matter. Indeed I am almost sorry that I mentioned it; but don't give any more extracts without my consent.

Tell our divan, the first time you all meet in Ambrose's, to remember me in their prayers; as I am sure that I never empty a tumbler or two, *solus*, without toasting them all alternately; and, as I allow each a bumper, it sometimes obliges me to have a third brewing. Let them know that I will see them all in July, and that I have a budget of famous anecdotes and rencontres to entertain them with; some of them out-hector Hector, and they are all personal, *ipso teste*, as Maturin says. But I shall drop the subject, as I do not wish to promise. "There's a braw time coming," as the deacon's son observes.

What would you think of it? I have been amusing myself with some imitations of the living authors. It was during the time I was confined to my room, from having sprained my left ankle in leaping over a five-bar gate for a wager, and I intend to make a complete cabinet of them. I have already allowed Hazlitt a complete ration of epigram, antithesis, and paradox. Godwin sails in a parachute of theory, suspended to a balloon inflated with sulphuretted hydrogen ; Cobbett writes an official document, *currente calamo*, with all the courtier-like dignity becoming a secretary to her Majesty ; and Charley Phillips, with his fists tied into large bladders, knocks arguments from off their feet by repeated douces on either side of the chops, with his unceasing one, twos.   I have, likewise, a complete set of the poets, good, bad, and indifferent.   The Cockneys I found it desperately hard to imitate, as I could not make my genius to descend so low. I do not know but that I have caricatured some of them a little ; but this was unintentional, as they have fairly baffled me in many particulars.

As you seem interested in my literary doings, I will treat you with two or three short specimens, as I see you are already in for a double postage.   To begin with the mightiest man of our age, do you think that in the following I have caught the chivalrous flow, the tone of the olden time —the grace, and the harmony, and the strength, that characterise the poetry of the Ariosto of the North?   The Lay of the Last Minstrel and Marmion form eras in the mind of every true living admirer of poetical excellence.

> The hounds in the kennel are yelling loud,
>   The hawks are bound for flight ;
> For the sun hath burst from his eastern shroud,
> And the sky is clear, without a cloud,
>   And the steed for the chase is dight :
> The merry huntsmen, up in the morn,
> Crack the long whip and wind the horn.
>
> Lord Timothy rubbed his eyes, and rose
>   When he heard the merry crew ;
> He scarce took space to don his clothes,
>   And his night-cap quick he threw
> Back on the pillow, and down the stair,
> Disdaining brush or comb for hair,
>   With lightning speed he flew ;
> And, in the twinkling of a fan,
> With frock and cap, the gallant man,
> Caparisoned all spick and span,
>   Was with the waiting crew.

Sir Abraham rode his bonny grey ;
  Sir Anthony his black ;
Lord Hector hath mounted his sprightly bay ;
Lord Tom, Lord Jack, and all are away ;
Curvet, and demivolte, and neigh,
Mark out their bold and brisk array,
With buckskins bright, and bonnets gay,
  And bugles at each back.

They had hardly ridden a mile, a mile,
  A mile but barely ten,
As each after each they leaped a stile,
When their heart played pit-a-pat the while,
  To see a troop of armed men,
A troop of gallant men at drill,
With well-soaked locks and stiffened frill ;
Each in his grasp held spear or sword,
Ready to murder at a word,
And ghastly was each warrior's smile,
Beneath his barred aventayle ;
Buff belts were girt around each waist ;
Steel cuisses round each thigh were braced ;
Around each knee were brazen buckles ;
And iron greaves to save their knuckles ;
High o'er each tin-bright helmet shone
The casque, and dancing morion,
Which reached to where the tailor sets,
On shoulder, woollen epaulettes ;
Their blades were of Toledo steel,
Ferrara, or Damascus real ;
  Yea ! human eye did never see,
  Through all the days of chivalry,
Men more bedight from head to heel, &c.

Lady Alice she sits in the turret tower,
  A-combing her raven hair ;
The clock hath tolled the vesper hour,
Already the shadows of evening lower
  To veil the landscape fair.
To the jetty fringe of her piercing eye
She raised her opera-glass,
For she was anxious to espy
  If her worthy knight should pass.
" Lo ! yonder he comes," she sighed and said,
Then with a rueful shake of head—
" Shall I my husband ne'er discover?
'Tis but the white cow eating clover! "
She looked again, " Sure yon is he,
That gallops so fast along the lea!

Alas ! 'tis only a chestnut tree ! !
Standing as still as still can be ! ! ! "
" Come hither, come hither, my little foot-page,
And dance my anguish to assuage ;
And be it jig, or waltz, or reel,
I care not, so it doth conceal
The ghosts that of a thousand dyes
Float evermore before mine eyes :
And I, to make thee foot it gay,
With nimble finger, by my fay,
Upon the tambourine will play ! " &c.

But I must not give you too much of it, as it will spoil
the interest of the work, which will shortly appear in three
octavo volumes, printed uniformly, and with portraits ; something like Peter's Letters.   The imitation extends to three
cantos, together with an introductory epistle to my friend
Dr. Scott.   Under the head of Coleridge you will find the
continuation of Christabel, and the Auncient Waggonere ;
both of which were ushered into public notice by your
delightful and discriminating work, together with the
following

FRAGMENT OF A VISION.

A dandy on a velocipede
  I saw in a vision sweet,
Along the highway making speed,
  With his alternate feet.
Of a bright and celestial hue
Gleamed beauteously his blue surtout ;
While ivory buttons, in a row,
Showed like the winter's caverned snow,
Which the breezy North
Drives sweeping forth
To lodge in the cave below :
Ontario's beaver, without demur,
To form his hat did lend its fur :
His frill was of the cambric fine,
And his neckcloth starched and aquiline ;
And oh, the eye with pleasure dwells
On his white jean indescribables ;
And he throws the locks from his forehead fair,
And he pants, and pants, and pants for air ;
What is the reason I cannot tell,
There is a cause—I know it well ;

Too firmly bound, too tightly braced,
The corsets grasp his spider waist,
Till his coat-tails are made to fly
Even from the back they glorify.
Look again, he is not there—
Vanished into the misty air !
Look again ! do you see him yet
Ah no ! the bailiff hath seized him for debt
And to and fro, like a restless ghost,
When peace within the grave is lost,
He paces as far, as far he should,
Within the bounds of Holyrood !

His lordship of Byron I have not handled roughly enough ; I cannot yet forget the tower of Babel. What a speech ! as if we were a parcel of jackasses ! ' I shall yet have at him for it.   What do you think of The Galiongee : a fragment of a Turkish Tale ?

THE GALIONGEE :

A Fragment of a Turkish Tale.

Advertisement.—The author of this tale begs to inform the public that the scattered fragments which it presents were collected from an improvisatore who recited during the time that the author drank his fifth cup of Mocha with that civillest of all gentlemen, Ali Pacha.

The Pasha sat in his divan,
With silver-sheathed ataghan ;
And called to him a Galiongee,
Come lately from the Euxine Sea
To Stamboul ; chains were on his feet,
    And fetters on his hands were seen,
    Because he was a Nazarene :
When, duly making reverence meet,
With haughty glance on that divan,
And curling lip he thus began :

    " By broad Phingari's silver light,
When sailing at the noon of night,
Bismillah ! whom did we descry
    But dark corsairs, who, bent on spoil,
    Athwart the deep sea ever toil !
We knew their blood-red flags on high :
The Capitan he called, belike,
With gesture proud, to bid us strike,

And told his Sonbachis to spare
Of not one scalp a single hair,
'Though garbs of green showed Emirs there!
It boots not, Pacha, to relate
　　What souls were sent to Eblis throne,
How Azrael's arrows scattered fate,
　　How wild, wet, wearied, and alone,
When all my crew were drenched in blood,
Or floated lifeless on the flood,
I fought unawed, nor e'er thought I
To shout ' Amaun!' the craven's cry.
　　I took my handkerchief to wipe
　　My burning brow, and then I took,
With placid hand, my long chibouque,
That is to say, my Turkish pipe,
And having clapped it in my cheek,
Disdaining e'er a word to speak,
I shouted to the pirate, ' Now,
You've fairly beat me, I allow,' " &c.

Perhaps, as I know that Childe Harold's Pilgrimage is
one of your first favourites, you will find an account of his
step-brother, Childe Paddy's * banishment to New Holland,
more to your taste.   This is the commencement:

Oh! mortal man, how varied is thy lot,
　Thy ecstasies of joy and sorrow; how
Chilled, sunk, and servile art thou, or how hot
　Flashes indignant beauty from thy brow!
　Times change, and empires fall; the gods allow
Brief space for human contemplation, and
　Above all partial dictates disavow
Unequal love; how can we, at their hand,
For individual fate a gentler boon demand?

Childe Paddy parted from his father's cot.
　It was not castle proud, nor palace high,
Extraneous symmetry here glittered not,
　But turf-built walls and filth did meet the eye;
　Loud was the grumph and grumble from hog-stye;
Swans gleamed not here, as on the Leman lake,
　But goose and ducklings, famed for gabbling cry,
With quack, quack, quack, did make the roofs to shake,
Till in their utmost holes the wondering rats did quake!

---

* It was first written " Childe Raddy," but I was afraid of angering the
Scotsman.—M. OD.

He thought of father, whom he loved and left ;
   He thought of mother at her booming wheel ;
He thought of sister, of his care bereft ;
   He thought of brethren dear ; and, to conceal
   The endless pangs that o'er his brain did reel,
As through the vale his pensive way he took,
   For fear his onward purpose would congeal,
He sung, while pacing with right-forward look,
" Sweet Kitty of Coleraine," and " Fair of Donabrooke ! "

I rejoice that your prophecy as to the popularity of Hogg's Tales has been abundantly verified. Natural power and genius will fight their way in spite of opposition, and "disdainful of help or hindrance." I doubt not that his better half has had a hand in the purgation of the new edition. Give my compliments to him ; tell him I shall never forget the kindness I experienced at Eltrive Lake ; and, above all, ask him how he likes the following stanzas, the opening of a ballad as long as " Kirkmabreck," that celebrated modern Timon, or rather she-Timon, or woman-hater :

Theyre wals ane Brounie offe mucle faime
   Thatte ussit too cumme too ane aulde fairme housse,
Ande evir the maydes fro theyre beddes came,
   Alle theyre werke wals dune, soo cannye and douce.

The cauppis wure cleanit ; the yerne wals spunne,
   Ande the parritche aye maide forre the oulde guidman,
The kye wure milkit, the yill wals runne,
   Ande shininge lyke goude wals the ould brasse pan.

Ande mickle they wonderit, and mair theye thocht,
   But neivir ane wurde too theyre minny spake theye,
Theye lukit aye too the braas theye hadde cofft,
   Too buske theyre hayre, and to maike theme gaye.

Then outte spake Jennye, the youngeste ane,
   " I'm shure to mye Jocke itte wull gie delyghte,
Ande maike the laddye a' fidginge faine,
   Too see the luffes offe mye handes soe whyte."

Thenne outte spake Kirstene, as doune she satte
   Before the glasse toe kaim herre hayre,
" Oh ! luke," quoth she, " I amme gettinge soe fatte,
   Thatte I offe idlesse muste beware.

> "The neiburs theye wille kenne noe mee,
>   Forre I'm scrimply aible to gaung aboutte,
> Iffe I gette on soe, ye wulle brieflye see
>   A hurlye cofft toe carrye mee outte," &c.

Speaking of Wordsworth, what is he dreaming about? The published part of the Excursion does not extend to a week, and we have had no more of it for the last seven years. If the poet's life and peregrinations are to occupy an equally proportionate space, published at the same distance of time, the world may expect to see the conclusion of the work at much about the same time when *Blackwood's Magazine* intends retiring from public notice, that is to say, somewhere about the year 3000.   The following is a small portion of a fifty-page episode.   It is entitled

THE KAIL POT.

If e'er, in pensive guise, thy steps have strayed
At eve or morn along that lofty street
Yclept the Canongate, exalt thine eyes,
And lo ! between thee and the azure sky,
Dangling in negro blackness beautiful,
A kail pot hangs, upon an iron bar
Suspended, and by iron chains hung down.
Beneath it yawns a threshold, like the den
Of Cacus, giant old, or like the caves
Of sylvan satyrs in the forest green ;
There enter, and, amid his porter butts,
In conscious wisdom bold, sits Nathan Goose,
Worshipping the Muses and a mug of ale !

Sweet are the songs of Nathan Goose, and strong,
Yea, potent is the liquor that he sells ;
On many a cold and icy winter night,
When stars were sparkling in the deep-blue sky,
Have, circling round his board, a jovial throng
Tippled until the drowsy chime of twelve.
Strange has it seemed to me that we, who breathe
Vapours as watery as the cooling drops
Of Rydal Mere, should drink combustibles,
And perish not ; yet, thereby, of the soul
The cogitations are disturbed ; its dreams
Are hollows by reality and time
Fulfilled not, and the waking spirit mourns,

When shines the sun above the eastern sea,—
The ocean seen from Black Comb's summit high,
And throws his yellow light against the pane
Of chamber window,—window deep embowered
With honeysuckle blossoms ;—o'er the wrecks
Of such fantastical and inane stuff,
Shadows, and dreams, and visions of the night.
Then follow headaches dreadful, vomitings
Of undigested biscuit, mingled with
The sour and miserable commixture of
Hot aqua vitæ with the mountain lymph,—
If city water haply be so called,—
The lymph of Fountain-well hard by the shop
Where seeds and roots are sold, above whose door
The black-eyed eagle spreads his golden wings.

Hard is the lot of him whom evil fates
Have destined to a way of life unmeet ;
Whose genius and internal strength are clogged
By drudgery, and the rubs of common men.
But I have gazed upon thee, Nathan Goose,
Gazed on the workings of thy inward soul—
Hailed with delight thy planet in the sky,
And mid the constellations planted thee ! &c.

As you are one of the prime admirers of the Lyrical Ballads—as who, with the smallest pretensions to poetical taste, does not acknowledge most of them to be extremely fine, and studded over with the very pearls of poetry ?—I have copied over for you a lyrical ballad of the true breed. I do not know but that you will like it almost as well as the Waggoner, or Peter Bell :

BILLY BLINN.

I knew a man that died for love,
    His name, I ween, was Billy Blinn ;
His back was humped, his hair was grey,
And on a sultry summer day
    We found him floating in the linn.

Once as he stood before his door
    Smoking, and wondering who should pass,
Then trundling past him in a cart
Came Susan Foy ; she won his heart,
    She was a gallant lass.

And Billy Blinn concealed the flame
　That burned and scorched his very blood ;
But often was he heard to sigh,
And with his sleeve he wiped his eye,
　In a dejected mood.

A party of recruiters came
　To wile our cottars, man and boy ;
Their coats were red, their cuffs were blue,
And boldly, without more ado,
　Off with the troop went Susan Foy !

When poor old Billy heard the news,
　He tore his hair so thin and grey ;
He beat the hump upon his back,
And ever did he cry, "Alack,
　Ohon, oh me!—alas a-day ! "

His nights were spent in sleeplessness,
　His days in sorrow and despair :
It could not last—this inward strife ;
The lover he grew tired of life,
　And sauntered here and there.

At length, 'twas on a moonlight eve,
　The skies were blue, the winds were still :
He wandered from his wretched hut,
And, though he left the door unshut,
　He sought the lonely hill.

He looked upon the lovely moon,
　He looked upon the twinkling stars ;
" How peaceful all is there," he said,
" No noisy tumult there is bred,
　And no intestine wars."

But misery overcame his heart,
　For all was waste and war within ;
And rushing forward with a leap,
O'er crags a hundred fathoms steep,
　He plunged into the linn.

We found him when the morning sun
　Shone brightly from the eastern sky ;
Upon his back he was afloat—
His hat was sailing like a boat—
　His staff was found on high.

Oh reckless woman, Susan Foy,
　To leave the poor, old, loving man,
And with a soldier, young and gay,
Thus harlot-like to run away
　To India or Japan.

> Poor Billy Blinn, with hair so white,
>   Poor Billy Blinn was stiff and cold ;
> Will Adze he made a coffin neat,
> We placed him in it head and feet,
>   And laid him in the mould !

I dare say you will suppose that there is no end to my prosing. But hold, my pen ! For the present I am determined to have done.   As to Southey, Lamb, Milman, Croly, Shelley, Wastle, Wilson, Campbell, Hunt, Montgomery, Bowles, Dr. Scott, Frere, Rogers, Bloomfield, Herbert, Thurlow, Willison Glass, &c., you shall have more of them in my next ; and meantime believe me, more than ever has been yet professed by

Yours, &c.,

MORGAN ODOHERTY.

COLERAINE, RED COW INN, *April* 30.

The Man in the Bell.

In my younger days bell-ringing was much more in fashion among the young men of —— than it is now. Nobody, I believe, practises it there at present except the servants of the church, and the melody has been much injured in consequence. Some fifty years ago, about twenty of us who dwelt in the vicinity of the cathedral formed a club, which used to ring every peal that was called for; and, from continual practice and a rivalry which arose between us and a club attached to another steeple, and which tended considerably to sharpen our zeal, we became very Mozarts on our favourite instruments. But my bell-ringing practice was shortened by a singular accident, which not only stopped my performance, but made even the sound of a bell terrible to my ears.

One Sunday I went with another into the belfry to ring for noon prayers, but the second stroke we had pulled showed us that the clapper of the bell we were at was muffled. Some one had been buried that morning, and it had been prepared, of course, to ring a mournful note. We did not know of this, but the remedy was easy. "Jack," said my companion, "step up to the loft, and cut off the hat;" for the way we had of muffling was by tying a piece of an old hat or of cloth (the former was preferred) to one side of the clapper, which deadened every second toll. I complied and, mounting into the belfry, crept as usual into the bell, where I began to cut away. The hat had been tied on in some more complicated manner than usual, and I was perhaps three or four minutes in getting it off; during which time my companion below was hastily called away, by a message from his sweetheart, I believe; but that is not

material to my story. The person who called him was a
brother of the club, who, knowing that the time had come
for ringing for service, and not thinking that any one was
above, began to pull. At this moment I was just getting
out, when I felt the bell moving; I guessed the reason at
once—it was a moment of terror; but by a hasty, and almost
convulsive, effort I succeeded in jumping down, and throwing myself on the flat of my back under the bell.

The room in which it was, was little more than sufficient
to contain it, the botton of the bell coming within a couple
of feet of the floor of lath. At that time I certainly was not
so bulky as I am now, but as I lay it was within an inch of
my face. I had not laid myself down a second when the
ringing began. It was a dreadful situation. Over me swung
an immense mass of metal, one touch of which would have
crushed me to pieces; the floor under me was principally
composed of crazy laths; and if they gave way, I was precipitated to the distance of about fifty feet upon a loft, which
would, in all probability, have sunk under the impulse of
my fall, and sent me to be dashed to atoms upon the marble
floor of the chancel, an hundred feet below. I remembered,
for fear is quick in recollection, how a common clock-wright,
about a month before, had fallen and, bursting through the
floors of the steeple, driven in the ceilings of the porch, and
even broken into the marble tombstone of a bishop who
slept beneath. This was my first terror, but the ringing
had not continued a minute before a more awful and
immediate dread came on me. The deafening sound of
the bell smote into my ears with a thunder which made me
fear their drums would crack. There was not a fibre of my
body it did not thrill through: it entered my very soul;
thought and reflection were almost utterly banished; I only
retained the sensation of agonising terror. Every moment
I saw the bell sweep within an inch of my face; and my
eyes—I could not close them, though to look at the object
was bitter as death—followed it instinctively in its oscillating
progress until it came back again. It was in vain I said to

myself that it could come no nearer at any future swing than
it did at first; every time it descended, I endeavoured to
shrink into the very floor to avoid being buried under the
down-sweeping mass; and then, reflecting on the danger of
pressing too weightily on my frail support, would cower up
again as far as I dared.

At first my fears were mere matter of fact. I was afraid
the pulleys above would give way, and let the bell plunge on
me. At another time, the possibility of the clapper being
shot out in some sweep, and dashing through my body, as
I had seen a ramrod glide through a door, flitted across my
mind. The dread also, as I have already mentioned, of
the crazy floor tormented me; but these soon gave way to
fears not more unfounded, but more visionary, and of course
more tremendous. The roaring of the bell confused my
intellect, and my fancy soon began to teem with all sorts of
strange and terrifying ideas. The bell pealing above, and
opening its jaws with a hideous clamour, seemed to me at
one time a ravening monster, raging to devour me; at another,
a whirlpool ready to suck me into its bellowing abyss. As
I gazed on it, it assumed all shapes; it was a flying eagle,
or rather a roc of the Arabian story-tellers, clapping its wings
and screaming over me. As I looked upward into it, it
would appear sometimes to lengthen into indefinite extent,
or to be twisted at the end into the spiral folds of the tail
of a flying-dragon. Nor was the flaming breath or fiery
glance of that fabled animal wanting to complete the picture.
My eyes, inflamed, bloodshot, and glaring, invested the supposed monster with a full proportion of unholy light.

It would be endless were I to merely hint at all the
fancies that possessed my mind. Every object that was
hideous and roaring presented itself to my imagination. I
often thought that I was in a hurricane at sea, and that the
vessel in which I was embarked tossed under me with the
most furious vehemence. The air, set in motion by the
swinging of the bell, blew over me nearly with the violence
and more than the thunder of a tempest; and the floor

seemed to reel under me as under a drunken man. But the most awful of all the ideas that seized on me were drawn from the supernatural. In the vast cavern of the bell hideous faces appeared, and glared down on me with terrifying frowns, or with grinning mockery, still more appalling. At last the Devil himself, accoutred, as in the common description of the evil spirit, with hoof, horn, and tail, and eyes of infernal lustre, made his appearance, and called on me to curse God and worship him, who was powerful to save me. This dread suggestion he uttered with the full-toned clangour of the bell. I had him within an inch of me, and I thought on the fate of the Santon Barsisa. Strenuously and desperately I defied him, and bade him be gone. Reason, then, for a moment resumed her sway, but it was only to fill me with fresh terror, just as the lightning dispels the gloom that surrounds the benighted mariner, but to show him that his vessel is driving on a rock, where she must inevitably be dashed to pieces. I found I was becoming delirious, and trembled lest reason should utterly desert me. This is at all times an agonizing thought, but it smote me then with tenfold agony. I feared lest, when utterly deprived of my senses, I should rise; to do which I was every moment tempted by that strange feeling which calls on a man, whose head is dizzy from standing on the battlement of a lofty castle, to precipitate himself from it; and then death would be instant and tremendous. When I thought of this I became desperate;—I caught the floor with a grasp which drove the blood from my nails; and I yelled with the cry of despair. I called for help, I prayed, I shouted: but all the efforts of my voice were, of course, drowned in the bell. As it passed over my mouth, it occasionally echoed my cries, which mixed not with its own sound, but preserved their distinct character. Perhaps this was but fancy. To me, I know, they then sounded as if they were the shouting, howling, or laughing of the fiends with which my imagination had peopled the gloomy cave which swung over me.

You may accuse me of exaggerating my feelings; but I

am not.   Many a scene of dread have I since passed through, but they are nothing to the self-inflicted terrors of this half hour.   The ancients have doomed one of the damned, in their Tartarus, to lie under a rock which every moment seems to be descending to annihilate him; and an awful punishment it would be.   But if to this you add a clamour as loud as if ten thousand Furies were howling about you, a deafening uproar banishing reason and driving you to madness, you must allow that the bitterness of the pang was rendered more terrible.   There is no man, firm as his nerves may be, who could retain his courage in this situation.

In twenty minutes the ringing was done.   Half of that time passed over me without power of computation, the other half appeared an age.   When it ceased I became gradually more quiet ; but a new fear retained me.   I knew that five minutes would elapse without ringing ; but at the end of that short time the bell would be rung a second time for five minutes more.   I could not calculate time.   A minute and an hour were of equal duration.   I feared to rise, lest the five minutes should have elapsed, and the ringing be again commenced ; in which case I should be crushed, before I could escape, against the walls or framework of the bell. I therefore still continued to lie down, cautiously shifting myself, however, with a careful gliding, so that my eye no longer looked into the hollow.   This was of itself a considerable relief.   The cessation of the noise had, in a great measure, the effect of stupefying me, for my attention, being no longer occupied by the chimeras I had conjured up, began to flag.   All that now distressed me was the constant expectation of the second ringing, for which, however, I settled myself with a kind of stupid resolution.   I closed my eyes, and clenched my teeth as firmly as if they were screwed in a vice.   At last the dreaded moment came, and the first swing of the bell extorted a groan from me, as they say the most resolute victim screams at the sight of the rack, to which he is for a second time destined.   After this, however, I lay silent and lethargic, without a thought.   Wrapt in the defensive armour of stupidity, I defied the bell and its intonations. When it ceased, I was roused a little by the hope of escape. I did not, however, decide on this step hastily; but, putting up my hand with the utmost caution, I touched the rim. Though the ringing had ceased, it still was tremulous from the sound, and shook under my hand, which instantly recoiled as from an electric jar. A quarter of an hour probably elapsed before I again dared to make the experiment, and then I found it at rest. I determined to lose no time, fearing that I might have lain then already too long, and that the bell for evening service would catch me. This dread stimulated me, and I slipped out with the utmost rapidity, and arose. I stood, I suppose, for a minute, looking with silly wonder on the place of my imprisonment, penetrated with joy at escaping, but then rushed down the stony and irregular stair with the velocity of lightning, and arrived in the bell-ringer's room. This was the last act I had power to accomplish. I leant against the wall, motionless and deprived of thought; in which posture my companions found me, when, in the course of a couple of hours, they returned to their occupation.

They were shocked, as well they might be, at the figure before them. The wind of the bell had excoriated my face, and my dim and stupefied eyes were fixed with a lack-lustre gaze in my raw eyelids. My hands were torn and bleeding, my hair dishevelled, and my clothes tattered. They spoke to me, but I gave no answer. They shook me, but I remained insensible. They then became alarmed, and hastened to remove me. He who had first gone up with me in the forenoon met them as they carried me through the churchyard, and through him, who was shocked at having, in some measure, occasioned the accident, the cause of my misfortune was discovered. I was put to bed at home, and remained for three days delirious, but gradually recovered my senses. You may be sure the bell formed a prominent topic of my ravings; and, if I heard a peal, they were instantly increased to the utmost violence. Even when the delirium abated, my sleep was continually disturbed by imagined ringings, and my dreams were haunted by the fancies which almost maddened me while in the steeple. My friends removed me to a house in the country, which was sufficiently distant from any place of worship to save me from the apprehensions of hearing the church-going bell; for what Alexander Selkirk, in Cowper's poem, complained of as a misfortune was then to me as a blessing. Here I recovered; but even long after recovery, if a gale wafted the notes of a peal towards me, I started with nervous apprehension. I felt a Mahometan hatred to all the bell tribe, and envied the subjects of the Commander of the Faithful the sonorous voice of their Muezzin. Time cured this, as it cures the most of our follies; but even at the present day, if by chance my nerves be unstrung, some particular tones of the cathedral bell have power to surprise me into a momentary start.

The Embalmer.

No. I.

Pero contodo esto me parece, que el traducir de una lengua en otra, como no sea de las Reynas de las lenguas, Griega y Latina, es como quien mira los tapices Flamencos por el revés que aunque se veén las figuras son llenas de hilos que las obscurecen, y no se ven con la lisura y tez de la haz; y el traducir de lenguas faciles ni arguye ingenio, ni elocucion, como no le arguye el que traslada ni el que copia un papel de otro papel; y no por esto quiero inferir que no sea loable este exercicio del traducir porque en otras cosas peores se podria occupar el hombre, y que menos provecho le truxessen.

Don Quixote, p. 2, c. 62.

DEAR CHRISTOPHER,—In spite of the angry motto against translators which I have prefixed to my letter, I yet must say that I look upon them as a very valuable body of men ; and you may take my word for it, that my respect for the corps is not at all diminished by the circumstance of my having occasionally figured in it myself. But I do not much value those of our brotherhood who are contented with oversetting, as the Germans phrase it, works into the mere vernacular. They are only writers for a day—nothing but ephemerals. *Non sic itur ad astra.* If the original be worth knowing, people will read it in its native tongue, so that there is no good done for any but the ignorant or lazy part of mankind.

My department, I flatter myself, is rather higher. It has been long complained that all living languages are in a state of such continual flux that it is almost wasting a man's talents to write in them. Geoffry Crayon, if I do not mistake, most pathetically laments this affair in his Sketch Book. Chaucer strikes us as more antique reading than Homer; and a man finds more difficulty in getting through Gawain Douglas than through Virgil. It is a melancholy reflection for the thousand-and-one writers of the present day, that even such of them as have the good luck to survive half a dozen centuries must submit to the misfortune of being read through the musty medium of comments and glossaries.

I have often turned my thoughts towards the prevention of this calamitous event, but, until a few days ago, in vain. An idea then suddenly struck me, as I lay in bed one morning, so felicitous that I instantly jumped up, and set about putting it into execution. My project is, to translate all works of modern tongues at once into ancient; a dead language, as my Lord Byron very properly remarks in his late gossiping pamphlet, being the only immortal thing in this world. By this means we should embalm our authors; and I intend to take upon me at once the office of EMBALMER GENERAL, in which capacity I may perhaps appear at the coronation, and offer the king a mummy case, as an appropriate homage fee. The works of our poets—for our prose writers I leave to Dr. Bellendus—will, I trust, be preserved by my preparations, at least as effectually as bodies are by the antiseptic drugs or gross unguents of Sir Everard Home, or that most magnificent personage William Thomas Brande, Esquire, Secretary to the Royal Institution, and chief concocter of that highly amusing and agreeably authentic miscellany, the *Quarterly Journal of Science.*

It may be said that translations always fall far short of the original, and sacrifice numberless graces. Perhaps this is true of all other translators now extant; but, in my particular case, all that I am afraid of is that I may beautify the original too much, and that the charms of my style and composition may make the readers of my translations apt to value inferior productions too highly, from the beauty of the amber in which I shall enwrap them. For instance, I translated a song by Willison Glass the other day, and I passed it on the Bailie, a man of letters, you know, for Tibullus. However, as in such cases the originals will perish, the world will be the better for having my versions in their place; and a regard to the general interest of mankind ought to pervade the breast of every good and benevolent person.

I had some doubt as to what language I should patronise. Hebrew is by far too crabbed to write, and is, besides, lying under high professorial censure. I understand, indeed, that a gentleman in Italy has translated the Satires of Horace successfully into the language of Zion ; and that it is capable of beautiful and harmonious melody, everybody who has read the pathetic dirge in your thirty-eighth Number, by the vice-provost of Trinity College, Dublin, must acknowledge. But, in spite of all this, a man's fingers get horribly cramped in jotting and dotting. It is tiresome work to be meddling with the kings and emperors of Hebrew accentuation—with Zakeph-Katons, Telisha Gedolas, Schalschelets, and other grim-titled little flourishes. And if the thing were to be done at all, it should be done Masoretically ; for I look on the Anti-Masorites to be complete Whigs (*i.e.* very contemptible persons) in literature. With respect to Greek, it is a very fit language. We all remember Porson's elegant translation of Three Children Sliding on the Ice ; and I have read two or three neat versions of Shakespeare, done by Cambridge men for the prize founded by him. God save the King, too, has been done for the Classical Journal passably ; and Mr Cæcilius Metellus has given the commencement of John Gilpin so well, in the same periodical, that I wish he would finish it ; after which he might try his hand at the celebrated imitation of Cowper's philosophical poem, Lord Byron's Mazeppa. I was inclined to follow these examples, but it most unluckily happened that, in the very first poem I took up, I had occasion to look for the precise signification of a word beginning with omega, which I wanted to use ; and not being quite satisfied with Stephanus's interpretation, I am obliged to wait until I see the opinion of the new *Thes.* on the point, which will delay my Greekish intentions until somewhere in the year 1835. Latin, then, being all that remained, I have commenced operations on a grand scale. Vincent Bourne, honest dear fellow, has done a great deal already in that way, but I shall soon surpass his labours.

I was dubious, too, with respect to the metres,·whether I should only use those of ancient Rome, or conform myself to the modern versification. There are great authorities on both sides. Dr Aldrich translated

> " A soldier and a sailor,
> A tinker and a tailor," &c.

into Latin of similar structure with the English, and Dr. Petre has done Chevy-Chace in the same way. Many inferior names might be also adduced. The objection to it is, that Latin lines to English tunes are as much out of place as English lines of Latin form. But that objection, not more than bare assertion at best, whatever might have been its weight formerly, is of no avail now, since the splendid success of the Laureate, and the much grander effort of the great poet who addressed you, Mr. North, in that divine hymn, have proved that the hexameter may be naturalised in our language. By a parity of reasoning our verses might be naturalised in Latin—at least the experiment is worth trying.

I send a few fragments, sweepings of my portfolios, as samples. The great works I am employed in I shall keep for your private inspection. Below are a part of "Take thy old cloak about thee," of "July the First," of "The Groves of Blarney," of "Mary Ambree," of "Sir Tristrem," and the epitaphs on Sir Patrick Sarsfield, John, Duke of Marlborough, Henry, Duke of Grafton, Robin Hood, Earl of Huntingdon, and Sir Daniel Donnelly, champion of Ireland. I have used both Latin and English metres.

I.

VERSE OF "TAKE THY OLD CLOAK ABOUT THEE." *

Sung by Iago in the Second Act of Othello.

King Stephen was a worthy peer,
    His breeches cost him but a crown,
He held them sixpence all too dear,
    And so he called the tailor loon.
He was a king, and wore a crown,
    Thou art a squire of low degree ;
'Tis pride that pulls the country down,
    So take thy old cloak about thee.

Rex Stephanus princeps fuit illustrissimus olim,
    Sexque decem braccæ constiterunt obolis.
Assibus hoc pretium reputans sex charius æquo,
    Sartorem jurgat nomine furciferi.
Ille fuit dominus celso diademate cinctus,
    Et tu demissi nil nisi verna loci ;
Eheu! sternit humi nunc nostra superbia regnum :
    Veste igitur trita contege terga, precor.

II.

VERSES OF JULY THE FIRST, THE GREAT ORANGE SONG IN IRELAND.

July the first, in old Bridge town,
    There was a grievous battle,
Where many a man lay on the ground,
    And the cannon they did rattle.
King James, he pitched his tents between,
    His lines for to retire,†
But William threw his bomb-balls in,
    And set them all on fire.†

*   *   *   *

The horse and cannon crossed the stream,
    And the foot came following a'ter,

---

* After a diligent collation of MSS. I have fixed on readings which differ
somewhat from the received text of this poem.—M. OD.

† To be pronounced—more Hibernico—reti-er, fi-er.—M. OD.

But brave Duke Schomberg lost his life
In crossing the Boyne Water.

*   *   *   *

A bullet from the Irish came,
    And grazed King William's arm—*
They thought his majesty was slain,
    But it did him little harm.†

*   *   *   *

The Protestants of Drogheda
    Have reason to be thankful,
That they were all preserved that day,
    Though they were but a handful.

———

In veteris pontis vico, Julique calendis
Atrox pugna fuit, morientia millia campum
Sternebant : Sonitum horribilem tormenta dedere.
In medio spatio tendebat rex Iacobus,
Posset ut ex acie subducere longius,† autem
Igniferos jecit glandes Gulielmus in hostem,
Exussitque statim flammis tentoria cuncta.

*   *   *   *

Flumen transivere equites tormentaque primum,
His instant pedites ; Dux Schonenbergius acer,
Dum transit, vitam deperdit in amne Bubinda.

*   *   *   *

Strinxit mox humerum Gulielmi glans ab Hibernis ;
Nil nocuit, quanquam de regis morte timerent.

*   *   *   *

Sint Protestantes Drohedæ super omnia læti,
Quod parvi numero, salvi tunc Marte fuerunt.

———

* To be pronounced—more Hibernico—ar-rum, har-rum.—M. OD.
† I fear I may have misunderstood this line, the original being rather
obscure—something like Sir R. Phillips's common sense.—M. OD.

III.

GROVES OF BLARNEY.*

The groves of Blarney they are most charming ——
   Blarnæi nemora † sunt jucundissima visu.

But I prefer the next verse :

   'Tis Lady Jeffries that owns this station,
     Like Alexander or Helen fair ;
   There is no lady in all the nation
     For emulation can with her compare.
   She has castles round her, that no nine-pounder
     Can dare to plunder her place of strength ;
   But Oliver Cromwell he did her pummel,
     And made a hole in her battlement.

———

   Jeffrisa castellum regit, perpulchra virago,
     Par et Alexandro pulchræ Helenæque simul,
   Cui cunctas inter peperit quas dulcis Ierne
     Dicere se similem fœmina nulla potest.

---

* Blarney certainly is a most interesting part of the world. Its famous old castle—"the statues gracing this noble place in"—its Charles the Twelfth, &c.—the various stories connected with it—but, above all, its celebrated stone, render it highly worthy of public attention. The stone is on the top of the battlements of the castle, and is bound with iron ; being struck, as it is mentioned in the above quoted verse, by a cannon shot when Oliver Cromwell attacked the place ; but we believe the story of his being there rests on rather weak foundations. Any person who kisses that stone is privileged to talk blarney all his life ; and many a gentleman we have seen from Ireland who has proved the efficacy of the ceremony. It is said, but the doctrine is not quite so authentic, that a dip in the Shannon gives the privilege of never blushing while in the act of committing blarney. Certain specimens, however, have come under our notice of ingenious Irishmen who, all unbaptized, were quite free from the sin of changing complexion. Blarney (not the place, but the thing) is quite a distinct affair from humbug, as lexicographers must well know. Its fame is widely extended all over the world, as it was the only English word that the King of Abyssinia was acquainted with, as you may see by Salt's Travels. Would Mr. O'Fogarty, on his recovery, favour us with an article on the place of his nativity?—M. OD.

† Nemora—a long by cæsura.—See Dr. Carey.—M. OD.

Hæc castella tenet quæ non tormenta timerent,
  Quæ ter tres libras horrida ferre solent.
Sed Cromwellus eam graviter concussit, hiatum
  In nido patulum conficiens dominæ.

IV.

VERSE OF MARY AMBREE.*

When our brave commanders, whom death could not daunt,
Marched off to the siege of the city of Gaunt ;
They counted their forces by two and by three,
But the foremost in battle was Mary Ambree.

———

Cum nostri ductores qui mortem spernebant
Ad Gantii turres cingendas pergebant,
Et copias legebant per duos et tres,
Fuit prima in pugna Maria Ambres.

V.

VERSE OF SIR TRISTREM.

[*I have translated the entire poem.*]

Geten and born was so
  The child was fair and white,
Nas never Rohand so wo,
  He wist not what to wite ;
To childbed ded he go,
  His owhen wiif al so tite,
Said he had children to, ,
  On hem was his delite.
    Bi Crist,
In court men cleped him so,
Tho Tram bifor the Trist.,

———

Sic genitus et satus,
  In mundum infans it ;
Rohantius contristatus
  Quid facere non scit.

---

* In Percy's Reliques. The lady is mentioned also by Ben Jonson, as
Mary Ambree, who marched so free, &c.—M. OD.

In lecto qui fuit stratus,
  Partus uxoris fit,
Quasi filius fuit natus
  Quem multum dilexit.
    Per Christum
Et fuit appellatus
Cum Tramo ante Tristum.

VI.

ON SIR P. SARSFIELD.*

Oh! Patrick Sarsfield, Ireland's wonder,
Who fought in field like any thunder,
One of King James's chief commanders,
Now lies the food of crows in Flanders.
              Ohone!

———

O! Patrici Sarsfield, decus mirantis Iernes,
  Cui tonitru simili cernere usus erat:
Jacobi heroas quo non præstantior inter,
  Belgarum corvis mortuus esca jaces.
             Eheu!

VII.

ON JOHN, DUKE OF MARLBOROUGH.

By Doctor Evans.

Here lies John, Duke of Marlborough,
Who ran the Frenchmen thorough and thorough;
Married Sarah Jennings, spinster,
Died in Saint James's, and was buried in Westminster.

———

Hic jacet Dux Marleburiensis,
Qui Gallos secuit tanquam ensis;
Virginem duxit Jenningiam Saram;
Mortuus Jacobi ad regiam claram,
Sepultus ad Stephani Martyris aram!

---

* Under a very fine print of Sir Patrick—engraved, if I do not mistake, by Lady Bingham, his daughter. If she also wrote the epitaph, it reflects great credit on her poetical powers. Sir Patrick fought gallantly for James II. in Ireland, and left it on the overthrow of his party. On the Continent he continued his aversion to William III., and was killed in the battle of Landen, in which that monarch was defeated. He was a brave man.—M. OD.

I must apologise for introducing a supernumerary line, and also for bringing "regiam claram " *rhythmi gratiâ*. Both practices, however, are justifiable by high poetic authority in this and other countries.

VIII.

CONCLUSION OF THE EPITAPH ON HENRY, DUKE OF GRAF-
    TON, SON OF CHARLES II., KILLED AT THE SIEGE OF
    CORK, 1690.*

Yet a bullet of Cork
It did his work,
Unhappy pellet !
With grief I tell it,
It has undone
Great Cæsar's son !
A statesman's spoiled ;
A soldier foiled ;
God rot him
Who shot him,—
A son of a——,†
I say no more,
Here lies Henry, the Duke of Grafton !

——————

Sed glans Corcensis stravit, miserabile telum,
    Heu ! natum rapuit Cæsaris egregii,
Excelsum pariter vel bello consiliisve :—
    Cædentis manus occupet atra lues !
Dispereat scorti soboles.—Nil amplius addam.
    Hic sunt Henrici Graftonis ossa Ducis.

* Shot by a blacksmith, who turned out, quoth the *Cork Remembrancer*, from a forge in the Old Post Office lane, as he was crossing the river Lee. The place where he fell is called Grafton's Alley. The epitaph is taken from a book published in 1702, called Poems on Affairs of State, &c, 2 vols. It is written by Sir F. S——d.—M. OD.

† There is a pleasant equivoque here. We are left in the dark whether this opprobrious name is applied to the blacksmith, or the Duke, of whom we know it was quite true. Verbruggen, the comedian, cracked a similar joke on the Duke of Saint Albans, which I believe is in Joe Miller. I have endeavoured to preserve the equivoque.—M. OD.

IX.

ON ROBIN HOOD.*

Underneath this little stone
Lies Robert, Earl of Huntingdon ;
IIe was in truth an archer good,
And people called him Robin Hood.
Such outlaws as he and his men
England never will see again.
[*Alcaics.*]
Parvo Robertus hic situs est comes
Huntingdonensis sub lapide obrutus ;
    Nemo negabit quam peritus
      Missilibus fuerit sagittis.
Vulgo vocatus Robin a Hoodius,
Exlex in agris vivere maluit ;
    In Anglia nunquam Roberto
      Vel sociis similes videbis.

X.

ON SIR DANIEL DONNELLY, C. I.†

Underneath this pillar high
Lies Sir Daniel Donnelly ;
IIe was a stout and handy man,
And people called him buffing Dan.
Knighthood he took from George's sword,
And well he wore it by my word !
He died at last, from forty-seven
Tumblers of punch he drank one even.
O'erthrown by punch, unharmed by fist,
He died unbeaten pugilist.
Such a buffer as Donnelly
Ireland never again will see.

Hic jacet, sub columnâ stratus,
Daniel Donnellius eques auratus ;
Fortis et acer ab omnibus ratus,
Plagosus Daniel cognominatus,

---

* In Percy's Reliques.
† From that great work, *Blackwood's Magazine*, No. XXXVIII.—M. OD.

Eques a Georgio fuit creatus,
Ornavitque ordinem equitatus ;
Quadraginta septem trucidatus,
Cantharis punchi hic est allatus ;
Potu, non pugno, ita domatus,*
Cecidit heros nunquam æquatus ;
Hiberniæ insulæ quâ fuit natus
Vir talis non erit posthac datus,

Enough of these. *Manum quod aiunt de tabula.*

I strongly recommend any poet who wishes for immortality to take advantage of my recipe. I am ready to translate for any gentleman at a fair and reasonable rate. Nor shall I be over hard in requiring any conditions from him, except that there be a slight degree of intelligibility in what he writes, say about four degrees above Maturin's Universe ; which, I hope, is not too much.

* More antique for *domitus.*—M. OD.

Song in Praise of Wastle and North.

Where'er Odoherty with casual foot
   Winds through this weary world his varied way,
Still be it his with vigour to recruit
   His toil-worn frame, and moistify his clay
   With—any potent dram his taste will suit,
To toast the health of friends beside the Forth—
The dauntless Wastle and the peerless North !

Let Southey sing of Thalaba and Roderick,
   And Scott chaunt forth his epic strains, to tell
How Bruce's vessel left the Bay of Broderick,
   And how, at Flodden, Scotland's ensign fell :
   Let simple Wordsworth tune on Peter Bell ;
And Coleridge curdle blood, and stiffen hair,
Telling how spirits plagued the Mariner.

Let Crabbe rhyme on 'bout vagabonds and flunkeys,
   Tailors and cobblers, gipsies and their brats,
Riding on wicker creels or half-starved donkeys,
   Their black eyes glancing 'neath their bits of hats ;
   Let Wilson roam to Fairyland : but that's
An oldish story ; I'll lay half a crown
The tiny elves are smothered by his gown.

Let missions go to Greenland with Montgomery ;
   Let green-sick ladies sonnetize with Bowles ;
Let Leigh Hunt sing of cabbages and flummery,
   And currant-bushes blooming on green knowls ;
   Let Keats draw out his whinings into growls ;

Let Corney Webbe write sonnets by the score,
" And trample wounded Time upon the floor."

Let Shelley sing of darknesses and devilry,
    Till earth grows Pandemonium at his touch ;
Let Tommy Moore, that son and soul of revilry,
    Praise Indians and fire-worshippers, and such :
    To stretch our thoughts so far is rather much ;
Although to spend an hour we do not grudge
With Twopenny Post-bags, Crib, and Betty Fudge.

Let Mrs. Hemans chaunt historic tales
    Till Cader Idris echoes back the strain ;
Let Missy Mitford spread adventurous sails
    Far south, and sing Cristina of the Main ;
    Miss Horford now may visit Falkirk plain
In safety ; as the only danger there
Is meeting with wild cattle at the fair.

Let Mrs. Opie sing of orphan boys,
    Whose sires were shot with slug at Trafalgar ;
Let Lady Morgan cant, and make a noise,
    With Lindley Murray and good sense at war ;
    Miss Baillie no doubt is a shining star :
But unto none I will attend, unless—
What is the *sine quâ non* ?   Only guess.

Unless in *Blackwood's* pine-tree grove he flourish,
    Writing an article for every number,
With fun and frolic.   These are things that nourish
    The heart of man, and keep his eyes from slumber.
    I like none of your melancholy lumber,
Your sonnets and your sentimental tales,
As tardy of digestion as brass nails.

You see I'm tainted with the metromanie,
    And not a little proud of innovation :

I'll have original verse as well as any,
  And not think there's any great occasion
  To write like Frere and Byron.   When the nation
Talks of the seven-line stanza, they shall cry—
Aye! that's the stanza of Odoherty!

𝔖𝔬𝔫𝔤,

On being asked who wrote " The Groves of Blarney."

" Who,"—ask ye !   No matter.—This tongue shall not tell
    O'er the board of oblivion the name of the bard ;
Nor shall it be uttered but with the proud spell
    That sheds on the perished their only reward.

No, no ! look abroad, sir, the last of October,
    In the pages of *Blackwood* that name shall be writ,
For Christopher's self, be he tipsy or sober,
    Was not more than his match, in wine, wisdom, or wit.

Ye Dowdens and Jenningses, wits of Cork city,
    Though mighty the heroes that chime in your song,
Effervescing and eloquent, more is the pity
    Ye forget the great poet of Blarney so long.

I mean not the *second*, O'Fogarty hight,
    Who can speak for himself, from his own native Helicon ;
I sing of an elder, in birth and in might,
    (Be it said with true deference)—honest *Dick Millikin.*

Then fill up, to his mem'ry, a bumper, my boys :
    'Twill cheer his sad ghost, as it toddles along
Through Pluto's dark alleys, in search of the joys
    That were dear upon earth to this step-son of song.

And this be the rule of the banquet for aye,
    When the goblets all ring with " Och hone, Ullagone ! "
Remember this pledge, as a tribute to pay
    To the name of a minstrel so sweet, so unknown.

September 1, 1821.

Specimens of a Free and Easy Translation.

In which HORACE *is done (for) into English, and adapted to the Taste of the Present Generation.*

PRELIMINARY LETTER.— Private.

DEAR NORTH,—I am sorry to learn, by your last, that you have had such a severe twitch this time; keep warm in Welch flannel, live soberly, and no more desperate attempts with the Eau Medicinale d'Husson. It will be no farce, I assure you, if the gout fly bolt into your stomach, like a Congreve rocket into the ditto of a whale, and carry you off in the twinkling of a walking-stick. Then there would be wiping of eyes, and blowing of noses; crape, weepers, and long cravats, throughout the land. Then there would be a breaking up of the glorious divan. Wastle would leave his High Street lodgings, and retire to his "airy citadel;" Morris would sell his shandrydan, and keep house at Aberystwith for life; Kempferhausen would pack up for Allemagne; Eremus would commence grinder to the embryo divines at Aberdeen; the Odontist would forswear poetry, take a large farm, and study Malthus on Population; Delta would take parson's orders; Paddy from Cork would fall into "a green and yellow melancholy," toss the remaining cantos of his epic to Beelzebub, and button his coat behind; Mullion would sell butter and eggs at his provision-warehouse, Grassmarket, and sedulously look forward to the provostship; while poor Odoherty (alas, poor Yorick!) would send his luggage to Dunleary harbour, and away to the fighting trade in South America. Then would there be a trumpeting and tantararaing among the Whigs,—

"Quassha ma boo! Our masters are no more!" would be echoed by every lip among them; and then, but not till then, with some shadow of hope might they look forward to their holding the reins of government, though, after all, most of them, if they did not hold well by the mane, would fall off the steed's back into the mire, they are such shocking bad riders; while the Radicals would press forward, and tread on their ribs in turn; Glasgow weavers would spin ropes to hang up whoever was obnoxious to them; Sheffield cutlers would grind razors to cut throats; and the Ribbon-men of Erin, and all "the ragged, royal race of Tara" would look forward to seats in the Cabinet. Then, indeed, would there be a complete revolution in Church and State; churchmen would be cut shorter by the head, the national debt washed out with a dishclout, and taxes abolished; and then, instead of election being fettered, and parliaments septennial, there would be universal suffrage, and no parliaments at all. Then would the Saturnian age return to bless the world; then would Lucifer hawk about his golden pippins, and find abundant sale for them; then would all property be common, and pickpockets left without a trade; while no person would have anything to do—at least, any right to do anything, except smoking his pipe, draining his mug, and snoring in his hammock.

My dear North, take care of the damp weather, and I warrant that, for many a long year to come, you shall keep death and the doctor at complete defiance; behold the cause of true freedom and loyalty prospering around you; and, were it not that you are a bachelor, rejoice in the caresses of your children's children.

From you, my revered friend, I shall descend to a humbler topic; "one on which," to use the words of Byron, "all are supposed to be fluent, and none agreeable—self."

1stly, With regard to health, I find myself as well as I wish all others to be. My sprained ancle is now quite convalescent, poor thing; and, by persevering in rubbing a tea-spoonful of opodeldoc upon it every morning, it will soon be as strong as a bedpost.   I occasionally take a Seidlitz powder to keep my stomach in order; for, depend upon it, the stomach of a literary man is almost of as much consequence as his head. Talking of the top-piece, I have an occasional headache; that is to say, after being too late out at night; but which I effectually remove and rectify by a bottle of sodawater—our friend Jennings' if possible; for it excels all others as much as his poetry the common run of verses, and stands, in relation to every other compound of the kind, in the same degree of excellence and superiority as Day and Martin's patent blacking to that made with soot, saliva, and small beer.

2dly, With respect to my intellectual pursuits.   Pray, what makes you so earnest to learn what a retired and obscure man like me is about, and whose poor contributions to literature are but a drop in the bucket, compared with what you every day receive from the bright luminaries of the age? But I value your partiality as I ought; and, though I am to these as a farthing candle to a six-in-the-pound, you generously dip my wick in your own turpentine, to make it blaze brighter.

I blush scarlet (God bless the army, and their coats of scarlet!) when I confess, on my knees (by the by, there is no need of kneeling, when you cannot see me), that I have been for some time notoriously idle.   Salamanca is such a noble beast that I could not resist taking him out to the hounds (I have won the brush thrice); and then partridges were so plenty, I said it would waste little powder and shot daily to fill and replenish my bag; and then there was sometimes cricket in the morning, and loo in the afternoon, and blows-out at night, and all that.   *Horresco referens.*   I have been shamefully idle; but I am determined to stick to it like rosin this winter; and hang me if I do not astonish the natives; I shall make some of them gaze up to the clouds in wonder, and others to shake in their shoes.   In the interim, I enclose specimens of a new, free, and easy translation (I should say, imitation) of Horace.   I have got finished with

the Odes, and am busy with the Satires, writing at the rate
of four hundred lines a day. Let me know, when convenient, what you think of them ; make a church and a mill
of them afterwards. Give my best respects to Mr. Blackwood,
when you see him, and believe me, while I have breath in
my nostrils,

Yours devoutly,

MORGAN ODOHERTY.

DUBLIN, *2d December* 1821.

HORACE, BOOK FIRST.

ODE I.

To Christopher North, Esq.

Ad Maecenatem.

Maecenas, atavis edite regibus, O et praesidium et dulce decus meum !	HAIL ! Christopher, my patron dear, Descended from your grandfather ; To thee, my bosom friend, I fly, Brass buckler of Odoherty !
Sunt quos curriculo pulverem Olympicum Collegisse juvat, metaque fervidis Evitata rotis, palmaque nobilis Terrarum dominos evehit ad deos :	Some are who all their hours consume With well-trained horse and sweated groom, Who, if the Doncaster they gain, Or, coming first, with lightened rein, At the St. Leger, bear away Elate the honours of the day, Pull up their collars to their ears, And think themselves amid the spheres. Such art thou, Lambton, Kelburne, Pierse, And more than I can name in verse.
Hunc, si mobilium turba Quiritium Certat tergeminis tollere honoribus :	Another tries, with furious speech, The bottoms of the mob to reach : Here on the hustings stands Burdett, With trope and start their zeal to whet ; While jackal Hobhouse, sure to tire on Tracking alway the steps of Byron, Stands at his arm, with words of nectar, Determined to out-hector Hector. Preston, with rosin on his beard, Starts up, determined to be heard, And swears destruction to the bones Of those who will not hear Gale Jones ; While Leigh Hunt, in the *Examiner*, About them tries to make a stir, And says (who doubts him ?) men like these Shame Tully and Demosthenes.

Illum, si proprio condidit hor-
    reo
Quidquid de Libycis verritur
    areis :
Gaudentem patrios findere sar-
    culo
Agros,

    Attalicis conditionibus
Nunquam dimoveas, ut trabe
    Cypria
Myrtoum pavidus nauta secet
    mare.

Luctantem Icariis fluctibus
    Africum
Mercator metuens, otium et
    oppidi
Laudat rura sui : mox reficit
    rates
Quassas, indocilis pauperiem
    pati.

Est qui nec veteris pocula
    Massici,
Nec partem solido demere de
    die,
  Spernit,

    nunc viridi membra sub
    arbuto
Stratus, nunc ad aquae lene
    caput sacrae.

Multos castra juvant, et lituo
    tubae
Permixtus sonitus,

    bellaque matribus
Detestata.

    Manet sub Jove frigido
Venator, tenerae conjugis im-
    memor ;
Seu visa est catulis cerva
    fidelibus,
Seu rupit teretes Marsus aper
    plagas.

A third, like Sir John Sinclair, tries
To hold the harrow to the skies ;
And thinks there is no nobler work
Than scattering manure with the fork,
Except (as Mr. Coke prefers)
To catch the sheep, and ply the shears :
Although you'd give, in guineas round,
A plum (*i.e.*, one hundred thousand pound),
You could not get these men, I know,
Aboard the northern ships to go,
Through frozen latitudes to stroll,
And see if ice surrounds the pole.
They wish success to Captain Parry,
But yet at home would rather tarry.
In slippers red, before the fire,
With negus to his heart's desire,
The merchant sits ; he winks and snores,
The north wind in the chimney roars ;
Waking, he bawls aloud—"Od rot 'em,
I fear my ships are at the bottom !
The crews are trifles to be sure,
But then the cargoes a'n't secure :
'Change will be changed for me to-morrow,
Alack ! for poverty and sorrow !"
Men are—I know them—let that pass,
Who crack a joke, and love a glass,
Whether, like Falstaff, it be sack,
Champagne, old hock, or Frontiniac,
Or whisky-punch, which, jovial dog,
Is true heart's-balsam to James Hogg.
Like Wordsworth, under pleasant trees
Some take delight to catch the breeze ;
Or lie amid the pastoral mountains,
And listen to the bubbling fountains.
Many in camps delight to hear
The fife and bugle's music clear,
While hautboy sweet, and kettle-drum,
Upon the ear like thunder come.
Though youngsters love a battle hot,
Their anxious mothers love it not :—
While in the fray a son remains out,
Some erring ball may knock his brains out.
O'er hedge and ditch, through field and thicket,
With buckskin breeches and red jacket,
On spanking steed the huntsman flies,
Led by the deep-mouthed stag-hounds' cries :
Meanwhile his spouse, in lonely bed,
Laments that she was ever wed ;

And, tossed on wedlock's stormy billow,
Like the M'Whirter, clasps her pillow,
And sighs, while fondling it about,
" Thou art my only child, I doubt !"

Me doctarum hederae praemia frontium
Dis miscent superis ;

—For me a laurel crown, like that
Used for a band to Southey's hat
(Not such as Cockney Will abuses,
And Leigh Hunt for a night-cap uses),
Would make me, amid wits, appear
A Sampson and a grenadier !

me gelidum nemus,
Nympharumque leves cum Satyris chori
Secernunt populo:

Then many a nymph, with sparkling eye,
Would crowd around Odoherty ;
Swift at the tune which Lady Morgan
Would play upon the barrel organ ;
MacCraws, and all my second cousins,
And light-heeled blue-stockings by dozens,
With nimble toe would touch the ground,
And form a choral ring around.

si neque tibias
Euterpe cohibet, nec Polyhymnia
Lesboum refugit tendere barbiton.

Oh that James Hogg, my chosen friend,
His glowing fancy would me lend—
His restless fancy, wandering still
By lonely mount and fairy rill !
That Dr. Scott, with forceps stout,
Would draw my stumps of dulness out ;
Exalt my heart o'er churlish earth,
And fill me with his fun and mirth ;

Quod si me lyricis vatibus inseris,
Sublimi feriam sidera vertice.

Then, Anak-like, 'mid men I'd stray,
Men that like mice would throng my way,
Rise high o'er all terrestrial jars,
And singe my poll against the stars.

ODE FIFTH, BOOK FIRST.

Ad Pyrrham.

To Molly M' Whirter.

Quis multa gracilis te puer in rosa
Perfusus liquidis urguet odoribus
Grato, Pyrrha, sub antro?
Cui flavam religas comam,

What exquisite, tell me, besprinkled with civet,
With bergamot, and *l'huile antique a la rose,*
Now presses thee, Molly (I scarce can believe it),
To march to the parson, and finish his woes?

Simplex munditiis ? Heu ! quoties fidem
Mutatosque deos flebit, et aspera

For whom do ye comb, brush, and fillet your tresses?
Whoever he be has not sorrows to seek ;

Nigris aequora ventis
　Emirabitur insolens,

Thou daily shalt bring him a peck of dis-
　　tresses;
　Then kick him, and kiss a new gallant next
　　week.

Qui nunc te fruitur credulus
　　aurea;
Qui semper vacuam, semper
　　amabilem,
　Sperat, nescius aurae
　　Fallacis! Miseri, quibus

He trusts that you'll love him, and doat on him
　　ever,
　And thinks you a goddess reserved for
　　himself:
But, Molly, there's too much red blood in your
　　liver,
　And antlers shall soon grace the poor silly elf.

Intentata nites! Me tabula
　　sacer
Votiva paries indicat uvida
　Suspendisse potenti
　　Vestimenta maris deo.

To some Johnny Raw thou wilt shine like a
　　planet,
　For lecturing Magnus has left thee behind;
And since I have escaped thee (oh! blessings
　　be on it),
　I will hang up an old coat in St. Mary's Wynd.

ODE NINTH, BOOK FIRST.

Ad Thaliarchum.

To Dr. Scott.

Vides, ut alta stet nive candi-
　　dum
Soracte, nec jam sustineant
　　onus
　Silvae laborantes, geluque
　Flumina constiterint
　　acuto.

Look out, and see old Arthur's Seat
　Dressed in a periwig of snow:
Cold sweeps the blast down Niddry Street,
　And through the Netherbow.

Dissolve frigus, ligna super
　　foco
Large reponens; atque be-
　　nignius
　Deprome quadrimum Sa-
　　bina,
　O Thaliarche! merum
　　diota.

Sharp frost, begone! haste, send the maid
　With coals two shovelsful and more;
Fill up your rummers—why afraid?—
　And bolt the parlour door.

Permitte divis caetera; qui
　　simul
Stravere ventos aequore fer-
　　vido
　Depraeliantes, nec cup-
　　ressi
　Nec veteres agitantur
　　orni.

Leave all to Fortune, Dr. Scott,
　Though tempests growl amid the trees.
While we have rum-punch smoking hot,
　We sha'n't most likely freeze.

Quid sit futurum cras, fuge
　　quaerere, et,
Quem Fors dierum cumque
　　dabit, lucro
　Appone; nec dulces
　　amores
　Sperne puer, neque tu
　　choreas,

A fig about to-morrow's fare!
　A twenty thousand prize, my buck
(Nay, do not laugh), may be my share:
　Won't that be rare good-luck?

Donec virenti canities abest
Morosa. Nunc et campus, et
   areae,
    Lenesque sub noctem su-
     surri
     Composita repetantur
      hora :

Doctor, I'm sure you'll toast the fair ;
   Shame to the tongue would say me nay ;
You'll toast them, till the very hair
   Of your peruke turn grey.

St. Giles's spire with snow is white,
   And every roof seems overgrown ;
Sharp winds that come, at fall of night,
   Down High Street closes moan ;

Nunc et latentis proditor in-
   timo
Gratus puellae risus ab angulo,
   Pignusque dereptum la-
   certis,
    Aut digito male perti-
    naci.

There, battering police officers,
   Hark how the mad jades curse and ban,
While Polly cuffs some spoonie's ears,
   And cries, "Sir, I'm your man !"

Inishowen.

1.

I care not a fig for a flagon of flip,
  Or a whistling can of rumbo ;
But my tongue through whisky-punch will slip
  As nimble as Hurlothrumbo.
So put the spirits on the board,
  And give the lemons a squeezer,
And we'll mix a jorum, by the Lord !
  That will make your worship sneeze, sir.

2.

The French, no doubt, are famous souls,
  I love them for their brandy ;
In rum and sweet tobacco-rolls
  Jamaica men are handy.
The big-breeched Dutch in juniper gin,
  I own, are very knowing ;
But are rum, gin, brandy, worth a pin
  Compared with Inishowen ?

3.

Though here with a lord 'tis jolly and fine
  To tumble down Lachryma Christi,
And over a skin of Italy's wine
  To get a little misty ;
Yet not the blood of the Bourdeaux grape,
  The finest grape-juice going,
Nor clammy Constantia, the pride of the Cape,
  Prefer I to Inishowen.

𝔄 Twist=imony in favour of Gin=twist.

*An humble imitation of that admirable Poem, the Ex-ale-tation of Ale,
attributed by grave authors to Bishop Andrews, on which point is to
be consulted Francis, Lord Verulam, a celebrated Philosopher, who has
been lately be-scoped-and tendencied by Macvey Napier, Esq.*

Running
Index of
Matters.

I.

Præm.

At one in the morn, as I went staggering home,
  With nothing at all in my hand but my fist,
At the end of the street a good youth I did
      meet,
  Who asked me to join in a jug of gin-twist.

2.

Gin-twist.'

" Though 'tis late," I replied, "and I'm muggy
      beside,
  Yet an offer like this I could never resist;
So let's waddle away, *sans* a moment's delay,
  And in style we'll demolish your jug of gin-
      twist."

3.

Wines.

The friends of the grape may boast of rich
      Cape,
  Hock, Claret, Madeira, or Lachryma Christi,
But this muzzle of mine was never so fine
  As to value them more than a jug of gin-twist.

4.

Brandy.

The people of Nantz, in the kingdom of France,
  Bright brandy they brew, liquor not to be
      hissed;

It may do as a dram, but 'tis not worth a damn,
  When watered, compared with a jug of gin-
    twist.

5.

Antigua, Jamaica, they certainly make a   *Rum.*
  Grand species of rum, which should ne'er be
    dismissed ;
It is splendid as grog, but never, you dog,
  Esteem it as punch, like a jug of gin-twist.

6.

Ye bailies of Glasgow ! Wise men of the West !   *Cold Punch.*
  Without your rum bowls you'd look certainly
    tristes ;
Yet I laugh when I'm told that liquor so cold
  Is as good as a foaming hot jug of gin-twist.

7.

The bog-trotting Teagues in clear whisky de- *Potsheen.*
    light,
  Preferring potsheen to all drinks that exist ;
I grieve, ne'ertheless, that it does not possess
  The juniper smack of a jug of gin-twist.

8.

Farintosh and Glenlivet, I hear, are the boast   *Farintosh.*
  Of those breechesless heroes, the Sons of the
    Mist ;
But may I go choke if that villainous smoke
  I'd name in a day with a jug of gin-twist.

9.

Yet the Celtic I love, and should join them, by *The Celtic.*
    Jove !
  Though Glengarry should vow I'd no right to
    enlist ;

For that chief, do you see, I'd not care a bawbee,
    If strongly entrenched o'er a jug of gin-twist.

10.

Kilts.

One rule they lay down is the reason, I own,
    Why from joining their plaided array I desist;
Because they declare that no one shall wear
    Of breeches a pair, o'er their jugs of gin-twist.

11.

Breeches.

This is plainly absurd, I give you my word,
    Of this bare-rumped reg'lation I ne'er saw the
        gist;
In my gay corduroys, can't these philabeg boys
    Suffer me to get drunk o'er my jug of gin-twist?

12.

Rack.

In India they smack a liquor called rack,
    Which I never quaffed (at least that I wist);
I'm told 'tis like tow in its taste, and, if so,
    Very different stuff from a jug of gin-twist.

13.

Porter and ale.

As for porter and ale—'fore Gad, I turn pale,
    When people on such things as these can in-
        sist;
They may do for dull clods, but, by all of the
        gods!
They are hog-wash when matched with a jug of
        gin-twist.

14.

Tea.

Why tea we import I could never conceive;
    To the Mandarin folk, to be sure, it brings grist;
But in our western soils the spirits it spoils,
    While to heaven they are raised by a jug of gin-
        twist.

15.

Look at Hazlitt and Hunt, most unfortunate
    pair !
  Black and blue from the kicks of a stern
    satirist ;
But would Mynheer Izzard once trouble their
    gizzard,
  If bohea they exchanged for a jug of gin-twist ?

Hazlitt, Hunt, Bohea. Z.

16.

Leibnitz held that this earth was the first of all
    worlds,
  And no wonder the buck was a firm optimist ;
For 'twas always his use, as a proof to adduce
  Of the truth of his doctrine, a jug of gin-twist.

Leibnitz.

17.

It cures all the vapours and mulligrub capers ;
  It makes you like Howard, the philanthro-pist ;
Woe, trouble, and pain, that bother your brain,
  Are banished out clean by a jug of gin-twist.

Howard.

18.

You turn up your nose at all of your foes,
  Abuse you, traduce you, they may if they list ;
The lawyers, I'm sure, would look very poor,
  If their clients would stick to their jugs of gin-
    twist.

Law of libel.

19.

There's Leslie, my friend, who went ramstam to
    law
  Because Petre had styled him a poor Hebraist ;
And you see how the jury, in spite of his fury,
  Gave him comfort far less than one jug of gin-
    twist.

Mr. Leslie and Dr. Olinthus Petre.

20.

Leslie and
Kit North.

And therefore, I guess, sir, the *celebre* Professor,
    Even though culpably quizzed as a mere sciolist,
Would have found it much meeter to have laughed
    at old Petre,
And got drunk with Kit North o'er a jug of gin-
    twist.

21.

Stranguary.

Its medical virtues   *   *   *   *
     *   *   *   *   *   *   *
     *   *   *   *   *   *   *
     *   *   *   *   *   *   *
     *   *   *   *   a jug of gin-twist.

22.

Brockden
Brown.

By its magical aid a toper is made,
    Like Brockden Brown's hero, a ventriloquist ;
For my belly cries out, with an audible shout,
    " Fill up every chink with a jug of gin-twist."

23.

Cosmogony.

Geologers all, great, middling, and small,
    Whether fiery Plutonian or wet Neptunist,
Most gladly, it seems, seek proofs for their schemes
    In the water, or spirit, of a jug of gin-twist.

24.

Geology.

These grubbers of ground (whom God may
    confound !),
    Forgetting transition, trap, hornblende, or schist,
And all other sorts, think only of quartz—
    I mean, of the quarts in a jug of gin-twist.

25.

Parnassus.

Though two dozen of verse I've contrived to
    rehearse,
    Yet still I can sing like a true melodist ;

For they are but asses who think that Parnassus
  In spirit surpasses a jug of gin-twist.

26.

It makes you to speak Dutch, Latin, or Greek ;   The Massora.
  Even learning Chinese very much 'twould assist :
I'll discourse you in Hebrew, provided that ye brew
  A most Massorethical jug of gin-twist.

27.

When its amiable stream, all enveloped in steam,   The Picturesque.
  Is dashed to and fro by a vigorous wrist,
How sweet a cascade every moment is made
  By the artist who fashions a jug of gin-twist !

28.

Sweet stream ! There is none but delights in thy   Whiggery.
    flow,
  Save that vagabond villain, the Whig atheist ;
For done was the job for his patron, Sir Bob,*
  When he dared to wage war 'gainst a jug of
    gin-twist.

29.

Don't think by its name, from Geneva it came,   John Calvin.
  The sour little source of the Kirk Calvinist—
A fig for Jack Calvin ! My processes alvine
  Are much more rejoiced by a jug of gin-twist.

30.

Let the *Scotsman* delight in malice and spite,   Michael Angelo;
  The black-legs at Brooks's in hazard or whist ;   Taylor, Esq. M.P. &c.
Tom Dibdin in books, Micky Taylor in cooks :
  My pleasure is fixed in a jug of gin-twist.

* Sir R. Walpole ; justly turned out for taxing gin. He was the last
decent man who committed Whiggery, nevertheless.—M. OD.

31

<table>
<tr><td>Precious
stones.</td><td>

Though the point of my nose grow as red as a rose
    Or rival in hue a superb amethyst,
Yet no matter for that, I tell you 'tis flat,
    I shall still take a pull at a jug of gin-twist.

</td></tr>
</table>

32.

<table>
<tr><td>Wise men of
Greece.</td><td>

There was old Cleobulus, who, meaning to fool us,
    Gave out for his saying, ΤΟ ΜΕΤΡΟΝ ΑΡΙΣΤ';
But he'd never keep measure, if he had but the
        pleasure
Of washing his throat with a jug of gin-twist.

</td></tr>
</table>

33.

<table>
<tr><td>Kisses.</td><td>

There are dandies and blockheads, who vapour
    and boast
Of the favours of girls they never have kissed;
That is not the thing, and therefore, by jing!
    I kiss while I'm praising my jug of gin-twist.

</td></tr>
</table>

34.

<table>
<tr><td>Plato.</td><td>

While over the glass I should be an ass
    To make moping love like a dull Platonist;
That ne'er was my fashion : I swear that my passion
    Is as hot as itself for a jug of gin-twist.

</td></tr>
</table>

35.

<table>
<tr><td>Θαλαττα
θαλαττα.</td><td>

Although it is time to finish my rhyme,
    Yet the subject's so sweet I can scarcely desist;
While its grateful perfume is delighting the room,
    How can I be mute o'er a jug of gin-twist?

</td></tr>
</table>

36.

<table>
<tr><td>God save
the King.</td><td>

Yet since I've made out, without any doubt,
    Of its merits and glories a flourishing list,

</td></tr>
</table>

Let us end with a toast, which we cherish the most :
   Here's "GOD SAVE THE KING!" in a glass of
      gin-twist.

37.

Then I bade him good-night in a most jolly plight, **Moral.**
   But I'm sorry to say that my footing I missed ;
All the stairs I fell down, so I battered my crown,
   And got two black eyes from a jug of gin-twist.

Odoherty on Werner.*

WE are exceedingly sorry for Mr. John Murray. Time was when it was the finest thing in the world to be Lord Byron's publisher. The whole reading population of Great Britain and Ireland was in a breathless state—

"One general hush expectant reigned from shore to shore"—

when a new work of the gifted peer was announced. When it appeared, ten or twelve thousand copies were disposed of in a week or ten days ; the copy-money was thus cleared in the twinkling of an eye, and fine pickings remained in the subsequent editions for the worthy bibliopolist's own private benefit and advantage. Now, alas! how are the mighty fallen ! A new tragedy of Lord Byron's is degraded ere it comes forth, for it receives as many preliminary puffs, in the shape of advertisements, as even a new "Voyage" of Mother Morgan's. But out comes the production, and there is an end of even this little buzz. Very few copies are sold at the first brush—not a great many more, perhaps, than of a new book by Southey or Wordsworth. Nobody buys the pig in a poke,—that is, nobody orders the tragedy merely because that name is on the title-page. In short, that *prestige* is among the things that have gone by. Lord Byron is no longer—we do not say *the* author of the day—he is no longer among the first, scarcely even among the second-rate favourites.

Meantime (and it is on this account we so much pity Murray) the noble scribe is probably by no means convinced of the extent to which his reputation has "progressed" the wrong way. His demands of money, for he is well known

* Werner: a Tragedy. By Lord Byron. 8vo. Murray, London.

to like cash almost as well as fame, still continue to be on the same sort of scale; and the unfortunate bookseller must be refunding, in the shape of *honorariums* for bulky tragedies, the very shiners which he pocketed years ago as his own fair share of the profits arising from tales, charming little tales, to which the said tragedies bear no more resemblance than the Newcastle-waggon does to Lord Fife's phæton and four.

But this is not all the extent of the evil. Every new affair of this mediocre and unpopular sort acts as a terrible drag upon the sale of Lord Byron's works as collected in volumes. "No," says the hesitating customer, "no, my good friend, I won't bite. I think I shall wait a little, and see whether he mends again. If it were only Lara, and the Corsair, and so forth, I would have bought your books; but, Lord love you! have not I got Sardanapalus, and his brethren, some of them at least—by themselves? and do you really expect me to buy *them* over again, merely because you have got them printed on a smaller type?" In fact, a book, even a book of great merit, is unsaleable when it grows too big. What, therefore, must be the fate of such a book as the "Works of Lord Byron" now constitute? The booksellers have always sold Milton's poetry apart from Milton's prose; and in like fashion Mr Murray must ere long, in common prudence, separate Lord Byron's early works of genius from the masses of Balaam under which he has of late been doing his best to bury all our recollections of their brightness.

There are a set of blockheads, such as "the Council of Ten" (who, by the way, are the gravest asses going), who pretend to think that the sale of Byron's works has been knocked down merely by the public indignation against the immoralities of his Don Juan, and the baseness and blasphemy of his Pisan production, "The Liberal." But this is mere humbug. The public curiosity is always stimulated to an astonishing degree by clever blackguardism; and a book of real wickedness and real talent, although it may not always be exhibited in the boudoir, is pretty sure to find its way into every house that has any pretensions to be "*comme il faut*." The book that cannot "be passed into families" is your stupid, your dull, your uninteresting and unreadable one—your "Hallam's Middle Ages," for example, your "Southey's History of the Peninsular War," your "Book of the Church," your "Doge of Venice," your "Pretyman's Life of Pitt," *et hoc genus omne quod odi*. These, indeed, are works which the most hungry reader can take his chance of borrowing from the circulating library the next time he is rheumatical at a watering-place. This is not the sort of thing that turns the penny in a moment. It is precisely that clumsy kind of manufacture that breaks the back of the bookseller with its leaden weight. Therefore, look sharp, Mr. Murray, and don't you buy your pigs in the poke any more than other people.

This bookseller has published a list of forthcoming works just now, that fills us with many and grievous apprehensions. The "Narrative" of Captain Franklin will do very well in hotpressed, to a moderate extent. The second series of D'Israeli's Curiosities, if it be as good a book as the first, will answer the turn to a hair; but if, like most second serieses, it is inferior, it will weigh down its elder brother, just as the Marino Falieros have oppressed the Giaour and Parasina. The "Suffolk Papers"!!! We wonder, after the total failure of the "Walpole Memoirs," anybody has ventured on them. The "Connection of Christianity with Human Happiness" will not go down. The "Latin Grammar of Scheller" is a capital book, and, if it is well translated, may have as great a run as Mrs. Rundle, and put many a cool thousand in Mr. Murray's pocket. The "Welsh Scenery" will not pass—remember Boydell! The "General Officer" is a fair travelling name for a book. "Vestiges of Ancient Manners and Customs discoverable in Italy and Sicily, by the Rev. James Blunt, A.M., Fellow of St. John's College, Cambridge, and late one of the Travelling Bachelors of that University," is another smooth title, and probably three hundred may be disposed of. About fifty will be the utmost sale of the "Expedition to Dongola." The "Abridgment of Paradise Lost, by Mrs. Siddons" ! ! !—What shall we say of such a notion? The next thing, no doubt, will be an abridgment of Pope's Homer by Sam Rogers. Really, really, these literary Christmas boxes should be left to " Family Bowdler."

But enough of this. The plain truth of the matter is, that many of the works in this long list *may* turn out to be very good ones, in their several ways, and we hope they will do so. But is there one of them that has the least chance of being considered AN ADDITION TO THE LITERATURE OF ENGLAND? Certainly not, unless indeed it be " Ada Reis," which, being a novel, may of course, for aught we know, be as fine as " Anastasius," or as poor as " Grahame Hamilton." With this exception, and surely we are the very soul of candour in considering it as one, Mr. Murray does not announce any new book that *can* make a noise. Now, our fear is that, hampered as he is with Lord Byron's prolific and yet unproductive cacoethes, this liberal and naturally enterprising publisher is really compelled to keep out of other speculations that might, under such able management as his, have brilliant and triumphant success. He is like old Michael Scott, with the rashly-conjured fiend to whom he was *obliged* to furnish work ; and who, after having cleft mountains in twain, and hung eternal bridges by the touch of his wand over the most terrific torrents, was at last fain to wear out his time " in the weaving of rope-sands ;" an allegorical expression, no doubt, to designate the manufacture of threadless, knotless, endless, useless mysteries, tragedies, and dramas.

When Lord Byron first announced himself as a tragedian in regular form, there is no doubt that public curiosity was strongly, most strongly, excited. " Marino Faliero, Doge of Venice," was a sad damper, yet nobody could deny that there was great and novel beauty in the conception of one character, that of the old Doge's young wife ; and we all said, this is a first attempt, and Byron may hereafter write a tragedy

worthy of Byron.   Then came Sardanapalus—on the whole
a heavy concern also; but still there was *Myrrha*, and there
was the Vision of Nimrod and Semiramis, and there was the
noble arming of the roused voluptuary; and these fine things
in so far checked the frown of reprehension.   "The two
Foscari" was greatly inferior; in fact, it contained a plot
than which nothing could be more exquisitely absurd and
unnatural, characters strained almost to the ludicrous, versification as clumsy as the grinding of the tread-mill, and
one splendid passage, just one.   "Cain, a Mystery," was worse
and worse.   Byron dared to measure himself with Milton, and
came off as poorly as Belial might have done from a contest
with Michael.   Crude metaphysics, as old as the hills, and
as barren—bald, threadbare blasphemies and puerile ravings
formed the staple of the piece.   The only tolerable touches,
those of domestic love and the like, were visibly borrowed
from Gesner's DEATH OF ABEL : and, in short, one of the
most audacious of all the insults that have ever been heaped
upon the faith and feelings of a Christian land was also one
of the most feeble and ineffectual.   Thank God! Cain was
abandoned to the Radicals, and, thank God! it was too
radically dull to be popular even among them.

Nevertheless, it is not to be denied that even in Cain
some occasional flashes of Lord Byron's genius were discernible; there was some deep and thrilling poetry in Cain's contemplation of the stars, enough to recall for a moment the
brighter and more sustained splendours of Manfred.

But now at last has come forth a tragedy by the same
hand, which is not only worse than any of those we have
been naming, but worse, far worse, than we, even after
reading and regretting them, could have believed it possible
for the noble author to indite—a lame and mutilated *rifaccia-
mento* of one of Miss Lee's Canterbury Tales ; a thing which,
so far from possessing, scarcely even claims, any merit beyond
that of turning English prose into English blank verse—a
production, in short, which is entitled to be classed with no
dramatic works in our language that we are acquainted with,
except, perhaps, the common paste-and-scissors dramas from

the Waverley Novels. Ye gods! what a descent is here for the proud soul of Harold!

We are not so absurd as to say, or to think, that a dramatist has no right to make free with other people's fables. On the contrary, we are quite aware that that particular species of genius which is exhibited in the construction of plots never at any period flourished in England. We all know that Shakespeare himself took his stories from Italian novels, Danish sagas, English chronicles, Plutarch's lives, from anywhere rather than from his own invention. But did he take the whole of Hamlet, or Juliet, or Richard III., or Anthony and Cleopatra, from any of these foreign sources? Did he not *invent*, in the noblest sense of the word, all the *characters* of his pieces? Who dreams that any old Italian novelist could have formed the imagination of such a creature as Juliet? Who dreams that the HAMLET of Shakespeare, the princely enthusiast, the melancholy philosopher, that spirit refined even to pain, that most incomprehensible and unapproachable of all the creations of human genius, is the same being, in anything but the name, with the rough, strong-hearted, bloody-handed, old AMLETT of the North? Or who is there that supposes Goethe to have taken the character of *his* FAUST from the old ballads and penny pamphlets about the Devil and Doctor Faustus? Or who, to come nearer home, imagines that Lord Byron himself found *his* Sardanapalus in Dionysius of Halicarnassus?

But here Lord Byron has *invented* nothing, absolutely, positively, undeniably NOTHING. There is not one incident in his play, not even the most trivial, that is not to be found in the novel from which it is taken; occurring exactly in the same manner, brought about by exactly the same agents, and producing exactly the same effects on the plot. And then as to the characters, why, not only is every one of them to be found in the novel, but every one of them is to be found there far more fully and powerfully developed. Indeed, but for the preparation which we had received from our old familiarity with Miss Lee's own admirable work, we rather incline to think that we should have been altogether unable to comprehend the gist of her noble imitator, or rather copier, in several of what seem to be meant for his most elaborate delineations. The fact is that this undeviating closeness, this humble fidelity of IMITATION, is a thing so perfectly new in *literature*, in anything worthy of the name of literature, that we are sure no one who has not read the Canterbury Tales will be able to form the least conception of what it amounts to. Again we must come back to the arras-work; and we now most solemnly assure our readers that unless our worthy friend, Mr. Daniel Terry, is entitled to be called a poet for *his* Rob Roy, or *his* Guy Mannering, my Lord Byron has no sort of title, none in the world, to be considered as having acted the part of a poet in the concoction and execution of *his* WERNER.

Those who have never read Miss Lee will, however, be pleased with this production; for, in truth, the story is one of the most powerfully-conceived, one of the most picturesque, and at the same time instructive stories that we are, or are ever likely to be, acquainted with. Indeed, thus led as we are to name Harriet Lee, for the first time, in these pages, we cannot allow the opportunity to pass without saying that we have always considered her works as standing upon the very verge of the very first rank of excellence in the species to which they belong; that is to say, as inferior to no English novels whatever, excepting only those of Fielding, Sterne, Smollett, Richardson, Defoe, Radcliffe, Godwin, Edgeworth, and *the Great Known*. It would not, perhaps, be going too far to say that the Canterbury Tales exhibit more of *that* species of invention which, as we have remarked a little above, was never common in English literature, than any of the works even of those first-rate novelists we have named, with the single exception of Fielding himself. Suppose almost any one of the Canterbury Tales to have been put in MS. into the hands of Miss Edgeworth, or *the Known*, and suppose the work to have been rewritten with that power and the various excellence which these two great living writers possess, and there can be little question that we should have had something worthy of casting even NIGEL or

THE ABSENTEE into the shade; that is to say, in so far as these books are to be considered as serious delineations of human feeling and passion. For example, take this very tale of "Kruitzner," or "The Landlady's Story." Considering them merely as fables, we have no hesitation in saying that they are far better fables than any original and invented one that can be found in any of the works of any of our living poets or novelists. This is high praise; but we feel that we are doing no more than justice in bestowing it.

After speaking in such terms of Miss Lee's fable we shall not, of course, be so daring as to attempt an analysis of it here. Let it be sufficient to say that we consider it as possessing mystery, and yet clearness, as to its structure: strength of characters, and admirable contrast of characters; and, above all, the most lively interest blended with and subservient to the most affecting of moral lessons.

The main idea which lies at the root of it is: *the horror of an erring father (who, having been detected in vice by his son, has dared to defend his own sin, and so to perplex the son's notions of moral rectitude) in finding that the son, in his turn, has pushed the false principles thus instilled to the last and worst extreme, in hearing his own sophistries flung in his teeth by a—*MURDERER. The scene in which the first part of this idea is developed in Lord Byron's tragedy is by far the finest one in it; and we shall quote alongside of it the original passages in the novel, in order that our readers may be enabled to form their own opinion.

LORD BYRON.	MISS LEE.
Ulric. I think you wrong him, (Excuse me for the phrase); but Stralenheim *Is not what you prejudge him, or, if so,* *He owes me something both for past and present:* *I saved his life, he therefore trusts in me;* *He hath been plundered too, since he came hither;*	" ' Stralenheim,' said Conrad, ' does not appear to me altogether the man you take him for:—but were it even otherwise, he owes me gratitude not only for the past, but for what he supposes to be my present employment. I saved his life, and he therefore places confidence in me. He has been robbed last night, is sick, a stranger, and in no condition to discover the villain who has plun-

LORD BYRON.

*Is sick, a stranger, and as such not
　now
Able to trace the villain who hath
　robbed him:
I have pledged myself to do so; and
　the business
Which brought me here was chiefly
　that:* but I
Have found, in searching for an-
　other's dross,
My own whole treasure—you, my
　parents!
　Werner. (agitatedly) *Who
Taught you to mouth that name of
　"villain"?*
　Ulric. What
More noble name belongs to com-
　mon thieves?

　Werner. Who taught you thus to
　brand an unknown being
With an infernal stigma?
　Ulric. *My own feelings
Taught me to name a ruffian from
　his deeds.*
　Werner. *Who taught you*, long-
　sought, and ill-found boy! *that
It would be safe for my own son to
　insult me?*
　Ulric. *I named a villain.　What
is there in common
With such a being and my father?*
　Werner. *Everything!
That ruffian is thy father!
Josephine.* Oh, my son!
Believe him not—and yet!——(*her
　voice falters.*)
　Ulric (*starts, looks earnestly at
　Werner, and then says slowly*)
And you avow it?
　Werner. *Ulric, before you dare
　despise your father,
Learn to divine and judge his actions.*
　Young,

MISS LEE.

dered him.　I have pledged myself
to do it, and the business on which
I sought the Intendant was chiefly
that.'"

"'The Count felt as though he had
received a stroke upon the brain.
Death in any form, unaccompanied
with dishonour, would have been
preferable to the pang that shot
through both that and his heart.
Indignantly had he groaned under
the remorse of the past: the humiliation thus incurred by it he would
hardly have tolerated from any human being; yet was it brought home
to him through a medium so bitterly afflicting as defied all calcula-
tion.　At the word *villain* his lips
quivered, and his eyes flashed fire.
It was the vice of his character ever
to convert the subjects of self-re-
proach into those of indignation.

"'And who,' said he, starting furiously from his seat, 'has entitled
you to brand thus with ignominious
epithets a being you do no know?
Who,' he added *with increasing
agitation*, '*has taught you that it
would be safe even for my son
to insult me?*'

"'*It is not necessary to know the
person of a ruffian*,' replied Conrad
indignantly, 'to give him the appellation he merits: *and what is there
in common between my father and
such a character?*'

"'*Everything*,' said Siegendorf
bitterly, 'for that ruffian was your
father!'

"Conrad started back with in-
credulity and amazement, then measured the Count with a long and
earnest gaze, as though, unable to
disbelieve the fact, he felt inclined
to doubt whether it were really his
father who avowed it.

"'Conrad,' exclaimed the latter,

LORD BYRON.

*Rash, new to life, and reared in
  luxury's lap,
Is it for you' to measure passion's
  force,
Or misery's temptation? Wait—
  (not long,
It cometh like the night, and quickly)
  Wait!—
Wait till, like me, your hopes are
  blighted—till
Sorrow and shame are handmaids
  of your cabin;
Famine and poverty your guests at
  table;
Despair your bedfellow—then rise,
  but not
From sleep, and judge! Should that
  day e'er arrive—
Should you see then the serpent, who
  hath coiled
Himself around all that is dear and
  noble
Of you and yours, lie slumbering in
  your path,
With but his folds between your steps
  and happiness,
When he, who lives but to tear from
  you name,
Lands, life itself, lies at your mercy,
  with
Chance your conductor; midnight
  for your mantle;
The bare knife in your hand, and
  earth asleep,
Even to your deadliest foe; and he
  as 't were
Inviting death, by looking like it,
  while
His death alone can save you:—
  Thank your God!
If then, like me, content with petty
  plunder,
You turn aside——I did so.*
  Ulric. *But*——
  Werner. (abruptly) *Hear me!
I will not brook a human voice—
  scarce dare*

VOL. I.

MISS LEE.

interpreting his looks, and in a tone
that ill disguised the increasing anguish of his own soul, ' before you
thus presume to chastise me with
your eye, learn to understand my
actions! Young and experienced in
the world—reposing hitherto in the
bosom of indulgence and luxury, is
it for *you* to judge of the force of the
passions, or the temptations of misery? Wait till like me you have
blighted your fairest hopes—have
endured humiliation and sorrow,
poverty and famine—before you pretend to judge of their effect on you.
Should that miserable day ever arrive
—should *you* see the being at your
mercy who stands between you and
everything that is dear or noble in
life; who is ready to tear from
you your name, your inheritance,
your very life itself; congratulate
your own heart if, like me, you are
content with petty plunder, and are
not tempted to exterminate a serpent, who now lives, perhaps, to
sting us all!

LORD BYRON.

Listen to my own (if that be human
   still)—
Hear me! you do not know this man
   —I do.
He's mean, deceitful, avaricious.
   You
Deem yourself safe, as young and
   brave; but learn
None are secure from desperation,
   few
From subtilty. My worst foe, Stra-
   lenheim,
Housed in a prince's palace, couched
   within
A prince's chamber, lay below my
   knife!
An instant—a mere motion—the least
   impulse—
Had swept him and all fears of mine
   from earth.
He was within my power—my knife
   was raised—
Withdrawn—and I'm in his:—are
   you not so?
Who tells you that he knows you not?
   Who says
He hath not lured you here to end
   you? or
To plunge you, with your parents, in
   a dungeon?

               (He pauses.

Ulric. *Proceed, proceed!*
Werner. Me he hath ever known,
And hunted through each change of
   time—name—fortune—
And why not you? Are you more
   versed in men?
He wound snares round me; flung
   along my path
Reptiles whom, in my youth, I would
   have spurned
Even from my presence; but, in
   spurning now,
Fill only with fresh venom. Will
   you be
More patient? Ulric—Ulric!—
   there are crimes

MISS LEE.

" 'You do not know this man,' continued he with the same incoherent eagerness, and impetuously silencing Conrad, who would have spoken—'I do! I believe him to be mean, sordid, deceitful! You will conceive yourself safe because you are young and brave! Learn, however, from the two instances before you, none are so secure but desperation or subtilty may reach them! Stralenheim in the palace of a prince was in my power! My knife was held over him! A single moment would have swept him from the face of the earth, and with all my future fears: I forbore—and I am now in his. Are you certain that you are not so too? Who assures you he does not know you? Who tells you that he has not lured you into his society, either to rid himself of you for ever, or to plunge you with your family into a dungeon? *Me*, it is plain, he has known invariably through every change of fortune or of name—and why not you? *Me* he has entrapt—are you more discreet? He has wound the snares of Idenstein around me :—of a reptile whom, a few years ago, I would have spurned from my presence, and whom, in spurning now, I have furnished with fresh venom :—Will *you* be more patient !—— Conrad, Conrad, there are crimes rendered venial by the occasion, and temptations too exquisite for human fortitude to master or endure.' The Count passionately struck his hand on his forehead as he spoke, and rushed out of the room.

"Conrad, whose lips and countenance had more than once announced an impatient desire to interrupt his father during the early part of his discourse, stunned by the wildness and vehemence with which it was

LORD BYRON.

Made venial by the occasion, and
temptations   [forbear.
Which nature cannot master or
Ulric (looks first at him, and then at
Josephine).
My mother!
  Werner. Ay! I thought so: you
  have now
Only one parent. I have lost alike
Father and son, and stand alone.
  Ulric. But stay!
    (*Werner rushes out of the*
    chamber.
  Josephine (to Ulric). Follow him
  not, until this storm of passion
Abates. Think'st thou that, were it
  well for him,
I had not followed?
  Ulric. I obey you, mother,
Although reluctantly. My first act
  shall not
Be one of disobedience.
  Josephine. Oh! he is good!
Condemn him not from his own
  mouth, but trust
To me, who have borne so much
  with him, and for him,
That this is but the surface of his
  soul,   [things.
And that the depth is rich in better
  Ulric. These then are but my
  father's principles?
My mother thinks not with him?
  Josephine. Nor doth he
Think as he speaks. Alas! long
  years of grief
Have made him sometimes thus.
  Ulric. *Explain to me*
More clearly, then, these claims of
  Stralenheim.

MISS LEE.

pursued, had sunk towards the close of it into profound silence. The anxious eyes of Josephine, from the moment they lost sight of her husband, had been turned towards her son; and, for the first time in her life, she felt her heart a prey to divided affections: for, while the frantic wildness of Siegendorf almost irresistibly impelled her to follow him, she was yet alive to all the danger of leaving Conrad a prey to reflections hostile to every sentiment of filial duty or respect. The latter, after a long silence, raised his inquiring looks to hers; and, whatever the impression under which his mind laboured, he understood too well the deep and painful sorrow imprinted on her countenance not instantly to conceal it.

" 'These are only the systems of my father,' said he, continuing earnestly to gaze on her. 'My mother thinks not with him!'

"Josephine spoke not: there was an oppression at her heart that robbed her of the power. Conrad covered his face with his hand, and reclined it for a moment on her shoulder.

" 'Explain to me,' said he, after a second pause, 'what are the claims of Stralenheim.'"

If this be not enough, pass to the only other scene in the play which can be supposed to possess equal interest; that, namely, in which the unhappy father is reproached by the son, whose bloody guilt he has just learnt to believe—from whose countenance he is shrinking in the most exquisite of horrors. The *supposed* murderer stands before father and son; HE has told the terrible truth, and dreads violence; the father reassures him, and he goes on thus—

<table>
<tr><td>

LORD BYRON.

Gabor. I have still a further
  shield.
I did not enter Prague alone; and
  should I
Be put to rest with Stralenheim,
  there are
Some tongues without will wag in
  my behalf.
Be brief in your decision!

</td><td>

MISS LEE.

"'I have yet an additional security,' replied the Hungarian, after a moment's meditation. 'I did not enter Prague a solitary individual; and there are tongues without that will speak for me, although I should even share the fate of Stralenheim! Let your deliberation, Count, be short,' he added, again glancing towards Conrad, 'and be the future at your peril no less than mine! Where shall I remain?'

"Siegendorf opened a door that admitted to one turret of the castle, of which he knew all other egress was barred; the Hungarian started, and his presence of mind evidently failed him. He looked around with the air of a man who is conscious that, relying on a sanguine hope, he has ventured too far, and neither knows how to stand his ground nor to recede; yet he read truth and security in the countenance of Siegendorf, although not unmingled with contempt. By an excessive effort of dissimulation, he therefore recovered his equanimity, and made a step towards the spot pointed out to him.

</td></tr>
<tr><td>

Siegendorf. I will be so.
My word is sacred and irrevocable
Within *these* walls, but it extends no
  further.

Gabor. I'll take it for so much.
Siegendorf (points to Ulric's sabre,

</td><td>

"'My promise is solemn, sacred, irrevocable,' said Siegendorf, seeing him pause again upon the threshold. 'It extends not, however, beyond my own walls.'

"'I accept the conditions,' replied the other. His eye, while speaking,

</td></tr>
</table>

LORD BYRON.

still upon the ground). Take
also *that*—
I saw you eye it eagerly, and him
Distrustfully.
  Gabor (*takes up the sabre*). I will;
and so provide
To sell my life—not cheaply.
  [*Gabor goes into the turret,
which Siegendorf closes.*]
  Siegendorf (*advances to Ulric*).
Now, Count Ulric!
For son I dare not call thee—What
say'st thou?
  Ulric. His tale is true.
  Siegendorf. True, monster!
  Ulric. Most true, father;
And you did well to listen to it; what
We know, we can provide against.
He must
Be silenced.
  Siegendorf. Ay, with half of my
domains;
And with the other half, could he
and thou
Unsay this villainy?
  Ulric. It is no time
For trifling or dissembling. I have
  said   [silenced.
His story's true; and he too must be
  Siegendorf. How so?
  Ulric. As Stralenheim is. Are
you so dull
As never to have hit on this before?
When we met in the garden, what
except
Discovery in the act could make me
know
His death? Or had the prince's
household been
Then summoned, would the cry for
  the police   [should I
Been left to such a stranger? Or
Have loitered on the way? Or could
  you, *Werner*,   [fears,
The object of the Baron's hate and

MISS LEE.

fell on the sabre of Conrad; and the
Count, who perceived it did so,
invited him by a look * to possess
himself of it. He then closed the door
of the turret upon him, and advanced
hastily towards his son.

" ' You have done well,' said the
latter, raising his head at the near
approach of his father, ' to listen to
this man's story. The evil we cannot
measure, we cannot guard against;
but it would be fruitless to temporise
further. He must be silenced more
effectually.' The Count started.
' With you,' pursued Conrad, drawing nearer and dropping his voice,
' it would be unwise longer to dis-
semble. His *narration is true.*
Are you so credulous as never to have
guessed this?' added he, on perceiv-
ing the speechless agony of his father,
' or so weak as to tremble at the acknowledgment? Could it escape you
that, at the hour we met in the garden at M——, nothing short of a
discovery during the very act could
have made the death of Baron Stralenheim known to any but him who
caused it? Did it appear probable,'
continued he, with the tone of a man
who is secretly roused to fury by a
consciousness of the horror he in-
spires, 'that if the Prince's household
had really been alarmed, the care of
summoning the police should devolve
on one who hardly knew an avenue

* How much better is this *look* than its dilution into language in the opposite
column! But *sic fere omnia.*

LORD BYRON.

Have fled—unless by many an hour
  before
Suspicion woke? I sought and
  fathomed you,
Doubting if you were false or
  feeble; I
Perceived you were the latter; and
  yet so
Confiding have I found you that I
  doubted
At times your weakness.

Siegendorf. Parricide! no less
Than   common   stabber!   What
  deed of my life,
Or thought of mine, could make you
  deem me fit
For your accomplice?
Ulric. Father, do not raise
The devil you cannot lay, between
  us. This
Is time for union and for action, not
For family disputes. While *you*
  were tortured,
Could *I* be calm? Think you that
  I have heard
This fellow's tale without some feel-
  ing? You
Have taught me feeling for *you* and
  myself;
For whom or what else did you ever
  teach it?
Siegendorf. Oh! my dead father's
  curse! 'Tis working now.
Ulric. Let it work on! The grave
  will keep it down!
Ashes are feeble foes: it is more easy
To baffle such than countermine a
  mole,
Which winds its blind but living path
  beneath you.
Yet hear me still!—If *you* condemn
  me, yet

MISS LEE.

of the town? Or was it credible that such a one should, unsuspected, have loitered on the way? Least of all could it be even possible that Kruitzner, already marked out and watched, could have escaped unpursued had he not had many hours the start of suspicion? I sounded, I fathomed your soul both before and at the moment; I doubted whether it was feeble or artificial.   I will own that I thought it the former, or I should have trusted you.   Yet such has been the excess of your apparent credulity that I have even at intervals disbelieved its existence!'

"'Monster!' exclaimed Siegendorf, frantic with emotion, 'what action of my life, what sentiment of my soul, ever authorised you to suspect that I would abet a deed thus atrocious?'

"'Father, father,' interrupted Conrad abruptly, and his form seemed to grow before the astonished eyes of the Count, 'beware how you rouse a devil between us that neither may be able to control! We are in no temper nor season for domestic dissension. Do you suppose that while your soul has been harrowed up, mine has been unmoved? or that I have really listened to this man's story with indifference? I too can feel for myself; for what being besides did your example ever teach me to feel? Listen to me!' he added, silencing the Count with a wild and alarming tone. 'If your present condemnation of me be just, I have listened to you at least once too often! Remember *who* told me, when at M——, that there were crimes rendered venial by the occasion; *who* painted the excesses of passion as the trespasses of humanity; *who* held the balance suspended

LORD BYRON.

Remember *who* hath taught me once too often
To listen to him? *Who* proclaimed to me
That *there were crimes* made venial by the occasion?
That passion was our nature? that the goods
Of Heaven waited on the goods of Fortune?
Who showed me his humanity secured
By his *nerves* only? *Who* deprived me of
All power to vindicate myself and race
In open day? By his disgrace which stamped
(It might be) bastardy on me, and on
Himself—a *felon's* brand! The man who is
At once both warm and weak invites to deeds
He longs to do, but dare not. Is it strange
That I should *act* what you could *think?*
We have done
With right and wrong: and now must only ponder
Upon effects, not causes. Stralenheim,
Whose life I saved from impulse, as, *unknown,*
I would have saved a peasant's or a dog's, I slew
Known as our foe—but not from vengeance. He
Was a rock in our way which I cut through,
As doth the bolt, because it stood between us
And our true destination—but not idly.
As stranger I preserved him, and he *owed me*

MISS LEE.

before my eyes between the goods of fortune and those of honour: *who* aided the mischief-stirring spirit within me, by showing me a specious probity, secured only by an infirmity of nerves. Were you so little skilled in human nature as not to know that the man who is at once intemperate and feeble engenders the crimes he does not commit? or is it so wonderful that *I* should dare to act what *you* dared to think? I have nothing now to do with its guilt or its innocence. It is our mutual interest to avert its consequences. We stood on a precipice down which one of three must inevitably have plunged; for I will not deny that I knew my own situation to be as critical as yours. I therefore precipitated Stralenheim! *You* held the torch! *You* pointed out the path! Show me now that of safety; or let me show it you!'

LORD BYRON.

His *life;* when due, I but resumed
  the debt.
He, you, and I stood o'er a gulf
  wherein
I have plunged our enemy. *You*
  kindled first
The torch—*you* showed the path ;
  now trace me that
Of safety—or let me !
  Siegendorf. I have done with life.
  Ulric. Let us have done with that
    which cankers life—
Familiar feuds and vain recrimina-
  tions
Of things which cannot be undone.
  We have
No more to learn or hide : I know
  no fear,
And have within these very walls
  men who
(Although you know them not) dare
  venture all things.

You stand high with the State ; what
  passes here
Will not excite her too great curiosity.
Keep your own secret, keep a steady
  eye,
Stir not, and speak not ;—leave the
  rest to me :
We must have no *third* babblers
  thrust between us.

MISS LEE.

" ' Let us have done with retro-
spection,' said Conrad, lowering his
tone, as not wholly insensible to the
effect his words had produced on his
father. 'We have nothing more
either to learn or to conceal from
each other. I have courage and
partisans ; they are even within the
walls, though you do not know them !
Siegendorf shuddered. Alas ! these
then had been the substitutes for
those affectionate and innocent
hearts whose welcome had rendered
his return to his native domain, in
the first instance, so delightful !
these were the baleful spirits before
whose influence virtue and industry
alike had withered !

" ' You are favoured by the State,'
pursued Conrad, 'and it will, therefore, take little cognizance of what
passes within your jurisdicion ; it is
for me to guard against distrust
beyond it. Preserve an unchanged
countenance. Keep your own secret,'
he added, glancing emphatically
towards the turret, 'and without
your further interference I will for
ever secure you from the indiscretion
of a third person.' So saying he
left the hall."

Now we have to inform our readers that in every part of
this performance the imitator has trod with almost the same
degree of painful and humiliating exactness in the footsteps
of his precursor ; and, having done so, we have just one

question to ask: Could not Virginius Knowles, could not Conscience Shiel, could not any common setter of sixpenny claptraps, have done this feat quite as well as the author of Childe Harold and Don Juan?

Even the passages we have quoted for a different purpose may suffice to show (what, if it were worth while, we could easily show more largely) that in this new play Lord Byron retains the same nerveless and pointless kind of blank verse which was a sorrow to everybody in his former dramatic essays. It is indeed "most unmusical, most melancholy." "Ofs," "tos," "ands," "fors," "bys," "buts," and the like, are the most common conclusions of a line; there is no ease, no flow, no harmony "in linked sweetness long drawn out." Neither is there anything of abrupt fiery vigour to compensate for these defects. In a word, as to invention, this performance is nothing; as to composition, it is raw, poor, and unfinished; and while the modest cost of this servile thing is five shillings and sixpence sterling, there is nothing more easy than, by spending twopence in the nearest circulating library, to enjoy the perusal of the very same story as told by its original author gracefully, vigorously, and with all the alike indescribable and inalienable charm of originality.

WERNER, then, is, without all doubt, the most commonplace and unworthy production which Lord Byron has ever yet put forth. "Heaven and Earth," which we see advertised, and which, if we may credit the whispers of the literary circles, is nothing more than a dramatised edition of our friend Fogarty's excellent poem of Daniel O'Rourke, seems not unlikely to carry the declension of this once pre-eminent star even further. In a word, we have at length lost all hopes of Lord Byron's ever doing anything in the drama; and therefore, the sooner he gives that affair up, the better it will be for himself and for "all concerned."

The extremely heavy effect, speaking generally, of his lordship's quizzical "Vision of Judgment" may probably have been, in one point of view, consolatory to Mr. Murray's feelings; for it would have been doubly sad to be obliged to

print Lord Byron's bad things, and see other and inferior
people publishing good things of his (however blackguard)
under one's nose. But we, who have ever been among
the sincerest and humblest admirers of anything that
bears the stamp of true genius, are, we must fairly confess it, constrained to regard the whole affair with a very
gloomy eye.

The sum of all we have to say is, that we think Lord
Byron is in the fair way to dish both himself and his publisher if he goes on at the same rate for another season
or two. Let him pause now, and retrieve all he has lost—
and more than retrieve it—by one effort worthy of himself.
This is yet in his power; ere long it may not be so.

Pococurante.

I do not care a farthing about any man, woman, or child in the world. You think that I am joking, Jemmy; but you are mistaken. What! You look at me again with those honest eyes of yours staring with wonder, and making a demi-pathetic, demi-angry appeal for an exception in your favour. Well, Jemmy, I *do* care about you, my honest fellow; so uncork the other bottle.

Did you ever see me out of humour in your life for the tenth part of a second? Never, so help me, God! Did you ever hear me speak ill of another? I might, perhaps, have cracked a joke—indeed, I have cracked a good many such in my time—at a man's expense behind his back; but never have I said anything which I would not say to his face, or what I would not take from him with treble hardness of recoil, if it so pleased him to return it; but real *bonâ fide* evil-speaking was never uttered by me. I never quarrelled with any one. You are going to put me in mind of my duel with Captain Maxwell. I acknowledge I fought it, and fired three shots. What then? Could I avoid it? I was no more angry with him, when I sent the message, than I was at the moment of my birth. Duelling is an absurd custom of the country, which I must comply with when occasion requires. The occasion had turned up, and I fought of course. Never was I happier than when I felt the blood trickling over my shoulders, for the wise laws of honour were satisfied, and I was rid of the cursed trouble. I was sick of the puppyism of punctilio and the booby legislation of the seconds, and was glad to escape from it by a scratch. I made it up with Maxwell, who was an honest though a hot-headed and obstinate man, and you know I was executor to his will. Indeed he dined with me the very day-week after the duel. Yet, spite of this equanimity, I repeat it that I do not care for any human being on earth (the present company always excepted) more than I care for one of those filberts which you are cracking with such laudable assiduity.

Yes, it is true; I have borne myself towards my family unexceptionably, as the world has it. I married off my sisters, sent my brothers to the colleges, and did what was fair for my mother. But I shall not be hypocrite enough to pretend to high motives for so doing. My father's death left them entirely to me, and what could I do with them? Turn them out? That would be absurd, and just as absurd to retain them at home without treating them properly. They were *my* family. My own comforts would have been materially invaded by any other line of conduct. I therefore executed the filial and fraternal affections in a manner which will be a fine topic of panegyric for my obituary. God help the idiots who write such things! *They* to talk of motives, and feelings, and the impulses that sway the human heart—they, whose highest ambition it is to furnish provender, at so much a line, for magazine or newspaper! Yet from them shall I receive the tribute of a tear. The world shall be informed in due time, and I care not how soon, that "Died at his house, &c. &c., a gentleman, exemplary in every relation of life, whether we consider him as a son, a brother, a friend, or a citizen. His heart," and so on to the end of the fiddle-faddle. The winding-up of my family affairs, you know, is, that I have got rid of them all; that I pay the good people a visit once a month, and ask them to a humdrum dinner on my birthday, which you are perhaps aware occurs but once a year. I am alone. I feel that I am alone.

My politics, what then? I am, externally at least, a Tory, *à toute outrance*, because my father and my grandfather (and I cannot trace my genealogy any higher) were so before me. Besides, I think every gentleman should be a Tory;

there is an easiness, a suavity of mind, engendered by Tory-ism, which it is vain for you to expect from fretful Whiggery or bawling Radicalism, and such should be a strong dis-tinctive feature in every gentleman's character. And I admit that, in my youth, I did many queer things, and said many violent and nonsensical matters. But that fervour is gone. I am still outside the same; but inside how different! I laugh to scorn the nonsense I hear vented about me in the clubs which I frequent. The zeal about nothings, the bustle about stuff, the fears and the precautions against fancied dangers, the indignation against writings which no decent man thinks of reading, or against speeches which are but the essence of stupidity; in short, the whole tempest in a teapot appears to me to be ineffably ludicrous. I join now and then, nay very often, in these discussions; why should not I? Am I not possessed of the undoubted liberties of a Briton, invested with the full privilege of talking nonsense? And, if any of my associates laugh inside at me, why, I think them quite right.

But I have dirtied my fingers with ink, you say, and daubed other people's faces with them. I admit it. My pen has been guilty of various political *jeux d'esprit*, but let me whisper it, Jemmy, on *both* sides. Don't start; it is not worth while. My Tory quizzes I am suspected of; *suspected*, I say, for I am not such a goose as to let them be any more than mere matters of suspicion; but of quizzes against Tories I am no more thought guilty than I am of petty larceny. Yet such is the case. I write with no ill feeling; public men or people who thrust themselves before the public in any way I just look on as phantoms of the imagination, as things to throw off commonplaces about. You know how I assassinated Jack —— in the song which you transcribed for me; how it spread in thousands, to his great annoyance. Well, on Wednesday last he and I supped *tête-à-tête*, and a jocular fellow he is. It was an accidental rencontre; he was sulky at first, but I laughed and sung him into good humour. When the second bottle had loosened his tongue, he looked at me most sympathetically, and said, "May I ask you a question?" "A thousand," I replied, "provided you do not expect me to answer them." "Ah," he cried, "it was a shame for you to abuse me the way you did, and all for nothing; but, hang it, let bygones be bygones; you are too pleasant a fellow to quarrel with." I told him he appeared to be under a mistake. He shook his head, emptied his bottle, and we staggered home in great concord. In point of fact, men of sense think not of such things, and mingle freely in society as if they never occurred. Why then should I be supposed to have any feeling whatever, whether of anger or pleasure, about them?

My friends? Where are they? Ay, Jemmy, I do understand what that pressure of my hand means. But where is the other? Nowhere! Acquaintances I have in hundreds—boon companions in dozens, fellows to whom I make myself as agreeable as I can, and whose society gives me pleasure. There's Jack Meggot, the best joker in the world; Will Thomson, an unexceptionable ten-bottle-man; John Mortimer, a singer of most renowned social qualities; there's —but what need I enlarge the catalogue? You know the men I mean. I live with them, and that right gaily; but would one of them crack a joke the less, drink a glass the less, sing a song the less, if I died before morning? Not one—nor do I blame them, for, if they were engulfed in Tartarus, I should just go through my usual daily round, keep moving in the same monotonous treadmill of life, with other companions to help me through, as steadily as I do now. The friends of my boyhood are gone, ay! all—all gone! I have lost the old familiar faces, and shall not try for others to replace them. I am now happy with a mail-coach companion, whom I never saw before, and never will see again. My cronies come like shadows, so depart. Do you remember the story of Abou Hassan in some of the Oriental tales? He was squandering a fine property on some hollow friends, when he was advised to try their friendship by pretending poverty and asking their assistance.

It was refused, and he determined never to see them more, never to make a friend—nay, not even an acquaintance; but to sit, according to the custom of the East, by the way-side, and invite to his board the three first passers-by, with whom he spent the night in festive debauchery, making it a rule never to ask the same persons a second time. My life is almost the same. True it is that I know the exterior conformation, and the peculiar habits of those with whom I associate, but our hearts are ignorant of one another. They vibrate not together ; they are ready to enter into the same communication with any passer-by. Nay, perhaps, Hassan's plan was more social. He was relieved from inquiries as to the character of his table-mates. Be they fair, be they foul, they were nothing to him. I am tormented out of my life by such punctilios as I daily must submit to. I wonder you keep company, says a friend—*friend !* well, no matter—with R. He is a scoundrel ; he is suspected of having cheated fifteen years ago at play ; he drinks ale ; he fought shy in a duel business; he is a Whig, a Radical, a Muggletonian, a jumper, a moderate man, a Jacobin; he asked twice for soup, he wrote a libel, his father was a low attorney, nobody knows him in good society, &c. &c. &c. Why, what is it to me ? I care not whether he broke every commandment in the decalogue, provided he be a pleasant fellow, and that I am not mixed up with his offences. But the world will so mix me up in spite of myself. Burns used to say, the best company he was ever in was the company of professed black-guards. Perhaps he was right. I dare not try.

My early companions I *did* care for, and where are they ? Poor Tom Benson, he was my class-fellow at school; we occupied the same rooms in college, we shared our studies, our amusements, our flirtations, our follies, our dissipations together. A more honourable or upright creature never ex-isted. Well, sir, he had an uncle, lieutenant-colonel of a cavalry regiment, and at his request Tom bought a cornetcy in the corps. I remember the grand-looking fellow strutting about in the full splendour of his yet unspotted regimentals,

the cynosure of the bright eyes of the country town in which
he resided. He came to London, and then joined his
regiment. All was well for a while; but he had always an
unfortunate itch for play. In our little circle it did him no
great harm; but his new companions played high, and far
too skilfully for Tom; perhaps there was roguery, or perhaps
there was not: I never inquired. At all events, he lost all
his ready-money. He then drew liberally on his family; he
lost that too. In short, poor Tom at last staked his commission, and lost it with the rest. This, of course, could
not be concealed from the uncle, who gave him a severe
lecture, but procured him a commission in an infantry
regiment destined for Spain. He was to join it without
delay; but the infatuated fellow again risked himself, and
lost the infantry commission also. He now was ashamed or
afraid to face his uncle, and enlisted (for he was a splendid-
looking young man, who was instantly accepted) as a private
soldier in the Twenty-sixth Foot. I suppose that he found
his habits were too refined and too firmly fixed to allow him
to be satisfied with the scanty pay, and coarse food, and low
company of an infantry soldier. It is certain that he
deserted in a fortnight after enlistment. The measure of
poor Tom's degradation was not yet filled up. He had not
a farthing when he left the Twenty-sixth. He went to his
uncle's at an hour when he knew that he would not be at
home, and was with difficulty admitted by the servant, who
recognised him. He persuaded him at last that he meant
to throw himself on the mercy of his uncle, and the man,
who loved him—everybody of all degrees who knew him loved
him—consented to his admission. I am almost ashamed to
go on. He broke open his uncle's escritoire, and took from
it whatever money it contained, a hundred pounds or thereabouts, and slunk out of the house. Heavens! what were
my feelings when I heard this, when I saw him proclaimed
in the newspapers as a deserter and a thief! A thief! Tom
Benson a thief! I could not credit the intelligence of my
eyes or my ears. He whom I knew only five months before—

for so brief had his career been—would have turned with scorn and disgust from any action deviating a hair's-breadth from the highest honour. How he spent the next six months of his life I know not; but about the end of that period a letter was left at my door by a messenger, who immediately disappeared. It was from him. It was couched in terms of the most abject self-condemnation and the bitterest remorse. He declared he was a ruined man in character, in fortune, in happiness, in everything, and conjured me, for the sake of former friendship, to let him have five guineas, which he said would take him to a place of safety. From the description of the messenger, who, Tom told me in his note, would return in an hour, I guessed it was himself. When the time came, which he had put off to a moment of almost complete darkness, I opened the door to his fearful rap. It was he; I knew him at a glance as the lamp flashed over his face; and, uncertain as was the light, it was bright enough to let me see that he was squalid and in rags; that a fearful and ferocious suspicion, which spoke volumes as to the life he had lately led, lurked in his side-looking eyes—those eyes that a year before spoke nothing but joy and courage; and that a premature greyness had covered with piebald patches the once glossy black locks which straggled over his unwashed face, or through his tattered hat.

I had that he asked, perhaps more, in a paper in my hand. I put it into his. I had barely time to say "O Tom!" when he caught my hand, kissed it with burning lips, exclaimed "Don't speak to me, I am a wretch!" and, bursting from the grasp with which I wished to detain him, fled with the speed of an arrow down the street, and vanished into a lane. Pursuit was hopeless. Many years elapsed, and I heard not of him—no one heard of him. But about two years ago I was at a coffee-house in the Strand, when an officer of what they called the Patriots of South America staggered into the room. He was very drunk. His tawdry and tarnished uniform proclaimed the service to which he

belonged, and all doubt on the subject was removed by his
conversation. It was nothing but a tissue of curses on
Bolivar and his associates, who, he asserted, had seduced him
from his country, ruined his prospects, robbed him, cheated
him, and insulted him. How true these reproaches might
have been I knew not, nor do I care; but a thought struck me
that Tom might have been of this army, and I inquired, as,
indeed, I did of everybody coming from a foreign country, if
he knew anything of a man of the name of Benson. "Do
you?" stammered out the drunken patriot. "I do," was my
reply. "Do you care about him?" again asked the officer.
"I did—I do," again I retorted. "Why then," said he, "take
a short stick in your hand, and step across to Valparaiso; there
you will find him two feet under ground, snugly wrapt up in
a blanket. I was his sexton myself, and had not time to
dig him a deeper grave, and no way of getting a stouter
coffin. It will just do all as well. Poor fellow, it was all
the clothes he had for many a day before." I was shocked
at the recital, but Holmes was too much intoxicated to
pursue the subject any further. I called on him in the
morning, and learned that Benson had joined as a private
soldier in this desperate service, under the name of Maberly—
that he speedily rose to a command—was distinguished for
doing desperate actions, in which he seemed quite reckless
of life—had, however, been treated with considerable ingratitude—never was paid a dollar—had lost his baggage, was
compelled to part with almost all his wearing apparel for sub-
sistence, and had just made his way to the seaside, pur-
posing to escape to Jamaica, when he sunk, overcome by
hunger and fatigue. He kept the secret of his name till the
last moment, when he confided it, and a part of his unhappy
history, to Holmes. Such was the end of Benson, a man
born to high expectations, of cultivated mind, considerable
genius, generous heart, and honourable purposes.

Jack Dallas I became acquainted with at Brazenose.
There was a time that I thought I would have died for him,
and I believe that his feelings towards me were equally

warm. Ten years ago we were the Damon and Pythias—the Pylades and Orestes—of our day. Yet I lost him by a jest. He was wooing most desperately a very pretty girl, equal to him in rank, but rather meagre in the purse. He kept it, however, a profound secret from his friends. By accident I found it out, and, when I next saw him, I began to quiz him. He was surprised at the discovery, and very sore at the quizzing. He answered so testily that I proceeded to annoy him. He became more and more sour, I more and more vexatious in my jokes. It was quite wrong on my part; but God knows I meant nothing by it. I did not know that he had just parted with his father, who had refused all consent to the match, adding injurious insinuations about the mercenary motives of the young lady. Dallas had been defending her, but in vain; and then, while in this mood, did I choose him as the butt of my silly witticisms. At last something I said, some mere piece of nonsense, nettled him so much that he made a blow at me. I arrested his arm, and cried " Jack, you would have been very sorry had you put your intentions into effect." He coloured as if ashamed of his violence, but remained sullen and silent for a moment, and then left the room. We never have spoke since. He shortly after went abroad, and we were thus kept from meeting and explaining. On his return we joined different coteries, and were of different sides in politics. In fact I did not see him for nearly seven years until last Monday, when he passed me with his wife; a different person from his early passion, the girl on account of whom we quarrelled, leaning on his arm. I looked at him, but he bent down his eyes, pretending to speak to Mrs. Dallas. So be it.

Then there was my brother—my own poor brother, one year younger than myself. The verdict, commonly a matter of course, must have been true in this case. What an inward revolution that must have been which could have bent that gay and free spirit, that joyous and buoyant soul, to think of self-destruction. But I cannot speak of poor Arthur. These were my chief friends, and I lost the last of them about ten years ago; and since that time I know no one, the present company excepted, for whom I care a farthing. Perhaps, if they had lived with me as long as my other companions, I would have been as careless about them as I am about Will Thomson, Jack Meggot, or my younger brothers. I am often inclined to think that my feelings towards them are but warmed by the remembered fervour of boyhood, and made romantic by distance of time. I am pretty sure, indeed, that it is so. And, if we could call up Benson innocent from the mould of South America—could restore poor dear Arthur—make Dallas forget his folly—and let them live together again in my society, I should be speedily indifferent about them too. My mind is as if slumbering, quite wrapped up in itself, and never wakes but to act a part. I rise in the morning to eat, drink, talk, to say what I do not think, to advocate questions which I care not for, to join companions whom I value not, to indulge in sensual pleasures which I despise, to waste my hours in trifling amusements or more trifling business, and to retire to my bed perfectly indifferent as to whether I am ever again to see the shining of the sun. Yet is my outside gay and my conversation sprightly. Within I generally stagnate, but sometimes there comes a twinge, short indeed, but bitter. Then it is that I am, to all appearance, most volatile, most eager in dissipation; but, could you lift the covering which shrouds the secrets of my bosom, you would see that, like the inmates of the hall of Eblis, my very heart was fire.

Ha—ha—ha! Say it again, Jemmy—say it again, man—do not be afraid. Ha—ha—ha! Too good, too good, upon my honour. I was crossed in love! *I* in love; you make me laugh; excuse my rudeness—ha—ha—ha! No, no, thank God, though I committed follies of various kinds, I escaped *that* foolery. I see my prosing has infected you, has made you dull. Quick! Unwire the champagne; let us drive spirits into us by its generous tide. We are growing muddy over the claret. *I* in love! Banish all gloomy thoughts.

> "A light heart and a thin pair of breeches
> Goes thorough the world, my brave boys."

What say you to that? We should drown all care in the bowl—fie on the plebeian word—we should dispel it by the sparkling bubbles of wine, fit to be drunk by the gods; that is your only true philosophy.

> " Let us drink and be merry,
>   Dance, laugh, and rejoice,
> With claret and sherry,
>   Theorbo and voice.
>
> " This changeable world
>   To our joys is unjust ;
> All pleasure's uncertain,
>   So down with your dust.
>
> " In pleasure dispose
>   Your pounds, shillings, and pence,
> For we all shall be nothing
>   A hundred years hence."

What, not another bottle? Only one more! Do not be so obstinate. Well, if you must, why, all I can say is, good-night.

* * * * * * * * *

He is gone. A kind animal, but a fool, exactly what is called the best creature in the world. I have that affection for him that I have for Towler, and I believe his feelings towards me are like Towler's, an animal love of one whom he looks up to. An eating, drinking, good-humoured, good-natured varlet, who laughs at my jokes when I tell him they are to be laughed at, sees things exactly in the light that I see them in, backs me in my assertions, and bets on me at whist. I had rather than ten thousand pounds be in singleness of soul, in thoughtlessness of brain, in honesty of intention, in solid contented ignorance, such as Jemmy Musgrove. That I cannot be. *N'importe.*

Booby as he is, he did hit a string which I thought had lost its vibration, had become indurated like all my other feelings. Pish! It is well that I am alone. Surely the claret has made me maudlin, and the wine is oozing out at my eyes. Pish! What nonsense! Ay, Margaret, it is exactly ten years ago. I was then twenty, and a fool. No, not a fool for loving you. By Heavens, I have lost my wits to talk this stuff! The wine has done its office, and I am maundering. Why did I love you? It was all my own perverse stupidity. I was, am, and ever will be a blockhead, an idiot of the first water. And such a match for her to be driven into. She certainly should have let me know more of her intentions than she did. Indeed! Why should she? Was she to caper after my whims, to sacrifice her happiness to my caprices, to my devotions of to-day, and my sulkinesses, or, still worse, my levities of to-morrow? No, no, Margaret; never, never, never, even in thought, let me accuse you, model of gentleness, of kindness, of goodness, as well as of beauty. I am to blame myself, and myself alone.

I can see her now, can talk to her without passion, can put up with her husband, and fondle her children. I have repressed that emotion, and, in doing so, all others. With that throb lost went all the rest. I am now a mere card in the pack, shuffled about eternally with the set, but passive and senseless. I care no more for my neighbour than the king of diamonds cares for him of clubs. Dear, dear Margaret, there is a lock of your hair enclosed, unknown to you, in a little case which lies over my heart. I seldom dare to look at it. Let me kiss its auburn folds once more, and remember the evening I took it. But I am growing more and more absurd. I drink your health then, and retire.

> Here's a health to thee, Margaret,
> Here's a health to thee ;
> The drinkers are gone,
> And I am alone,
> So here's a health to thee.

Dear, dear Margaret.

The Last Words of Charles Edwards, Esq.

DEAR NORTH,—I shall be obliged by your sinking scruples, and giving a place in your next number to the enclosed paper, entitled "The Last Words of Charles Edwards, Esq." The production will of itself sufficiently explain who the writer *was*. I knew him in the Peninsula as a dashing fellow; and, notwithstanding all he says, he was a great favourite with his mess. Bad as he was, he did not want some good points: he was not a scoundrel to the core. He is gone! May the history of his errors do good to one young and unhardened sinner! I think it may well be expected to do good to hundreds of them.

Some people will say you act wrongly in giving publicity to such a record. Don't mind this; it is mere cant. The paper is a transcript—I have no doubt a faithful one—of the feelings of a man who had strong passions himself, who understood human passion, who understood the world, and who lived miserably, and died most miserably, because he could not, or would not, understand himself; and therefore derived no benefits from his acute perceptions as to others. Is not this a lesson? I think it is not only a lesson, but a lesson of lessons; and I request you to print the thing as it stands.

I received the paper from an old friend of mine, who at one time served in the same troop with Edwards. The packet was left at his house on Christmas night, 1822. He was home at the time, and did not reach London until a week had elapsed. The handwriting was disguised, but he recognised it notwithstanding; and the newspapers of the day sufficiently confirmed the import.—Yours truly,

MORGAN ODOHERTY.

CHAPTER I.

I am, or, more properly speaking, I have been, a man of pleasure. I am now forty years, less some few months, of age; and I shall depart this life at twelve o'clock to-night. About that hour it is that I propose to shoot myself through the head. Let this letter be evidence that I do the act advisedly. I should be sorry to have that resolution confounded with madness, which is founded upon the coolest and maturest consideration. Men are coxcombs even in death; and I will not affect to disguise my weakness. I would not forfeit the glory of triumphing over broken-spirited drunkards and half-crazy opium-chewers—of being able to die grateful for the joys I have experienced, and of disdaining to calumniate pleasures after they have ceased to be within my reach. I do assure you, Mr.——, that I should wait personally upon you with this epistle; but that I think the mere reasonableness of my suicide must carry conviction with it of my sanity; but that I trust to lay before you such facts, and such arguments, as shall approve me not only justifiable, but most philosophic, in destroying myself. Hear what I have done; weigh what I mean to do; and judge if I deserve the name of madman.

I was born of a family rather ancient than rich; and inherited, with something like the handsome person of my father, his disposition to expend money rather than to acquire it. To my own recollection, at eighteen I was of a determined temper rather than of a violent one; ardent in the prosecution of objects rather than sudden to undertake them; not very hasty either in love or in quarrel. I had faculty enough to write bad verses,—not industry enough to write anything else; and an aptitude for billiards and horse-riding to a miracle.

Now I desire to have this considered not as a *confession*, but as a statement. As I plead guilty to no fault, I make a declaration, not an acknowledgment. I am not lamenting anything that is past. If I had to begin again to-morrow, I would begin again in the same way. I should vary my course, perhaps, something, with the advantage of my present experience; but take it in the main, and it would be the race that I have run already.

At eighteen, with an education, as Lord Foppington has it, " rather at large ;" for (like Swift's captain of horse) my tutors were the last people who expected any good of me— at eighteen, it became necessary for me to think of a profession. My first attempt in life was in the Navy. I was anxious to *go*, and cared very little whither ; and a school-boy midshipman of my acquaintance cajoled me into a Mediterranean voyage by promises of prize-money and descriptions of Plymouth harbour.

If I were to speak from my feelings at the present moment, I should say that the life of a sailor has its charms. I am bankrupt in appetite as well as in estate; if I have nothing left to enjoy, I have little capacity left for enjoyment ; and I now know how to appreciate that exuberance of spirit with which a man dashes into dissipation on shore after six weeks' restraint from it at sea. But I know also that these are the feelings of situation and of circumstance. The past seems delightful where no hope lives for the future. I am cherishing most fondly the recollection of those sensations which are now the most completely lost to me for ever. But it is the act of the moment which forms the index to the true impression. A ship of war may seem abstract liberty to him who pines in the dungeons of the Inquisition. But confinement, monotony, coarse society, and personal privation— the simple fact is worth all the argument. After a cruise of two months I quitted the navy for ever.

Charmed almost as much with my change of society as with my change of dress, I quitted the sea-service, and entered a regiment of light dragoons ; and for two years from the time of my joining the army I led the life which lads commonly lead in the outset of a military career. And even to the occurrences of those two years, rude and unintellectual as they were, my memory still clings with pleasure and with regret. Toys then, however trifling, pleased; the most refined enjoyments could have done no more. Is there a man living, past thirty, who does not sometimes give a sigh to those days of delicious inexperience and imperception, when the heart could rest content with the mere gratification of the senses; when the intimacies of the dinner-table passed current for friendship; when the woman who smiled on all was to all, nevertheless, charming; and when life, so long as health and money lasted, was one uninterrupted course of impulse and intoxication?

It was my fate, however, to continue but a short time a mere follower of opera *figurantes*, and imbiber of strong potations. Just before I was one-and-twenty, a woman eight years older than myself in great measure fixed my destiny, and entirely formed my character.

Boys who run riot commonly attach themselves, I think, to married women. Wives, where by ill fortune they incline to irregularity, are more understanding, and more accessible, than girls; and hope is your only food for an incipient passion. Many a woman becomes an object of desire, when there seems to be a probability of success; upon whom, but for such foreknowledge or suspicion, we should not perhaps bestow a thought.

Louisa Salvini was eight-and-twenty years of age, a Sicilian by birth, full of the climate of her country. Hers was the Spanish, or Italian, style of beauty; small rather as to figure, yet of exquisite proportion. She had a shape which but to behold was passion;—a carriage, such as nothing but the pride of her own loveliness could have suggested. Her eyes! Their glance of encouragement was fascination. Her lips confused the sense to look upon them. And her voice! —If there be (passing attraction either of face or form) one charm about a woman more irresistible than every other, it is that soft—that mild, sweet, liquid tone, which soothes even in offending and, when it asks, commands; which shakes conviction with its weakest word, and can make falsehood (ay, though known for such) so sweet that we regard the

truth with loathing.   O Heaven! I have hearkened to the
delicious accents of such a voice till, had my soul's hope
been asked from me, it would have been surrendered without
a struggle!—To-night, at midnight, I shall hear such a voice
for the last time!   I shall hear it while I gaze upon features
of loveliness; while my soul is lulled with music, and when
my brain is hot with wine; and the mere melody of that
voice will go farther to raise the delirium I look for than   *
*   *   *   *   *   *   *   *   *
But enough of this now.   My tale should be of that which
was.   Let that which shall come hereafter give some other
historian material.

My acquaintance with Lousia Salvini was of her seeking
rather than of mine.   Accident threw me, under favourable
circumstances, in her way; but it so happened that, at the
moment, I did not perceive I had excited her attention.
The manner of our subsequent introduction was whimsical.
I was not a man (at twenty) to decline an adventure blind-
fold; a well played upon old lady carried me, as a visitor, to
Salvini's house; and my fate was decided from the first
moment that I entered it.

Gracious Heaven! When I reflect that the woman of whom
I speak;—whom I recollect one of the loveliest creatures
that Nature ever formed;—whose smile I have watched, for
its mere beauty, even in the absence of passion;—at whose
feet I have sat for hour after hour, intoxicating myself with
that flattery which is the only flattery true manhood can
endure;—when I reflect that this woman, at the moment
while I write, is a withered, blasted, aged creature of fifty!
Madness, annihilation, is refuge from such a thought.   I met
her, scarce a month since, after an absence of years.
Those eyes, which once discoursed with every rising emotion, retained still something of their original brightness; but
it now only added horror to their expression.   That hand,
which I had pressed for hours in mine, was now grown bony,
shrunken, and discoloured.   Her once cloudless complexion
reeked with paint, through which the black furrow of Time

showed but more deep and ghastly. Her lips, *oh !* they were the same lips which—— The voice too—more dreadful than all !—that voice which had once been sweetest music to my soul ; that voice which memory still is sounding in my ears ; that voice which I had loved, had worshipped ; that voice was gone ; it was no more ; and what remained was harsh, tremulous, broken, discordant ! And this is the woman whom I so adored ?   It is she, and she is unconscious of change ! And I shall be, must be, the thing that she now is !   Hold, brain ! The blow of this night saves me from such a fate !

My love for Louisa Salvini endured two years without satiety.   An attachment of equal duration has never befallen me since.   But, at the time to which I refer, all circumstances were in my favour.   I was glowing with all the fervour of youth, and with all the vigour of unwasted constitution.   My mistress's beauty delighted my senses ; her avowed preference gratified my vanity ; she was charming to me (love apart), taken merely as a companion ; and, what conduced still farther to the keeping alive our passion, she was not (being another's) constantly in my presence.

Contentment, however, is not the lot of man.   Give a Mahometan his paradise, and in six weeks he would be disgusted with it.   My affection for my charming mistress was just beginning to be endangered, when the regiment to which I belonged was ordered to the Continent.   The fact was that I met in Louisa's society a variety of women of principles as free as her own, and the very jealousy which each lady entertained of her friends made success with herself the more easy and certain.   A little while longer, and Louisa and I had severed ; my embarkation, parting us by necessity, saved us probably from a parting by consent.

I left England very poor as to pecuniary means, but rich in every other advantage which (to me) made life desirable. Youth, O youth ! could I but recall the years that I have lived !   I would rather stand now upon the barrenest plain in Europe, naked, friendless, penniless, but again sixteen, than possess, as the thing I am, the empire of the world.

Is there a fool so besotted as to trust the cant he utters, to believe that MONEY can really purchase all the blessings of this life? Money can buy nothing; it is worth nothing. I have rioted in its abundance; I have felt its total deprivation; and I have enjoyed more, I believe, of happiness in the last state than in the first.

Shall I forget the first event of my career on the Continent—that event which, in the end, led to its premature termination? Shall I forget the insolent superiority with which I looked down upon my brother officers, men to whom play, excess of wine, and mercenary women seemed, and indeed were, delights sufficient?

Wine, until after thirty, from choice, I seldom tasted. My spirits, when sober, were too vivid for control; wine only troubled their serenity, without heightening their level. Of play, I touched it once; and I shall speak of it hereafter. But women? such women as these men could admire? Even my more cultivated sense rejected them; two years of intimacy with Salvini and her companions had chastened my taste, and made delicate my perceptions. Can I ever, I repeat, forget that exquisite moment, that moment which secured to me at least one enemy for life, when I, the poorest cornet in our regiment, defeated my colonel in the favour of the first beauty in Lisbon? By Heaven, the recollection of that single hour past warms my spirits to high pitch for the hour that is to come! The envy, the hate—the burning hate—which my success engendered in the bosoms of half my acquaintance! The sensation of hating is one which I have never fully experienced; but the pleasure of being hated—oh, it is almost equal to the pleasure of being beloved!

To a man of habits and temperament like mine the Peninsula was a delightful residence in 1808. I remember the gay appearance of the capital; which, taken by moonlight from the river, is perhaps one of the most imposing in the world.   I remember the striking panoramic *coup-d'œil* of its church and convent spires innumerable ; its marble fountains, its palaces, its towers, and its gardens ; its streets and squares of white and yellow buildings, each gaudily appointed from the basement to the roof, with *jalouise* lattices, balconies, and verandahs ; the whole city, too, throwing itself (from the irregular site upon which it rises) full, at a single glance, upon the eye ; and every feature in the prospect seeming, like an object in a picture, disposed artfully with a view to the general beauty of the scene.

Then the free spirits of the women ; their passions concentrated, almost to madness, by the restraint under which they live !   Honour, for aiding the hopes of a lover, be to systems of restriction, severity, and *espionage!*   Opportunity to an English woman wants the piquancy of novelty.   As it is constantly recurring, it is constantly neglected.   In Spain they seize it when it does present itself ; for, once rejected, it may never be found again.

But beyond the beauty of Lisbon as a city, beyond even the brightness of those souls that inhabited it, there was a laxity of law and manner in it at the period to which I speak— a license inseparable from the presence of a foreign force in a prostrate, shackled, and dependent country—an absence as much of moral as of physical police which, to a disposition such as mine, was peculiarly acceptable.   Add to this the further fact, that I was fresh in a strange capital ; among a people to whose manners, and almost to whose language, I was a stranger ; where, little being fully understood, all had credit for being as it ought to be ; and where the mere novelty of my situation was a charm almost inexhaustible.   Such allurements considered, could I fail to be charmed with the Peninsula ?

My stay in this land of delight, then, was something short of three years.   I was present at the famous battle of Talavera ; and, afterwards, at the desperate contest of Albuera, under Beresford, where the Polish lancers first tried their strength against our English cavalry.   I was a sharer, too, in the more partial affair of Busaco, and took part in the duty of covering the retreat that followed—a retreat in which the whole of the southern line of Portugal, from the Spanish frontier to Lisbon, was depopulated and laid waste ; in which convents were deserted, cities consumed by fire, and women born to rank and affluence compelled to seek protection from the meanest followers of the British army.

The evacuation of Coimbra (the Bath, if I may so call it, of Portugal) is present to me now, as though it had occurred but yesterday. I see the immense population, men, women, and children, of all ranks and of all ages, pouring out, at an hour's notice, through the Lisbon gate of the city ; and rushing upon a journey which not one in five of them could hope to accomplish. It was little to have abandoned home and property ; to have set forth on foot (for the army had seized all conveyance)—on foot, and unprovided, in a long and rapid march, through a distracted, ravaged, lawless tract of country. If to have suffered this was much, the trial was still to come. I saw these multitudes, spent with travel and with hunger, reach towns in which every hovel, every shed was filled with troops. I saw families upon families yet new upon their pilgrimage,—not yet so tamed and beaten down by suffering as willingly to carry their daughters into the guardrooms of an infuriated soldiery ; I saw them lying (for even the churches were filled with our sick and wounded)—lying unsheltered all night in the fields and open squares ; waiting, with feverish restlessness, the appearance of morning, as though new light (repose apart) would to them be an accession of new strength.

The vast column rolled forward on the high road to the capital, collecting the population of the country over which it passed. Behind were left the weak, the aged, and the dying ; and some few wretches, of profession, who, tempted by the hope of gain, took their chance (and lost it) of mercy from the enemy. But, though every step over which the mass advanced gave addition to its numbers, there were

drains at work, and fearful ones, to counteract the reinforcement. Cold dews at midnight, burning suns by day, scanty
provisions, and fatigue unwonted—these ministers did their
work, and especially among the females. Towards the
close of the second day's march, the women began to fail
rapidly. At first, when a girl grew faint, and unable to
proceed, her sister would stay by her. This feeling, however,
was not fated to last long : soon the sister dashed desperately
forward ; to sink herself, and meet her own fate, some few
leagues farther on.

I saw one company halted between Leiria and Pombal,
which must have consisted of eight hundred or a thousand
individuals. These people came from the neighbourhoods
of Coimbra and Condeixa ; some of them from as far up as
Mongoalde and Vizeu. There were girls of fourteen or fifteen,
clad in their gayest apparel, their only means of carrying or,
as they said, of "saving" it. There were old men, and
grandames ; peasants, male and female ; friars, artisans,
servants and *religieuses.* After travelling, most of them,
more than fifty miles on foot, and passing two or three nights
in the open air, they were lying upon the banks of a river,
waiting for the sunrise, as I rode past them. I never can
forget this scene ; and yet I feel that it is impossible for me
to describe it. The stream (I believe it was a branch of the
Mondego) was dark and swollen, from the effect of recent
rains ; and it rushed along between the willows which grew
on either bank, as though sharing in the hasty spirit which
animated every object about it. On the road, which lay to
the right of the river, troops and fugitives were already in
motion. It was just dawn when I came up. A light breeze
was half clearing off the fog from the surface of the water.
I saw the living figures imperfectly as I approached ; all
white and shrouded, like spectres, in the mist. The light
dresses of the girls were saturated with wet. Their flowers
and feathers were soiled, drooping, broken. Their hair—
(the Spanish women are remarkable for the beauty of that
feature)—their dark long hair hung neglected and dishevelled.

Their feet, which cardinals might have kissed, were, in many instances, naked, wounded, bleeding. And, worse than all, their spirit and their strength was gone. Of those whom I saw lying on the banks of that water, a fearful proportion lay there to rise no more. And yet many had gold and jewels: but gold could not help them. And their loveliness remained; and they looked in eloquent, though in mute, despair upon British officers who passed by; and yet those men, who would have fought knee-deep for the worst of them, they could not help them. I overtook, after this, a beautiful girl of fifteen, travelling alone, out of the high road, from apprehension of insult. This girl had been separated from her friends in the general confusion. She had money and diamonds to a considerable amount about her; and had accomplished half her journey, but felt unable to proceed farther. She begged on her knees for a horse, for any conveyance; to be allowed to travel near me, with my servants, anywhere, anyhow, to be protected, and to get on. I had not the means of aiding that girl. I could not help her. Every Englishman had already done his utmost. I had then three women under my protection. I see the figure, the countenance, the tears of that girl at this moment. I thought at one time that I must have stayed and been made prisoner along with her. I could not carry her away in my arms. I could not leave her—no man could have left her to her fate. Fortunately an officer came up, who was less encumbered than myself, and she was provided for. And in such way (and in ways a thousand times more dreadful) great numbers of women got on to the capital. They escaped for a time the lot of their friends and relatives; but, eventually, what was to be their fate? What *was* their fate? What if I saw these women afterwards—women born to affluence—reared in the very lap of luxury and softness— what if I saw many of them begging in the public streets of Lisbon? I did see them in that state; but it is a subject that I must not dwell upon.

The conclusion of my peninsular campaign was not favourable to my fortunes. As a soldier, I did my duty in the field; but opportunity for a man to distinguish himself cannot always be commanded. I had a project once, with a few fellows as desperate or as careless as myself, for dashing at the enemy's military chest: but our scheme fell to the ground, for we never got a chance of carrying it into execution. In the meantime, as regarded promotion, my general conduct was not such as to make friends. Repeated successes, in one peculiar pursuit, inspired me with an excessive confidence in myself, and with a very contemptuous estimate of most other persons. I saw men, whom at all points I ranked far below myself, graced with the favour of superiors, and rich in the gifts of fortune. When a chance did occur for making such usurpers feel their proper place, was it in human nature to resist the temptation? All hope of patronage under such a *régime* was of course out of the question. I interfered with everybody; and, at last, began to take a pride in doing so. The recompense of these good offices was in due time to be paid.

A Spanish officer, with whom I was associated in the convoy of certain treasure, proposed to me one night, after our halt upon the march, to take a trip down the Tagus, and bring his wife upon the journey. I had met this lady, a short time before, in Lisbon, and (according to my invariable custom in such cases) fancied that she had a liking for my person. It was a fine moonlight evening when we left Villa Nova, and we ran down with the tide to the *Quinta* of my friend; but no sooner had we taken the Signora on board than the aspect of the weather suddenly changed, and we were exposed, during the whole night, to considerable danger.

From the moment almost that we left Silveira's house the weather began to be unfavourable. The darkness, after the moon had gone down, was extreme. The wind, which set in squalls across a rapid and contrary tide, seemed to acquire greater force at every successive gust, and was accompanied, from time to time, with heavy showers of rain.

Our boat, though capacious enough, was undecked and slightly rigged, evidently unfit for rough treatment of any kind; and, to make matters worse, our sailors became alarmed, and Silveira, who knew the river, was ill from sea-sickness. How curiously, in the arrangement of the human heart and mind, do our passions balance and compensate each other! A man might reasonably, perhaps, be expected to keep his wits about him in such a dilemma as this. For myself, I had some little nautical experience; and, besides, my companions were afraid; and it helps a man's valour greatly to see other people frightened. But Silveira's wife, who was as little of a heroine as any woman I ever met with —I was compelled to support her during almost the whole of the night; for the sea kept dashing into our open boat, and her husband, from illness, could scarcely take care of himself; and yet, under these circumstances, while she expected, I believe, to be washed overboard every half minute, I could perceive that I had not been quite mistaken in my suspicion of her good opinion of me.

Whatever interest, however, I might have felt in the progress of this little excursion, its termination was such as I certainly had not contemplated. With the utmost exertions both of the Spaniard and myself, we did not get back to our halting-place until evening on the day after we had started. At daybreak (twelve hours before) a treacherous quarter-master had marched forward with our escort; my friend the colonel did not let slip so favourable an opportunity to get rid of a man whom he doubtless considered as a trouble-some coxcomb; and, to avoid the inevitable result of a court-martial, I asked and obtained permission to resign.

Chapter II.

Upon home service my affairs, in a pecuniary point of view, would have been very little affected by the loss of my commission. On service abroad, however, the consequence was different. As a soldier, I enjoyed many advantages and immunities which a civil individual could scarcely even for money procure. Besides, though no discredit attached to my fault (for Silveira, indeed, had never been brought to any account), still I was, up to a certain point, a man placed in the shade. I had not lost my rank dishonourably; but still I *had* lost it, and the military world felt that I had. I missed the visits of some men with whom I had been upon terms of intimacy, and received advances from others of whose acquaintance I was not ambitious. One friend asked casually when I intended to go to England; another mentioned some new Spanish levies, in which commissions were easily to be obtained. One fellow, to whom I had never spoken in my life, and who had been dismissed from the navy for gross insubordination and misconduct, had the presumption to write to me about "jobs" in "high quarters," "favouritism," "injustice," and "public appeal;" but I horsewhipped him in an open coffee-room, while the waiter read his letter to the company. These, however, were teazing, not to say distressing, circumstances; and, to avoid seeming at a loss (particularly as I was very much at a loss indeed), it became necessary to do something, and with the least possible delay.

I could have married Portuguese ladies; but their means were in supposition. Ready money, in Portugal, there was little; rents, in the existing state of the country, were hopeless; and I had not much reliance upon a title to land, which to-day was in our possession, to-morrow perhaps in that of the enemy. Misfortunes, as the adage declares, are gregarious. Meditating which course, out of many, I should adopt, I fell into a course which I had never meditated at all.

The Peninsula, during the war, was the scene of a good deal of high play. In quarters distant from the capital the difficulty of killing time drove all but professed drinkers to gaming; and the universal employment of specie, for paper was used only in commercial transactions, gave an aspect peculiarly tempting to the table. Silver, in dollars and Portuguese crowns, was the common run of currency; the army was paid entirely in that metal; and it was no unusual thing to see an officer come down to a gaming-house absolutely bending under the weight of a couple of hundred pounds which he had to risk; or sending for a servant (hackney coaches were scarce), in case of a run of luck, to carry away his winnings.

Hazard and faro were the favourite games. Of billiards people were shy—people commonly dread faculty in any shape. There was some danger in going home, after being very successful, at night; but the games of chance were in general very fairly played. The bank, of course, had a certain, and a considerable, advantage; but as all the houses were public and open, there was little, if any, opportunity for fraud. And it was not by the assumed advantage of the table, or by any process so tedious, that my stripping was effected. In luck I was unfortunate. I lost at my first sitting more money than I could afford to part with, and in hope of recovering it was compelled to persevere. I have heard, among many dogmas as to the seductiveness of play (a passion, by the way, no more invincible, though perhaps more rapidly destructive, than most of the other passions to which the human mind is subject), that a losing gamester may stop, but that a winning one never can. Perhaps this axiom is meant to apply peculiarly to your gamester *de cœur ;* and possibly (though *de tête* would be the more "germane" illustration)—possibly, as Gall or Spurzheim would say, the "organ" of winning and losing was not in me strongly developed. As far as my own feeling goes, it certainly negatives the principle. Had I at any time regained my own, I think I should have stopped. I lost every shilling I possessed; horses, jewels, and even pistols, in the attempt.

I have stated, I think, that I was an only child; but, up to this point, I have said very little about my parents. Thank Heaven (for their sakes) they no longer exist. My father died in my arms about seven years since, exhorting me, with his last breath, against the habits he had lived in all his life. I can understand this. My father died what is called "a natural death." Sickness had enervated his mind; terrors, the mere weakness of nerve, oppressed him. The ague of a month effected that change to which the argument of years had been unequal; after fifty years of infidelity he fancied he died a believer. Were I to live ten years longer, I should probably die as he did.

But I name my relatives in this place, merely for the sake of observing that, at the time to which I refer, I was very much estranged from them. My father held himself pretty well relieved from anxiety as to the fate of a man over whose conduct he had no control; and it was a draft only for fifty pounds which I received from him in Lisbon after the loss of my commission, accompanied by a letter, which determined me never to apply to him again.

So, with twenty guineas only in my pockets, and with experience enough to know how little twenty guineas would do for me, I again landed in England in the year 1812; but I have not time, nor would the world have patience, for the adventures which, in three months, conducted me to my last shilling. I wrote a novel, I recollect, which no bookseller would look at;—a play, which is still lying at one of the winter theatres. Then I sent proposals to the commander-in-chief for altering the taste of our cavalry accoutrements and harness; next, drew a plan (and seriously too) for the invasion of China; and after these, and a variety of other strange efforts, each suggested by my poverty, and all tending to increase it, the clocks were striking twelve on a dreary November night, as I walked along Piccadilly without a penny in the world.

It is at twelve o'clock this night that my earthly career must terminate; and, looking back to the various changes with which my life has been chequered, I find crisis after crisis connecting itself with the same hour. On the evening to which I allude, I wandered for hours through the streets; but it was not until midnight that I thought very intently on my situation. There is something, perhaps, of appalling in the aspect of London at that hour;—in the gradual desertion of the streets by reputable passengers; and in the rising, as it were from their depths of earth, of forms repulsive, horrible, and obscene. This change of object and association is sometimes peculiarly striking in the Parks. As the evening draws in, the walking parties and well-dressed persons disappear one by one, and the benches become peopled with an array of fearful creatures, who seem to glide from behind the trees,—to be embodied, as it were, out of the air. I have myself turned round suddenly, and seen a squalid shape beside me, which had not been there but the moment before. And I knew not how it came, nor from what quarter it approached; but it came on through the dark like some pale meteor, or unwholesome exhalation, which was not visible till the good light was gone. The closing, too (in the town), of the shops, one after the other,—the honester and safer houses first, and so on until the haunts even of guilt and infamy shut up their doors, as seeing no farther prospect through the gloom. And the few animated objects which break the general stillness, more revolting and fearful even than that stillness itself! Starving wretches, huddled together in holes and corners, seeking concealment from the eye of the police; thief-takers making their stealthy rounds, and eyeing every casual wanderer with suspicious and half-threatening glances. Then the associations which present themselves to the mind in such a situation. Thoughts of burglars, murderers, wretches who violate the sanctity of the grave, and lurking criminals of still darker dye ;—the horror being less of injury from such creatures than of possible approximation to them ;—the kind of dread which a man feels, he can scarcely tell why, of being touched by a rat, a spider, or a toad.

But I wandered on till St. James's bell tolled twelve ; and the sound awakened some curious recollections in my memory. A mistress of mine had lived in Sackville Street once, and twelve o'clock (at noon) was my permitted hour to visit her. I had walked up and down a hundred times in front of St. James's Church waiting impatiently to hear that clock strike twelve, which now struck twelve upon my ruin, my degradation. The sound of the bell fell upon my ear like the voice of an old acquaintance. My friend yet held his standing; my estate had something changed.

I did wander on, however, after St James's clock told twelve, and while the rain, falling in torrents, drove even beggars to their shelter. I had neither home nor money. There were acquaintances upon whom I might have called, and from whom a supper and a bed would have been matters of course; but I felt that my spirits were rapidly rising to the right pitch for considering the situation in which I stood. Nothing sharpens the perceptions like the pressure of immediate danger. Had I slept and awoke at daylight, I must again have waited for the hour of darkness. Men succeed over and over again, upon the spur of emergency, in enterprises which, viewed calmly, they would never have undertaken.

I strolled onwards down Piccadilly through the wet dark night (to avoid the hackney coachmen, who kept teasing me with offers of their services), and leaned against one of those splendid houses which stand fronting the Green Park. The strong bright glare of the door-lamps below showed the princely proportion of the building. Night was now growing fast into morning, but lights were still visible in the show-apartments of the mansion. Presently I heard the sound of a pianoforte, and a voice which I thought was familiar to me. I listened; and in a moment the singer went on :

1.

The setting sun with crimson beam
　　Now gilds the twilight sky ;
And evening comes with sportive mien,
　　And cares of daylight fly :
Then deck the board with flowers, and fill
　　My glass with racy wine ;
And let those snowy arms, my love,
　　Once more thy harp entwine.
　　　　Oh ! strike the harp, my dark-haired love,
　　　　　And swell that strain so dear.
　　　　Thine angel form shall charm mine eye,
　　　　　Thy voice delight mine ear.

Surely, said I, I have heard these words before ; but the song continued :

2.

The glasses shine upon the board,
　　But brighter shines thine eye ;
The claret pales its ruby tint,
　　When lips like thine are nigh ;
The tapers dim their virgin white
　　Beside thy bosom's hue ;
And the flame they shed burns not so bright
　　As that I feel for you.
　　　　Then strike the harp ! Each note, my love,
　　　　　Shall kindle fresh desire ;
　　　　Thy melting breath shall fan that flame,
　　　　　Thy glowing charms inspire.

It was the voice of a man whom I had known intimately for years. I cast my eye upon the door, and read the name of his family. My old companion, my *friend*, was standing almost within the touch of my hand. I thought on the scene in which he was an actor; on the gaiety, the vivacity, the splendour and the sparkle, the intrigues and the fierce passions, from which a few feet of space divided me. I was cold, wet, and penniless; and I had to choose.

It may be asked, why did not suicide then present itself as a rallying point? It did present itself at once; and, on the instant, I rejected it. Destitute as I was, I had still a confidence in my own powers—I may almost say, in my own fortune. I felt that, wealth apart, I had a hundred pleasurable capabilities which it would be folly to cast away. Besides, there were relatives, whose deaths might make me rich. I decided not to die. My next supplies, however, were to arise out of my own personal exertions ; and, in the meantime, the approach of light reminded me that I was still wet and in the street. I had no fastidious apprehensions about degrading myself. If I could have held a plough, or digged in a mine, I should not have hesitated to have performed either of those duties. But, for holding a plough, I had not the skill ; and, for the mines, there were none in the neighbourhood of London. One calling, however, there was, for which I was qualified. Within four-and-twenty hours after my dark walk through Piccadilly, I was a private dragoon in the 31st regiment, and quartered at Lymington Barracks.

Chapter III.

I have denied, I do still deny, the overpowering influence commonly attributed to rank and fortune ; and let me not be accused of offering opinions, without at least having had some opportunities for judgment. If there be a situation in which, beyond all others, a man is shut out from all probability of advancement, it is the situation of a private soldier. But the free undaunted spirit which sinks not in extremity can draw even from peculiar difficulty peculiar advantage ; where lead only is hoped for grains of gold excite surprise ; a slender light shows far when all is dark around it.

Twelve months passed heavily with me in the 31st Dragoons. My apparently intuitive dexterity in military exercises saved me from annoyance or personal indignity, and might, in a certain way, have procured me promotion. But a halberd, as it happened, was not my object. I looked for deliverance from my existing bondage to the falling in

with some wealthy and desirable woman.   And in the strict
performance of a soldier's duty—active, vigilant, obedient,
and abstaining—I waited with patience for the arrival of
opportunity.

I waited till my patience was exhausted half a dozen times
over; but the interim certainly was not passed in idleness.
He whose prospect lies straight forward is seldom content
to look about him; but there was matter for analysis and
curious investigation on every side of me.   As an officer, I
had seen little of the true character or condition of the
soldiery; and a regiment of cavalry is really a machine of
strange constitution—I say, "of cavalry," *par preference*,
because there is generally about a dragoon regiment a more
lofty, though perhaps not more just, style and feeling than
belongs (from whatever cause) to our regiments of infantry.

The 31st Regiment was remarkable for the splendour of
its uniform and appointments, an attribute rather anything
than advantageous to the soldier; but which always, nevertheless, operates powerfully in the recruiting of a corps.   We
had men amongst us from almost every class of society.
There were linen-weavers from Ireland, colliers from War-
wickshire and Shropshire, ploughmen, gamekeepers, and
poachers from every quarter and county.   There were men
too of higher rank, as regarded their previous condition;
and that in a number very little imagined by the world.
There were men of full age, who had run through fortunes—
lads who had quarrelled with, or been deserted by, their families—ruined gamblers, *ci-devant* fortune-hunters, ex-officers,
and strolling players.   In a company so heterogeneous it
would have been difficult to keep the peace but for that law
which visited the black eye as a breach of military discipline.
As men, those who had been "gentlemen" were incompar-
ably the worst characters.   Some of them vapoured, or at
least talked, about their origin, and so exposed themselves
to the ridicule which waits upon fallen dignity.   Others made
use of their patrician acquirements to seduce the wives or
daughters of their more plebeian comrades.   They were

dissipated in their habits, ribald in their discourse, and destitute even of any remnant of honest or decent principle.

The poachers among us were another party, almost of themselves; for the gamekeepers, the same animals domesticated, never cordially agreed with them. Idle in their habits, slovenly in their appearance, these fellows were calculated, nevertheless, to make admirable soldiers in the field. Their courage was peculiarly of the true English character; slow something to be excited, but, when excited, impossible to be overcome. I remember one of them well, for his anecdotes used to amuse me, who for two years had been the scourge of every preserve within ten miles of his parish; and who had, with difficulty, escaped transportation by enlisting as a soldier. He was a strong, muscular lad, about two or three and twenty; not of large stature, or of handsome appearance, but of a resolution, or rather of an obduracy, which nothing short of death could have subdued. I saw him once fight, after repeated provocation, with a fourteen-stone Irishman of the 18th, who was the lion of his troop. The battle lasted, without any etiquette of the prize-ring, in constant fighting, more than an hour. My acquaintance was knocked down in every round for the first thirty minutes, but the blows made no more impression upon him than they would have done upon a man of iron. That he had the worst of the battle never seemed to occur to him; he fell, and rose, fell, rose again, and struck on. Nothing but the loss of sight or of life could have subdued him; and I firmly believe he would have destroyed himself if he had been compelled to give up. At length his antagonist's confidence gave way before his obstinacy; and there was something almost staggering to the senses in the appearance of it. The man seemed to get no worse for a beating that might have destroyed half-a-dozen. He spoke very little, never broke his ground, and rose with a smile after such falls as might have crushed him to pieces. Both parties suffered severely, my friend rather the most; but, at the end of an hour's fighting, the Hibernian owned himself vanquished.

But whatever might be the qualities of these men individually, taken as a body they were amenable, reasonable beings. To have made them individually discontented would have been difficult, to have tampered with them *en masse* quite impossible. The sound of the word "discipline" had a sort of magical effect upon their minds. Their obedience (from its uniform enforcement) became perfectly mechanical; and severity excited little complaint, for it was understood to be the custom of the service.

We had three different commanding officers during the time of my stay at Lymington, but there was only one who ever disturbed the temper of the garrison, and even he failed to excite any feeling beyond great personal hatred to himself.

The first commandant was a man who had himself been a private soldier, and who had risen by degrees to the rank of lieutenant-colonel. Corporal punishment was his reliance. He punished seldom, but severely. And this man, though a strict disciplinarian, was universally popular.

Our second leader was a well-meaning man, but a theorist; and he seemed to have been sent as a punishment for the sins of the whole garrison. He was strongly opposed to the practice of corporal punishment, as tending to degrade and break the spirit of the soldier; and being puzzled, as a wiser head might be, in the substitution of other penalties, he actually put his men through a course of experiments upon the subject. For example, having heard that Alfred the Great made an arrangement by which every man became, to a certain degree, answerable for his neighbour, Major W—— resolved to introduce the same system into his own depôt; and whenever, accordingly, any soldier was absent from barracks without leave—and, in a garrison of a thousand men, some one or other was pretty sure to be always absent— he confined the remaining nine hundred and ninety-nine to their barracks until he returned. Indeed without, I believe, the least feeling of cruelty or malice, this man passed half his time in devising inflictions, and the other half in practising them upon us. And, besides this, he fatigued us with eternal inspections; wasted more paper in writing rules and regulations than might have made cartridges for a whole battalion; and after compelling us, even in cold weather, to go through a tedious parade on a Sunday, was so merciless as always to make a long speech at the end of it.

Our third commandant, and the only one whom I ever dreaded—for the whims of the second hardly passed what might be called vexations—our third commandant was a fool; and, of course, being a soldier, a martinet. Quite incompetent to the discussion of any possible matter beyond the polish of a carbine-barrel, or the number of paces in which a regiment ought to cross the parade-ground, he gave his whole attention to what he termed the "military" appearance of his troops. A speck upon a man's uniform— a hair too much or too little in a whisker—a spot, or a drop of water, upon the floor of a room in which thirty men inhabited, ate, drank, and slept; these were crimes which never failed to call down heavy retribution. And perfection, with this gentleman, was almost as much a fault as negligence. He lived only upon orders, reprimands, and whippings. The man who could not do his duty was to be tortured, as a matter of course; the man who did it well was corrected as "a conceited fellow." Every process under his jurisdiction was conducted at the point of the "damme." He attempted to make his officers cut their hair in a particular shape. He forbad a staff-adjutant, who could not afford to give up his place, ever to quit the barrack-yard without stating where he was going to. I have known him set three hundred men to pick straw off a stable-yard, where every fresh puff of wind left them their labours to begin again. Eventually the fellow joined a regiment in India; and fell in a skirmish, by a ball, it was supposed, from one of his own soldiers.

But I was weary of examining characters and avoiding

persecutions. I was tired of being a favourite among the nursery girls of Lymington, and even of enjoying the enmity of the young gentlemen of the neighbourhood. I had become weary of the honour and discomfort of endurance— I sighed, in the midst of exertion, for exertion's reward— I never doubted that talent must in time find its level; but I had begun to doubt whether man's life would be long enough to afford the waiting, when the chance that I was hoping and wishing for appeared.

How constantly do men ascribe to momentary impulse acts which really are founded in deep premeditation! Mistakes, surprises, jokes, and even quarrels pass current as accidental which are in truth matters of *malice prepense.* My object at Lymington was to introduce myself to persons of consideration; and with that view for months I carried my life, as it were, in my hand. Every moment that I could snatch from the routine of military duty was systematically devoted to searching after adventure. There was not a family of condition within five miles of the depot, but I had my eye upon their motions and arrangements. How often, while watching their gay parties on the river, did I pray for some dreadful accident which might give me an opportunity of distinguishing myself! How often have I wished, in riding night picquet or express, that some passing equipage would be attacked by robbers, that I might make my fortune by defeating them! I saw by chance one evening a mill on fire in the distance; and, making sure it was a nobleman's seat, swam through two rivers to arrive at it. At length, the commonplace incident—I had looked for it, though, a hundred times—the commonplace incident of two tipsy farmers, on a fair day, affronting an officer in Lymington market-place, who had a lady on his arm, gave me the chance I had so long sought. This affair gave me an opportunity of being useful to Captain and Mrs. Levine.

The Honourable Augustus Levine, who had joined the garrison but a few days when this accident befell him, was one of those men of fortune who seem born for no purpose than to put poor fellows in contentment with their destiny. He was an abject creature, both in heart and mind ; despicable (there be more such) in person as in principle. And yet the worm was brother to an earl—he was master of a fine estate—he commanded an hundred soldiers; and (a man may have too many blessings) he had a young and handsome wife.

When I declare that Lymington Barracks were full of stripling officers, who, in addition to wealth and station, possessed (many of them) all personal advantages, my venturing even to think of Mrs. Levine upon the credit of such a service as I had performed may appear to savour not a little of presumption. Setting the event apart, I should maintain a different opinion. A hundred qualifications, which would only have been of course in a man of rank, in a peasant would excite surprise, and, consequently, interest. My encounter in the market-place, though a vulgar one, had given me some opportunity for display; and a private soldier, who possessed figure, accomplishment, and deportment—who could make verses, make love, and, moreover, fight like a Turk—such a man would secure attention ; and love follows very easily. I cannot afford now to dwell upon details; but, whatever be the value of my general principle, consequences, in the particular instance, did approve my dream. Within six months I had disclosed my real name and rank—eloped with Mrs. Levine—fought a duel with her husband—and had a verdict entered against me in the Court of King's Bench, with damages by default to the amount of £10,000.

There is this circumstance, among a thousand others, to attach us to the female sex, that a man can scarce, in any case, whatever the degree of friendship, receive a favour from his fellow-man without some feeling of inferiority ; while from a woman each new act of kindness, or of bounty, seems but a tribute to his merit, and a proof of her affection.

My encounter with Levine produced very trifling consequences. Both parties were slightly wounded at the first fire, and neither appeared anxious to try the fortune of a second. The penalty of £10,000 was a more serious matter to deal with. Mrs. Levine possessed, independent of her husband, an income exceeding £800 a-year; but that property formed no fund for the payment of a large sum in damages. Our only alternative was to quit England immediately.

I enter here with pain upon an epoch in my history which filled up sadly and wearily a period of five years. Isabella Levine was a woman whose personal charms were perhaps among the weakest of the attractions she possessed. If I had sought her in the beginning from interested motives, I did not long profess a passion without really entertaining it. That she had deserted such a husband as Levine seemed to me no stain upon her virtue. He had been forced upon her by the command of an uncle on whom she depended. and who himself had felt so little confidence in the man of his selection that, in giving his niece a large fortune, he reserved it principally within her own control. Was it a crime in Isabella that she quitted a being whom she could not love? Was she a companion for stupidity, for slovenliness, for brutality? Was she a subject for neglect and for coarse infidelity? Was it fit that her tenderness, her beauty, and her youth should be wasted upon a creature who could not appreciate what he was possessing? She did not sell herself to me for title or for fortune. She was not seduced by a fashion or a feather. If she loved me— and I think she did love me—it was for myself alone.

Impressed with these feelings, I left England a second time for Lisbon. The war had now been carried into the heart of France, and the Peninsula had a prospect of sufficient security. If by law I was prevented from marrying Isabella, by gratitude, as well as by affection, I held myself bound to her for ever. I took it as an admitted principle that every man must settle at some time, and deliberately formed my plan of lasting domestic happiness.

I had not then ascertained that the very thought of a set

system is destruction to everything in the nature of enjoyment. I had yet to discover that it was better even to die at once than await in one fixed posture the wearing of unprofitable vacancy.

I set out with a wish as well as a resolution to act well. I had seen the errors of married men, and I determined to avoid them. I will treat a woman, said I, with that attention which she is entitled to demand : I will not render her miserable by my dissipations ; I will not insult her by slighting her society ; I will love none but Isabella, and with her my hours shall be passed. I now see ill omen in these my first resolutions. A man does not put himself upon the defensive unless he feels cause to apprehend attack. I suspect that, like the wolf in the fable, the sight of the collar already made me uneasy.

I shall never forget, for my time indeed is almost come, the torture which it cost me to carry my good resolutions into effect : the days, the weeks, the years that I suffered of satiety, weariness, indifference, disgust. I am convinced that the decline of my passion for Isabella was only hastened by my efforts to conceal and to resist it. The love of full liberty, which I had been used freely to indulge, acquired now tenfold force from the restraint to which I subjected myself. The company of the plainest woman of my acquaintance would have been delightful to me compared with the uniformity of beauty.

I bore up against these inclinations until my very brain became affected. My senses grew morbid from excess of inflammation. And withal I could perform but half the task I had imposed on myself. I might refuse to love other women, but I could not compel myself to love Isabella. My attentions continued ; but they were the attentions of a prescribed duty. The feelings I had once entertained towards her, the letters I had written to her, for I chanced once by accident to fall on some of them, the whole seemed a dream, a delusion, a delirium from which I had recovered, and the remembrance of which excited wonder.

Steadily to pursue the course upon which I had determined was not to cheat myself of the conviction that that course was destroying me.   In vain did I recollect what I owed to Isabella: her uniformly excellent conduct, the sacrifices she had made for me.   These images refused to dwell upon my imagination.   They were as shadows in the water, which eluded my grasp when I would have seized them.   I found only a woman who now was in my way, who no doubt meant to bestow happiness upon me, but who in fact drove me to frenzy.   I would again have been left destitute ; I would have returned to my ration and my broadsword ; I would have submitted to anything to have been once more a free man ; but to desert Isabella, or to be deserted by her;— I was not (Heaven be praised !) quite villain enough to take the first course ; my pride could not have endured that she should take the second.

There are limits to the capacity of human endurance. We are none of us so far from insanity as we believe ourselves.   My temper had suffered in the course of these conflicts a shock from which, I think, it never afterwards recovered, when a train of new circumstances, unforeseen and unexpected, broke, for good or ill, the trammels which entangled me.

We had been five years together,. and I had been four years miserable, when a habitual depression which I had perceived but neglected to speak of,—for, in the fever of my own soul, I had no thought for the distress of others,—this terminated in the serious illness of Isabella.   At first, supposing her indisposition to be transient, I treated it as an affair of domestic routine, taking every precaution for her safety rather as a matter of course than from any feeling of anxiety ; but an intimation from my physician that she was in a state of real danger aroused me from that apathy with which I contemplated all passing events.

"Danger? What danger? There could be no danger; the man must be mistaken."

"He was not mistaken. My wife's complaint was low,

nervous fever, brought on, as it seemed to him, by some cause operating upon the mind; and, if her spirits could not be kept up, her peril was immediate."

I never received any intelligence with greater discomposure in my life. A variety of recollections, very like accusations, crowded one after the other suddenly upon my memory. My heart awoke from that lethargy into which long suffering had plunged it. Still, I thought, the thing must be exaggerated. "Her spirits kept up?" Why, they must be kept up. "What was to be done to keep them up?" That the adviser left to me.

I visited Isabella with feelings which I could scarce acknowledge even to myself. She sent for me as I was going to her chamber, and my purpose of going almost changed. I know not how to describe the sensation which her message produced. I was going to her at the very moment unsummoned, and yet the summons compelled me to turn back. It was not the feeling of a man who is detected in a crime, for that must suppose a previous consciousness that he was committing one; it was the alarm rather of a child who plays with a forbidden bauble, and suddenly discovers that the last whirl has broken it.

I had seen Isabella on the preceding evening, but I found her much worse than I had expected. I leaned upon her bed; it was some time before she could gather firmness to express herself. At length she spoke, and I hear her accents at this moment.

She spoke with apparent confidence of her approaching death. "She regretted it for my sake, because her fortune would die with her." "Could she but have secured my future happiness and safety, as she had nothing left in life to hope for, so she would have had nothing to desire."

These are commonplace expressions, perhaps I shall be be told. The fact may be so. *Death* is very commonplace. But those who, in the midst of a course decidedly evil, have been cursed with sufficient perception to abhor the guilt they could not abstain from, such only can appreciate my feelings at that moment. The mere mention of Isabella's death as possible carried distraction to my soul. She told me that she had long seen the decline of my affection; "her only wish was that it could have lasted while she lived!" I stood before her a convicted villain. I could not lie, I could not speak; at last I wept, or I had died.

I must not dwell upon the particulars of this interview. She thanked me for the uniform kindness I had shown her; for the effort with which I had avoided connections which she had but too plainly seen my desire to form. "Could I pardon her for the pain that she had caused me? I should be happier after her death; for, if it left me poor, it would at least restore me to my liberty."

Let me do myself justice here as I have visited justice upon myself elsewhere. I was not quite a wretch. If my passions were habitually fierce and ungovernable, their impulse in the good cause was as powerful as in the cause of ill.

I knelt beside Isabella's bed. I confessed the truth of all she charged me with. I invoked curses on my restless temper; swore that all my former love for her was rekindled; that I would not survive her death; that I should esteem myself her murderer! Nor did I at that moment, so help me Heaven, utter any sentiment which I did not feel. If I did not at that moment love Isabella passionately, I would have laid my life down with pleasure for her safety, for her happiness. And I trusted that I had in some measure restored her peace of mind; and I was seriously resolving to *like* a peaceful life, when a circumstance occurred well calculated again to put my resolution to the proof.

Chapter IV.

Had I been asked for which of my virtues I should ever have a fortune given me, I might have had some difficulty, and should have had, in answering the question. It was my fate, however, for once to be enriched by my irregularities. My grandfather, penetrated on a sudden with admiration of the man who had brought his family name so much into discussion, died, after making twenty wills in favour of twenty different people, and, passing over my father, bequeathed a property of £4000 a year to me.

I premised that about this time some unforeseen occurrences befel me. Two of these I have already described; the third was of all the most unexpected. While I was busy in preparations for returning to England, and devising schemes out of number for pleasures and splendour when I should arrive there, Isabella left me.

It was a blow for which, less than for a miracle, I was prepared. Returning one evening from shooting (we were then living at Condeixa), I found a letter in her hand lying sealed upon my table. The sight of the address alone paralysed me. What had happened flashed in an instant across my mind. The contents of the letter were these:—

"If I have used deception towards you, Charles, believe me, it is now for the first time. · I wish to spare you the needless agony of bidding me farewell; I wish to secure myself against the danger of being diverted from a course which reflection has convinced me is the best. I cannot forget that you have ceased to love me; I have known the fact long, but circumstances have kept me silent. I acquit you—Heaven is my witness—of unkindness or ingratitude; esteem, affection, regard, compassion, I know you give me these; and love is not at our command. There are men from whom I could be satisfied with kindness and esteem; but I cannot fall so low as to accept pity, Charles, from you. You always will, you always must, love some woman. Can I know this, and yet live with you, and be conscious that you do not love me?

" For three years I have endured to see you wretched, and to feel myself the cause of your distress. Could I feel this, and yet be happy? What did I gain by depriving others of your heart when I knew that to me your heart was lost for ever? A thousand times have I wished that your scruples would give way, and that you would be happy in a course which could have added nothing to my misery. I have borne all this long, but my motive for bearing it is at an end. Your accession of fortune makes my presence no longer necessary. You have now open before you that career for which you have so long panted ; I believe that you are capable of sacrificing it for me ; but can I accept such a sacrifice from you, Charles? Can I exact it? Do you think I could value it ?

" Farewell! I will no longer continue to hang upon you, interrupting enjoyments in which I am forbidden to participate. Farewell! My pen trembles as I write the word ; but be assured that I write it irrevocably.

" Do not distract us both by vain endeavours to recall me. If love were yours to give, I know, I feel, that you would give it to me ; but it is not, Charles, at your disposal. Farewell, once more ; for I had intended but to say, ' Farewell!' May you be happy, though my day of happiness is over. Thank Heaven, your impetuous temper is no longer likely to be excited by want of means to those enterprises which might not always be successful ; but, if ever chance should place you again in such emergency as to make Isabella's fortune, her life, her love, worth your acceptance, then, and then only, will she consent again to hear from you."

She is living yet—I trust she is ! If the last prayers of one who has prayed but too seldom ; if those prayers may be heard which merit nor hearing nor value ; if mercy for another can be granted to him who dares not, cannot, ask it for himself—then may every blessing she can wish for, every blessing which can wait on life, be hers! May she know that in my last hour my thoughts were upon her; that my latest wishes were breathed for her safety, for her happiness!

How merely is man the creature of events over which he has no control! When I kissed Isabella's forehead scarce six hours before she wrote that letter, how far was I from imagining that I then beheld her for the last time! And what a turn did our separation give probably to my destiny! I despise the pedantic dogma which says "No one can be missed." Ill as I think of human nature, I think that assertion is a libel upon it. Among creatures who have as little of discrimination as of feeling, to whom the newest fool is always the most welcome friend; by such beings it may be true that "no one can be missed;" but I deny that any man of common sensibility or perception can part *for ever*, even from a mere companion, without remembrance and regret.

I paused, for my brain was giddy after reading Isabella's letter. My first thought was to follow her, but, on reflection, I abandoned the design. I felt that I could not hope to overcome her fixed belief that the continuance of our connection would on my part be a sacrifice. She had retired into a convent, the Lady Superior of which had long been known to us, and I felt that she must be happier there or anywhere than with me. Should it seem that my decision was, under the circumstances, a convenient one, I swear that it was a decision in which my wishes had no part. No honourable or feeling man will doubt my candour in this statement. He will know, if not from experience, from instinct, that had I listened to my own wishes I should only have thought of recovering Isabella. He will know that her absence left a blank in my heart; that, spite of philosophy, axiom, or authority, I felt there was a something missing, wanting—a reliance, a consolation, a *point d'appui* to the mind which nothing but the society of woman could supply.

And, if I have loved other women, Isabella has not been forgotten. In the maddest moments of gaiety, in the wildest hours of license, the doubt of her existence, the certainty of her wretchedness, has dashed across my mind and poisoned the cup of pleasure at my lips. Before I quitted Portugal I wrote her letter after letter, intreating, promising, imploring her return. If it was not for my love that I desired to change her resolution, I swear that for my mere quietude, for my peace of mind, I wished to do it. Ah! what have I to regret in being compelled to quit a world where to possess feeling or reflection is to be eternally unhappy; where passion leaves its victim no choice but in his own wretchedness, or in the misery of those whom, at his soul's hazard, he would shield from harm; and where the being who enjoys the most of gratification himself is the creature who is most callous to the sufferings of all around him!

It was not, however, until I had completed my dispositions as to Isabella's fortune, until I was about to embark for England, to place distance—seas—between us; I did not fully until that moment feel what it was to part from her for ever. I wrote to her once more, even while my vessel was under sail. Though I was sensible of the folly, I wrote the letter with my blood. I entreated that she would follow me, and follow me without delay. I declared that I should expect her, that I would take no denial, that I should wait for her at the first English port. With that strange confidence which men often have when their hopes are totally desperate, I went so far even as to appoint the hotel at which I should stay. I really did expect that Isabella would follow me to England. I wronged her firmness. The ship in which I had embarked met with contrary winds. A subsequently sailing vessel reached England before us. I found, on landing at Falmouth, a packet from Isabella; but it contained only her picture, and these words,—" Do not forget me."

That picture hangs about my neck at the moment while I write. I will die with it next my heart. As the magnet, catching eagerly each particle of iron, lets golden sands roll on unheeded by, so memory treasures up our moments of

misfortune long after those of happiness and gaiety are forgotten.   Isabella lost was to be remembered for ever.

But these are recollections which unhinge me for detail.
I have a blow to strike, and almost within this hour, for
which every corporal and mental agent must be nerved.
And my senses rush along in tide as furious and rapid as
my fate ! I cannot dwell, amid this whirl of mind and fancy,
upon the measures which in seven years dispossessed me
of £70,000.   I am not lamenting that which I have done.
I began with a resolution to *live* while I did live.   Uncertain
of the next moment, the passing hour was all to me.   What
mattered it, since my course must cease, whether it ceased
sooner or later; provided, while it lasted, I was in all
things content ?   I scorned the confined views of men who,
possessing means, submitted to let " I dare not " wait upon
" I would ; " and vowed when I put myself at the head of my
fortune, that no expenditure of wealth, no exposure of person,
should ever have weight to disappoint my inclination.

Yet my estate lasted longer than, under such a resolution,
might be·expected.   The rich, for the most part, either
lavish their money without enjoying it, or, to maintain what
is called a certain " state," suffer dependents to lavish it for
them.   As it happened that I had no wish for commonplace
distinctions, nor was very desirous of anything which money
alone could buy, I escaped all those rapidly ruinous contests
in which the longest purse is understood to carry the day.
I saw something of the absurdities of fashion, but I entered
very little into them.   Curiosity, want of employment, and
that natural desire which even the silliest man feels to laugh
at the follies of those about him, made me associate sometimes with fine gentlemen ; but I never became a fine gentleman myself.

And yet it was amusing, in the way of *chasse ennui*, to glide
along with the frequenters of Bond Street and with the
loungers at the opera ; and to observe the excessive, the
monstrous self-delusion of men who had been born to
ample means, and were not encumbered much with under-

standing. Their talk was such feather, and yet even in what they uttered they were generally mistaken. If they were vicious, it was from thoughtlessness; if honest, from accident. Their conversation was so easy, and yet (to themselves) so entertaining; the jest so weak; the laugh so hilarious. Their belief, too, was so facile,—I did envy them that faculty! Not one of them ever doubted anything that he was at all interested in crediting. All about them was fudge, and yet they never seemed to be aware of it. Their Bond Street dinners were *not* good. They would talk all day about the fancied merits of particular dishes, and yet at night be put off with such wine and *cuisine* as really was sad stuff, and could not have passed but upon men of fashion.

But the most striking feature in their characters was their utter want of self-respect. I have seen a young man literally begging for half-crowns who but a few months before had driven his curricle and been distinguished for his insolence.

Another would borrow small sums and never pay them, until not even a servant was left who would lend him a shilling. Others would endure to be insulted by their tradesmen; to be poisoned at coffee-houses where they could not pay their bills; to truck and barter their clothes and valuables for ready-money with waiters at hotels; and all this to obtain supplies which in reality they did not want, and because they knew no mode of dissipating time but in dissipating a certain quantity of specie.

These were the people who went to fights—to races; wore large hats, and garments of peculiar cut; with little of taste or fancy in their devices; and of true conception of splendour or of elegance, none.

Then their hangers-on were a set of men fit to be classed *per se* in history; fellows culled from all ranks and stations, but all rascals alike; their avocations various, but all infamous. There were among them cashiered officers, or men who had left the army to avoid that infliction; fraudulent waiters and markers from billiard tables; shopkeepers' sons, black-leg attorneys, and now and then the broken-down heir of a respectable name and family.

I recollect one or two of these fellows who were characters for posterity in their way. There was one Mr. M'Grath in particular, a native of the sister kingdom, with whose history in full it fell to my lot to be acquainted. I traced him back to his leaving Dublin, where he had acted as collecting clerk to a distiller, and from whence, on account of some trifling embezzlements, he had come over to England with about twenty pounds in his pocket. This man on his arrival had not a friend nor a connection to back him ; his address was bad ; his person not prepossessing ; and he had an unconquerable aversion to anything like honest labour ; but he began with a little, and by industry rose.

His first step in London was into a second-floor lodging in Jermyn Street, Piccadilly, for he laid himself out as an appendage to men of fortune from the beginning. The woman of the house dwelt herself in a single apartment, waited upon her guests as a servant, and fleeced them, because her house was " in a situation ! "

This woman had a hump-backed daughter who stood a grade above her mother. I saw her afterwards in a workhouse, to which I went for the purpose of ascertaining the truth of M'Grath's history. She did the better kind of labour, while her mother attended to the drudgery, and by parsimony and great exertion they had acquired near £2000.

M'Grath's second step in life, having heard of the £2000, was to marry his landlady's hump-backed daughter ; and with part of the money he bought a commission in the Guards. Here he remained but a short time, his real character being discovered. Within twelve months he deserted his newly acquired wife. The furniture of the mother's house was next seized for his debts. The two miserable women then came for support upon the parish ; and with the wreck of the £2000 M'Grath commenced gentleman.

And, with the appointments of respectable station about him, this fellow had gone on for more than twenty years when by accident I met with him, the most handy and universally applicable creature in the world. Latterly he had found it convenient to call himself a conveyancer, and undertook to act as an agent on all occasions. He was a money-lender, an assistant in borrowing money or in investing it. He bought or sold a horse; could obtain patronage (upon a deposit) for a curacy or a colonel's commission. Then he dealt among the bankrupts; could indorse a bill; get it cashed. He would arrange a provision for a distressed lady; wait upon a betrayer at the hazard of being kicked downstairs; threaten law proceedings; introduce a new face; in short, wherever there was distress and helplessness, there, as if by instinct, you were sure to find M'Grath.

I met with the gentleman under circumstances (for him) peculiarly unlucky. He had been settling with a certain peer the terms upon which he was to be freed from the importunity of a female from whom importunity ought not to have been necessary. I chanced shortly afterwards to fall in with the lady; and (she really had been unfortunate) to become interested for her. M'Grath in this case had gone to work with less than his usual prudence. He had received at the end of his negotiation £500 from the nobleman in question, upon a written promise that the applicant should trouble him no more; of which £500 he accounted for £200 in cash, giving his own note to his client as security for the rest. This was a safe £300 gained; but M'Grath was not content. Distress within a short time obliged the same woman to dispose of some jewels and other personal property which she possessed; and this property, with a fatuity apparently unaccountable even after what had happened, she employed M'Grath to find a purchaser for. The monstrous apparent folly of such an act made me doubt the truth of the whole story when I heard it. In Heaven's name, I asked, why had she trusted such a fellow as M'Grath even in the first transaction? "And who but such a man," was the answer, "would have undertaken such an office?"

M'Grath, however, probably had his necessities as well as other people, for on this occasion he took a measure of very questionable safety. Relying upon the lady's dread of public exposure, he pawned the whole of her jewels, and converted the money to his own use. I caused him merely to be arrested, although his offence was, I believe, a criminal one ; and eventually he was liberated from prison by the Insolvent Act, for he had judged rightly so far the exposure of a prosecution could not be borne ; but, by a singular coincidence, I had afterwards to kick him out of my own house, on his calling for the particulars (he did not know upon whom) of a next presentation to a living advertised for sale.

Women, however, of course, among the true spendthrifts of my acquaintance, were the principal objects of discourse and of attention. But their arrangements even upon this point were of so odd a description that the ridiculous overpowers every other feeling when I think of them. I forget the man's name who told a certain king that there was no royal road to the knowledge of mathematics. I doubt he would have failed to impress my acquaintances with that truth. *On achete le tout* seemed to be their conviction. One loved in order that he might be affirmed a person in the world ; another for the fashion of a particular lady ; a third because a mistress was a good point to show "style" in ; and a fourth because it was necessary to have one. The *nonchalance* of this last set was the most exquisite thing in nature. They affected (and I believe felt) a perfect indifference towards their *protegées ;* introduced all their acquaintance, without a jot of jealousy, at their houses ; and I saw a letter from a peer to a French woman who transacted love affairs for him, stating that he meant to form an attachment of some duration when he came to town ; and describing (as to person) the sort of lady upon whom he should wish to fix his affections.

The nature of such connections may well be imagined. No regard was ever dreamed of for the feelings of the women; the men were, of course, appreciated and abused. It was a sacrifice on both sides; but the sacrifice of the man was merely a sacrifice of money of which he did not know the value: and that sacrifice neither obtained nor deserved any gratitude, for the same individual who would ruin himself in keeping a splendid *etat* for his mistress would lavish nothing upon her that did not redound to his own "fashionable" notoriety.

For myself, if I did not enter into the spirit of what was called *ton*, it did not arise from any want of general good reception. As soon as it was found that I cared about no coterie, all coteries were open to me. But, if it was much to be one of the few, I thought it would be even more to stand alone. And therefore, although I kept fine horses, I did not race them to death. I had a handsomely furnished house; but I refused to have a *taste;* that is to say, I did not lie awake fourteen nights together imagining a new scroll pattern for the edge of a sofa, nor decide (still in doubt), after six weeks' perplexity, which was the properest tint of two-and-twenty for the lining of a window-curtain. In short, my private arrangements were no way guided by ambitious feeling; whether I rode, drove, drank, or dressed, I did the act merely because it was an act gratifying to myself, not because it had been done by Lord Such-a-one or was to be done by Mr. So-and-so; and although my fortune was small compared with the fortunes of some of my companions, yet, as it mattered not how soon the whole was expended, I generally seemed upon emergency to be the richest man of the circle I was moving in.

And a race for some to envy has my career been to this moment! If the last few months have shown note of coming evil, that evil could not terrify me when I was prepared to elude it. If I have not enjoyed, in the possession of riches, that absolute conviction (my solace under poverty) that what tribute I did receive was paid entirely to myself,

yet the caution and experience which poverty taught me
has preserved me from gross and degrading imposition.
Let me keep up my spirits, even with egotism, in a moment
like this.   I have not been quite an object to court imposition.   The same faculties and powers which availed me
when I was without a guinea continued at my command
throughout my high fortune.   I have not been, as an old
man, wasting property which I could not spend; I have
not been a wretched pretender by purchase to place and
to circumstance to which desert gave me no title; I have
not been the thing that I am, to die, because I will not be.

Gold is worth something, inasmuch as it gives certain
requisites for continued enjoyment which can be obtained
from no other source.   Apart from all pretension to severe
moral principle, I had ever this feeling in its fullest extent
—that the man was thrice a villain, a wretch thrice unfit to
live, who could plunge any woman that trusted him into
poverty, into disgrace.   To this principle I would admit
neither of exception nor evasion.   I do not say that every
man can command his passions, but every man can meet
the consequences of them.   Again and again, in my days
of necessity, did I fly from connections which seemed to
indicate such termination.   Money, however, as society is
constituted, can do much.   My subsequent wealth relieved
me from all obstacles.

Yet, let me redeem myself in one point—I shall not
attempt it in many—my power was in no instance (as I
believe) employed cruelly.   For my fellow-men I had little
consideration.   I knew them merciless; I had felt them so.
Still, upon man, if I recollect well, I never wantonly inflicted
pain; and in no one instance, as Heaven shall judge me,
did I ever sacrifice the feelings of a woman.

A portion of my wealth was given to relieve my father
from debts which he had incurred in expectation of the
whole.   Another portion, I trust, will have placed in security
beings whose happiness and safety form my latest wish on
earth.   A third portion, and a large one, has been consumed

in idle dissipation; but if I have often thrown away a hundred guineas, I have sometimes given away ten.

The whole, however, at last is gone. Parks, lordships, manors, mansions, not a property is left. As my object was always rather pleasure than parade, this change in my circumstances is little known to the world. I am writing, and I shall die so, in elegant apartments, with liveried servants, splendid furniture—all the paraphernalia of luxury about me. The whole is disposed of and the produce consumed. To-morrow gives the new owner possession. A hundred persons make account to nod to me to-morrow. I have for to-morrow four invitations to dinner. I shall die to-night.

Let me not be charged with flying this world because I fear to meet the loss of fortune. Give me back the years that I have spent, and I can deem lightly of the money. But my place, my station among my fellow-men? It totters, it trembles. Youth, hope, and confidence, these are past; and the treasures of the unfathomed ocean could not buy them back.

Life of life, spirit of enjoyment, to what has it not fallen! Does it still spring in the heart, like the wild flower in the field, the native produce of a vigorous soil, which asks no tillage, defies eradication, and rears its head alike amid the zephyr and the storm? No; it is this no longer. It is an exotic now, a candle-light flower, the sensitive plant with the hue of the rose; love is its sunshine, wine the dew that cherishes it; it blossoms beneath the ray of the evening star, and blooms in the illuminated garden at midnight; but in the cool breeze of morning it droops and it withers; and day, which brings life to all else, destroys it for ever.

Then, if I had the Indies still in my grasp, would I endure to descend in the scale of creation? Would I join the class of respectable old men, and sit spectator of a conflict which I am no longer able to engage in? Would I choose the more disgusting course of some I see around me, and let the vices of manhood degenerate into the weaknesses of age? Would I struggle to maintain a field in which victory is past my hope; dispute a palm which, of necessity, must be wrested from my hand? Would I endure to have men whom I have been accustomed to see as children, push me insolently from the stage of life, and seize the post which I have occupied?

If I could not bear this, still less could I endure the probable, the inevitable, consequences of living to extreme old age. To be, if not distasteful to my own depraved and doting sense, conscious of being distasteful to all the world beside!—to die worn out with pains and aches! helpless in body, feebler still in mind!—the tottering victim of decrepitude and idiotcy, cowering from that fate which by no effort I can avoid!

I will not come to this. I will not make a shirking, ignominious end of life when I have the power within myself to die as may become a man. To this hour I have had strength to keep my station in the world. In a few moments it would be gone, but I shall go before it. And what do I lose by thus grappling with my fate? A few years at most of uncertainty or uneasiness. That man may die to-morrow I know afflicts him little; but let him reflect in his triumph that he must die on the next day. Let him remember that when he has borne to hear people inquire after his health, listen to his answer with impatience, and go to be happy out of his reach; when he has borne to close the eyes of the last friend of his youth, to lose all his old connections, and to find himself incapable of forming new ones; when he has endured to be a solitary, excommunicated wretch, and to read, in the general eye, that he is an in-truder upon earth,—he is still but as a ball to which a certain impetus is given, which, moving in a fixed track, can neither deviate nor pause, and which has but (to an inch) a marked space to pass over, at the end of which comes that fall from which the world's worth cannot save it.

I can write no more. My hour is fast approaching. Now am I greater, in my own holding, than an emperor!

He would command the fate of others, but I command my own. This is in very choice the destiny which I would embrace. There is something sublime in thus looking in the face of Death; he sits over against me as I write, and I view him without terror. If I have a predominant feeling at this moment, it is a feeling of curiosity.

One full glass more and I am prepared. Wine is wanting only to aid the nerve, not to stimulate the courage or the will. My pistols lie loaded by my side. I will seal this packet, nevertheless, with a steady hand, and you who receive it shall bear witness that I have done so.

Now within this half hour I will forget even that care must be the lot of man. I will revel for a moment in the influence of wine and in the smile of beauty—I will live for one moment longer the being I could wish to live for ever.

The clock strikes eleven. Friend, whom I have selected to receive my parting words, I must conclude. I shall send this letter to you instantly. You will receive it while I still exist, and yet you will be unable—the world would be unable—to prevent the act I meditate. Do me justice, and farewell! When chimes tell twelve to-night I shall be uppermost in your mind. You will wonder, you will be troubled, you will doubt. And when you sit at breakfast to-morrow morning, some public newspaper, recording my death, will give you perhaps the real name of

TITUS.

Chevy Chase;

A POEM—IDEM LATINE REDDITUM.

BEING of Sir Philip Sidney's opinion, that the ballad of Chevy Chase stirs the heart like the sound of a trumpet, and being moreover willing that other nations should have at least some idea of that magnificent poem, I have translated it into the universal language of Europe—Latin; and I send you my translation of the first fitte. You will perceive that I have retained the measure and structure of the verse most religiously; I wish I could say that I have preserved also the fire and spirit of the original. Bold, at the desire of Bishop Compton, translated into Latin the more modern ballad of Chevy Chase, as also did Anketeil, a Presbyterian clergyman (I believe) in the north of Ireland. Lord Woodhouselee, in his excellent Essay on Translation, has quoted the first verse of Anketeil's translation apparently without knowing the author. But to say nothing of the inferiority of the poem they translated, I flatter myself that I out-top them by the head and broad shoulders in the superior richness and melody of my double rhymes. Print this, then, by all means; so no more from your servant at command.   O. P.

I.

The Percy out of Northumberland,*
  And a vow to God made he,
That he would hunt in the mountains
  Of Cheviot within days three,
In the mauger of doughty Douglas,
  And all that with him be.

I.

PERSÆUS ex Northumbria
  Vovebat, Diis iratis,
Venare inter dies tres
  In montibus Cheviatis,
Contemtis forti Douglaso
  Et omnibus cognatis.

---

* I have modernised the spelling of the old ballad.

2.

The fattest harts in Cheviot
  He said he'd kill and carry away :
" By my faith," said doughty Douglas,
  " I'll let that hunting if I may."

2.

"Optimos cervos ibi," ait,
  " Occisos reportabo ;"
" Per Jovem," inquit Douglãsus,
  " Venatum hunc vetabo."

3.

The Percy out of Bamborough came,
  With him a mighty meany ;
With fifteen hundred archers bold ;
  They were chosen out of shires three.

3.

Ex Bamboro Persæus it,
  Cum agmine potenti ;
Nam tribus agris lecti sunt
  Sagittarii ter quingenti.

4.

This began on Monday at morn,
  In Cheviot the hills so high ;
The child may rue that is unborn ;
  It is the more pity !

4.

Ad Cheviatos graditur,
  In Lunæ die mane ;
Puer nondum natus fieret hoc ;
  Quod est dolendum sane !

5.

The drivers through the woods went,
  For to raise up the deer ;
Bowmen bickered upon the bent
  With their broad arrows clear.

5.

Viri, qui cervos agerent,
  Per nemora pergebant ;
Dum sagittarii spiculas
  Ex arcubus fundebant.

6.

Then the wild through the woods went,
  On every side sheer ;
Greyhounds through the groves glent,
  For to kill their deer.

6.

Tum diffugerunt * penitus
  Per omnem sylvam feræ ;
Et eas canes Gallici
  Sequentes percurrère.

7.

This began in Cheviot the hills above,
  Early on a Monday ;
By that it drew to the hour of noon,
  A hundred fat harts dead there lay.

7.

Hunc matutino tempore
  Venatum sic cœperunt ;
Et centum sub meridiem
  Pingues cervi ceciderunt.

8.

They blew a mort upon the bent ;
  They 'sembled on sides sheer :
To the quarry then the Percy went,
  To see the brittling of the deer.

8.

Tum tubæ taratantara †
  Convocat dissipatos ;
Comes Persæus visum it
  Cervos dilaniatos.

---

* Percy's translation of *sheer*.
† So Ennius : At tuba terribili sonitu *taratantara* dixit.

9.

He said—" It was the Douglas' promise
　This day to meet me here,
But I wist he would fail verament : "
　A great oath the Percy sware.

9.

Dicens, " Promisit Douglasus
　Mî hic occursum ire,
Sed * scivi quod non faceret."
　His dictis jurat mirè.

10.

At last a squire of Northumberland
　Looked at his hand full nigh—
He was ware of the Douglas coming,
　With him a mighty meany ;

10.

Tandem armiger Northumbriæ
　Aspexit venientem
Prope ad manum Douglasum,
　Et agmina ducentem.

11.

Both with spear, bill, and brand,
　It was a mighty sight to see ;
Hardier men of heart and hand
　Were not in Christianity.

11.

Cum hastis, pilis, ensibus,
　Magnifici iverunt ;
Fortiores in fidelibus
　Domini non fuerunt.

12.

They were twenty hundred spearmen
　　good,
　Withouten any fail ;
They were borne along by the water of
　　Tweed,
　In the bounds of Tividale.

12.

Bis mille procul dubio
　Hastati bonæ notæ,
Ad aquas Tuedæ nati sunt,
　In finibus Tiviotæ.

13.

" Leave off the brittling of the deer," he
　　said,
　" And to your bows take heed ;
For never since you were on your mothers
　　born
　Had ye such meikle need."

13.

" Mittite cervos, sumite
　Sagittas nullâ morâ ;
Nunquam tam opus fuit, ex
　Nostrâ natali horâ."

14.

The doughty Douglas on a steed
　He rode his men beforne ;
His armour glittered as did a glede—
　A bolder bairn was never born.

14.

In primo fortis Douglasus
　Equitans veniebat ;
Lorica prunæ similis
　Ardenti resplendebat.

---

* Consult the Edinburgh Reviewer of Falconer's Strabo for this construction of *scio quod*. The " paltry " dog will remember something about it,
as sure as my name is not Copplestone.

15.

"Tell me what men ye are," he says,
  "Or whose men that ye be ;
Who gave ye leave to hunt in this
  Cheviot Chase in spite of me?"

16.

The first man that an answer made,
  It was the Lord Percy—
"We will not tell what men we are,
  Nor whose men that we be ;
But we will hunt here in this chase,
  In spite of thine and thee.

17.

"The fattest harts in Cheviot
  We have killed, and cast to carry
    away."
"By my troth," said the doughty Douglas,
  "Therefore the one of us shall die this
    day."

18.

Then said the doughty Douglas
  Unto the Lord Percy,
"To kill all these guiltless men,
  Alas! it were great pity.

19.

"But, Percy, thou art a lord of land,
  I am an earl in my own country ;
Let all our men upon a party stand,
  And do the battle of thee and me."

20.

"Now Christ's curse on his crown," said
    the Lord Percy,
  "Whosoever thereto says nay!
By my troth, doughty Douglas," he says,
  "Thou shalt never see that day,

21.

"Neither in England, Scotland, nor
    France,
  Nor for no man of woman born ;
But an fortune be my chance,
  I dare meet him one for one."

15.

Et, "Quinam estis, cedo," ait,
  "Aut cujus viri sitis?
Quis misit vos venatum hic,
  Nobis admodum invitis?"

16.

Persæus autem Douglaso
  Respondit longe primus,
"Qui sumus haud narrabimus,
  Aut cujus viri simus ;
Sed hic, invitis omnibus,
  Venatum statim imus.

17.

"Cervorum hic pinguissimos
  Occisos auferemus."
"Idcirco," dixit Douglasus,
  "Necesse est ut pugnemus."

18.

Et dixit fortis Douglasus
  Hæc verba nunc Persæo,
"Necare hos innoxios
  Non esset gratum deo ;

19.

"Sed tu, Persæe, princeps es,
  Sum ego comes quoque ;
Cernamus soli, agmine
  Manente hic utroque."

20.

Persæus inquit, "Pereat is
  Qui huic vult obviam ire,
Nam, hercle, dies aderit
  Nunquam, Douglàse dire,

21.

Quum Angliâ, Scotiâ, Galliâ,
  Negaverim tentare
Sortem cum ullo homine
  In pugnâ singulari."

22.

Then bespake a squire of Northumber-
land,
  Rog. Witherington was his name—
It shall never be told in South England
  To King Harry the Fourth for shame,

22.

Tunc armiger Northumbriæ
  R. Withringtonus fatur,
" Nunquam Henrico principi
  In Anglia hoc dicatur ;

23.

" I wot ye be great lords two,
  I am a poor squire of land,
I will never see my captain fight in a
  field
  And look on myself and stand ; *
But while I may my weapon wield,
  I will not fail both heart and hand."

23.

" Vos estis magni comites
  Et pauper miles ego,
Sed pugnaturum dominum,
  Me otioso, nego :
Sed corde, manu, enseque,
  Pugnabo quamdiu dego."

24.

That day, that day, that dreadful day—
  The first fytte here I find ;
An ye will hear more of the hunting of
  Cheviot,
Yet there is more behind.

24.

O dies ! dies, dies trux !
  Sic finit cantus primus ;
Si de venatu plura vis,
  Plura narrare scimus.

FINIS PARTIS PRIMÆ.

P. S.—I am aware that " Douglassius " is consecrated ; but I am not
without authority for Douglasus.—I have also translated this into Greek,
and I send you the first verse as a specimen.

$$\Pi\epsilon\rho\sigma\alpha\hat{\iota}os\ \dot{\epsilon}\kappa\ No\rho\theta o\acute{\upsilon}\mu\epsilon\rho\iota as$$
$$E\check{\upsilon}\chi\epsilon\tau o\ \tau o\hat{\iota}s\ \vartheta\epsilon o\hat{\iota}\sigma\iota,$$
$$\Theta\eta\rho\hat{q}\nu\ \dot{\epsilon}\nu\ \tau\rho\iota\sigma\dot{\iota}\nu\ \dot{\eta}\mu\acute{\epsilon}\rho a\iota s$$
$$\text{'}E\nu\ o\check{\upsilon}\rho\epsilon\sigma\iota\ X\epsilon\epsilon\iota a\tau o\hat{\iota}\sigma\iota,$$
$$K\check{a}\nu\ \dot{a}\nu\tau\acute{\epsilon}\chi\eta\sigma\iota\ \Delta o\acute{\upsilon}\gamma\lambda a\sigma os$$
$$\Sigma\dot{\upsilon}\nu\ \pi\hat{a}\sigma\iota\nu\ \dot{\epsilon}\tau\acute{a}\rho o\iota\sigma\iota.$$

Don't say a word of this, however, to Hallam—" classic Hallam, much
renowned for Greek," as Lord Byron justly styles him—lest he should mistake
my verses for Pindar's, and consequently declare them not Greek. *A propos,*
is it not a good joke to see Hallam putting a Greek motto to his book on
the Middle Ages after all ? I was thinking of translating old Chevy into
Hebrew—for I am a Masorite ; but as Professor Leslie has declared Hebrew
to be a " rude and poor dialect " in his book on Arithmetic, I was afraid to
come under the censure of that learned gentleman. To be sure he does
not know (*as I can prove from his writings*) even the alphabet of the
language he abuses, but still I am afraid he would freeze me if I had anything to do with it.

---

* In Bishop Percy—" And stand myself and look on." But correct it,
meo periculo.

Chevy Chase.

<table>
<tr><td>Second Fytte.</td><td>Pars Secunda.</td></tr>
</table>

1.	**1.**

* THE English men had their bows bent,
   Their hearts were good enow,
The first † of arrows that they shot off,
   Seven score spearmen they slew.

ANGLI perstrenui animis
   Tunc arcus intenderunt,
Et vicies septem homines
   Primo jactu necaverunt.

2.

Yet bides Earl Douglas on the bent,
   A captain good enough :
And that was seen verament,
   For he wrought them wo and wouch.

Attamen mansit Douglasus
   In boni ducis morem ;
Quod patuit cum perniciem
   Effudit et dolorem.

3.

The Douglas parted his host in three,
   Like a chief chieftain of pride ;
With sure spears of mighty tree,
   They came in on every side.

Trifariam struxit aciem,
   Periti ducis arte ;
Cum hastis ligni validi
   Ruunt ex omni parte.

4.

Through our English archery
   Gave many a wound full wide ;
Many a doughty they made to die,
   Which gained them no pride.

Ediderunt stragem plurimam
   Per ordines Anglorum :
Heroum vitas dempserunt ‡
   Non amplius superborum.§

---

* I have, as before, modernised the spelling of the old ballad, and in a few places the language.—W. M.

† *i.e.*, first flight. Percy.—W. M.

‡ Dr. Carey (Prosody, p. 199, &c.) condemns this license. I therefore give him leave to alter my systolated præterites into preterpluperfects, as he has done in all the passages which stand in the way of his rule. I have no doubt that he will discover some new picturesque mood and tense beauty in the change quite unknown to the author.—W. M.

§ I hope I have hit the sense of my original.—W. M.

5.

The English men let their bows be,
  And pulled out brands that were
      bright ;
It was a heavy sight to see
  Bright swords on helmets light.

5.

Stringunt, omissis arcubus,
  Angli gladios fulgentes :
Quos miserum fuit cernere
  In cassibus descendentes.

6.

Through rich mail and myne-ye-ple *
  Many stern they struck down straight ;
Many a ficke that was full free
  There under foot did light.

6.

Armorum plicas splendidas
  Mucro strictus penetravit :
Et multos quondam nobiles
  Pes vilis conculcavit.

7.

At last the Douglas and the Percy met,
  Like two captains of might and main ;
They swept together, till they both sweat,
  With swords of fine Milain. †

7.

Persæus mox et Douglasus
  (Dux contra vires ducis)
Pugna concurrunt ensibus
  Mediolani cusis.

8.

These worthy fickes for to fight,
  Thereto they were full fain,
Till the blood out of their helmets
      sprung,
  As ever did hail or rain.

8.

Hi comites fortissimi
  Perstiterunt pugnando,
Donec cruor saliit cassibus,
  Ut imber vel ut grando.

9.

"Hold thee, Percy," said the Douglas,
  "And i' faith I will thee bring,
Where thou shalt have an earl's wages
  Of James, our Scottish king :

9.

"Si cedas," inquit Douglasus,
  "Perducam te, Persæe,
Ubi ut comes viveres
  Sub rege Scotiæ meæ :

10.

"Thou shalt have thy ransom free—
  I bid thee hear this thing ;
For the manfullest man art thou,
  That ever I conquered in field-fight-
    ing."

10.

"Et lytrum ‡ nullum peterem,
  Nam vere potest dici,
Te virum esse optimum,
  Quem prælio unquam vici."

---

* "Perhaps many plies or folds. Monyple is still used in this sense in the north, according to Mr. Lambe." Bp. Percy. I have followed him.—W. M.

† Swords made of Milan steel. Percy.—W. M.

‡ Græce, λύτρον. Ennius uses it, or rather its plural, lytra, as the name of a play concerning the ransom of Hector's body. If this be not thought sufficient authority, the reader may substitute *prætium* in the text with all my heart.—W. M.

11.

" Nay, then," said the Lord Percy,
  " I told it thee beforne,
That I would never yielded be
  To no man of woman born."

11.

Dixit Persæus, " Iterum,
  Quod antea dixi, edam ;
Id est, quod nunquam homini
  Ex fæmina nato cedam."

12.

With that there came an arrow hastily
  Forth of a mighty one ;
It hath stricken the Earl Douglas
  In at the breast-bone.

12.

Ex forti arcu calamus
  Tum rapide volavit,
Et inter verba Douglasum
  In pectore vulneravit.

13.

Through liver and lungs both
  The sharp arrow is gone ;
That never after in his life days
  He spake more words than one : *
" Fight ye my merry men while you may,
  For my life days are gone."

13.

In jecore et pulmonibus
  Hæsit sagita cita ;
Et postea verbum unicum
  Hoc tantum dixit ita :
" Pugnate strenue, socii,
  Nam ego cedo vita."

14.

The Percy leant upon his brand,
  And saw the Douglas die ;
He took the dead man by the hand,
  And said, " Woe is me for thee.

14.

Persæus nitens gladio
  Douglassi vidit mortem,
Et manu captu mortui
  Ploravit ejus sortem :

15.

" To have saved thy life I'd have
    parted with
My lands for years three ;
For a better man of heart nor hand
  Was not in all the north country."

15.

" Tribus annis agros dederem
  Servare virum talem ;
Nam fortior nemo fuit per
  Regionem borealem."

16.

Of all that saw a Scottish knight,
  Was named Sir Hugh Montgomery ;
He saw the Douglas to death was dight ;
  He spanned a spear a trusty tree.

16.

Hugo Montgomoræus hunc
  Cæsum vulnere indigno
Vidit, et hastam arripit
  Ex strenuo factam ligno.

---

* From this it appears that Jerry-Benthamism is of an older date than the superficial commonly imagine. Fight-you-my-merry-men-while-you-may-for-my-life-days-are-gone ; or, as the original has it, Fyghte-ye-my-merry-men-whylles-ye-may-for-my-lyff-days-ben-gan, is as pretty a *single* word as any we can find in the lucid pages of this most Euphuistical radical, and most radical Euphuist, who commonly passes in our days for the inventor of the many-words-clubbing-to-make-one style. We have here a much older authority ; so that Jerry must be set down as one of the *servum pecus* in that instance.—W. M.

17.

He rode upon a courser
  Through an hundred archery;
He never stinted nor never stopped
  Till he came to the good Lord Percy.

18.

He set upon Lord Percy
  A dint that was full sore,
With a sure spear of a trusty tree,
  Clean through the body he the Percy
    bore.

19.

At the other side that a man might see
  A large cloth-yard and mare.
Two better captains were not in Chris-
    tianty
  Than that day slain was there.

20.

An archer of Northumberland
  Saw slain was the Lord Percy;
He bare a bent bow in his hand,
  Was made of trusty tree.

21.

An arrow that a cloth-yard long,
  To the hard steel haled he;
A dint that was both sad and sore
  He set on Sir Hugh Montgomery.

22.

The dint it was both sad and sore
  That he on Montgomery set;
The swan-feathers that his arrow bore
  With his heart's-blood were wet.

23.

There was never a ficke one foot would
    fly,
  But still in storm did stand,
Hewing on each other while they might
    drie
  With many a baleful band.

17.

Et equitavit fortiter
  Per sagittarios centum;
Donec ad Anglum comitem
  Ab eo erat ventum.

18.

Persæum gravi vulnere
  Dicto citius sauciavit,
Nam corpus hasta rigidâ
  Penitus perforavit.

19.

Hasta ex læso corpore
  Exivit ulnæ spatio;
Meliores cæsis ducibus
  Non tenuit ulla natio.

20.

Sagittarius ex Northumbria
  Vidit dominum necatum;
In manu arcum tenuit
  Ex arbore fabricatum.

21.

Tres pedes longum calamum
  Perduxit ad mucronem,
Et vulnere mortifero
  Interimit Hugonem.

22.

Pertriste fuit vulnus, quod
  Hugo accipiebat:
Sagittæ alas cygneas
  Cor sanguine tingebat.

23.

Nulli volebant fugere;
  Sed strenue simul stantes *
Dimicabant quamdiu licuit,
  Se mutuo laniantes.

---

* An attempt at imitating the alliteration of the original. —W. M.

<table>
<tr><td>

24.

This battle began on Cheviot,
  An hour before the noon,
And when even song-bell was rung,
  The battle was not half done.

</td><td>

24.

Cœperunt hora cernere
  Antemeridiana ;
Et prælium sæviit vesperis
  Cum sonuit campana.

</td></tr>
</table>

25.

They took on, on either hand,
  By the light of the moon ;
Many had no strength to stand,
  In Cheviot the hills aboun.

25.

Etiam sub Lunæ radiis
  Perstabant sic pugnare ;
Donce sauciati plurimi
  Non potuerunt stare.

26.

Of fifteen hundred archers of England
  Went away but fifty and three :
Of twenty hundred spearmen of Scot-
    land
  But even five and fifty.

26.

Quinquaginta tres rediere ex
  Anglorum ter quingentis ;
Quinquaginta quinque tantum ex
  Bis millibus Scotæ gentis.

27.

But all were slain, Cheviot within,
  They had no strength to stand on high ;
The child may rue that is unborn ;
  It was the more pity.

27.

Ceciderunt sane cæteri
  In montibus Cheviatis ;
Puer nondum natus fleret hoc
  Quod est dolendum satis.

28.

There was slain with the Lord Percy
  Sir John of Agerstone,
Sir Roger, the kind Hartley,
  Sir William the bold Heron.

28.

Occisi cum Persæo sunt *
  Johannes Agerstonus,
Rogerus initis Hartlius,
  Gulielmus et Heronus ;

29.

Sir George the worthy Lovel,
  A knight of great renown,
Sir Ralph, the rich Rokeby,
  With dints were beaten down.

29.

Et Georgius dignus Lovelus,
  Bellator famæ veræ,
Rodolphus dives Rokebius
  Confossi cecidere.

---

* How beautifully Homeric ! How like the catalogues of the slain in the
lines of the prince of poets ! Particularly, how like the following :

> Καὶ σύν Περσαίῳ ἐδάμεν Ἀγαστώνος ἀμύμων,
> Ἀρτλείος τ' ἀγαθὸς, Ἡρώνος θ' ἱππότα δῖος ;
> Καὶ Λοβέλος κρατερὸς αἰχμητῆς, ἠδέ Ῥοβαῖος
> Ἀφνειος βιότοιο πέσον χαλκοῖο τυπῇσι.

The names in the Greek are not expressed so roughly as in the English,
but there is a manifest resemblance between the passages.—W. M.

30.

For Withrington my heart is wo,	Pro Withringtono doleo
That ever he slain should be:	Quem fatum triste stravit;
For when his legs were hewn in two,	Nam binis fractis cruribus
He knelt, and fought upon his knee.	In genibus pugnavit.

31.

There was slain with the doughty Douglas	Montgomoræus cecidit
Sir Hugh Montgomery,	Cum Douglaso die eo;
Sir David Liddel, that worthy was,	Atque Liddelus, dignus vir
His sister's son was he.	Nepos Montgomeræo.*

32.

Sir Charles Murray in that place,	Moræus, virtus bellica
That never a foot would fly;	Quem fugere non sivit;
Sir Hugh Maxwell, a lord that was,	Hugo Maxwellus dominus
With the Douglas did he die.	Cum Douglaso obivit.

33.

So on the morrow they made them biers	Feretra luce postera
Of birch and hazel gray;	Ex betula fecerunt;
Many widows, with weeping tears,	Et lachrymantes viduæ
Came to fetch their mates away.	Maritos avexerunt.

34.

Tividale may carp of care!	Tiviotæ vallis lugeat!
Northumberland may make great moan!	Northumbris sint dolores!
For two such captains, as slain were there,	Nam nunquam erunt finibus
Of the march party shall never be none.	Principes meliores.

35.

Word is come to Edinburgh,	Edinam regi Scotico
To James the Scottish king,	Mox nuncium est relatum,
That doughty Douglas, lieutenant of the march,	Marchiarum præsidem Douglasum
He lay slain Cheviot within.	Esse collibus necatum.

36.

His hands did he weal and wring,	Fœdavit pugnis pectora,
He said, "Alas! and wo is me!	Exclamans voce tristi,
Such another captain Scotland within,"	"Væ mihi! quis in Scotia
He said, "I'faith shall never be."	Est comparandus isti?"

---

* I confess that I am not sure whether the author means that Sir David Liddel was nephew to Earl Douglas or Sir H. M.; but, as the latter is more syntactical, I have preferred it.—W. M.

37.

Word is come to lovely London,
  To the Fourth Harry our king,
That Lord Percy, lieutenant of the
      marches,
  He lay slain Cheviot within.

38.

"God have mercy on his soul," says King
      Harry,
  " Good Lord if thou will it be !
I have a hundred captains in England
  As good as ever was he.
But, Percy, an I brook my life,
  Thy death well quit shall be."

39.

As our noble king made his avow,
  Like a noble prince of renown,
For the death of the Lord Percy,
  He did the battle of Humbledown.

40.

Where six-and-thirty Scottish knights
  On a day were beaten down ;
Glendale glittered with their armour
      bright,
  O'er castle, tower, and town.

41.

(This† was the hunting of the Cheviot ;
  That tear began this spurn ;

37.

Londinumque amabilem *
  Henrico est relatum,
Persæum finium præsidem
  Esse collibus necatum.

38.

" Salus sit animæ," inquit Rex,
  Si ita placeat deo !
Sunt pares fortitudine
  Centum duces regno meo ;
Sed tamen Scotos puniam
  Pro nobili Persæo."

39.

Et Homilduni fortis rex
  Patravit id quod dixit ;
Ubi propter cæsum comitem
  Cum hostibus conflixit.

40.

Ubi quater novem equites
  Scoti simul periere ;
Glendalæ turres castraque
  Sparsis armis micuere.

41.

Et causam dedit prælii
  Venatio Cheviata ;

---

* Another Homerism, Αὐγειὰς ἐρατεινὰς. *Iliad*, B. 532, 583. Ἀρήνην ἐρατεινὴν. 591. Μαντινέην ἐρατεινὴν. 607, and a thousand other places. The author had manifestly made Homer his study.—W. M.

† Bp. Percy suspects these two verses, 41, 42, to be spurious. So do I, as they stand at present ; but I think we might make a good verse out of the two, thus :

    This was the hunting of the Cheviot,
      Upon a Monday ;
    There was the doughty Douglas slain,
      The Percy never went away.

This will get off the confusion with regard to the battle of Otterburn, and strange language of these verses. Percy's interpretation of " That tear began this spurn," is, " That tearing or pulling occasioned this spurn or kick." I have followed him, though I confess I am not satisfied with it. —W. M.

Old men, that knew the ground well
    enough,
  Call it the battle of Otterburn.

Pugna, loci gnaris senibus,
  Otterburni est vocata.

42.

At Otterburn began this spurn
  Upon a Monday ;
There was the doughty Douglas slain,
  The Percy never went away.)

Otterburni die Lunæ sic
  Incepi hic venatus ;
Ibi Persæus cecidit,
  Et Douglasus est stratus.

43.

There never was a time on the march
    parties,
  Since the Douglas and the Percy met,
But it was marvel an the red blood ran
    not
As the rain does on the street.

Cum se in marchiis Douglasus
  Persæo obviam daret,
Fuit mirum, si effusius
  Cruor imbre non manaret.

44.

Jesus Christ our *bales bete,
  And to the bless us bring !
This was the hunting of the Cheviot ;
  God send us all good ending !

Miserere nostrum Domine,
  Et nos salute dona !
Venatio ista finiit sic ;
  Sit nobis finis bona !

𝕰xpliceth Richard Sheale † temp. Henr. VI.

𝕰xplicit O. P. temp. Geo. IV.

---

* *i.e.* Better our bales, remedy our evils. Bp. Percy.—W.M.

† The author of this ballad, as the reader may see by the expliceth, is RICHARD SHEALE, a gentleman not to be confounded, as honest old Tom Hearne has done, with a Richard Sheale who was living in 1588. Nor is he to be confounded with a Richard Sheil who is alive in 1820, writing tragedies and other jocose performances. I waive the objection arising from Chronology, as that is a science I despise, therein imitating Lady Morgan, the Edinburgh Reviewers, Major Cartwright, and various other eminent persons. For (to take one instance from the works of the first-cited authority) might not Mr. Richard Sheil of 1820 be as capable of writing a ballad in the days of Henry VI. as the wife of the Grand Condé of intriguing with a king who was dead before she was born? (See, if extant, Lady Morgan's France.) My objections to their identity are of a graver and more critical nature. 1st, Richard Sheil of Chevy Chase is an original writer, which nobody accuses Richard Sheil of Evadne of being. 2ndly, Although in verse 33, Second Fytte, the ballad-monger had an opportunity of bringing up the children with their mothers, to serve as a clap trap, he has not done so ; an omission of which the tragedy-monger of Ballemira would never have been guilty. 3dly, The people in the poem of the rhymester are decent men, who talk plain language ; whereas the people in The Apostate are stalking-talking rogues, who discourse in the

PERORATIO.

I.

Vale! I, carmen meum. i,
  Pulcherrimam Edinam,
Et ibi pete illico
  Blackwodi Magazinam.

2.

Invenias tum Christophorum
  A Borea nominatum ;
Cui tuum spero numerum
  Rhythmicum fore gratum.

3.

Quid agam si interroget,
  Respondeas, " Nihil sane ;
Est, bibit, garrit, dormitat,
  Meridie, vespere, mane."

4.

Et addas, " Te, Christophore
  (Ut liquido juravit),
In tribus, cum me mitteret,
  Cantharis propinavit."

5.

Finiamus nunc.   Lectoribus
  (Si ulli sint lectores)
Arrideant. precor, veneres,
  Et gratiæ, et amores.

I have done with Chevy Chase ; but, as I am in a garrulous disposition, I wish to add a few words. Every true lover of English literature must acknowledge the great benefit conferred on it by Bishop Percy, in publishing his Relics. That work has breathed a spirit of renovated youth over our poetry, and we may trace its influence in the strains of higher mood uttered by the great poets of our own days. The Bishop was qualified for this task by exquisite poetical feeling, a large share of varied antiquarian knowledge, and general literary acquirements—united accomplishments which he possessed in a greater degree perhaps than any of his contemporaries. But since his time, and in a great measure in consequence of his work, and those which it called forth, so much more is known with respect to early English literature—I might say with respect to early English history—and the taste of the public

---

most sarsenet phraseology. *4thly* and *lastly*, The ballad of the Percy and Douglas (teste Sir P. Sidney) moves the heart like the sound of a trumpet, whereas the tragedy of Adelaide puts one to sleep more effectually than a double dose of diacodium. Wherefore I am of opinion that Mr. R. Sheil now extant is *not* the author of Chevy Chase. Q. E. D.—W. M.

is so much more inclined to such studies, that I think a general collection of our old English ballads, comprising of course those of Percy, Ritson, and others, which may merit preservation, is a great desideratum. Little skilled as I am in such subjects, I could point out deficiencies in the plan or the details of every work of the kind I have ever seen; deficiencies, however, which I have not had time to notice, nor perhaps would this be the proper place to do it, or I the proper person, after travestying the first of the old ballads into Monkish Latin. I should require in the editor high poetic taste, a deep and minute knowledge of the history and antiquities of the country, a profound acquaintance with the customs, the language, the heraldry, the genealogy of our ancestors, a critical judgment with respect to ancient poetry, and a perfect familiarity with all our poetic stores, ancient and modern—besides, what are not so common as may be imagined, undeviating honesty and fidelity.—Yours, &c. &c. O. P.

DUBLIN, *May* 31, 1820.

The Pewter Quart.

A New Song to an old Tune.

Written and Composed for the Jollification of Bibbers of Beer,
Porter, Ale, Stout, Nappy,
And all other Configurations of Malt and Hop.

Preface to the reader, which serves also for invocation.

Gentle reader!
Poets there were, in ages back,
Who sung the fame of the bonny black jack;
Others tuned harmonious lays
In the leathern bottle's praise.
Shall not I then lift my quill
To hymn a measure brighter still?
Maidens, who Helicon's hill resort,
Aid me to chant of the pewter quart.

1.

Here, boy, take this handful of brass ;
Across to the Goose and Gridiron pass,
Count the coin on the counter out,
And bring me a quart of foaming stout :
Put it not into bottle or jug,
Cannikin, rumkin, flagon, or mug ;
Into nothing at all, in short,
Except the natural pewter quart.

2.

As for the glass, though I love it well,
Yet the quart I take to be prefera—ble ;

For it is solid and stout, like what
Bubbles and froths inside the pot :
Why should anything, brittle or frail,
Fence ENGLAND'S liquor, VALOROUS ALE !
  He was a man of taste and art,
   Who stowed it away in a pewter quart.

3.

In the bowels of ENGLAND'S ground
Its materials all are found ;
From its sides should flow again
What cheers the bowls of ENGLAND'S men :
Can the same be said, I ask,
In favour of foreign flagon or flask ?
  None can of them the good report
   We can of our national pewter quart.

4.

Pleasant it is their shine to see
Like stars in the waves of deep Galilee ;
Pleasant it is their chink to hear
When they rattle on table full charged with beer ;
Pleasant it is, when a row's on foot,
That you may, when you wish to demolish a brute,
  Politely the lad to good manners exhort,
   By softening his skull with a pewter quart.

5.

As for the mallet-pate, pig-eye Chinese,
They may make crockery if they please ;
Fit, perhaps, may each vehicle be
For marrowless washes of curst Bohea ;
That is a liquor I leave to be drunk
By Cockney poet and Cockney punk ;
  Folks with whom I never consort,
   Preferring to chat with my pewter quart.

6.

Silver and gold no doubt are fine,
But on my table shall never shine ;
Being a man of plain common sense,
I hate all silly and vain expense,
And spend the cash these gew-gaws cost,
In washing down gobbets of boiled and roast
  With stingo stiff of the stiffest sort,
   Curiously pulled from a pewter quart.

7.

Beakers and bowls, I am told, of wood,
For quaffing water are counted good ;

They give a smack, say the wat'ry folks,
Like drinking after artichokes.
Devil may care ! I never use
Water in either my belly or shoes,
    And shall never be counted art or part
    In putting the same in a pewter quart.

8.

Galvani one day, skinning a frog,
To pamper his paunch with that pinchgut prog,
Found out a science of wonderful wit,
Which can make a stuck pig kick out in a fit,
Make a dead thief dance a Highland reel,
And butcher a beast without cleaver or steel ;
    And he proves by this science, with erudite art,
    That malt must be drunk from a pewter quart.

9.

If hock then loves the glass of green,
And champagne in its swan-necked flask is seen ;
If Glasgow punch in a bowl we lay,
And twist off our dram in a wooden quaigh ;
If, as botanical men admit,
Everything has its *habitat* fit,
    Let Sir John Barleycorn keep his court,
    Turban'd with froth in his pewter quart.

10.

So, boy, take this handful of brass,
Across to the Goose and Gridiron pass,
Count the coin on the counter out,
And bring me a quart of foaming stout ;
Put it not into bottle or jug,
Cannikin, rumkin, flagon, or mug—
    Into nothing at all, in short,
    Except the natural pewter quart.

HERE FOLLOWS A DISSERTATION ON THE LEATHER BOTTLE AND THE BLACK JACK.

IN the works of the ingenious D'Urfey, which he who studies not with nocturnal and diurnal attention is worthy of infinite reprobation, not to say worse, will be discovered two poems, which have not, as yet, excited the notice of the learned in the manner which they deserve. I shall therefore, as briefly as the importance of the matter will admit of, dissertate somewhat upon them ; inviting the attention of the sage and erudite to my remarks, perfectly regardless of the approbation or disapprobation of those whom my friend the Reverend Edward Irving calls "the flush and flashy spirits of the age," thereby making an agreeable and euphuistical alliteration at head and tail.

In the third volume of "Pills to Purge Melancholy," the two hundred and forty-seventh page and first verse, will be found these words :—

The Leather Bottle.

Now God above, that made all things,
Heaven and earth, and all therein :
The ships upon the seas to swim,
To keep foes out, they come not in.
Now every one doth what he can
All for the use and praise of man.
   I wish in Heaven that soul may dwell
   That first devised the leathern bottle.

A more splendid exordium is not in the whole compass of our poetry. The bard, about to sing of a noble invention, takes high ground. His eye, with a fine frenzy rolling, glances at the origin of the world, the glories of heaven and the utilities of earth ; at old ocean murmuring with its innumerable waves, and the stately vessels walking the waters in all their magnificence ; and then, by a gradual and easy descent, like Socrates bringing philosophy from the abodes of the gods to the dwellings of men, chants the merits of him who, for the use and praise of man, devised the leathern bottle. Compare Pindar's celebrated opening with this, and you will see how short is the flight of the Bœotian muse contrasted with that of our own swan. Observe, moreover, the solid British feeling of the illustrious poet. No sooner does he mention ships than the national spirit breaks forth.

The ships upon the seas to swim,
To keep foes out, they come not in.

Had the man who wrote this one idea inconsistent with the honour and glory of Britain? I lay a thousand pounds he had not. Had he lived in our days he would have consigned the economists to the Devil and the *Scotsman*. Conceive for a moment this great man, big with beer, and thoroughly impressed with veneration for our walls of wood, reading that article in the *Edinburgh* on the Navigation Laws. What an up-curled lip of indignation would he not display! How hearty would be his guffaw of contempt! How frequent his pulls at the vessel inserted in his dexter paw, in order to wash down the cobweb theories he was endeavouring to swallow! How impatiently would the pigtail turn under his nether-gum, until at last, losing patience, he would fling the Balaam over the bannisters, and exclaim, " Here, John, take it away from me, and put it in the only place where it can be at all for the use and praise of man." What place that is it is not necessary for me to mention.

> Now what do you say to the cans of wood?
> Faith they are nought, they cannot be good.
> When a man for beer he doth therein send
> To have them filled, as he doth intend,
> The bearer stumbleth by the way,
> And on the ground his liquor doth lay;
> Then straight the man begins to ban,
> And swears it 'twas long of the wooden can;
> But had it been in a leathern bottle,
> Although he stumbled all had been well;
> So safe therein it would remain
> Until the man got up again.
> And I wish in Heaven, &c.

The ambling pace of the verse cannot be sufficiently commended. Here we go on jog-trot, as Sancho Panza on Dapple. Nothing stops the full gush of poetry poured out in a ceaseless, murmuring flow, like a brook rolling at the feet of two lovers by moonlight. Remark, too, the insight this verse gives us of the manners of the poet. His habits are completely anti-domestic; they have what King Leigh calls "all the freshness of out-of-doors life." He has no store at home. When he wants to drink, he sends for the quantity required. All the bother of butlers is done away with. The whole tribe of tapsters are his footmen, and the wide world his cellar. You perceive, too, the habit of his household : it is in a state of perpetually blissful intoxication. Nothing can be more a matter of course than that any messenger of his should stumble by the way : it is a regular affair of ordinary speculation. And then see his magnanimity. Grieved as he is at the loss of his liquor, he has no indignation against the drunken bearer, but transfers his wrath to the vessel, resolving henceforward to alter his measures. In all this there is something Christian-like and philanthropic.

> Now for the pots with handles three,
> Faith they shall have no praise of me.
> When a man and his wife do fall at strife
> (As many, I fear, have done in their life),
> They lay their hands upon the pot both,
> And break the same, though they were loth ;
> Which they shall answer another day
> For casting their liquor so vainly away ;
> But had it been in a bottle filled,
> The one might have tugged, the other have held ;
> They both might have tugged till their hearts did ake,
> And yet no harm the bottle would take.
> And I wish in Heaven, &c.

The philosophy of this verse is worthy of Lord Bacon or his commentator. The philosopher, knowing the pugnacity of human nature, feels no surprise at a matrimonial scuffle ; but instantly his great object occurs to his mind, "fight it out," quoth he, "fight it out by all means ; but don't spill the drink." The whole forms a pleasant domestic picture ; the husband on one side of the table, warming his bunions at the fire ; the wife, mending a pair of breeches at the other ; and a three-handled pot, lying in quiet serenity between them, upon a deal table. Suddenly arises a storm, occasioned by what we are not informed by the poet, but most probably by an unequal division of the contents of the aforesaid pot—and a combat ensues. Both seize the pot, and the liquor is spilt. How touchingly, and yet with a just indignation, does our friend reflect on this !

> For which they shall answer another day
> For casting their liquor so vainly away.

The solemnity of this threat is awfully impressive. It sounds like a voice from Delphi, or like a deep-toned imprecation uttered from the mystic groves of Eleusis. There is nothing like it in all Paradise Lost.

> Now what of the flagons of silver fine?
> Faith they shall have no praise of mine.
> When a nobleman he doth them send
> To have them filled as he doth intend,
> The man with his flagon runs quite away,
> And never is seen again after that day.
> Oh then his lord begins to ban,
> And swears he hath lost both flagon and man.
> But it ne'er was known that page or groom
> But with a feathern bottle again would come.
> And I wish in Heaven, &c.

You see here the touches of a fine archaic simplicity. The silver flagon indicating that its possessor is a nobleman; the provision for life which it affords the flying footman, *who never again is seen after that day;* the baronial swearing of his lordship, and his regret at the loss of his property, first in the flagon, and then in the man,—all take us back to the feudal times, and make us think of beetle-browed castles frowning over foaming cataracts ; of knights clad in the panoply of plate and mail pricking forth upon the plain ; of ladye love and chivalrye ;

> *Of tilting furniture, emblazoned shields,*
> *Impresses quaint, caparisons and steeds,*
> *Bases and tinsel trappings, gorgeous knights,*
> *At tilt and tournament; then marshall'd feast,*
> *Served up in hall with sewers and seneschals.*

It is agreeable to yield the mind occasionally to these soft delusions of fancy, and to let our souls revel in the beauties and splendours of times past by. But, alas! as Burke says, "the day of chivalry is gone, and the glory of Europe is departed." I agree with that great orator, but shall nevertheless proceed with the Leathern Bottle.

> Now what do you say to these glasses fine?
> Faith they shall have no praise of mine.
> When friends are at a table set,
> And by them several sorts of meat,
> The one loves flesh, the other fish;
> Among them all remove a dish:
> Touch but a glass upon the brim,
> The glass is broke; no wine left in.
> Then be your table-cloth ne'er so fine,
> There lies your beer, pour ale, your wine.
> And doubtless for so small abuse
> A young man may his service lose.
> And I wish, &c.

I am sorry the poet wrote this verse. There is something flunkyish and valleydeshammical in the whole passage; something, in fact, Moorish—I mean Peter-Moorish; and I suspect an interpolation. What need we care for the discarded skip, or the stained diaper? Get it washed. Warrant it will not add a shilling to your washerwoman's bill in the twelvemonths. But perhaps you are afraid of the stains remaining to offend your optic nerve. Make your mind easy on the subject. You will find your remedy in the two hundred and ninety-ninth page of the Book of Rundell. "Rub your part," says that she-Kitchener, "on each side with yellow soap; then lay on a mixture of starch in cold water, very thick; rub it well, and expose the linen to the sun and air, till the stain comes out. If not removed in three or four days, rub that off, and renew the process. When dry, it may be sprinkled with a little water." Observe, it *may* be sprinkled; for she does not insist on *that* with dogged pertinacity. Nothing can be more simple than the process; and I am sorry the matter was mentioned.

If it really be a *bona-fide* part of the composition, I must only class it among the follies of the wise, and mourn over the frail condition of human nature.

> Now when this bottle is grown old,
> And that it will no longer hold,
> Out of the side you may cut a clout
> To mend your shoe when worn out,
> Or hang the other side on a pin ;
> 'Twill serve to put many odd trifles in,
> As nails, awls, and candles' ends ;
> For young beginners need such things.
>   I wish in Heaven his soul may dwell
>   That first invented the leathern bottle.

This is a brilliant verse, and displays a genius for mechanical invention which would do honour to a Perkins. The thrifty management, too, is highly commendable ; and the care he manifests for young beginners marks a parental and humane disposition, which converts our admiration of the poet into love for the man. He appears to be of the opinion of that eminent statesman—the Mr. Maberley of his day—who declared that there is nothing like leather. Much may be, and indeed has been said on both sides of the question, but though the controversy is far from being set at rest, I shall not agitate it on the present occasion.

Let me now turn to the second head of my discourse ; namely, the BLACK JACK.

> 'Tis a pitiful thing that now-a-days, sirs,
> Our poets turn leathern-bottle praisers.
> But if a leathern theme they did lack,
> They might better have chosen the bonny black jack ;
> For when they are both now well worn and decayed,
> For the jack than the bottle much more can be said.
>   And I wish his soul much good may partake
>   That first devised the bonny black jack.

I for one am free to admit that I do not like this commencement. There is something, as Leigh Hunt says, base and reviewatory in it. Why need he disparage the valuable labours of his predecessor bard? The world was large enough for them both. But the poetic tribe is irritable. This very moment there is barbarous civil war going on among them. Southey calls Byron Satan, and Byron compliments the Laureate with the soothing title of rogue. Bernard Barton has been heard to declare that he did not think ODoherty's poetry had anything Miltonian about it,— to be sure it was in private,—and he qualified the assertion by adding that he gave it merely as matter of opinion ; but, after all, it was shabby on the part of Broadbrim. I say nothing, and mention the business just in illustration.

And now I will begin to declare
What the conveniences of the jack are.
First, when a gang of good fellows do meet,
As oft at a fair or a wake you shall see't ;
They resolve to have some merry carouses,
And yet to get home in good time to their houses.
Then the bottle it runs as slow as my rhime,
With jack they might have all been drunk in good time.
   And I wish his soul in peace may dwell
   That first devised that speedy vessel.

The writer of this is evidently an intensely moral and domestic man. It being an object of necessity to get drunk, the question arises how this is to be done with the most decorous propriety. Arguing then with Macbeth that when a thing is to be done, 'twere well that it were done quickly, and anxious to delight the family at home with an early visit, he naturally prefers the jack, or, as he most poetically calls it, the speedy vessel. He manifestly hates loitering and lingering in any work in which he is engaged, and is quite shocked at the idea of intruding on domestic arrangements by any absence of his. He feels the duties of the head of a household too keenly ; he is too much interested in the proper ordering of affairs at home. Certain I am that family prayers were the regular order of the day in his establishment.

And therefore leave your twittle twattle,
Praise the jack, praise no more the leathern bottle;
For the man at the bottle may drink till he burst,
And yet not handsomely quench his thirst.
The master hereat maketh great moan,
And doubts his bottle has a spice of the stone;
But if it had been a generous jack,
He might have had currently what he did lack.
   And I wish his soul in Paradise
   That first found out that happy device.

The lament of the unsated beer-bibber is given here with a pathos which must draw tears from the eyes even of the most hard-hearted. No words are thrown away. We see him endeavouring to effect his purpose at the bottle's mouth; and, finding his efforts vain, he "*hereat maketh great moan.*" How simple, yet how tender! Had Shiel, or any poetaster of that stamp, such a passage in his hands, into what a bladder of wordy amplification would he not have blown it! We should infallibly have had the wife and children drawn in to participate in the father's sorrow; but here we have a strain of higher mood:

Be your liquor small or thick as mud,
The cheating bottle that cries good, good;
Then the master again begins to storm,
Because it said more than it could perform:
But if it had been in an honest black jack,
It would have proved better to sight, smell, and smack.
   And I wish his soul in Heaven may rest
   That added a jack to Bacchus's feast.

On this verse I make no remark, as I am sure that by this time the reader of moderate abilities or proper application will be able to discover its scope and tendency.

No flagon, tankard, bottle, or jug,
Is half so fit, or so well can hold tug;
For when a man and his wife play at thwacks,
There is nothing so good as a pair of black jacks:
Thus to it they go, they swear, and they curse,
It makes them both better, the jack's ne'er the worse;

For they might have banged both till their hearts did ake,
And yet no hurt the jacks could take:
    And I wish his heirs may have a pension
    That first produced that lucky invention.

I am afraid my friend Joe Hume would hardly agree with this last prayer, but it is evident that Joseph has no taste for the fine arts.   The philological student will discover in this verse the origin of the phrase, " leathering a man's wife."   On the moral propriety of conjugal fistycuffery I had prepared some copious remarks, when I received information from a sure hand that my Lord Holland has a folio on the subject nearly ready for the press, and I bow to his lordship's superior talents and experience.

Socrates and Aristotle
Sucked no wit from a leathern bottle;
For surely I think a man as soon may
Find a needle in a bottle of hay.
But if the black jack a man often toss over,
'Twill make him as drunk as any philosopher;
When he that makes jacks from a peck to a quart,
Conjures not, though he lives by the black art.
    And I wish, &c.

I care not a fig for the black art, and defy the foul fiend, Prince Hohenlohe, and Ingleby the Emperor of the Conjurors, so shall make no remark on the last two lines.   It would lead us into too deep a historico-metaphysical disquisition were I to enter into a history of the fortunes of the Aristotelian philosophy.   During the life of Aristotle, he was looked on as the prince of philosophers, and such did his estimation continue as long as there were minds in the world manly enough to understand him.   While Europe was sunk in darkness, he was taken up by the acute Arabians, then at the head of the intellect of the earth.   From them the schoolmen caught him, badly translated and imperfectly understood; and, when their day was over, the puny whipsters who had got possession of the ear of the metaphysical world thought nothing could be finer than to disparage, because he had been caricatured, him whom they could not read; and we see, in our own day, Stewart mumping and mumbling pretty little nothings, with full assurance that the Peripatetic whom he cannot construe, or who, if construed for him, is far above any reach of thought he could bring to the consideration, is unworthy to unloose the latchet of his shoe. But to his fortune in our poetry I may briefly advert: it is a fine illustration of the elder Mr. Shandy's theory of the .influence of a name. That he was a hard drinker I hope, for he was a great man; but, whether he was or not, no name of the ancients occurs so often in juxtaposition with the bottle. See the verse above. So also the eminent Harry Carey:

> *Zeno, Plato, Aristotle*
> *All were lovers of the bottle.*

So in MS. *penes me :*

> *To moisten our throttle,*
> *We'll call the third bottle,*
> *For that was the practice of wise Aristotle.*

All owing to the two last syllables of his name. With respect to the remark in the text, that

> If the black jack a man often toss over,
> 'Twill make him as drunk as any philosopher,

I can vouch, from my own experience, that the illustration is correct, for I have had the honour of being intimately acquainted with fifteen of the first philosophers of the age, fourteen of whom went to bed drunk as widgeons every night of their lives, and the fifteenth retired when he found himself tipsy.

> Besides, my good friend, let me tell you, that fellow
> That framed the bottle his brains were but shallow.

> The case is so clear, I nothing need mention,
> The jack is a nearer and deeper invention.
> When the bottle is cleaned, the dregs fly about
> As if the guts and the brains flew out;
> But if in a cannon-bore jack it had been,
> From the top to the bottom all might have been clean.
> And I wish his soul no comfort may lack
> That first devised the bouncing black jack.

I am not antiquarian enough to decide on the correctness of the above objurgation against the uncleanliness of the bottles of the olden time, and willingly leave the consideration of the matter to Mr. John Nichols, who presides (and long may he preside!) over the archæologists who wield the pen for the *Gentleman's Magazine*, in which, perhaps, he will favour us with an engraved likeness of a leathern bottle, as I think churches are running rather low. But be that as it may, he must have little gusto for the sublime who can fail to admire the splendid epithet of the CANNON-BORE Jack. What vast ideas of stupendous bibosity does not it excite? Conceive a nine-pounder-like machine charged with ale, levelled on your table, in full range against your brains! Nay, the very word is good. It makes us think of battle and blood—of square column and platoon mowed down in unrelenting sweep—of Sir William Congreve, the Duke of Wellington, and the field of Waterloo—of Buonaparte, St. Helena, and Sir Hudson Lowe—and thence, by the association of ideas, of Barry O'Meara, and the horse-whipping of old Walter of the *Times*. I shall lump my dissertation on the four following verses :—

> Your leather bottle is used by no man
> That is a hair's-breadth above a plowman;
> Then let us gang to the Hercules pillars,
> And there let us visit those gallant jack swillers.
> In these small, strong, sour, mild, and stale,
> They drink orange, lemon, and Lambeth ale:
> The chief of heralds there allows
> The jack to be of an ancienter house.
> And may his successors never want sack
> That first devised the long leather jack.

Then for the bottle, you cannot well fill it,
Without a tunnel, but that you must spill it.
'Tis as hard to get in as it is to get out:
'Tis not so with a jack, for it runs like a spout.
Then burn your bottle, what good is in it?
One cannot well fill it, nor drink, nor clean it;
But if it had been in a jolly black jack,
'Twould come a great pace and hold you good tack.
  And I wish his soul, &c.

He that's drunk in a jack looks as fierce as a spark
That were just ready cockt to shoot at a mark;
When the other thing up to the mouth it goes,
Makes a man look with a great bottle nose.
All wise men conclude that a jack, new or old,
Though beginning to leak, is however worth gold;
For when the poor man on the way does trudge it,
His worn-out jack serves him for a budget.
  And I wish his heirs may never lack sack
  That first contrived the leather black jack.

When bottle and jack stand together, fie on't,
The bottle looks just like a dwarf to a giant;
Then have we not reason the jack for to choose,
For they can make boots when the bottle mends shoes;
For add but to every jack a foot,
And every jack becomes a boot:
Then give me my jack, there's a reason why
They have kept us wet, they will keep us dry.
I now shall cease, but as I am an honest man,
The jack deserves to be called Sir John.
  And may they ne'er want for belly nor back
  That keep up the trade of the bonny black jack.

Amen! and virtue be its own reward!

On the above four things are to be particularly noticed—

I. That the Hercules Pillars is the *ne plus ultra* of signs.

II. That the progress of time has extinguished various sorts of ales; for who nowadays drinks orange, lemon, or Lambeth? They sleep with the Chians and Falernians of the days of Greece and Rome.

III. That a partiality for a man's favourite pursuit may lead him to bestow on it unjust and undeserved praise; for after various and repeated experiments in drinking out of every vessel under the sun, I can give it as my unbiassed opinion that the shape of the instrument imparts no additional value to the liquor drunk, and that therefore the idea that he who imbibes from a black jack acquires a superior fierceness or martiality of aspect must be classed among such innocent delusions as induced the barber to recommend white-handled razors as the best fitted for abrading of beards.

Lastly and finally, we cannot help being pleased by the vein of genuine and unaffected piety which runs through both these dignified compositions. The prayers which in both conclude each verse, though more varied and poetical in the latter, are not more solemn and impressive than the solitary ejaculation of blessing bestowed on the earlier production. There is something striking which sinks into the soul in the constant choral-like repetition of the one formulary which amply compensates for the picturesque diversity which excites our admiration but fills us not with awe. The one goes to the head, the other to the heart. To conclude, if the brows of the inventors of the bottle and jack deserve to be bound with snow-white fillets, as being men who civilised life by new productions of art and genius, the bards who hymned their exploits may justly claim the same honour as being pious poets, who spoke things worthy of Apollo.   M. OD.

The Night Walker.

" Midnight ! yet not a nose, from Tower Hill to Piccadilly, snored ! "

IN a crowded and highly cultivated state of society like that of London, the race of exertion against time is incessant. Take a distant village, although a populous one (as in Devonshire or Cornwall), and even discord, during the hours of darkness, is found forgetting herself in rest. The last alehouse closes before the clock strikes ten, sending the very scapegraces of the hamlet in summer to bed by daylight ; no lady would choose after curfew hour (even by beating her husband) to disturb her neighbours ; and unless some tailor happens to be behindhand with a wedding pair of small clothes, or some housewife prolongs the washing-day and gives an extra hour to her lace caps, or unless the village be a post-stage, where the " first-turn-boy " must sleep in his spurs, or where, the mail changing horses, some one sits up to give the guard his glass of rum, no movable probably like a lighted candle is known to such a community from eleven o'clock on the Saturday night to six o'clock on the Monday morning. In London, however, the course of affairs is widely different. As the broad glare of gas drives darkness even from our alleys, so multitudinous avocations keep rest for ever from our streets. By an arrangement the opposite to that of Queen Penelope, it is during the night that the work of regeneration in our great capital goes on ; it is by night that the great reservoirs which feed London and Westminster repair the vast expenditure which they make during the day. As the wants of twelve hundred thousand persons are not ministered to with a wet finger, this operation of replenishment does not proceed in silence.   Its action is best observable (as regards the season) towards the end of spring ; when, the town being at the fullest, the markets are most abundantly supplied.   Then every succeeding hour of the four-and-twenty brings its peculiar business to be performed, and sets its peculiar agents into motion.

Between half-past eleven and twelve o'clock at night the several theatres of the metropolis discharge themselves of their loads, and at that hour it is (unless the House of Commons happens to sit late) that the last *flush* of passengers is seen in the streets of London.   The forth-rushing multitudes of Covent Garden and Drury Lane pass westward in divisions by King Street and Leicesterfields, eastward by Catherine Street, the Strand, and Temple Bar ; they are crossed at the points of Blackfriars and St. Martin's Lane by the Middlesex-dwelling visitors of Astley's and the Circus, and may be distinguished from the chance travellers (pedestrians) of the same direction by their quick step, hilarious mood, and still more by that style of *shouldering* in which Englishmen when they walk in a body always indulge towards the single-handed.   About this time, too, the hackney horses put their best feet (where there is a choice) foremost, knowing of old that whence comes one lash there as easily come two.   The less public and more peaceful districts of town are next flattered for some twenty minutes by the loud knocks of coachmen, occasionally commuted into " touches of the bell " for the sake of " the lodgers," or " the children," or sometimes " the old lady opposite."   And before the stroke of midnight, in these comparatively pacific regions the tom-cats and the watchmen reign with undisputed sway.

In the greater thoroughfares of London, however, and especially about Fleet Street and the Strand, the tumult of evening does not subside so easily.   From twelve by Paul's clock until after two in the morning the Gates of the Temple, and the nooks under St. Dunstan's Church, the corners of Bell Yard, Star Court, and Chancery Lane, the doors of the Rainbow, the Cock, and the other minor coffee-houses of Fleet Street are beset by habitual idlers or late-stirring "professional people," members of spouting-clubs and second-rate actors, barristers without law and medical students guiltless of physic; besides these, there flourish a set of City "choice spirits," who can't get so far west as "Pedley's Oyster-rooms," or "The Saloon," in Piccadilly, but must take their "lark" (moving homewards) between the Adelphi Theatre and Whitechapel; and now and then, perhaps, some grocer of Farringdon falls (*vino gravidus*) into the irregularity of a "set-to," and pays thirty shillings "making-up" money to his Jew antagonist at St. Bride's Watch-house, to save a *jobation* at Guildhall from the sitting alderman next day.

This is the very "witching time," *par excellence*, of night,

> "When graves yield up their dead"

(because resurrection-men will have it so), when lamps are "rifled at," and sots pushed out of public-houses; and when the sober wayfarer starts ever and anon at the prolonged hilly-oh-ho-ho! that bellow, as it were, *crescendo*, peculiar I think to the throats of the English, which frightens watchmen into their hutches and quiet citizens into the kennel. This whoop by the way prolonged, which invites MANKIND, as it were, to clear the way, is with us a pure national, and not a local, characteristic. Both high and low affect the practice; both "good men" and bullies. We have it at Oxford and at Cambridge, where the gowns-men if opposed strip and buff to their work like stout "forty minutes" fellows; and again in London, where your flustered haberdasher, after defying perhaps a whole street, at last provokes somebody to thrash him, and is beat without a blow in his defence.

By two o'clock, however, the riotous get pretty well disposed of; some snug and flea-bitten in their own personal garrets, more (and still flea-bitten) in the compters of the police. The wickets of the night-houses after this open only to known customers, and the flying pieman ceases his call. The pickpockets, linked with the refuse of another pestilence of the town, are seen sauntering lazily towards their lurking-places in gangs of five and six together. And when these last stragglers of darkness have swept over the *pavé*, the *débris* of the evening may be considered as cleared off; and except an occasional crash of oyster-shells cast (*maugre* Angelo Taylor) from some lobster-shop, or the sharp rattle of a late billiard-ball echoing from the rooms over Mrs. Salmon's, silence, or something like it, obtains for some brief minutes, while the idlers of night give place to the dark-working men of business.

The earliest disturbers of London until within these few years were the market gardeners, who rolled lazily through the suburbs about three with their filled-up carts and waggons, some "well to do" and pompous, parading their four high-fed horses apiece, others poor (and modest) drawing with a single quadruped, and he, God wot, looking as though stray cabbage-leaves were his holiday-fare, that is, supposing (what is not supposable) that such a thing as a holiday ever happened to him ; all the *spring* vehicles, however, top-heavy with baskets of raspberries, strawberries, and currants; and followed by heavier machines bearing gooseberries, or frame potatoes ; the cauliflowers, peas, and such more ponderous and plebeian esculents having creaked into town (as they might) in the course of the preceding evening.

But two or three mild winters of late in succession have brought a new article of foreign trade into England. Ice, for the use of the confectioners, comes now to us all the way from Norway, where a gentleman, we understand, is making arrangements to send over even snow, at a far cheaper rate than it can afford to fall in this country ; so that frost, in fact (as regards Great Britain and Ireland), may consider itself discharged from further attendance ; and, with the help of a few more devices in the way of commercial arrangement, and perhaps a new improvement or two as to the application of steam, it shall go hard but we will shortly turn the seasons out of doors altogether. And this imported ice (jealous of sunshine) is foremost in our streets now of mornings, moving along, in huge cart-loads, from the below-bridge wharfs; and looking, as it lies in bulk, like so much conglutinated Epsom salts.

Meantime the river above bridge is not suffered to lie idle; but the fruits of Putney and Fulham walk upon the shoulders of porters, from Hungerford and the Adelphi stairs, to the great mart of vegetable matter, Covent Garden. And upon this spot (Covent Garden), which circumstances seem to have erected into a sort of museum for all the varied staple of a crowded capital city; to which all the patron friends of all the ills that scourge mankind seem to have rushed with one consent, day and night, to hold divan; where Luxury roams gorgeous through her long range of lighted taverns, and brims the bowl with wine, which Discord waits to dash with blood; where hunger, squalor, nakedness, and disease dance, antic, round our NATIONAL MONUMENTS of national wealth and superfluity; where vices, too hideous to be contemplated in detail, assert their royalty over us, alike in every class and every condition, blazing in transient lustre amid the splendid hotels of the Piazza, starving, in rags (yet scarce more abject) amongst the horrid fastnesses of Bedford Court!—upon this spot, where all things monstrous are crowded and jumbled together; where the sounds seem all confused, and the sights all anomalous; where the wild laugh of revelry, and the low moan of suffering, the subdued whisper of entreaty, and the hoarse bark of execration mingle and mix and blend, and half neutralise each other; upon this spot, Covent Garden— jovial Covent Garden, the darling haunt alike of folly and of wit, the great mart of all London for oranges, outcasts, and old clothes, where the jokes are mostly good, where the cookery is always excellent, where the claret is commonly the best in England, and the morality never failingly the worst—on this spot, one continued uproar of labour or dissipation has endured without intermission for nearly a century gone by; and here, so long as London shall keep her holding as a city, silence, probably, by night or day, shall never find a resting-place.

But we will tear ourselves from Covent Garden even in "the sweet" (as Falstaff calls it) "of the night," for we must take a peep at the other points of *provisional* concentration about town. We must look towards Cockspur Street, where the hay collects itself in such quantities that nothing but the stomach of a horse could ever hope to make away with it. And we must cross, too, into Smithfield, where herds of cattle keep coming in all night, and where it is amazing how anybody can get a wink of sleep for the barking of the dogs and the bellowing of the bulls, and, louder than all, the swearing of the drovers, against whom Heaven, Richard Martin, strengthen thine arm! Smithfield, however, to be seen to advantage, should be taken from its eastern bearing through the fogs of a November morning, when the lights in the west quadrangle at "The Ram," "The Goat," and "The Bull's Head" show like beacons (though they shine but dimly) amid the total darkness on all sides of them; and when, looking at the hubbub of traffic which roars through the outward street against the deep unheeding silence that reigns within the houses, a man might fancy he witnessed the rush of an invading army, or division, into a town which the inhabitants had the night before abandoned. Then pick your way round (for there is no venturing to cross) and peep through the steaming window-panes into the parlour of an inn, where graziers and salesmen, in their fantastic "auld world" dresses, flop-hatted and top-coated, booted and waist-be-girt; knee-capped, twenty-handkerchiefed, mud-be-splashed, and spurred, snore or smoke in arm-chairs; and, between whiles, drive bargains for thousands. Mark the huge bulk of these men, their bluff bearing and English countenances. Hark to their deep voices, strange dialects, and uncouth expression. Then take their attendant demons, the badged drovers, each his goad and cord in hand; and with garb so pieced together, patched, and tattered that it might pass for the costume of any age, being like the costume of none. Catch the style of the old-fashioned building before you, with its latticed windows and penthouse roof. Take the low ceiling of the sitting apartment, and the huge sea-coal fire that glows in it. Take the figures of the farmers within doors, and of the drovers hovering without; of the gaitered, smock-frocked hostlers, carriers, and carmen; of the ragged, patient, waiting ponies, and the still more ragged and patient sheep-dogs—the most faithful, intelligent, and ill-used beings of their species; take these objects amid the darkness of the hour and the exaggeration of the fog, and then, with a little natural romance and a lively recollection of Shakespeare, you may (almost) fancy yourself thrown back into the glorious rudeness of the thirteenth century, arriving from a recent robbery (ah! those indeed were days) rich with the spoils of " whoreson caterpillars," and calling for a light to walk between tavern and tavern !

But the sober clearness of a summer's morning is no nurse for these wild fancies. It shows all objects too plainly and distinctly for picturesque effect, the true secret of which lies in never exhibiting anything *fully*, but in showing just enough to excite the imagination, and in then leaving it room enough to act. So we will turn back from Smithfield, just in the cold grey light of daybreak, and cross Holborn to Chancery Lane, where the kennels by this time are overflowing; and rogues, with scoops, are watering the roads—that is, " making the *dust* one *mud !*" Now watchmen congregate round posts for a little sober conversation; old women make to their respective standings with hot saloop and bread and butter; and presently the light hung caravans of the fishmongers—built at first in imitation of the hearses, and now re-imitated into Paddington stage-coaches—begin to jingle along at a trot by Thames Street towards Billingsgate.

As the last stars fade in the horizon and the sun coquettes with the church spires, new actors in sundry shapes appear upon the scene. Milkwomen in droves clank along with their (to be filled) pails. The poorer fish-dealers, on their own heads, undertake the "care of *soles.*" Chimney-sweepers shuffle on, straining out a feeble cry. And parties walk home (rather chilly) from Vauxhall, flaunting in satin shoes, silk stockings, and ostrich feathers; stared at now and then by some gaping, slip-shod baker, who fetches spring water from the pump to cool his *sponge,* and looks like the statue in Don Juan, or a sack of flour truant from the kneading-trough; or hooted by some lost thing, all mad, and pale, and ghastly—some *creation* of gin, and carmine, and soiled muslin, which shows by daylight as a being of other time and place—an apparition, a prodigy, a denizen of some forbidden sphere—a foul lamp, thickly glimmering out its dregs, which the sun's light by some accident has omitted to extinguish.

Five o'clock, and the world looks as if stretching itself to awake. Coal-waggons and drays start forth upon "long turns," their country intent denoted by the truss of hay placed above the load. Butchers step sturdily towards Islington or Smithfield. Anglers, children of hope! stride fieldwards with baskets on their backs. And Holborn and Snow Hill are crowded with pony-carts (since the Chancellor of the Exchequer rides nothing under fourteen hands) bearing butter, cheese, poultry, sucking-pork, and eggs from Newgate market to the distant parishes of Marylebone and Pancras.

Six! And 'prentices begin to rub their eyes and curse their indentures. Maid-servants at "the Piccadilly end" of the town are not bound to stir just yet, but Russell Square and its dependencies set their spider-killers in motion betimes; for courts of law and counting-houses both sit at nine o'clock, and an advocate in practice of ten thousand a year must step into his carriage at five-and-thirty minutes past eight in the morning.

And now the different shops begin to open themselves for action. Our friend the baker is first, for he has been up all night, and he has to cool his loaves at the open windows as he draws them from the oven. Next comes the pastry-cook, lotting his remnant of cheese-cake, selling yesterday's dainties at half-price to-day, and still making money (as it is said) by the dealing. Then coaches, splashed and dirty, come labouring into town; and coaches, fresh and clean, drive out; and by this time the mercers and jewellers set their portals wide, in favour of sweeping, sprinkling, and window-cleaning; for the show-glasses (and here again sigh our friends the apprentices) must be emptied all, and polished and refurnished before breakfast.

The clock strikes eight, and the night-walker must be seen no more. Hurry and bustle and breakfast are on foot. The milkman cries in haste, and yet can scarce make his rounds fast enough. Maids with clean aprons (and sometimes with clean plates) step forth, key in hand, for the modicum of fresh butter; and hot rolls (walk as you will) run over you at every corner. By nine the clerks have got down to their offices—the attorneys have opened their bags, and the judges are on their benches; and the business of the *day* in London may now be said to have begun, which varies from hour to hour as strangely as the business of the night, and (to the curious observer) presents even a more ample field for speculation.

"Back and side go bare, go bare."

RENDERED INTO LATIN.

I.

Backe and side go bare, go bare,
  Both foote and hande go colde;
But bellye, God sende thee good ale
    ynoughe,
  Whether it be newe or olde.
I cannot eat but lytle meate,
  My stomacke is not good;
But sure I thinke that I can drynke
  With him that weares a hood.
Though I go bare, take ye no care,
  I am nothing a colde;
I stuff my skyn so full within
  Of jolly good ale and olde.
Backe and side go bare, go bare,
  Both foote and hande go colde;
But belly, God send thee good ale
    enoughe,
  Whether it be newe or olde.

I.

Sint nuda dorsum, latera—
  Pes, manus, algens sit;
Dum Ventri veteris copia
  Zythi novive fit.
Non possum multum edere,
  Quia stomachus est nullus;
Sed volo vel monacho bibere
  Quanquam sit huic cucullus.
Et quamvis nudus ambulo,
  De frigore non est metus;
Quia semper Zytho vetulo
  Ventriculus est impletus.
Sint nuda dorsum, latera—
  Pes, manus, algens sit;
Dum Ventri veteris copia
  Zythi novive fit.

2.

I love no rost, but a nut-browne toste,
  And a crab laid in the fyre;
A little breade shall do me stead,
  Much breade I not desyre.
No frost nor snow, nor winde, I trowe,
  Can hurt me if I wolde:
I am so wrapt, and throwly lapt,
  Of jolly good ale and olde.
    Backe and side go bare, &c.

2.

Assatum nolo—tostum volo—
  Vel pomum igni situm;
Nil pane careo—parvum habeo
  Pro pane appetitum.
Me gelu, nix, vel ventus vix
  Afficerent injuria;
Hæc sperno, ni adesset mî
  Zythi veteris penuria.
    Sint nuda, &c.

3.

And Tyb, my wyfe, that as her lyfe
  Loveth well good ale to seeke;
Full oft drynkes shee, tyll ye may see
  The teares run down her cheeke:

3.

Et uxor Tybie, qui semper sibi
  Vult quærere Zythum bene,
Ebibit hæc persæpe, nec
  Sistit, dum madeant genæ.

Then doth she trowle to mee the boule,
Even as a mault-worme shuld;
And sayth, "Sweete hart, I took my
    parte
  Of this jolly good ale and olde."
    Back and side go bare, &c.

Et mihi tum dat cantharum,
  Sic mores sunt bibosi ;
Et dicit "Cor, en ! impleor
  Zythi dulcis et annosi."
    Sint nuda, &c.

4.

Now let them drynke tyll they nod and
    winke,
  Even as good felowes should doe ;
They shall not mysse to have the blysse
  Good ale doth bringe men to.
And all poore soules that have scowr'd
    boules,
  Or have them lustely trolde,
God save the lyves of them and their
    wyves,
  Whether they be yonge or old.
    Backe and syde go bare, &c.

4.

Nunc ebibant, donec nictant
  Ut decet virum bonum ;
Felicitatis habebunt satis,
  Nam Zythi hoc est donum.
Et omnes hi, qui canthari
  Sunt haustibus lætati,
Atque uxores vel juniores
  Vel senes, Diis sint grati.
    Sint nuda, &c.

There's not a Joy that Life can give.

Tune—GRAND MARCH *in Scipio*.

1.

THERE'S not a joy that WINE *can give like that it takes away*,
When slight intoxication yields to drunkenness the sway ;
'Tis not that *youth's smooth cheek* its *blush* surrenders to the
    nose,
But the stomach turns, the forehead burns, and all our
    pleasure goes.

2.

Then the few who still can keep their chairs amid the
    smashed decanters,
Who wanton still in witless jokes and laugh at pointless
    banters—
The magnet of their course is gone, for let them try to walk,
Their legs they speedily will find as jointless as their talk.

3.

Then the mortal hotness of the brain like Hell itself is
    burning ;
It cannot feel, nor dream, nor think—'tis whizzing, blazing,
    turning.
The heavy wet, or port, or rum, has mingled with *our tears*,
And if by chance we're weeping drunk, each drop our
    cheek-bone sears.

4.

Though fun still flow from fluent lips, and jokes confuse our
    noddles
Through midnight hours, while punch our powers insidi-
    ously enfuddles,
'Tis but as ivy leaves were worn by Bacchanals of yore,
To make them still look fresh and gay while rolling on the
    floor.

5.

Oh could I walk *as I have* walked, *or* see *as I have* seen,
Or even roll as I have done on many a carpet green,
As port at Highland inn seems sound, all corkish though
    it be,
So would I the Borachio kiss, and get blind drunk with
    thee.

Farewell, Farewell, beggarly Scotland.

RENDERED INTO LATIN.

1.

FAREWELL, farewell, beggarly Scotland,
    Cold and beggarly poor countrie ;
If ever I cross thy border again,
    The muckle deil must carry me.
There's but one tree in a' the land,
    And that's the bonny gallows tree.
The very nowte look to the south,
    And wish that they had wings to flee.

2.

Farewell, farewell, beggarly Scotland,
    Brose and bannocks, crowdy and kale !
Welcome, welcome, jolly old England,
    Laughing lasses and foaming ale !
'Twas when I came to merry Carlisle
    That out I laughed loud laughters three ;
And if I cross the Sark again,
    The muckle deil maun carry me.

3.

Farewell, farewell, beggarly Scotland,
    Kilted kimmers wi' carrotty hair ;
Pipers who beg that your honours would buy
    A bawbee's worth of their famished air !

I'd rather keep Cadwallader's goats,
    And feast upon toasted cheese and leeks,
Than go back again to the beggarly North,
    To herd 'mang loons with bottomless breeks.

LATIN VERSION.

1.

Valedico, Scotia, tibi,
    Mendica, egens, frigida gens ;
Diabolus me reportet ibi
    Si unquam tibi sum rediens.
Arbor unus nascitur ibi,
    Isque patibulus est decens ;
Bos ipse Austrum suspicit, sibi
    Alas ut fugeret cupiens.

2.

Vale, vale, Scotia mendica,
    Avenæ, siliquæ, crambe, far !
Ridentes virgines, Anglia antiqua,
    Salvete, et zythum cui nil est par !
Cum redirem Carlilam lætam
    Risu excepi effuso ter :
Si unquam Sarcam rediens petam,
    Diabole ingens ! tu me fer !

3.

Vale popellus tunicatus
    Crinibus crassis, et cum his
Tibicen precans si quid afflatûs
    Famelici emere asse vis !
Capros pascerem Cadwalladero,
    Cui cibus ex cepis et caseo fit,
Potius quam degam cum populo fero,
    Cui vestis sine fundo sit.

On Irish Songs.

THERE is, I perceive, a disinclination becoming very visible on the part of the English to believe us Irish people when we tell them that they know nothing about us. They look upon it as a sort of affront, and yet nothing is more true; and, as example is much better than any theory, I shall just beg leave to prove my assertion by what they put into our mouths when they think fit to write as Irish.

The first book I lay my hand on will do. It is a collection of Irish songs, published in London without date, printed by Oliver & Boyd. It contains all the popular Irish songs which you hear sung at the theatres, public-houses, Vauxhall, and other such fashionable places of resort. There are ninety of them in all, and I shall patiently examine these specimens of Irish wit; these would-be flowers of the Hibernian Parnassus.

The first song is a great favourite—the Sprig of Shillelah, and it is not much amiss. It contains an immensity of blarney to us, which, of course, is palatable. I suspect the author of never having been in Ireland, nevertheless, from these lines :

> " Who has e'er had the luck to see Donnybrook Fair,
> An Irishman all in his glory is there ; "

for I have had the "luck" to see that fair, and I never could see any glory in it. It is a paltry thing, if compared with Bartholomew Fair, or any of the great fairs of London; and like them is a nuisance which gathers the blackguard men and women of a metropolis to indulge in all kinds of filth. I should call it the worst specimen of Ireland. Would a Scotchman think his national character would be favourably exhibited by a collection of the cadies and baker-boys and gutter-bloods of Edinburgh, with their trulls? And as Dublin is three times the size of Edinburgh, the sweepings of its streets must be three times as disgusting. The squalid misery, too, which is mixed up with the drunken riot of the fairs of Donnybrook, has always been quite revolting to my eyes, and I should rather see the magistracy of Dublin employed in suppressing it than hear silly song-writers using their rhymes in its panegyric.

The next is Paddy MacShane's Seven Ages—a stupid parody on Shakespeare. A great knowledge of Ireland is shown here. Mr. MacShane, it appears, was a native of Ballyporeen, and fell in love with a lady there; but

> "She asked me just once that to see her I'd come,
> When I found her ten children and husband at home,
> A great big whacking chairman of Ballyporeen!"

Now Ballyporeen (Heaven bless it!) is a dirty village of about fifty houses at the foot of the Kilworth mountains, as you enter Tipperary, on the mail-coach road from Cork to Dublin. When I passed through it last the only decent-looking house I saw there was the inn, and a poor one enough even that was. I leave it to yourself to judge what a profitable trade that of a chairman would be in such a place as that, or how probable it is that a woman with a husband and ten children could pass off, incog., as unmarried upon a native. You would walk from one end to the other of it in three minutes.

Again he tells us that

> "I turned servant, and lived with the great justice Pat,
> A big dealer in p'ratoes at Ballyporeen:
> With turtle and venison he lined his inside,
> Ate so many fat capons," &c.

Potatoes are somewhere about the price of three halfpence a stone in Ballyporeen, and they are cultivated by almost every one in it, so that this excellent justice had a fine merchandise of it. As for turtle, I imagine that the name of it was never heard of in the village ; indeed, as Tipperary is quite an inland county, it must be a rarity to every part of it. And capons ! I am quite sure the dish is unknown altogether. The bard shows great knowledge of the Irish magistracy even by the way he mentions his justice— Justice Pat !

We have then,

> " There was an Irish lad, who loved a cloistered nun."

A good song, and perhaps Irish. One verse is like the idiom. When the hero could not get at his mistress,

> " He stamped and raved, and sighed and prayed,
>   And many times he swore ;
>   The Devil burn the iron bolts!
>   The Devil burn the door ! "

Then follows :

> " Mulrooney's my name, I'm a comical boy,
>   A tight little lad at shillelah.
>   St. Patrick wid whisky he suckled me, *joy*,
>   Among the sweet bogs of Killalah."

I must protest that I never heard the word "joy" so used in Ireland by anybody, and yet it is a standing expression put into our mouths by every writer of Irish characters. Of the existence of Killalah I am ignorant. We have Killalah in Connaught, but it rhymes to tallow. But, àpropos of rhymes, listen to those put into Mr. Mulrooney's mouth :

> " But thinks I, spite of what fame and glory *bequeath*,
>   How conceited I'd look in a fine laurel *wreath*,
>   Wid my hand in my mouth, to stand picking my *teeth*."

I flatter myself that the " comical boy " would say *be-quaith* and *wraith*, rhyming to *faith*, and never think of screwing up his mouth to squeezing these into *bequeeth* and *wreeth*.

Of Dermot and Sheelah I shall quote only the chorus :

> " Beam, bum, *boodle*, loodle, loodle,
> Beam, bum, *boodle*, loodle, loo."

Pretty writing that, and very much on a par, in point of sense and interest, with Barry Cornwall's humbugs to Appollor, rather more musical I own. But is it Irish ? *Negatur.* I deny it poz ! Boodles ! Why, boodles is a club of good hum-drum gentlemen, kept by Cuddington and Fuller, at 31 St. James Street, but not particularly Hibernian. A chorus in the same taste concerning them would run thus :

> " Bow wow, boodle, noodle, doodle,
> Bow, wow, boodle, noodle, pooh ! "

Close following comes Paddy O'Blarney ; a misnomer on the face of it. Blarney is a village and baronial castle. You might as well say Sawney M'Linlithgow or Archy O'Goosedubs. The song is a brutal attempt at wit and mock-Irish, *e.g.* :

> " I found one who larnt grown-up *Jolmen* to write,
> Just to finish gay Paddy O'Blarney."

Jolmen ! What's that ? Put for *jontlemen*, I suppose. This fellow had a fresh idea of the tongue. Such a word never was heard among us. By the way, our plebeians generally say jintlemen, though the folks who write for us think otherwise.

Hear the next bard :

> " I'm a comical fellow."

En passant, I may remark that I never heard any one say he was a comical fellow that he did not prove an ass, and the rule holds here :

> " I'm a comical fellow, I tell you no fib,
> And I come from the bogs of Killaley ; "

a various reading, I suppose, of the celebrated unknown district commemorated in another song by the name of Killalah.

> " You see I'm the thing by the cut of my jib,
> And they christen'd me Teddy O'Reilly."

Observe the name O'Reilly rhymes plainly to "highly." Ask for O'Raly anywhere, and you will not be understood. But the Christian name is equally destructive to its Irish pretensions. Teddy! A Cockney vulgarism for Edward, and that too confined to the raff of Cockaigne. Thady is a common Irish name, which, as you know, is the abbreviation of Thaddeus, the name of one of the apostles, according to Saints Matthew and Mark. But Teddy is unheard of; yet it occurs in half a dozen songs of this volume.

What part of the world the next song comes from needs no ghost to tell us. One rhyme will denote it :

> " As the board they put out was too narrow to *quarter*,
> The first step I took I was in such a *totter*."

It is, you see, marked with the indelible damned Cockney blot, and, in all probability, proceeds from the pen of Leigh Hunt. An Irishman, who sounds the R as fiercely as ever that canine letter rung from human organ, could never have been guilty of it.

Cushlamachree, which succeeds, is, 'tis said, from the pen of Curran, and the first verse is, I think, a good and warm one :

> " Dear Erin, how sweetly thy green bosom rises,
> *An emerald set in the ring of the sea ;*
> Each blade of thy meadows my faithful heart prizes,
> Thou Queen of the West—the world's Cushlamachree."

We soon come to a strain of another mood in Sheelah's Wedding, which, for magnificent ignorance of the country in which the scene is laid, is just as good as can be conceived. I extract the whole second verse as a sample of various beauties :

> "Well, the time being settled, to *church* they were carried,
> With some more lads and lasses, to see the pair married,
> Who vowed that too long from the *parson* they tarried ;
> For who should such sweet things be scorning ?

> Then at *church*, arrah, yes, you may fancy them there;
> Sure the *priest* tied them fast, you may very well swear;
>   And when it was done,
>   Och, what laughing and fun
> Took place about something, and throwing the stocking,
>   While the blythe boys and GIRLS
>   Talked of ringing the BELLS
> On St. Patrick's day in the *morning*."

The rhyme here marks this brute to be a bestial Cockney. The mixture of the words "parson" and "priest" convicts him of not knowing Irish phraseology, which restricts the latter word to the Roman Catholic clergy, who are not parsons. By the name Sheelah the lady is decidedly Catholic; and then how consistently we have the talk about the "church" and the "bells"! Roman Catholic places of worship all through Ireland are called *chapels*, and they have no bells, very few having even one. And the morning marriage! There the ape, if he knew anything of Ireland, must have known that Catholic marriages there are celebrated in the *evening*. I have been at some hundreds of them. In the next song, and several others, we have "taef" for "thief;" which is enough. The vulgarism, inter Hibernos, is "teef." In the next we have the adventures of a certain Mr. *Teddy*, of whom I have already disposed. I may pass Mr. Grimgruffenhoff, and Bumper Squire Jones, for different reasons. The latter is a capital song indeed, and written by an Irish Baron of Exchequer. The breed of such judges is not extinct while we have Lord Norbury, whom God preserve.

Mr. O'Gallogher falls in love in the next song with a lady named Cicely: what part of Ireland he found her in is not mentioned. It never was my lot to meet with one of her name, and the same remark I must extend to the heroine of the following chant, the celebrated Looney Mactwolter's mistress, Miss Judy *O'Flannikin*, who is evidently transmuted from O'Flannegan, to rhyme the opening line,

> "Oh! whack, Cupid's a *Mannikin*."

Looney itself is a dubious *Christian* name. I have known

plebeians of that *surname*, and when they rise in society, if they ever do, they change it always to Loane.

"Murphy O'Casey" heads the next. Psha! The name will not pass muster. You might as well say Blackwood O'Jeffrey. Nor can I panegyrise in another song Father O'Rook, for an Irishman would certainly call him O'Rourke.

I skip a parcel of mere vulgarity to give you

> " I'm Larry O'Lashem, was born in Killarney,"

one of whose adventures is described in the following dialect:

> " I amused myself laughing, to see how the HINDER
> Wheels after the fore ones most furiously paid, [Qu?]
> Till a wheel broke its leg, spilt the coach out of the WINDER,
> While my head and the pavement at nut-cracking played."

Winder ! Poet of Cockneyland, the compliments of the season to you ! I disclaim you as a countryman. Nor shall I claim the bard, who, singing of the siege of Troy, tells you that

> " —— the cunning Ulysses, the Trojans to *cross*,
> Clapt forty fine fellows on one wooden *horse*."

From the theme of the poem—those old down-looking Greeks—and this rhyme, it is evident that it was written by the late Mr. Keats. May I be shot if *he* was an Irishman !

Molly Astore is a beautiful tune to namby-pamby New-Monthly-looking words, and the parody on it is quite a poor thing. I flatter myself I have made better.

A poet farther on treats us to the following description of a Kerryman :

> " His hair was so red and his eyes were so bright."

No doubt there are red-haired Kerrymen, but they are not one in fifty. The complexion is dark olive, and the hair black, they being in all probability descended from the Spaniards. The poet was thinking of a Highlander. Now the knights of Kerry wear breeches, and are in a small degree civilised.

Another Irishman from Cockneyshire sings of

> "———— Cormac O'Con,
> Of the great Con grandsire,
> With the son of Combal the Greek sire,
> Whose name sounded afar,
> As great Ossian's *papa*."

If I met this fellow, who has our Irish names so glib at his fingers' ends, at the top of the highest house of the city, I should kick him down-stairs. A Ludgate Hill pawnbroker could not be more impertinent if he wrote of the fine arts.

In the same *de haut en bas* fashion should I kick him who informs us that

> "I were astonished as much as e'er *man was*
> To see a sea-fight on an ocean of *canvass*."

You hear the barbarian saying canvass—I long to pull his nose.

I apprehend the author of the Irish Wedding (see Jon Bee) is a Scot:

> "First, book in hand, came Father Quipes."

What part of the world does that name belong to?—

> "———— came Father Quipes,
> With the bride's dada, the *Bailie, O.*"

Bailies we have none in Ireland ; and, if we had, they should be all Protestants, and thereby out of the pale of Father Quipes.

A piece of politics in another ditty is quite diverting to us who know a thing or two :

> "Though all taxes I paid, yet no vote I could pass O———"

and was in consequence, though

> "With principles pure, patriotic, and *firm*,
> Attached to my country, a friend to *reform*,"

obliged to fly. His case was certainly hard in not having a vote when every farmer or labourer in Ireland may have one if he likes, or rather if his landlord likes. In the county of Cork there are 25,000 voters, in Down about 20,000, and so on ; so that this grievance about the want of suffrage is rather singular.

There is no use in bothering the public with any more remarks on such a subject. I hope nobody will think I have any spleen against this collection of songs, which is just as good as any other similar one, but I wished to show that I had some ground for saying that we are not quite wrong in accusing our English friends of ignorance of our concerns. Some time or other, perhaps, I may in the same way get through the usual stage characters in which we figure, and prove them equally remote from truth.

It would, perhaps, be a good thing to go over some of the political speculations on Ireland in the same manner, but I never liked Irish politics, and now I particularly detest them. I frequently admire the intrepidity of the heads which John Black spins out for the edification of the Whigamores whenever he takes us in his hand. Evidently wishing to patronise us, he nevertheless treats us as mere barbarians. I remember reading one morning in the *Chronicle* that, except Dublin and Cork, there were no large towns in Ireland, which accounts for its want of civilisation, while Scotland was indebted for her superiority over us to her possessing such eminent cities as Edinburgh, Glasgow, Paisley, Aberdeen, Dundee, Inverness, and some others which I forget. Now Limerick is larger and more populous than any except the first two ; Waterford, Galway, Kilkenny, and Belfast, fall little short of them ; and, taking out the first half dozen of Scotch towns, you would seek in vain through Scotland for towns to compare with Drogheda, Sligo, Carlow, Clonmell, Derry, Youghall, and several others. This is but a small sample of his accuracy.

He of the *Courier* knows, *in his writings*, something more, but *personally* Mudford is quite horror-struck at the notion of us. The Roman Catholic Association, professedly friends of the liberty of the press, have brought an information against him for inserting some remarks of a correspondent on Maynooth College, and availed themselves of an obscure law to lay the venue against him in Cork. The very wind of the word has frightened my friend Mudford out of his seven senses. Some Cockney blackguard, with that spirit of personality so disgustingly the distinction of the Cockney school, once called him "a pile of fleecy hosiery," but that name is every day becoming less and less applicable. He looks on the Corkagians as no better than Ashantees, and no doubt anticipates from the jaws of long John Brixon, mayor of that beef-abounding city, the fate of poor Sir Charles M'Carthy. Let him be comforted. Cork, I can assure him, is well munitioned with victual and drink, and he has but a small chance of being eaten alive there, particularly as he remains but a fortnight. Nor let him dread the hostile countenances of a grand jury, empanelled by Jack Bagnell and Ned Colburn—best of little men—sheriffs of the aforesaid bailiwick. And even if that is improbable, the thing comes to a petit jury even before them—let him pluck up courage. Men there are to be found on all sides of the banks of

> "The spreading Lee, that like an island fayre
> Encloseth Corke with its divided flood,"

who would devour the boot, from the silk twist that hems its upper-leather to the iron horse-shoe which guards its heel, sooner than give a verdict against the right. Counselled by these reflections, let him devour turbot, hot (as the old cookery-books have it) from the bank in the harbour; let him swallow salmon, creaming in everlasting curd from the Lee; let Kinsale feed him with hake, fish of delicious flavour, unheard of in Augusta Trinobantum; from Cove let him gulp down oysters capacious as his well-fleshed hand. Kerry will supply him mutton to masticate, small but lively; Cork itself will offer its beef and butter, peerless throughout the land. Pork is, I own, inferior to the flesh of Anglia pigs; but Wicklow can send her turf-dried hams, easily procurable, that will scarce vail bonnet to those of Wiltshire. He may, no doubt, regret the crammed poultry of London, but a turkey in native flavour will smoke upon his board for two tenpennies. Does he long for dainties more rich and rare? In a harbour yawning for the West Indies he need not desiderate turtle; in a city within easy march of sporting hills and dales he need not be afraid of wanting game or venison. As for drink, is he fond of port? Vessels from Oporto will jostle the boat that brings him to the quay; if of claret, he must be unskilled in bibulous lore if he knows not the value set upon the claret of Ireland. But, as his stay is short, I recommend whisky-punch. *That* he cannot get for love nor money in London. Let him there ingurgitate that balmy fluid. There's Walker —there's Wise—there's Callaghan—there's Hewitt—excellent artists all; they will sell it to him for from 6s. 6d. to 7s. 6d. a gallon; and a gallon will make sixty-four tumblers —I have often calculated it—and that is three times as much as he should drink in an evening. So doing he will be happy and fearless of the act of Judge Johnson.

But what is this I am about? digressing from a disquisition on songs, pseudo-Irish, to the way in which a stranger who knows how could live in Cork. It can't be helped. I have lost the thread of my argument, so I think I had better conclude.

On English Songs.

I HAVE been tumbling over Ritson's songs listlessly this morning, for want of something better to do, and cannot help thinking that a much better selection and arrangement might be made. He assigns 304 pages to love-songs, and but 228 to all others. The collection of ancient ballads which concludes the volume is not very much in place in a book of *songs*, and besides is far inferior to what we now know such a collection ought to be. Now, I submit, without at all disparaging that " sublime and noble, that sometimes calm and delightful, but more frequently violent, unfortunate, and dreadful passion " of love, as Ritson calls it—it does not fill such a space in the good song-writing of any country as a proportion of fifteen to eleven against all other species. I say of good song-writing, for I know of namby-pamby it fills nine parts out of ten.

And precisely of namby-pamby are composed nine parts out of ten of Ritson's most pedantic divisions into classes —classes sillily planned at first, and not clearly distinguished in execution afterwards. The second song of the first class, by Miss Aiken, concludes with this verse :

> " Thus to the rising god of day
> Their early vows the Persians pay,
> And bless the spreading fire :
> Whose glowing chariot, mounting soon,
> Pours on their heads the burning noon :
> They sicken and expire."

This is not song-writing. It is only a bombastic repetition of a middling thought which had been already expressed ten thousand times. It is, in short, a verse out of a poor *ode* in the modern sense of the word.

In Otway's song, p. 4—

> "To sigh and wish is all my ease,
>   Sighs which do heat impart
> Enough to melt the coldest ice,
>   Yet cannot warm your heart."

Is this verse worth printing;—this frigid, trivial conceit, which has been tossed about by the verse-writers of all the nations in the world?

In the same page sings Viscount Molesworth:

> "Almeria's face, her shape, her air,
>   With charms resistless wound the *heart*,"

which, it is needless to say, is rhymed by "*dart.*"

In short, of the eighty-four songs of the first-class, with the exception of "Take, oh take those lips away!" "To all ye ladies now at land," "My time, O ye Muses, was happily spent," which, though far too long for a song, contains many ideas and lines perfectly adapted for that style of composition, and perhaps half-a-dozen others, all are of the same cast; and, what makes it more provoking, we see affixed to some of them the names of Dryden, Prior, &c., as if the editor had a perverse pleasure in showing us that these men could write as tritely and trivially as their neighbours on some occasions. Colin and Lucy, and Jemmy Dawson, which this class contains, are no more songs than Chevy Chace, or the Children of the Wood.

The second class, in which "love is treated as a passion," is better; for even attempts at writing in the language of passion are generally at least readable if they are often absurd. What we cannot tolerate is inanity. There is a kind of noisy gallantry about

> "Ask me not how calmly I
>   All the cares of life defy;
> How I baffle human woes,
>   Woman, woman, woman knows,"

which is pleasant. Song XII. is excellent. Compare the very sound of

> " Over the mountains,
>   And over the waves,
> Under the fountains,
>   And under the graves ;
> Under floods that are deepest
>   Which Neptune obey,
> Over rocks which are steepest,
>   Love will find out his way," &c.,

with the trim nothingness of the very next :

> " Oft on the troubled ocean's face
>   Loud stormy winds arise,
> The murmuring surges swell apace,
>   And clouds obscure the skies ;
> But when the tempests' rage is o'er "—

what follows ? Why,

> " Soft breezes smooth the main,
> The billows cease to lash the shore,
> And all is calm again " ! !

Compare, again, song XXII. :

> " Would you choose a wife for a happy life,
>   Leave the court, and the country take,
> Where Susan and Doll, and Hanny and Moll,
> Follow Harry and John, whilst harvest goes on,
>   And merrily, merrily rake," &c.,

with song XXIV. :

> " Happy the world in that blest age
>   When beauty was not bought and sold,
> When the fair mind was uninflamed
>   With the mean thirst of baneful gold."

What jejune trash ! And how absurd and abominable an attempt it is to put into this creeping dialect what we have read in Greek all but divine, and in Italian almost as delicious as Greek ! I say, compare such passages as these together, and if you be not thoroughly sensible of the vast inferiority of the songs by persons of quality, and the propriety of utterly ejecting them from collections of songs, you will be fit to comment on them in the style of Gilbert Wakefield, and to receive panegyrics accordingly from Tom Dibdin.*

* What is written above of English Songs, will, of course, apply to the songs of all nations.   I shall give a specimen in French.   I shall first quote a song by Antoine Ferrand, a Parisian, a Counsellor of the Court of Aids, who died in 1719 :—

Iris est plus charmante
Que l'Aurore naissante ;
La Jeunesse brillante
   N'eut jamais tant d'appas.
Tout le monde l'adore ;
     Flore

Est moins fraiche et moins belle.
     Qu' elle :
Venus même n'a pas
Tant d'amours qui marchent sur ses pas,
&c.

Here we have Venus, Flora, and Aurora, in full fig ; and, in the name of the three goddesses, is the song worth a farthing?   Now take a song which you may vote low if you have a mind, but it is a good song nevertheless, and worth a cart-load of the above rubbish.   I shall copy it all :—

1.
Malgré la bataille
  Qu' on donne demain,
Ca, faisons ripaille,
  Charmante Catein :
Attendant la gloire,
  Prenons le plaisir,
Sans lire au grimoire
  Du sombre avenir.

2.
Si la Hallebarde
  Je peux mériter,
Pres du corps du garde
  Je te fais planter ;
Ayant la dentelle,
  Le soulier brodé,
La blouque à l'oreille
  Le chignon cardé.

3.
Narguant tes compagnes,
  Méprisant leurs vœux,
J'ai fait deux campagnes
  Roti de tes feux.

Digni de la pomme,
  Tu reçus ma foi,
Et jamais rogome
  Ne fut bu sans toi.

4.
Tien, serre ma Pipe,
  Garde mon briquet ;
Et si la Tulipe
  Fait le noir trajet,
Que tu sois la seule
  Dans le régiment,
Qu' ait le brule-gueule
  De son cher amant.

5.
Ah ! retien tes larmes,
  Calme ton chagrin ;
Au nom, de tes charmes
  Achéve ton vin.
Mais, quoi ! de nos bandes
  J' entends les Tambours?
Gloire ! tu commandes,
  Adieu mes amours.

The author of this song is Christopher Mangenot, brother of the Abbe

The third class opens beautifully indeed with " He that loves a rosy cheek." Few poems in our language resemble so much as the first two verses of this song (the third is provokingly inferior) the admirable and indefinable beauty of the Greek epigrams. I, however, do not remember one exactly in point. Those following (except the jocular ones, as " Why so pale, fond lover?" "Tom loves Mary passing well," " My name is honest Harry," " My passion is as mustard strong," &c.) are not particularly worthy of applause. It contains, to be sure, " Mary, I believed thee true," " Still to be neat, still to be drest," and some others ; but the staple commodity is :

> " But passion's wild impetuous sea
>   Hurries me far from peace and thee—
>   'Twere vain to struggle more.
>   Thus the poor sailor slumbering lies,
>   While swelling tides around him rise,
>   And push his bark from shore :
>   In vain he spreads his helpless arms ;
>   His pitying friends, with fond alarms,
>   In vain deplore his state.
>   Still far and farther from the coast,
>   On the high surge his bark is tost,
>   And, foundering, yields to fate."

Is not this the quintessence of absurdity nowadays? Fine, pretty, good-for-nothing verses I admit them to be, never intended or fitted to be sung ; and, besides, have I not read somewhere—

> " Heu ! quoties fidem
> Mutatosque Deos flebit, et aspera
>   Nigris æquora ventis
>   Emirabitur insolens,
> Qui nunc te fruitur credulus aurea " ?

I own I have no patience when I see things which have

Mangenot of the Temple. It was written during our war with France in 1744. It was generally attributed to the pen of Voltaire, but I doubt if he could have written in this vein. I wish somebody would translate it into English.—M. OD. (Do it yourself.—C. N.)

been once beautifully expressed re-said in a manner blundering and diluted.

Class Fourth is devoted solely to expressions of love for the fair sex *—not a hopeful subject.   Love to them is too serious a thing to be jested with [see Lord Byron's Don Juan, and also see Ovid, from whom Lord Byron has *conveyed* the idea]; and they are too proud to complain if slighted. They would be wrong if they did.   It is *our* part to sue ; it is *theirs* to slight or to accept.   They should take the advice of Shakespeare :

> " Sigh no more, ladies, sigh no more :
>   Men were deceivers ever,
>   One foot at sea, and one on shore,
>   To one thing constant never.
>   Then sigh not so,
>   But let them go,
>   And be you blithe and bonny."

If the ladies *will* not write their feelings, I am afraid we *can* not.   At all events, this fourth class is completely *fadé*. There are some middling songs in it, but the majority are like those from Mr. Mosy Mendez :

> " Vain is every fond endeavour
>   To resist the tender dart ;
>   For examples move us never ;
>   We must feel to know the smart."

Which is just as much poetry as—

> " Vain, quite vain, the toil you spend is,
>   When your time in verse you pass ;
>   For, good Mr. Moses Mendez,
>   You are nothing but an ass."

The ideas in Soame Jenyns's song, No. X., are very pretty.   The appeal to a lover acknowledged triumphant—

> " Say would you use that very power
>   You from her fondness claim,

---

* In this class Ben Jonson's " Drink to me only " is inserted, I think wrongly, for it appears to be an address from a man, not a woman.   By Ritson's remark, p. lxxix, it would appear that he did not know it was from the Greek.

> To ruin, in one fatal hour,
>   A life of spotless fame?
> Ah! cease, my dear, to do an ill,
>   Because, perhaps, you may;
> But rather try your utmost skill
>   'To save me than betray,"

is elegantly thought and expressed. There is something like the idea in the life of Gilbert Earle, when the lady urges her lover not to take advantage of her tenderness to betray her honour.

In the Fifth Class are some very good songs. It contains, among others, three more especial favourites of mine—"Sally in our alley" by poor Harry Carey (Goldsmith's own song, by the way), "Black-eyed Susan," and Bishop Percy's "O Nanny, wilt thou gang with me?" But I rather think I am not peculiar in this taste. It contains also a good deal of very good nonsense. In general, of the 287 songs of the volume I think we might fairly, for one reason or another, dispense with at least 200.

Our second division is drinking. Ritson was a water-drinker, and therefore says, he candidly owns that he was "not sorry to find every endeavour used to enlarge this part of the collection with credit (and he may probably, as it is, have been too indulgent) prove altogether fruitless; a circumstance, perhaps, which will some time or other be considered as not a little to the honour of the English Muse." This is stuff. I shall not eulogise drinking, but I am not to be humbugged with the idea that *any* production of the English Muse ever soared within five hundred yards of him who sings of

"Ἡδὺν, θεσπεσιον, θειον ποτον:"

or that any *songs* we have can beat those of Anacreon. If future generations differ with this dictum of mine, they may with all my heart; but I shall retain to myself the privilege of thinking such generations asinine to a great degree. Ritson's selections, however, are tolerable. Drinking-songs may be divided pretty fairly into two classes;—the meditative, which in the Egyptian manner brings the skeleton into the banquet-room, and bids you think of the fleetingness of life as the chief stimulus to make the most of its enjoyments while it lasts.

> " Heu, heu, nos miseros, quam totus homuncio nil est,
>   Quam fragilis tenero stamine vita cadit!
> Sic erimus cuncti, postquam nos auferet Orcus,
>   Ergo vivamus, dum licet esse bene—"

as Trimalchio sings. The second class is the joyous, which bids us use the goods the gods provide us because we like them—because they exhilarate us; when the song bursts forth from mere animal spirits, or, to talk Pindarically, when

> " Θαρσαλέα δὲ παρὰ
>   Κρητῆρα φωνὰ γίγνεται :"

and we cry—

> " Ἐγκιρνάτω τίς μιν, γλυκὺν
>   Κώμου προφάταν."

Of the former kind, "An hundred years hence" has always appeared to me particularly good :

> " Let us drink, and be merry,
>   Dance, joke, and rejoice,
> With claret and sherry,
>   Theorbo and voice.
> The changeable world
>   To our joy is unjust,
> All treasures uncertain ;
>   Then down with your dust!
> In frolics dispose
>   Your pounds, shillings, and pence,
> For we shall be nothing
>   An hundred years hence."

Of the more roaring jovial songs, I do not see any worth extracting in Ritson. I think the pages of *Blackwood* contain some far superior to any which he sports.

What stories a commentator thoroughly versant with this subject could tell in every part of this department! I see here some of the ditties of Tom D'Urfey, whose whole life, properly written, would be a history of the joviality of

England for half a century. I see here some of the songs of Tom Brown, a fellow of deeper thought than generally is to be found among the bards of the bottle. Then we have " Ye Goodfellows all " by Baron Dawson, the friend of Carolan, last of the Irish bards, and the companion of Dr. King, poet of Cookery. We see the names of Gay, Lord Rochester, Harry Carey, old Sheridan the purple-snouted, Ben Jonson the rare, Milton, and the Duke of Wharton. Let any one who knows the literary history of the country just pause for a minute at the last names I have quoted, and run over at a mental glance the events of their lives ; and how various a blending of thoughts will he not experience ! I confess that reading convivial songs is to me a melancholy amusement. Every page I turn presents me with verses which I heard in merry hours from voices now mute in death, or removed to distant lands, or estranged in affection. But—

> " 'Tis in vain
> To complain,
> In a melancholy strain,
> Of the days that are gone, and will never come again."

Is the story true that Wolfe either wrote or sung " How stands the glass around," the night before the battle,

> " When that hero met his fate on the heights of Abram "?

I heard he did, but I forget my authority.

" The Ex-ale-tation of Ale " is not properly a song, but it is a pleasant extravaganza. There is one phenomenon mentioned in it, which I submit to Sir Humphry Davy or some other great chemist, for I cannot resolve it :

> " Nor yet the delight that comes to the sight
> To see how it flowers and mantles in graile,*
> *As green as a leek* with a smile on the cheek,
> The *true orient colour* of a pot of good ale."

How was it green ? I know not, neither can I conjecture. The third part of Miscellaneous Songs has our usual

* *i.e.*, small particles. Spenser uses the word for gravel.

favourites joined to others quite unworthy.   Strange to say, it contains neither "God save the King" nor "Rule Britannia."   Could this have arisen from the cankered Jacobinism of citizen Ritson?   If so, it was shabby even for a Jacobin.   I cannot pass over this list without thanking Tom Campbell for "Ye mariners of England."   I never read it without forgiving him all his Whiggery, and lamenting the Ritter Bann and Reullura.

As for the fourth part—the old ballads—I say nothing, except that it is poor enough, and I think uncalled for here. The last ballad is by Sir W. Scott; a translation from the Norman French, the original of which, the editor says, cannot now be retraced.   Had it ever any existence?   It is a splendid thing, and I do not recollect seeing it in his works. Therefore here it goes—

BALLAD

ON THE DEATH OF

SIMON DE MONTFORT,

EARL OF LEICESTER,

AT THE BATTLE OF EVESHAM, 1266.

(Literally versified from the Norman French.)

BY WALTER SCOTT, ESQ.

" In woful wise my song shall rise,
  My heart impels the strain ;
Tears fit the song, which tells the wrong
  Of gentle Barons slayn.
Fayr peace to gaine they fought in vayn ;
  Their house to ruin gave,
And limb and life to butcheryng knyfe,
  Our native land to save.

CHORUS.

" Now lowly lies the flower of pries,*
  That could so much of weir : †
Erle Montfort's scathe, and heavy death,
  Shall cost the world a tear.

---

* Price.   † War.

"As I here say, upon Tuesdaye,
    The battle bold was done ;
Each mounted knight there fell in fight,
    For ayd of foot was none :
There wounds were felt, and blows were dealt,
    With brands that burnished be,
Sir Edward stoute, his numerous route
    Have won the maisterie.
                    Now lowly lies, &c.

"But though he died on Montfort's side,
    The victorie remained ;
Like Becket's fayth, the Erle's in deathe
    The martyr's palm obtained ;
That holy saint would never graunt
    The church should fall or slyde ;
Like him, the Erle met deadly peril,
    And like him dauntless dyed.
                    Now lowly lies, &c.

"The bold Sir Hugh Despencer true,
    The kingdom's Justice he,
Was doomed to die unrighteouslye,
    By passynge crueltie ;
And Sir Henry, the son was he
    To Leister's nobile lord,
With many moe, as ye shall know,
    Fell by Erle Gloster's sword.
                    Now lowly lies, &c.

"He that dares dye in standing by
    The country's peace and lawe,
To him the Saint the meed shall graunt
    Of conscience free from flawe.
Who suffers scathe, and faces death,
    To save the poor from wrong,
God speed his end, the poor man's friend,
    For suche we pray, and long !
                    Now lowly lies, &c.

"His bosom nere, a treasure dere,
    A sackclothe shirt, they founde ;
The felons there full ruthless were
    Who stretched hym on the grounde.
More wrongs than be in butcherye
    They did the knight who fell,
To wield his sword, and keep his worde,
    Who knew the way so well.
                    Now lowly lies, &c.

> "Pray as is meet, my brethren sweet,
>   The maiden Mary's son,
> The infant fair, our noble heir,
>   In grace to guide him on.
> I will not name the habit's * claym,
>   Of that I will not saye ;
> But for Jesus' love, that sits above,
>   For churchmen ever pray.
>   Now lowly lies, &c.

> "Seek not to see, of chivalrye,
>   Or count, or baron bold ;
> Each gallant knight, and squire of might,
>   They all are bought and sold ;
> For loyaltie and veritie,
>   They now are done awaye—
> The losel vile may reign by guile,
>   The fool by his foleye.
>   Now lowly lies, &c.

> " Sir Simon wight, that gallant knight,
>   And his companye eche one,
> To Heaven above, and joye and love,
>   And endless life, are gone.
> May He on rood who bought our good,
>   And God, their paine relieve,
> Who, captive ta'en, are kept in chaine,
>   And depe in dungeon grieve !

> " Now lowly lies the flower of pries,
>   That could so much of weir ;
> Erle Montfort's scathe, and heavy death,
>   Shall cost the world a tear." †

On the whole, the really good songs of Ritson might be
gathered into a single volume. His preliminary dissertation
is pleasant enough, and might be retained with improve-
ments. Another volume of additional songs might be
collected, and then it would be tolerably complete. I
should agree with Ritson as to the propriety of rejecting all

---

* The clerical habit is obviously alluded to ; and it seems to be cautiously
and obscurely hinted that the Church was endangered by the defence of
De Montfort.

† It was the object of the translator to imitate, as literally as possible,
the style of the original, even in its rudeness, abrupt transitions, and
obscurity ; such being the particular request of Mr. Ritson, who supplied
the old French of this ballad minstrelsy.

political songs, for I think they should make a separate work, which is a desideratum in our literature. Songs of Freemasonry also I should exclude, though I do not think with him that they would disgrace the collection, some of them being pretty good, but because they are not intelligible to the uninitiated. The only one in favour of which I should break my rule that I recollect just·now is Burns's "Adieu, a heart-warm, fond adieu, dear brethren of the mystic tie."

Some time or other what I propose will be effected. Blackwood should publish it.

Twenty-one Maxims to Marry by.

> "To be thus is nothing;
> But to be *safely* thus—!"
> —SHAKESPEARE.

I NEVER knew a good fellow in all my life that was not, some way or other, the dupe of women. One man is an ass unconsciously, another with his eyes open; but all that are good for anything are saddled and bridled in some way, and at some time or other.

If a good fellow drinks—your best perhaps won't drink very much. now—but if he does drink, ten to one it is because he is out of humour with some woman. If he writes, what can he write about but woman? If he games, why is it but to get money to lavish upon her? For all his courage, ardour, wit, vanity, good-temper, and all other good qualities that he possesses, woman keeps an open market, and can engross them wholly! Why, then, after we have abused women—which we all of us do—and found out that they are no more to be trusted than fresh-caught monkeys—which the best of us are very likely to do;— after all, what does it come to but this—that they are the Devil's plagues of our lives, and we *must* have them?

For, if you are "five-and-twenty, or thereabouts," and good for anything, you'll certainly become attached to some woman; and—you'll find I'm right, so take warning in time—depend upon it, it had better be to an honest one. It's Cockney taste, lads—nasty, paltry, Bond Street stuff—to be seen driving about in a cabriolet with the mistress of half the town. And, for the attachment, never flatter yourselves that you are certain to get "tired" of any woman with whom you constantly associate. Depend upon it you are a great deal more likely to become very inextricably fond of her. Kick it all out of doors, the stale trash, that men are naturally "indifferent" to their wives. How the deuce should a fine woman be the worse for being one's wife? And are there not five hundred good reasons—to everybody but a puppy—why she must be the better? Then, as you must all of you be martyred, suffer in respectable company. MARRY, boys! It's a danger; but, though it is a danger, it is the best! It is a danger! I always feel thankful when a man is hanged for killing his wife; because I should not choose to kill a wife of my own : and yet the crying of the "dying speech "—"for the barbarous and inhuman murder !" &c. &c.—is a sort of warning to her—as one rat, losing his tail in the rat-trap, frightens the whole granaryful that are left. But, though marriage is a danger, nevertheless hazard it. Between evils, boys !—you know the proverb ?—choose the least. Marry, I say, all and each of you ! Take wives ; and take them in good time, that "your names may be long in the land." And then—seeing that you would, one and all of you, have wives—comes the question, how you should go about to get them ?

Then, in the first place, I shall assume that he who reads this paper and marries, marries for a wife. Because if he wants a "fortune" to boot, or a "place," or to be allied (being plebeian) to a "titled family," the case is out of my *métier ;* he had better apply to an attorney at once. Don't make these things indispensable any of you, if you can help it. For the fortune, a hundred to one—when you get it— if it does not override you with "settlements," and "trusts," and whole oceans of that sort of impertinence, which every proper man should keep clear of. No woman ought to be *able* to hold property independent of her husband. And if that is not the law, all I can say is that it ought to be so. Then for the "place ; " it's very well to have a place where you can get one, but it must be the very devil to have the donor eternally all your life afterwards reminding you how you came by it.   And for the " titled family," why shut the book this minute, and don't have the impudence to read another line that I write, if you wouldn't quoit a brother-in-law that was " right honourable " with one impetus from Charing Cross to Whitechapel, just as soon as a kinsman that was a clerk in the Victualling Office—provided he deserved it, or you took it into your head that it was convenient to do it ! Besides, a nice woman is worth all the money in the Bank. What would you do with it, after you had it, but give it all for one ?   Please your taste, my children ; and so that you get an honest woman, and a pleasing one, to the Devil send the remainder.   And then, to guide your choice, take the following maxims.   Those who have brains will perceive their value at a glance, and such as are thick-headed can read them three or four times over.   And let such not be too hastily disheartened, for it is the part of wit to bear with dulness; and one comfort is, when you have at last beaten anything into a skull of density, the very Devil himself can hardly ever get it out again.   " We write on brass," as somebody or other observes, and some-where, " less easily than in water, but the impression once made endures for ever."

MAXIM I.

Now in making marriage, as in making love and indeed in making most other things, the beginning it is that is the difficulty.   But the French proverb about beginnings—" C'est le premier pas qui *coute* "—goes more literally to the arrangement of marriage, as our English well illustrates the condition of love : " The first step over, the rest is easy." Because, in the marrying affair, it is particularly the " first step " that " costs," as to your cost you will find if that step happens to go the wrong way.   And most men, when they go about the business of wedlock, owing to some strange delusion begin the affair at the wrong end.   They take a fancy to the white arms (sometimes only to the kid gloves) or to the neat ankles of a peculiar school girl, and conclude from these premises that she is just the very woman of the world to scold a household of servants and to bring up a dozen children! This is a convenient deduction, but not always a safe one. Pleasant, like Dr. McCulloch's deductions in his Political Economy, but generally wrong. "Let not the creaking of shoes nor the rustling of silk betray thy poor heart," as Shakespeare says, &c. &c., "to woman!"—implying thereby that red sashes and lace flounces are but as things transitory, and that she who puts ornaments of gold and silver upon her own head may be a "crown to her husband," and yet not exactly such a "crown" as King Solomon meant a virtuous woman should be. He that has ears to hear (while he has nothing worse than ears), let him hear! A word to the wise should be enough. There are some particular qualities now and then very likely to lead a gentleman on the sudden to make a lady his wife, and after she has become so very likely again to make him wish that they had made her anybody else's.

MAXIM II.

White arms and neat ankles bring me naturally at once to the very important consideration of beauty; for don't suppose, because I caution you against all day-dishabilles, that I want to fix you with a worthy creature whom it will make you extremely ill every time you look at. No! Leave these to apothecaries, lawyers, and such, generally, as mean to leave money behind them when they die. You have health, a competence, a handy pull at a nose, or at a trigger: let them grovel. For the style of attraction please yourselves, my friends. I should say a handsome figure, if you don't get both advantages, is better than a merely pretty face. I don't mean by "handsome figure" forty cubits high, and as big round as the chief drayman at Meux's brew-house; but finely formed and set. Good eyes are a

point never to be overlooked.   Fine teeth—full, well-pro-
portioned limbs—don't cast these away for the sake of a
single touch of the small-pox, a mouth something too
wide, or dimples rather deeper on one side than the other.

MAXIM III.

It may at some time be a matter of consideration
whether you shall marry a maid or a widow.   As to the taste,
I myself will give no opinion.   I like both ; and there are
advantages and disadvantages peculiar to either.   If you
marry a widow, I think it should be one whom you have
known in the lifetime of her husband ; because then—*ab
actu ad posse*—from the sufferings of the defunct you
may form some notion of what your own will be.   If her
husband is dead before you see her, you had better be off
at once ; because she knows (the jade !) what you will like,
though she never means to do it ; and depend upon it, if
you have only an inch of *penchant*, and trust yourself to look
at her three times, you are tickled to a certainty.

MAXIM IV.

Marrying girls is a nice matter always, for they are as
cautious as crows plundering a corn-field.   You may "stalk"
for a week, and never get near them unperceived.   You
hear the caterwauling, as you go upstairs into the drawing-
room, louder than thunder ; but it stops as if by magic
the moment a (marriageable) man puts his ear to the key-
hole.   I don't myself, I profess, upon principle see any
objection to marrying a widow.   If she upbraids you at any
time with the virtues of her former husband, you only reply
that you wish he had her with him with all your soul.   If
a woman, however, has had more than three husbands, she
poisons them ; avoid her.

MAXIM V.

In widow-wiving it may be a question whether you should

marry the widow of an honest man or of a rascal.   Against the danger that the last may have learned ill tricks they set the advantage that she will be more sensible (from the contrast) to the kindness of a gentleman and a man of honour.   I think you should marry the honest man's widow, because with women habit is always stronger than reason.

MAXIM VI.

But the greatest point, perhaps, to be aimed at in marrying is to know before marriage what it is that you have to deal with.   You are quite sure to know this fast enough afterwards.   Be sure, therefore, that you commence the necessary requisitions before you have made up your mind, and not, as people generally do, *after*.   Remember there is no use in watching a woman that you *love* ; because she can't do anything, do what she will, that will be disagreeable to you.   And still less, in examining a woman that loves *you* ; because for the time she will be quite sure not to do anything that ought to be disagreeable to you.   I have known a hundred perfect tigresses as playful as kittens, quite more obliging than need be under such circumstances.   It is not a bad way, maid or widow, when you find yourself fancying a woman, to make her believe that you have an aversion to her.   If she has any concealed good qualities, they are pretty sure to come out upon such an occasion.

N.B.—Take care, nevertheless, how you make use of this suggestion ; because, right or wrong, it is the very way to make the poor soul fall furiously and fatally in love with you. *Vulnus alit venis, et cæco carpitur igni!*

MAXIM VII.

In judging *where* to look for a wife, that is, for the lady who is to form the " raw material " of one, very great caution is necessary.   And you can't take anything better with you, in looking about, as a general principle, than that good mothers commonly make tolerably good daughters.

Of course, therefore, you won't go, of consideration pre-pense, into any house where parents are badly connected, or have been badly conducted; nor upon any account at all into any house where you don't quite feel that if you don't conduct yourself properly you'll immediately be kicked out of it. This assurance may be troublesome while you are only a visitor; but, when you come to be one of the family, you'll find it mighty convenient. If you can find any place where vice and folly have been used to be called by their right names, stick to that by all means: there are seldom more than two such in one parish; and, if you see any common rascal let into a house where you visit as readily as yourself, go out of it immediately.

MAXIM VIII.

Mind, but I need hardly caution you of this, that you are not taken in with that paltry, bygone nonsense about "If you marry, marrying a fool." Recollect that the greatest fool must be sometimes out of your sight, and that she will yet carry you (for all purposes of mischief) along with her. A shrew may want her nails kept short; but, if you keep a strait waistcoat in the house, you may always do this your-self. And she is not of necessity, like your "bleating inno-cents," a prey to the first wolf who chooses to devour her.

MAXIM IX.

At the same time, while you avoid a fool, fly—as you fly from sin and death—fly from a philosopher! It is very dangerous to weak minds examining (farther than is duly delivered to them) what is right or wrong. I never found anybody yet who could distinctly explain what murder is if put to a definition.

All who find their minds superior to common rule and received opinion, value themselves on original thinking, talk politics, read Mary Wolstonecraft, or meddle with the mathematics—these are the unclean birds upon whom the protecting genius of honest men has set his mark that all may know; and pray do you avoid them.

MAXIM X.

If you marry an actress, don't let her be a tragedy one. Habits of ranting, and whisking up and down with a long train before a row of " footlamps," are apt to cast an undue ludicrousness (when transplanted) over the serious business of life.   Only imagine a castigation delivered to the cook, in " King Cambyses' vein," upon the event of an under-done leg of mutton at dinner; or an incarnation of Helen M'Gregor, ordering the cat to be thrown alive into the cistern if a piece of muffin was abstracted without leave at breakfast !

MAXIM XI.

If you do marry an actress, the singing girls perhaps are best; Miss Paton, I think, seems very soft, and coaxing, and desirable.   I myself should prefer Kitty Stephens to any of them; though she is a sad lazy slut—won't learn a line, and sleeps all day upon the sofa!   But I'm a teacher; and therefore the less I parade my own practice—at least so the belief goes—the better.

MAXIM XII.

Be sure, wherever you choose, choose a proud woman. All honesty is a kind of pride, or at least three-fourths of it.   No people do wrong, but in spite of themselves they feel a certain quantity of descent and self-degradation.   The more a woman has to forfeit the less likely she is to forfeit anything at all.   Take the pride although you have the virtue; the more indorsements you get, even on a good bill, the better.

MAXIM XIII.

I don't think the saints, after all is said and done, are the worst people in the world to match among. Nine-tenths of the mischief that women do arise less from ill design than from idle, careless, vagabond levity. It falls out commonly among the great card-players and play-hunters; very little among the Methodists and Presbyterians. Of course you won't contract for anything beyond going to church three times a-day, and such like public professions of faith and feeling. But, for the rest, I don't see why you should embarrass yourself about any system of belief, so long as it offends only against reason, and tends to the believer's temporal advantage.

MAXIM XIV.

At the same time, after the last sentence of the above exhortation, I need hardly tell you that you must not marry a Roman Catholic. Indeed I suppose it would be a little too much for any of you, who read *me*, to fancy a pleasant gentleman claiming the right to catechise your wives in private? For my part, God help any rascal who presumed to talk of law, human or divine, in my family; except the law which, like Jack Cade's law, came " out of my mouth !" I know something of these matters, having once con-templated being a monk myself—in fact, I had stolen a dress for the purpose. On the same principle—I rather think I mentioned this before—suffer no " guardianships " or " trusteeships " in your family to disturb your reign or fret your quiet. I knew a very worthy fellow who, having only a marriage settlement brought to him, broke the solici-tor's clerk's neck down stairs that brought it; and it was brought in " justifiable homicide." If a dog dares but to hint that there *is* such a thing as " parchment " in your presence, plump and rib him.

MAXIM XV.

I don't think, by the way, that there *ought* to be any parchment, except the petitions to the House of Commons, which are cut up to supply the tailors with measures. This is useful. Messrs Shiel and O'Connell's work takes the dimensions of my person once a month very accurately. I mention this because it has been said that no *measures*, in which the work of those gentlemen was concerned, ever could be taken accurately.

MAXIM XVI.

Talking of accuracy leads me to observe : Don't marry any woman hastily at Brighton or Brussels without knowing who she is, and where she lived before she came there. And, whenever you get a reference upon this or any other subject, always be sure and get another reference about the person referred to.

MAXIM XVII.

Don't marry any woman under twenty : she is not come to her wickedness before that time : nor any woman who has a red nose at any age ; because people make observations as you go along the street. " A cast of the eye "—as the lady casts it upon you—may pass muster under some circumstances ; and I have even known those who thought it desirable : but absolute squinting is a monopoly of vision which ought not to be tolerated.

MAXIM XVIII.

Talking of "vision" reminds me of an absurd saying—that such or such a one can "see as far through a millstone as those that picked it." I don't believe that any man ever saw through a mill-stone but Jeremy Bentham, and he looked through the hole.

MAXIM XIX.

One hears a great deal about "City taste." I must say I don't think an alderman's daughter by any means (*qua* Cornhill merely) objectionable. A fine girl may be charming, even though her father should be a Common Councilman. Recollect this.

MAXIM XX.

On the question of getting an insight into matters before marriage, if possible, I have dropped a word already. It is a point of very great importance, and there are two or three modes in which you may take your chance for accomplishing it. If you are *up to* hiring yourself into any house as a chambermaid—it requires tact, and close shaving ; but it would put you into the way of finding out a thing or two. I "took up my livery" once as a footman, and I protest I learned so much in three weeks that I would not have married any female in the family. An old maiden aunt, or sister, if you have one, is capable of great service. She will see more of a tomboy in five minutes than you would in six months ; because, having been in the oven herself, she knows the way. On the other hand there is the danger that she may sell you to some estate that she thinks lies convenient ; or even job you off to some personal favourite, without the consideration of any estate at all. The Punic faith of all agents—and especially one's own relatives—is notorious.

MAXIM XXI.

On the subject of accomplishments it is hardly my business to advise. I leave a great part—the chief part—upon this point to your own fancy. Only don't have any waltzing, nor too much determined singing of Moore's songs ; there is bad taste, to say the best of it, in all such publicities. For music, I don't think there is a great deal gained by a woman's being able to make an alarming jangle on the pianoforte, particularly under that unmerciful scheme of " duets," in which two tyrants are enabled to belabour the machine at the same time. Dancing a girl ought to be able to execute well ; but don't go anywhere where a *Monsieur* has been employed to give the instruction. As dancing is an art to be acquired merely from imitation, a graceful female—being the precise thing to be imitated— must be a far more efficient teacher than even Mr. Kick-the-Moon himself can be. Besides, I don't like the notion of a d—d scraper putting a girl of thirteen into attitudes. If I were to catch a ballet-master capering in my house, I'd qualify the dog to lead in the opera before he departed.

N.B.—Now we are on the subject of dancing, don't on any account marry a " lively " young lady ; that is, in other words, a " romp ;" that is, in other words, a woman who has been hauled about by half your acquaintance.

And now, my friends, my first twenty-one rules—just beginning your instruction, each of you, how to get a wife— are spoken out. And any directions how to manage one, if they come at all, must come at some future opportunity. Just two words, however, even upon this head ; for I would not leave you upon any subject too much unprovided.

In the first place, on the very day after your marriage, whenever you do marry, take one precaution. Be cursed with no more troubles for life than you have bargained for. Call the roll of all your wife's even speaking acquaintance ; and strike out every soul that you have—or fancy you ought to have—or fancy you ever shall have—a glimpse of dislike to.

Upon this point be merciless. Your wife won't hesitate— a hundred to one—between a husband and a gossip ; and, if she does, don't you. Be particularly sharp upon the list of women ; of course, men—you would frankly kick any one from Pall Mall to Pimlico who presumed only to recollect ever having seen her.

And don't be manœuvred out of what you mean by

cards or morning calls, or any notion of what people call "good breeding." Do you be content to show your ill-breeding by shutting the door, and the visitors can show their good-breeding by not coming again.

One syllable more to part. If you wish to be happy yourself, be sure that you must make your wife so. Never dispute with her where the question is of no importance; nor, where it is of the least consequence, let any earthly consideration ever once induce you to give way. Be at home as much as you can; be as strict as you will, but never *speak* unkindly; and never have a friend upon such terms in your house as to be able to enter it without ceremony. Above all, remember that these maxims are intrusted to all of you, as to persons of reason and discretion. A naked sword only cuts the fingers of a madman; and the rudder with which the pilot saves the ship would in the hands of the powder-monkey probably only force her upon the rocks. Recollect that your inquest as to matrimony is a matter of the greatest nicety, because either an excess of vigilance or a deficiency will alike compromise its success. If you don't question far enough, the odds are ten to one that you get a wife who will disappoint you. If you question a jot too far, you will never get a wife at all.

A Dozen Years Hence.

"LET's drink and be merry,
   Dance, sing, and rejoice "—
So runs the old carol,
   " With music and voice."
Had the bard but survived
   Till the year thirty-three,
Methinks he'd have met with
   Less matter for glee ;
To think what we were
   In our days of good sense,
And think what we shall be
   A dozen years hence.

Oh ! Once the wide Continent
   Rang with our fame,
And nations grew still
   At the sound of our name ;
The pride of Old Ocean,
   The home of the free,
The scourge of the despot
   By shore and by sea,
Of the fallen and the feeble
   The stay and defence—
But where shall our fame be
   A dozen years hence ?

The peace and the plenty
   That spread over all,
Blithe hearts and bright faces
   In hamlet or hall ;

A DOZEN YEARS HENCE.

Our yeomen so loyal
  In greenwood or plain,
Our true-hearted burghers,
  We seek them in vain ;
For loyalty's now
  In the pluperfect tense,
And *freedom's* the word
  For a dozen years hence.

The nobles of Britain,
  Once foremost to wield
Her wisdom in council,
  Her thunder in field ;
Her judges, where learning
  With purity vied ;
Her sound-headed Churchmen,
  Time-honoured and tried :
To the gift of the prophet
  I make no pretence,
But where shall they all be
  A dozen years hence ?

Alas ! for old Reverence,
  Faded and flown ;
Alas ! for the Nobles,
  The Church, and the Throne ;
When to Radical creeds
  Peer and Prince must conform,
And Catholics dictate
  Our new Church Reform ;
While the schoolmaster swears
  'Tis a usless expense,
Which his class won't put up with
  A dozen years hence.

Perhaps 'twere too much
  To rejoice at the thought,

That its authors will share
  In the ruin they wrought ;
That the tempest which sweeps
  All their betters away
Will hardly spare Durham,
  Or Russell, or Grey :
For my part I bear them
  No malice prepense,
But I'll scarce break my heart for't
  A dozen years hence.

When Cobbett shall rule
  Our finances alone,
And settle all debts
  As he settled his own ;
When Hume shall take charge
  Of the National Church,
And leave his own tools,
  Like the Greeks, in the lurch !
They may yet live to see
  The new era commence,
With their *own* " Final Measure,"
  A dozen years hence.

Already those excellent
  Friends of the mob
May taste the first fruits
  Of their Jacobin job ;
Since each braying jackass
  That handles a quill
Now flings up his heels
  At the poor dying Bill ;
And comparing already
  The kicks with the pence,
Let them think of the balance
  A dozen years hence.

When prisons give place
　To the swift guillotine,
And scaffolds are streaming
　Where churches have been ;
We too, or our children,
　Believe me, will shake
Our heads—if we have them—
　To find our mistake ;
To find the great measure
　Was all a pretence,
And be sadder and wiser
　A dozen years hence.

Béranger's "Monsieur Judas" versified.

Monsieur Judas est un drôle
Qui soutient avec chaleur,
Qu'il n' a joué qu'un seul rôle,
Et n'a pris qu'une couleur.
Nous qui détestons les gens,
Tantôt rouges, tantôt blancs,
    Parlons bas,
    Parlons bas :
Ici près j'ai vu Judas,
J'ai vu Judas, j'ai vu Judas.
	HERE Judas, with a face where shame
	    Or honour ne'er was known to be,
	Maintaining he is still the same,
	    That he ne'er ratted—no—not he.
	But we must spurn the grovelling hack,
	To-day all white—to-morrow black.
	    But hush ! He'll hear,
	    He'll hear, he'll hear ;
	Iscariot's near—Iscariot's near !

Curieux et nouvelliste,
Cet observateur moral
Parfois se dit journaliste,
Et tranche du libéral ;
Mais voulons-nous réclamer
Le droit de tout imprimer,
    Parlons bas,
    Parlons bas :
Ici près j'ai vu Judas,
J'ai vu Judas, j'ai vu Judas.
	The moral Surface swears to-day
	    Defiance to the priest and Pope ;
	To-morrow, ready to betray
	    His brother Churchmen to the rope.
	But let us trust the hangman's string
	Is spun for him—the recreant thing !
	    But hush ! He'll hear,
	    He'll hear, he'll hear ;
	Iscariot's near—Iscariot's near !

Sans respect du caractère,
Souvent ce lâche effronté
Porte l'habit militaire
Avec la croix au côté.
Nous qui faisons volontiers
L'éloge de nos guerriers,
    Parlons bas,
    Parlons bas :
Ici près j'ai vu Judas,
J'ai vu Judas, j'ai vu Judas.
	All character that knave has lost :
	    Soon will the neophyte appear,
	By priestly hands be-dipped, be-crossed,
	    Begreased, bechrismed, with holy smear.
	Soon may he reach his final home,
	"A member of the Church of Rome." *
	    But hush ! He'll hear,
	    He'll hear, he'll hear ;
	Iscariot's near—Iscariot's near !

Enfin, sa bouche flétrie
Ose prendre un noble accent,
Et des maux de la patrie
Ne parle qu'en gémissant.
	Now from his mouth polluted flows—
	    Snuffled in Joseph Surface tone—
	Lament o'er hapless Ireland's woes,
	    O'er England's dangerous state a groan.

---

* The ordinary conclusion of a gallows speech in Ireland—"I die an unworthy member of the Church of Rome."

Nous qui faisons le procès
A tous les mauvais Français,
　　Parlons bas,
　　Parlons bas :
Ici près j'ai vu Judas,
J'ai vu Judas, j'ai vu Judas.

Ere long beneath the hands of Ketch,
Sigh for thyself, degraded wretch !
　　But hush ! He'll hear,
　　He'll hear, he'll hear ;
Iscariot's near—Iscariot's near !

Monsieur Judas, sans malice,
Tout haut vous dit : " Mes
　　amis,
Les limiers de la police
Sont à craindre en ce pays."
Mais nous qui de mains bro-
　　cards
Poursuivons jusqu'aux mou-
　　chards,
　　　　Parlons bas,
　　　　Parlons bas :
Ici près j'ai vu Judas,
J'ai vu Judas, j'ai vu Judas.

Judas ! Till then the public fleece,
　For kin and cousins scheme and job,
Rail against watchmen and police,
　Inferior swindlers scourge or rob.
At last, another crowd before,
Thou shalt speak once—and speak no
　more !
　　But hush ! He'll hear,
　　He'll hear, he'll hear ;
Iscariot's near—Iscariot's near !

An Hundred Years Hence.

I.

"Let us drink and be merry,
   Dance, joke, and rejoice,
With claret and sherry,
   Theorbo and voice."
So sings the old song,
   And a good one it is;
Few better were written
   From that day to this:
And I hope I may say it,
   And give no offence,
Few more will be better
   An hundred years hence.

II.

In this year eighteen hundred
   And twenty and two,
There are plenty of false ones
   And plenty of true:
There are brave men and cowards,
   And bright men and asses;
There are lemon-faced prudes,
   There are kind-hearted lasses.
He who quarrels with this
   Is a man of no sense,
For so 'twill continue
   An hundred years hence.

III.

There are people who rave
　Of the National Debt:
Let them pay off their own
　And the nation's forget.
Others bawl for reform,
　Which were easily done,
If each would resolve
　To reform Number One.
For *my* part to wisdom
　I make no pretence :
I'll be as wise as my neighbours
　An hundred years hence.

IV.

I only rejoice that
　My life has been cast
On the gallant and glorious
　Bright days which we've past ;
When the flag of Old England
　Waved lordly in pride,
Wherever green Ocean
　Spreads his murmuring tide :
And I pray that unbroken
　Her watery fence
May still keep off invaders
　An hundred years hence.

V.

I rejoice that I saw her
　Triumphant in war,
At sublime Waterloo,
　At dear-bought Trafalgar ;
On sea and on land,
　Wheresoever she fought,
Trampling Jacobin tyrants
　And slaves as she ought :

Of CHURCH and of KING
　Still the firmest defence :
So may she continue
　An hundred years hence.

VI.

Why then need I grieve if
　Some people there be,
Who, foes to their country,
　Rejoice not with me ?
Sure I know in my heart
　That Whigs ever have been
Tyrannic, or turnspit,
　Malignant, or mean :
THEY WERE AND ARE SCOUNDRELS
　IN EVERY SENSE,
AND SCOUNDRELS THEY WILL BE
　AN HUNDRED YEARS HENCE.

VII.

So let us be jolly,
　Why need we repine ?
If grief is a folly,
　Let's drown it in wine !
As they scared away fiends
　By the ring of a bell,
So the ring of the glass
　Shall blue devils expel :
With a bumper before us
　The night we'll commence
By toasting true Tories
　An hundred years hence.

Vidocq's Slang Song Versified.

As from ken [1] to ken I was going,
   Doing a bit on the prigging lay,[2]
Who should I meet but a jolly blowen,[3]
   Tol lol, lol lol, tol derol, ay ;
Who should I meet but a jolly blowen,
   Who was fly [4] to the time o' day ? [5]

Who should I meet but a jolly blowen,
   Who was fly to the time o' day?
I pattered in flash,[6] like a covey [7] knowing,
   Tol lol, &c.
" Ay, bub or grubby,[8] I say."

I pattered in flash, like a covey knowing,
   " Ay, bub or grubby, I say."
" Lots of gatter," [9] quo she, " are flowing,
   Tol lol, &c.
Lend me a lift in the family way.[10]

1 *Ken*, shop, house.
2 *Prigging lay*, thieving business.
3 *Blowen*, girl, strumpet, sweetheart.
4 *Fly* (contraction of *flash*), awake, up to, practised in.
5 *Time o' day*, knowledge of *business*, thieving, &c.
6 *Pattered in flash*, spoke in slang.
7 *Covey*, man.
8 *Bub and grub*, drink and food.
9 *Gatter*, porter.
10 *Family*, the thieves in general. *The family way*—the thieving line.

" Lots of gatter," quo' she, " are flowing ;
   Lend me a lift in the family way.
You may have a crib [11] to stow in,
   Tol lol, &c.
Welcome, my pal,[12] as the flowers in May.

" You may have a bed to stow in ;
   Welcome, my pal, as the flowers in May."
To her ken at once I go in,
   Tol lol, &c.
Where in a corner out of the way ;

To her ken at once I go in,
   Where in a corner, out of the way,
With his smeller,[13] a trumpet blowing,
   Tol lol, &c.
A regular swell-cove [14] lushy [15] lay.

With his smeller, a trumpet blowing,
   A regular swell-cove lushy lay ;
To his clies [16] my hooks [17] I throw in,
   Tol lol, &c.
And collar his dragons [18] clear away.

[11] *Crib*, bed.

[12] *Pal*, friend, companion, paramour.

[13] *Smeller*, nose. *Trumpet blowing* here is not slang, but poetry for snoring.

[14] *Swell-cove*, gentleman, dandy.

[15] *Lushy*, drunk.

[16] *Clies*, pockets.

[17] *Hooks*, fingers ; in full, *thieving hooks*.

[18] *Collar his dragons*, take his sovereigns. On the obverse of a sovereign is, or was, a figure of St. George and the *dragon*. The etymon of collar is obvious to all persons who know the taking ways of Bow Street and elsewhere. It is a whimsical coincidence that the motto of the Marquis of Londonderry is " Metuenda *corolla draconis*." Ask the City of London, if " I fear I may not collar the dragons " would not be a fair translation.

To his clies my hooks I throw in,
   And collar his dragons clear away ;
Then his ticker [19] I set a-going,
   Tol lol, &c,
And his onions,[20] chain, and key.

Then his ticker I set a going,
   With his onions, chain, and key.
Next slipt off his bottom clo'ing,
   Tol lol, &c.
And his gingerhead topper gay.

Next slipt off his bottom clo'ing,
   And his gingerhead topper gay,
Then his other toggery [21] stowing,
   Tol lol, &c.
All with the swag [22] I sneak away.

Then his other toggery stowing,
   All with the swag I sneak away ;
Tramp it, tramp it, my jolly blowen,
   Tol lol, &c.
Or be grabbed [23] by the beaks [24] we may.

Tramp it, tramp it, my jolly blowen,
   Or be grabbed by the beaks we may ;
And we shall caper a-heel-and-toeing,
   Tol lol, &c.
A Newgate hornpipe some fine day.

And we shall caper a-heel-and-toeing,
   A Newgate hornpipe some fine day ;

---

[19] *Ticker*, watch. The French slang is *tocquanta*.
[20] *Onions*, seals.
[21] *Toggery*, clothes (from *toga*).   [22] *Swag*, plunder.
[23] *Grabbed*, taken.   [24] *Beaks*, police-officers.

With the mots [25] their ogles [26] throwing,
　　Tol lol, &c.
And old Cotton [27] humming his pray. [8]

With the mots their ogles throwing,
　　And old Cotton humming his pray ;
And the fogle-hunters [29] doing,
　　Tol lol, &c.
Their morning fake [30] in the prigging lay.

[25] *Mots*, girls.　　　[26] *Ogles*, eyes.
[27] *Old Cotton*, the Ordinary of Newgate.
[28] *Humming his pray*, saying the prayers.
[29] *Fogle-hunters*, pickpockets.
[30] *Morning fake*, morning thievery.

En roulant de vergne en vergne [1]
Pour apprendre à goupiner, [2]
J'ai rencontre la mercandière, [3]
Lonfa malura dondaine,
　Qui du pivois solisait, [4]
Lonfa malura dondé.

J'ai recontré la mercandière,
Qui du pivois solisait ;
. Je lui jaspine en bigorne, [5]
Lonfa malura dondaine,
　Qu'as-tu donc à morfiller ? [6]
Lonfa malura dondé.

Je lui jaspine en bigorne :
Qu'as-tu donc à morfiller ?
J'ai du chenu pivois sans lance ; [7]
Lonfa malura dondaine,
　Et du larton savonné, [8]
Lonfa malura dondé.

J'ai du chenu pivois sans lance
Et du larton savonné,
Une lourde, une tournante, [9]
Lonfa malura dondaine,
　Et un pieu pour roupiller, [10]
Lonfa malura dondé.

Une lourde, une tournante [11]
Et un pieu pour roupiller,
J'enquille dans sa cambriole,
Lonfa malura dondaine,
　Espérant de l'entifler, [12]
Lonfa malura dondé.

J'enquille dans sa cambriole,
Espérant de l'entifler,
Je rembroque au coin du rifle, [13]
Lonfa malura dondaine,
　Un messière qui pionçait, [14]
Lonfa malura dondé.

---

[1] City to city.　　　[2] To work.　　　[3] The shopkeeper.
[4] Sold wine.　　　[5] I ask him in slang.　　　[6] To eat.
[7] Good wine without water.　　　[8] White bread.
[9] A door and a key.　　　[10] A bed to sleep upon.
[11] I enter her chamber.　　　[12] To make myself agreeable to her.
[13] I observe in the corner of the room.　　　[14] A man lying asleep.

Je rembroque au coin du rifle
Un messière qui pionçait ;
J'ai sondé dans ses vallades,[15]
Lonfa malura dondaine,
Son carle j'ai pessigué,[16]
Lonfa malura dondé.

J'ai sondé dans ses vallades,
Son carle j'ai pessigué,
Son carle, aussi sa tocquante,[17]
Lonfa malura dondaine,
Et ses attaches de cé [18]
Lonfa malura dondé.

Son carle, aussi sa tocquante
Et ses attaches de cé,
Son coulant et sa montante,[19]
Lonfa malura dondaine,
Et son combre galuché,[20]
Lonfa malura dondé.

Son coulant et sa montante,
Et son combre galuché,
Son frusque, aussi sa lisette,[21]
Lonfa malura dondaine,
Et ses tirants brodanchés,[22]
Lonfa malura dondé.

Son frusque, aussi sa lisette
Et ses tirants brodanchés,
Crompe, crompe, mercandière,[23]
Lonfa malura dondaine,
Car nous serions bequillés,[24]
Lonfa malura dondé.

Crompe, crompe, mercandière,
Car nous serions bequillés ;
Sur la placarde de vergne,[25]
Lonfa malura dondaine,
Il nous faudrait gambiller,[26]
Lonfa malura dondé.

Sur la placarde de vergne
Il nous faudrait gambiller,
Allumés de toutes ces largues,[27]
Lonfra malura dondaine,
Et du trepe rassemblé,[28]
Lonfa malura dondé.

Allumés de toutes ces largues
Et du trepe rassemblé,
Et de ces charlots bons drilles,[29]
Lonfa malura dondaine,
Tous aboulant goupiner,[30]
Lonfa malura dondé.

---

[15] Search his pockets.
[16] I took his money.
[17] His money and watch.
[18] His silver buckles.
[19] His chain and breeches.
[20] Gold-edged hat.
[21] His cat and waistcoat.
[22] Embroidered stockings.
[23] Take care of yourself, shopkeeper.
[24] Hanged.
[25] On the Place de Ville.
[26] To dance.
[27] Looked at by all these women.
[28] People.
[29] Thieves ; good fellows.
[30] All coming to rob.

A Story without a Tail.

CHAPTER I.

HOW WE WENT TO DINE AT JACK GINGER'S.

So it was finally agreed upon that we should dine at Jack Ginger's chambers in the Temple, seated in a lofty story in Essex Court. There were, besides our host, Tom Meggot, Joe Macgillicuddy, Humpy Harlow, Bob Burke, Antony Harrison, and myself. As Jack Ginger had little coin and no credit we contributed each our share to the dinner. He himself provided room, fire, candle, tables, chairs, table-cloth, napkins—no, not napkins; on second thoughts we did not bother ourselves with napkins—plates, dishes, knives, forks, spoons (which he borrowed from the wig-maker), tumblers, lemons, sugar, water, glasses, decanters—by the by, I am not sure that there were decanters,—salt, pepper, vinegar, mustard, bread, butter (plain and melted), cheese, radishes, potatoes, and cookery. Tom Meggot was a cod's head and shoulders, and oysters to match; Joe Macgillicuddy, a boiled leg of pork with peas-pudding; Humpy Harlow, a sirloin of beef roast, with horse-radish; Bob Burke, a gallon of half-and-half, and four bottles of whisky, of prime quality ("Potteen" wrote the Whisky-man, "I say, by Jupiter, but of which *many*-facture *He* alone knows"); Antony Harrison, half a dozen of port, he having tick to that extent at some unfortunate wine merchant's; and I supplied cigars *à discretion*, and a bottle of rum, which I borrowed from a West-Indian friend of mine as I passed by. So that, on the whole, we were in no danger of suffering from any of the extremes of hunger and thirst for the course of that evening.

We met at five o'clock sharp, and very sharp. Not a man was missing when the clock of the Inner Temple struck the last stroke. Jack Ginger had done everything to admiration. Nothing could be more splendid than his turn-out. He had himself superintended the cooking of every individual dish with his own eyes, or rather eye, he having but one, the other having been lost in a skirmish when he was midshipman on board a pirate in the Brazilian service. "Ah!" said Jack often and often, "these were my honest days. Gad! did I ever think when I was a pirate that I was at the end to turn rogue, and study the law?" All was accurate to the utmost degree. The table-cloth, to be sure, was not exactly white, but it had been washed last week, and the collection of plates was miscellaneous, exhibiting several of the choicest patterns of delf. We were not of the silver-fork school of poetry, but steel is not to be despised. If the table was somewhat rickety, the inequality in the legs was supplied by clapping a volume of Vesey under the short one. As for the chairs,—but why weary about details, chairs being made to be sat upon?—it is sufficient to say that they answered their purposes, and whether they had backs or not, whether they were cane-bottomed or hair-bottomed or rush-bottomed, is nothing to the present inquiry.

Jack's habit of discipline made him punctual, and dinner was on the table in less than three minutes after five. Down we sate, hungry as hunters, and eager for the prey.

"Is there a parson in company?" said Jack Ginger from the head of the table.

"No," responded I from the foot.

"Then, thank God," said Jack, and proceeded, after this pious grace, to distribute the cod's head and shoulders to the hungry multitude.

CHAPTER II.

HOW WE DINED AT JACK GINGER'S.

THE history of that cod's head and shoulders would occupy but little space to write. Its flakes, like the snow-flakes on a river, were for one moment bright, then gone for ever; it perished unpitiably. "Bring hither," said Jack with a firm voice, "the leg of pork." It appeared, but soon to disappear again. Not a man of the company but showed his abhorrence to the Judaical practice of abstaining from the flesh of swine. Equally clear in a few moments was it that we were truly British in our devotion to beef. The sirloin was impartially destroyed on both sides, upper and under. Dire was the clatter of the knives, but deep the silence of the guests. Jerry Gallagher, Jack's valet-de-chambre, footman, cook, clerk, shoeblack, aide-de-camp, scout, confidant, dun-chaser, bum-defyer, and many other offices *in commendam*, toiled like a hero. He covered himself with glory and gravy every moment. In a short time a vociferation arose for fluid, and the half-and-half (Whitbread quartered upon Chamyton, beautiful heraldry!) was inhaled with the most savage satisfaction.

"The pleasure of a glass of wine with you, Bob Burke," said Joe Macgillicuddy, wiping his mouth with the back of his hand.

"With pleasure, Joe," replied Bob. "What wine do you choose? You may as well say port, for there is no other; but attention to manners always becomes a gentleman."

"Port, then, if you please," cried Joe, "as the ladies of Limerick say when a man looks at them across the table."

"Hobnobbing wastes time," said Jack Ginger, laying down the pot out of which he had been drinking for the last few minutes; "and besides, it is not customary now in genteel society to pass the bottle about."

[I here pause in my narrative to state, on more accurate recollection, that we had not decanters. We drank from the black bottle, which Jack declared was according to the fashion of the Continent.]

So the port was passed round, and declared to be superb. Antony Harrison received the unanimous applause of the company; and, if he did not blush at all the fine things that were said in his favour, it was because his countenance was of that peculiar hue that no addition of red could be visible upon it. A blush on Antony's face would be like gilding refined gold.

Whether cheese is prohibited or not in the higher circles of the West End, I cannot tell; but I know it was not prohibited in the very highest chambers of the Temple.

"It's double Gloucester," said Jack Ginger; "prime, bought at the corner. Heaven pay the cheesemonger, for I sha'n't; but, as he is a gentleman, I give you his health."

"I don't think," said Joe Macgillicuddy, "that I ought to demean myself to drink the health of a cheesemonger; but I'll not stop the bottle."

And, to do Joe justice, he did not. Then we attacked the cheese, and in an incredibly short period we battered in a breach of an angle of 45 degrees in a manner that would have done honour to any engineer that directed the guns at San Sebastian. The cheese, which on its first entry on the table presented the appearance of a plain circle, was soon made to exhibit a very different shape, as may be understood by the subjoined diagram :—

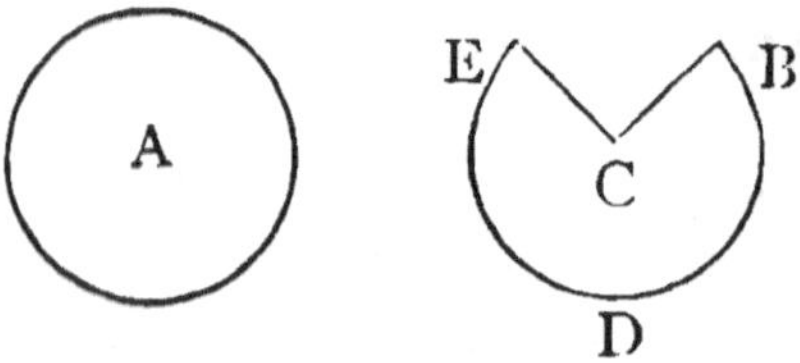

[A, original cheese; EBD, cheese after five minutes standing on the table; EBC, angle of 45°].

With cheese came and with cheese went celery. It is unnecessary to repeat what a number of puns were made on that most pun-provoking of plants.

"Clear the decks," said Jack Ginger to Jerry Gallagher. "Gentlemen, I did not think of getting pastry, or puddings, or dessert, or ices, or jellies, or blancmange, or anything of the sort for men of sense like you."

We all unanimously expressed our indignation at being supposed even for a moment guilty of any such weakness : but a general suspicion seemed to arise among us that a dram might not be rejected with the same marked scorn. Jack Ginger accordingly uncorked one of Bob Burke's bottles. Whop! went the cork, and the potteen soon was seen meandering round the table.

"For my part," said Antony Harrison, "I take this dram because I ate pork, and fear it might disagree with me."

"I take it," said Bob Burke, "chiefly by reason of the fish."

"I take it," said Joe Macgillicuddy, "because the day was warm, and it is very close in these chambers."

"I take it," said Tom Meggot, "because I have been very chilly all the day."

"I take it," said Humpy Harlow, "because it is such strange weather that one does not know what to do."

"I take it," said Jack Ginger, "because the rest of the company takes it."

"And I take it," said I, winding up the conversation, "because I like a dram."

So we all took it for one reason or another, and there was an end of that.

"Be off, Jerry Gallagher," said Jack. "I give to you, your heirs and assigns, all that and those which remain in the pots of half-and-half—item for your own dinners what is left of the solids ; and, when you have pared the bones clean, you may give them to the poor. Charity covers a multitude of sins.　Brush away like a shoeblack, and levant."

"Why, thin, God bless your honour," said Jerry Gallagher, "it's a small liggacy he would have that would dippind for his daily bread for what is left behind any of ye in the way of the drink, and this blessed hour there's not as much as would blind the left eye of a midge in one of them pots, and may it do you all good, if it a'n't the blessing of Heaven to see you eating.　By my sowl, he that has to pick a bone after you won't be much troubled with the mate.　Howsomever "——

"No more prate," said Jack Ginger.　"Here's twopence for you to buy some beer; but no," he continued, drawing his empty hand from that breeches-pocket into which he had most needlessly put it; "no," said he, "Jerry, get it on credit wherever you can, and bid them score it to me."

"If they will," said Jerry.

"Shut the door," said Jack Ginger in a peremptory tone, and Jerry retreated.

"That Jerry," said Jack, "is an uncommonly honest fellow, only he is the damnedest rogue in London.　But all this is wasting time, and time is life.　Dinner is over, and the business of the evening is about to begin.　So bumpers, gentlemen, and get rid of this wine as fast as we can.　Mr. Vice, look to your bottles."

And on this Jack Ginger gave a bumper toast.

CHAPTER III.

HOW WE CONVERSED AT JACK GINGER'S.

THIS being done, every man pulled in his chair close to the table, and prepared for serious action.　It was plain that we all, like Nelson's sailors at Trafalgar, felt called upon to do our duty.　The wine circulated with considerable rapidity; and there was no flinching on the part of any individual of the company.　It was quite needless for our president to remind us of the necessity of bumpers, or the impropriety of leaving heel-taps. We were all too well trained to require the admonition or to fall into the error. On the other hand, the chance of any man obtaining more than his share in the round was infinitesimally small. The Sergeant himself, celebrated as he is, could not have succeeded in obtaining a glass more than his neighbours. Just to our friends, we were also just to ourselves; and a more rigid circle of philosophers never surrounded a board.

The wine was really good, and its merits did not appear the less striking from the fact that we were not habitually wine-bibbers, our devotion generally being paid to fluids more potent or more heavy than the juice of the grape, and it soon excited our powers of conversation. Heavens! What a flow of soul! More good things were said in Jack Ginger's chambers that evening than in the House of Lords and Commons in a month. We talked of everything—politics, literature, the fine arts, drama, high life, low life, the opera, the cockpit—everything from the heavens above to the hells in St. James's Street. There was not an article in a morning, evening, or weekly paper for the week before which we did not repeat. It was clear that our knowledge of things in general was drawn in a vast degree from those recondite sources. In politics we were harmonious—we were Tories to a man, and defied the Radicals of all classes, ranks, and conditions. We deplored the ruin of our country, and breathed a sigh over the depression of the agricultural interest. We gave it as our opinion that Don Miguel should be king of Portugal, and that Don Carlos, if he had the pluck of the most nameless of insects, could ascend the throne of Spain. We pitched Louis Philippe to that place which is never mentioned to ears polite, and drank the health of the Duchess of Berri. Opinions differed somewhat about the Emperor of Russia, some thinking that he was too hard on the Poles, others gently blaming him for not squeezing them much tighter. Antony Harrison, who had seen the Grand Duke Constantine when he was campaigning, spoke with tears in his eyes of that illustrious prince, declaring him, with an oath, to have been a d—d good fellow. As for Leopold, we unanimously voted him to be a scurvy hound; and Joe Macgillicuddy was pleased to say something complimentary of the Prince of Orange, which would have no doubt much gratified his Royal Highness if it had been communicated to him, but I fear it never reached his ears.

Turning to domestic policy, we gave it to the Whigs in high style. If Lord Grey had been within hearing, he must have instantly resigned; he never could have resisted the thunders of our eloquence. All the hundred and one Greys would have been forgotten; he must have sunk before us. Had Brougham been there, he would have been converted to Toryism long before he could have got to the state of tipsyfication in which he sometimes addresses the House of Lords. There was not a topic left undiscussed. With one hand we arranged Ireland, with another put the Colonies in order. Catholic Emancipation was severely condemned, and Bob Burke gave the glorious, pious, and immortal memory. The vote of £20,000,000 to the greasy blacks was much reprobated, and the opening of the China trade declared a humbug. We spoke, in fact, articles that would have made the fortunes of half a hundred magazines, if the editors of these works would have had the perspicacity to insert them; and this we did with such ease to ourselves that we never for a moment stopped the circulation of the bottle, which kept running on its round rejoicing, while we settled the affairs of the nation.

Then Antony Harrison told us all his campaigns in the Peninsula, and that capital story how he bilked the tavern-keeper in Portsmouth. Jack Ginger entertained us with an account of his transactions in the Brazils; and, as Jack's imagination far outruns his attention to matters of fact, we had them considerably improved. Bob Burke gave us all the particulars of his duel with Ensign Brady of the 48th, and how he hit him on the waistcoat pocket, which, fortunately for the ensign, contained a five-shilling piece (how he got it was never accounted for), which saved him from grim death. From Joe Macgillicuddy we heard multifarious narrations of steeple-chases in Tipperary, and of his hunting with the Blazers in Galway. Tom Meggot expatiated on his college adventures in Edinburgh, which he maintained to be a far superior city to London, and repeated sundry witty sayings of the advocates in the Parliament House, who seem to be gentlemen of great facetiousness. As for me, I emptied out all Joe Miller on the company; and, if old Joe could have burst his cerements in the neighbouring church-yard of St. Clement Danes, he would have been infinitely delighted with the reception which the contents of his agreeable miscellany met with. To tell the truth, my jokes were not more known to my companions than their stories were to me. Harrison's campaigns, Ginger's cruises, Burke's duel, Macgillicuddy's steeple-chases, and Tom Meggot's rows in the High Street, had been told over and over; so often, indeed, that the several relaters begin to believe that there is some foundation in fact for the wonders which they are continually repeating.

"I perceive this is the last bottle of port," said Jack Ginger; "so I suppose that there cannot be any harm in drinking bad luck to Antony Harrison's wine-merchant, who did not make it the dozen."

"Yes," said Harrison, "the skinflint thief would not stand more than the half, for which he merits the most infinite certainty of non-payment."

(You may depend upon it that Harrison was as good as his word, and treated the man of bottles according to his deserts.)

The port was gathered to its fathers, and potteen reigned in its stead. A most interesting discussion took place as to what was to be done with it. No doubt, indeed, existed as to its final destination; but various opinions were broached as to the manner in which it was to make its way to its appointed end. Some wished that every man should make for himself; but that Jack Ginger strenuously opposed, because he said it would render the drinking unsteady. The company divided into two parties on the great questions of bowl or jug. The Irishmen maintained the cause of the latter. Tom Meggot, who had been reared in Glasgow, and Jack Ginger, who did not forget his sailor propensities, were in favour of the former. Much erudition was displayed on both sides, and I believe I may safely say that every topic that either learning or experience could suggest was exhausted. At length we called for a division, when there appeared—

<table>
<tr><td>For the jug.</td><td>For the bowl.</td></tr>
<tr><td>Bob Burke.</td><td>Jack Ginger.</td></tr>
<tr><td>Joe Macgillicuddy.</td><td>Humpy Harlow.</td></tr>
<tr><td>Antony Harrison.</td><td>Tom Meggot.</td></tr>
<tr><td>Myself.</td><td></td></tr>
</table>

Majority 1 in favour of the jug. I was principally moved to vote as I did because I deferred to the Irishmen as persons who were best acquainted with the nature of potteen, and Antony Harrison was on the same side from former recollections of his quarterings in Ireland. Humpy Harlow said that he made it a point always to side with the man of the house.

"It is settled," said Jack Ginger; "and, as we said of Parliamentary Reform, though we opposed it, it is now law, and must be obeyed. I'll clear away these marines, and do you, Bob Burke, make the punch. I think you will find the lemons good, the sugar superb, and the water of the Temple has been famous for centuries."

"And I'll back the potteen against any that ever came from the Island of Saints," said Bob, proceeding to his duty, which all who have the honour of his acquaintance will admit him to be well qualified to perform. He made it in a couple of big blue water-jugs, observing that making punch in small jugs was nearly as great a bother as ladling from a bowl; and, as he tossed the steamy fluid from jug to jug to mix it kindly, he sang the pathetic ballad of Hugger-mo-fane:

> " I wish I had a red herring's tail," &c.

It was an agreeable picture of continued use and ornament, and reminded us strongly of the Abyssinian maid of the Platonic poetry of Coleridge.

CHAPTER IV.

HOW HUMPY HARLOW BROKE SILENCE AT JACK GINGER'S.

THE punch being made, and the jug revolving, the conversation continued as before. But it may have been observed that I have not taken any notice of the share which one of the party, Humpy Harlow, took in it. The fact is that he had been silent for almost all the evening, being out-blazed and overborne by the brilliancy of the conversation of his companions. We were all acknowledged wits in our respective lines, whereas he had not been endowed with the same talents. How he came among us I forget, nor did any of us know well who or what he was. Some maintained he was a drysalter in the City; others surmised that he might be a pawnbroker at the West End. Certain it is that he had some money, which perhaps might have recommended him to us, for there was not a man in the company who had not occasionally borrowed from him a sum too trifling, in general, to permit any of us to think of repaying it. He was a broken-backed little fellow, as vain of his person as a peacock, and accordingly we always called him Humpy Harlow, with the spirit of gentlemanlike candour which characterised all our conversation. With a kind feeling towards him, we in general permitted him to pay our bills for us whenever we dined together at tavern or chop-house, merely to gratify the little fellow's vanity, which I have already hinted to be excessive.

He had this evening made many ineffectual attempts to

shine, but was at last obliged to content himself with opening his mouth for the admission, not for the utterance, of good things. He was evidently unhappy, and a rightly constituted mind could not avoid pitying his condition. As jug, however, succeeded jug, he began to recover his self-possession ; and it was clear, about eleven o'clock, when the fourth bottle of potteen was converting into punch, that he had a desire to speak. We had been for some time busily employed in smoking cigars, when, all on a sudden, a shrill and sharp voice was heard from the midst of a cloud, exclaiming, in a high treble key :—

" *Humphries told me* "—

We all puffed our Havannahs with the utmost silence, as if we were so many Sachems at a palaver, listening to the narration which issued from the misty tabernacle in which Humpy Harlow was enveloped. He unfolded a tale of wondrous length, which we never interrupted. No sound was heard save that of the voice of Harlow, narrating the story which had to him been confided by the unknown Humphries, or the gentle gliding of the jug, an occasional tingle of a glass, or the soft suspiration of the cigar. On moved the story in its length, breadth, and thickness, for Harlow gave it to us in its full dimensions. He abated it not a jot. The firmness which we displayed was unequalled since the battle of Waterloo. We sat with determined countenances, exhaling smoke and inhaling punch, while the voice still rolled onward. At last Harlow came to an end ; and a Babel of conversation burst from lips in which it had been so long imprisoned. Harlow looked proud of his feat, and obtained the thanks of the company, grateful that he had come to a conclusion. How we finished the potteen, converted my bottle of rum into a bowl (for here Jack Ginger prevailed), how Jerry Gallagher, by superhuman exertions, succeeded in raising a couple of hundred of oysters for supper ; how the company separated, each to get to his domicile as he could ; how I found in the morning my personal liberty outraged by the hands of that

unconstitutional band of gens-d'-armes created for the direct
purposes of tyranny, and held up to the indignation of all
England by the weekly eloquence of the *Dispatch;* how I
was introduced to the attention of a magistrate, and recorded
in the diurnal page of the newspaper—all this must be left
to other historians to narrate.

CHAPTER V.

WHAT STORY IT WAS THAT HUMPY HARLOW TOLD AT JACK GINGER'S.

AT three o'clock on the day after the dinner, Antony
Harrison and I found ourselves eating bread and cheese,
part of *the* cheese, at Jack Ginger's. We recapitulated the
events of the preceding evening, and expressed ourselves
highly gratified with the entertainment. Most of the good
things we had said were revived, served up again, and
laughed at once more. We were perfectly satisfied with
the parts which we had respectively played, and talked ourselves into excessive good-humour. All on a sudden, Jack
Ginger's countenance clouded. He was evidently puzzled ;
and sat for a moment in thoughtful silence. We asked him
with Oriental simplicity of sense, " Why art thou troubled ? "
and till a moment he answered :—

" What *was* the story which Humpy Harlow told us
about eleven o'clock last night, just as Bob Burke was
teeming the last jug ? "

" It began," said I, " with ' *Humphries told me.*' "

" It did," said Antony Harrison, cutting a deep incision
into the cheese.

" I know it did," said Jack Ginger ; " but what was it
that Humphries had told him ? I cannot recollect it if I
was to be made Lord Chancellor."

Antony Harrison and I mused in silence, and racked our
brains, but to no purpose. On the tablet of our memories

no trace had been engraved, and the tale of Humphries, as reported by Harlow, was as if it were not so far as we were concerned.

While we were in this perplexity Joe Macgillicuddy and Bob Burke entered the room.

"We have been just taking a hair of the same dog," said Joe. "It was a pleasant party we had last night. Do you know what Bob and I have been talking of for the last half hour?"

We professed our inability to conjecture.

"Why, then," continued Joe, "it was about the story that Harlow told last night."

"The story begins with '*Humphries told me*,'" said Bob.

"And," proceeded Joe, "for our lives we cannot recollect what it was."

"Wonderful!" we all exclaimed. "How inscrutable are the movements of the human mind!"

And we proceeded to reflect on the frailty of our memories, moralising in a strain that would have done honour to Dr. Johnson.

"Perhaps," said I, "Tom Meggot may recollect it."

Idle hope! dispersed to the winds almost as soon as it was formed. For the words had scarcely passed "the bulwark of my teeth" when Tom appeared, looking excessively bloodshot in the eye. On inquiry it turned out that he, like the rest of us, remembered only the cabalistic words which introduced the tale, but of the tale itself nothing.

Tom had been educated in Edinburgh, and was strongly attached to what he calls *metapheesicks;* and, accordingly, after rubbing his forehead, he exclaimed—

"This is a psychological curiosity which deserves to be developed. I happen to have half a sovereign about me" (an assertion which, I may remark in passing, excited considerable surprise in his audience); "and I'll ask Harlow to dine with me at the Rainbow. I'll get the story out of the humpy rascal, and no mistake."

We acquiesced in the propriety of this proceeding; and Antony Harrison, observing that he happened by chance to be disengaged, hooked himself on Tom, who seemed to have a sort of national antipathy to such a ceremony, with a talent and alacrity that proved him to be a veteran warrior, or what, in common parlance, is called an old soldier.

Tom succeeded in getting Harlow to dinner, and Harrison succeeded in making him pay the bill, to the great relief of Meggot's half-sovereign; and they parted at an early hour in the morning. The two Irishmen and myself were at Ginger's shortly after breakfast; we had been part occupied in tossing halfpence to decide which of us was to send out for ale, when Harrison and Meggot appeared. There was conscious confusion written in their countenances. "Did Humpy Harlow tell you *that* story?" we all exclaimed at once.

"It cannot be denied that he did," said Meggot. "Precisely as the clock struck eleven, he commenced with '*Humphries told me.*'"

"Well; and what then?"

"Why, there it is," said Antony Harrison. "May I be drummed out if I can recollect another word."

"Nor I," said Meggot.

The strangeness of this singular adventure made a deep impression on us all. We were sunk in silence for some minutes, during which Jerry Gallacher made his appearance with the ale, which I omitted to mention had been lost by Joe Macgillicuddy. We sipped that British beverage, much abstracted in deep thought. The thing appeared to us perfectly inscrutable. At last I said : " This will never do; we cannot exist much longer in this atmosphere of doubt and uncertainty. We must have it out of Harlow to-night, or there is an end of all the grounds and degrees of belief, opinion, and assent. I have credit," said I, "at the widow's in St. Martin's Lane. Suppose we all meet there to-night, and get Harlow there if we can?"

"That I can do," said Antony Harrison, "for I quartered myself to dine with him to-day, as I saw him home, poor little fellow, last night. I promise that he figures at the widow's to-night at nine o'clock."

So we separated. At nine every man of the party was in St. Martin's Lane, seated in the little back parlour; and Harrison was as good as his word, for he brought Harlow with him. He ordered a sumptuous supper of mutton kidneys interspersed with sausages, and we set to. At eleven o'clock precisely the eye of Harlow brightened; and, putting his pipe down, he commenced with a shrill voice :—

"*Humphries told me*"—

"Aye," said we all with one accord, "here it is—now we shall have it—take care of it this time."

"What do you mean ?" said Humpy Harlow, performing that feat which by the illustrious Mr. John Reeve is called "flaring up."

"Nothing," we replied, "nothing : but we are anxious to hear that story."

"I understand you," said our broken-backed friend. "I now recollect that I did tell it once or so before in your company, but I shall not be a butt any longer for you or anybody else."

"Don't be in a passion, Humpy," said Jack Ginger.

"Sir," replied Harlow, "I hate nicknames. It is a mark of a low mind to use them; and, as I see I am brought here only to be insulted, I shall not trouble you any longer with my company."

Saying this the little man seized his hat and umbrella and strode out of the room.

"His back is up," said Joe Macgillicuddy, "and there's no use of trying to get it down. I am sorry he is gone, because I should have made him pay for another round."

But he was gone, not to return again, and the story remains unknown; yea, as undiscoverable as the hiero- glyphical writings of the ancient Egyptians. It exists, to be sure, in the breast of Harlow; but there it is buried, never to emerge into the light of day. It is lost to the world, and means of recovering it there, in my opinion, exist none. The world must go on without it; and states and empires must continue to flourish and to fade without the knowledge of what it was that Humphries told Harlow. Such is the inevitable course of events.

For my part, I shall be satisfied with what I have done in drawing up this accurate and authentic narrative, if I can seriously impress on the minds of my readers the perishable nature of mundane affairs; if I can make them reflect that memory itself, the noblest, perhaps the characteristic, quality of the human mind will decay even while other faculties exist, and that, in the words of a celebrated Lord of Trade and Plantations of the name of John Locke, "we may be like the tombs to which we are hastening, where, though the brass and marble remain, yet the imagery is defaced, and the inscription is blotted out for ever!"

END OF VOL.

PRINTED BY BALLANTYNE, HANSON AND CO.
EDINBURGH AND LONDON.

www.ingramcontent.com/pod-product-compliance
Lightning Source LLC
Chambersburg PA
CBHW032141110726
47902CB00003B/655